When she's not writing fiction, Sarah Dunnakey writes and verifies questions for a variety of TV quiz shows including *Mastermind*, *University Challenge* and *Pointless*. She has an honours degree in history and has previously worked as a librarian, an education officer in a Victorian cemetery and an oral history interviewer.

Sarah has won or been shortlisted in several short story competitions and her work has been published in anthologies and broadcast on Radio 4. She won a Northern Writers' Award from New Writing North for her debut novel *The Companion*, and the NWA Arvon Award in 2019. She grew up in North East England but now lives in West Yorkshire. Follow her on Instagram and X @SarahDeeWrites.

By the same author:

The Companion

THE
12
MURDERS OF
CHRISTMAS

SARAH DUNNAKEY

avon.

Published by AVON
A division of HarperCollins*Publishers* Ltd
1 London Bridge Street
London SE1 9GF

www.harpercollins.co.uk

HarperCollins*Publishers*
Macken House,
39/40 Mayor Street Upper,
Dublin 1
D01 C9W8
Ireland

A Hardback Original 2024
1
First published in Great Britain by HarperCollins*Publishers* 2024

A catalogue copy of this book is available from the British Library.

ISBN: 978-0-00-872003-2 (HB)

Typeset in Bembo by HarperCollins*Publishers* India

Printed and bound in the UK using 100%
Renewable Electricity at CPI Group (UK) Ltd

MIX
Paper | Supporting
responsible forestry
FSC™ C007454
FSC
www.fsc.org

For my dad, Bill Dunnakey,
who loves stories, puzzles and puzzling stories

The Estate of the late Mr Edward Luddenham
cordially invites you to attend
Bracestone House, North York Moors
19th-24th December

Mr Luddenham's final will and testament
will be read on 24th December

Attendance mandatory for those with
expectations from the aforesaid

Full board, with all expenses met
Bring only yourself and a festive story of mystery
and murder to share

RSVP: law@brotherton.co.uk

INTRODUCTION

Can you solve the puzzles and unlock the final mystery?

At the end of each of the stories in this book, you will find a puzzle. The puzzles take several forms, including ciphers, anagrams, tests of logic and general knowledge. Each of the first eleven puzzles provides a single word clue. All these clues are needed to solve the final puzzle at the end of the book.

To add to the festive fun, some of the stories also have mini puzzles and 'goose eggs' – conundrums hidden within the stories themselves – for you to solve.

You may wish to have paper and a pen to hand.

BRACESTONE HOUSE

It looks like the scene of a murder, ironically, thought Judy, putting her suitcase down on the gravel and stepping back to get a fuller view of the façade of Bracestone House. Behind it no doubt lay the full complement of library, ballroom, study and billiard room, with numerous candlesticks and pieces of lead piping to hand.

The low December sun cast harsh shadows across the grey gritstone, giving a rugged edge to a building that was trying hard to look imposing. A short flight of wide steps led to a doorway built for giants. Its portico, etched with the Luddenham family crest, was supported on either side by barrelled columns. The door itself was a very dark wood, with elaborate ironwork hinges, the knocker held in the teeth of a grinning lion. Judy grasped it and rapped sharply three times. She was a tall woman with smooth dark skin that often had her mistaken for late forties rather than fifties. Her black hair, finely streaked with silver, was brushed back from her face in soft waves. A seasoned librarian, her finely arched eyebrows were used to good effect whenever silence or the payment of a fine was required. She was determined not to be daunted either by the house or the week that lay ahead.

On either side of the doorway, rows of multi-paned windows

betrayed the house's Jacobean origins. Although the corner turrets, she decided, glancing up at the cawing of a crow, must surely be a much later addition.

'Second floor, upper left.'

Judy turned to see a large-framed man in an ill-fitting sports jacket and ill-conceived denim jeans approaching through the archway to the car park where she had left her Fiat Panda. He was in his mid-sixties, she guessed. A broad jowly face, florid with a slightly bulbous nose and watery hazel eyes. Grey streaks in unkempt hair that reached his shoulders. She wondered if the blond bits were tinted.

'The room where Edward was killed,' the man continued, hoisting his large canvas holdall onto his shoulder. 'James Burton,' he said holding out his hand. 'Retired journo and, as of last week, bestselling author. You may have heard of my book *Private Life of a Public Man?*'

'I could hardly have missed it,' said Judy. 'Weren't you on the *Today* programme on Monday?'

'Yes, and *The One Show* last night.' James pushed out his chest like a proud songbird. His floral print shirt was open at the neck, revealing a tuft of hair. 'My phone's not stopped ringing. It's what the public crave, isn't it, a bit of dirt on the great and good?'

'Apparently so,' said Judy, 'We've got a reserve list a mile long for it at the library.' He was looking at her expectantly.

Waiting for my credentials? Judy thought. She'd prefer to leave him guessing what role a middle-aged Black woman in a smart navy trouser suit and red patent leather shoes had in Edward Luddenham's life. But there would be more than enough speculation and assumption-making over the next few days. There seemed little point starting the games already.

'Judy Monye,' she said. 'I'm the local history librarian at the Central …'

'Judy!' James exclaimed. '*The* Judy? Ed often mentioned you. We were on the board of the North Yorkshire Lit & Sci Society together. He called you his personal research assistant.'

'Did he indeed?' said Judy, well aware that her contribution to Edward's research had gone beyond that of helping him find the books he needed.

'He said many a time that he should have credited you on at least half of his articles,' James continued. 'I'm sure he would have given you a nod in *Notorious Northerners* if he'd only had the chance to finish writing the book. Damn shame, he was so close.'

'That would have been nice,' said Judy, with a small smile.

A slow creaking behind them heralded the opening of the front door. In the vast space stood a small round woman in a black dress, white apron and thick black stockings. A frilled white mobcap perched precariously on her pink-tinged silver curls.

'What-ho Magenta! Where's Riff-Raff?' asked James, bounding forward. 'Think we'll fit a "Time-Warp" in before tea?'

'Always the same joke, Mr Burton,' said the woman, without smiling. She had a strong Tyneside accent, which somehow added an extra note of contempt to her voice. 'I looked up that film after you said I should. You're daft as a bat if you think I look like that woman. And I'd thank you not to encourage Linden to watch it. He would not be amused.' She turned to Judy. 'Welcome to Bracestone House, Mrs Monye. I'm Mrs Linden, housekeeper, cook and generally at your service this week.'

They stepped into a spacious entrance hall, where the air was cold enough for their breath to cloud, but held a warm, welcoming scent. The room was two storeys high, unplastered, with a grey stone staircase leading up to a mezzanine landing.

To one side of the staircase stood an enormous baubled and

tinselled Christmas tree, its glittering silver star almost touching the mezzanine balcony.

James whistled. 'Bet you had to stand on Linden's shoulders to decorate that.'

'Don't be silly, Mr Burton. We got in the same company as last year – Xmas by Xander. They had the whole house done in three hours.' She smiled again at Judy. 'We didn't want any of you missing out on the festive spirit while you were here.'

Judy's hand went to the gold locket at her throat. It held photographs of her two grown-up sons. Curiosity had been her main reason for accepting the odd invitation to spend the week before Christmas among strangers, several miles from her family. It hadn't been an easy decision and she had been intending to delay any 'festive spirit' until she returned home.

'Shall I show you your rooms or would you like to meet the others first?'

'Rooms please,' Judy was about to say but James answered before she could. 'Why put off the inevitable, Mrs L? Throw us to the lions! Eh, Judy?'

Judy wondered if, behind the bluster, he was as nervous about this get together as she was.

They left their bags at the bottom of the stairs on the housekeeper's instructions. 'Linden will see to them,' she said and led them down a corridor to the right.

She knocked on a door and when a male voice called 'Come in,' opened it.

'This was Mr Luddenham's study,' she said to Judy as she ushered them both through, announcing 'Mr James Burton and Mrs Judith Monye,' before slipping back out and closing the door behind her.

The walls of the room were panelled in a warm-coloured wood. Books filled tall shelves on two of the walls and on a third an imposing wooden desk stood before crimson velvet curtains concealing the windows. A fire blazed in a hearth below green and blue ceramic tiles and a grey marble surround. A green leather sofa and two matching armchairs were arranged in a semi-circle close to the heat.

The sofa was occupied by a man and a woman dressed almost identically in neutrally toned jumpers and canvas jeans. They looked to be in their forties and both held mugs of herbal- smelling tea while having a subdued discussion. In one chair sat a man in an olive-green herringbone tweed suit and a sombre maroon tie. He was completely bald, the overhead chandelier shining on his polished dome, and wore a white goatee beard. Judy judged him to be slightly older than James, possibly in his early seventies. His slippered feet were resting on an embroidered footstool, the flames in the hearth observed through his whisky glass apparently taking all of his attention. Opposite him sat a large woman with a mass of jet-black curls pinned up in a haphazard fashion. She was wrapped in a shawl of many colours that merged with the rainbow stripes of her long velvet skirt. Several small balls of wool nestled in her lap. In her hands she held a slender hooked needle and a flat piece of intricately knotted turquoise crochet.

She looked up at the newcomers over half-moon glasses. 'Apologies for not getting up. I'm constructing a sea dragon and I'll likely lose his tail if I disturb my gatherings. I'm Dinah Garnett,' she added. 'Owner of Crafty Sew-and-Sew, in Malton.' She looked at Judy hopefully.

'Sorry, I don't know the shop,' Judy said, although she had visited the market town many times. Handicrafts had never agreed with her. She blamed a particularly traumatic macramé project at primary school: a hanging basket that had deconstructed itself back into strands of string as soon as she'd placed a potted spider plant in it.

'Ah, I hoped you might be a fellow crafter,' Dinah said nodding to the embroidered silk flower pinned to the lapel of Judy's jacket. 'That's lovely.'

'It was a present from … a friend,' Judy said. 'Last …' her words caught in her throat. 'Last Christmas.'

'A friend with very good taste,' said Dinah, her cheeks creasing as she smiled. Judith realised that despite Dinah's unsilvered hair, they were of a similar age.

The bald man had risen to his feet but left one hand laid possessively on top of the armchair.

'Good to see you, James, I believe congratulations are in order. Stuart Yorke,' he added briskly, addressing Judy. 'With an 'e'. Friend of Edward's since school. Been a god-awful year. A comfort to have everyone back here again.'

'Again?' asked Judy.

The two people on the sofa who had so far remained seated stopped their private conversation. The man acknowledged them with a nod; the woman scowled. He had dark close-cropped hair, touched with grey at the temples, his expression calm but serious. She had a shoulder-length blonde bob, and fine features that seemed harsh even in the soft light of the study.

'Edward's daughter, Helena and her partner Jon Gudmundsson, who hails from Iceland,' said James when the two failed to introduce themselves. 'They're Mindfulness Mentors.' He gave the two words a taunting emphasis. 'Be sure to ask them about the Wellness Centre they're going to open once they've found the right location. Come to think of it, chaps, this place might fit the bill, eh?' He winked at the stiff-faced couple before strolling over to a teak cabinet beside the fireplace, extracting a bottle of malt whisky and a glass and pouring himself a generous measure.

'We were all here last year,' Stuart explained. 'Except for Ms Garnett, of whom I've not previously had the pleasure.' He looked at Dinah with a curiosity that she ignored, her attention refocused on her crochet dragon.

James, returning with his already half-empty glass and carrying the wooden chair from the desk, was less subtle.

'Ms Garnett, you indisputably lend a splendid vibrancy to the occasion.' he said sitting down heavily. Was his voice already slightly slurred? wondered Judy. Had he stopped for a couple of crafty pints in a pub en route? Not that she was one to judge, being fond of a glass or two of wine herself, but even she hadn't found the need to start on the Dutch courage quite so early.

'I confess,' James continued, 'to being slightly baffled at your presence. Are you another old friend of Edward's? I don't recall him ever mentioning your name.'

'Yes, Dinah,' interjected Helena. 'Jon and I have been wondering why you were invited. But unlike James were too polite to ask?' She gave the former journalist a withering look.

'To add local colour?' Dinah suggested with a flutter of her shawl. 'Or more likely because Edward was one of Crafty Sew-and-Sew's best customers. Who else do you think provided the soft furnishings for this place? The lovely cushions and curtains. Not to mention keeping him supplied with socks and handknitted jumpers.'

'Father didn't wear handknitted ...' Helena hesitated. 'Although now you come to mention it, he was wearing one last Christmas.' She turned to Jon. 'You asked him if it was an Icelandic pattern.'

'And he replied, "No, 100 per cent Yorkshire",' said Jon.

'My very own handiwork,' said Dinah. 'Maybe he's put in his will that I can have it all back. I certainly don't want any of the socks returning. But there was a rather nice Fair Isle jumper that I was particularly pleased with ...'

'Let's not start dividing up my father's possessions just yet,' pleaded Helena.

I wonder if she's already made an inventory, thought Judy. Out loud she said, 'So except for Dinah you were all here last December?'

James nodded. 'Edward broke with the habit of a lifetime and requested a family Christmas. Rose was here, the daughter of his son, Tristan, who died in that dreadful climbing accident when she was only a kid. Not Tristan's widow though, Ed couldn't stand her. Rose brought her girlfriend along. Lovely girl, Indian heritage I believe. Stuart and his son, Barney, and I joined them for drinks and Mrs Linden's finest nibbles on the afternoon of Christmas Eve. What with Jon representing our friends in the far north and our housekeeper and manservant being natives of Geordie land, it was quite the global gathering.' He sat with his legs spread wide, holding his glass on one knee. 'Sheeting down with rain outside, the boiler on the blink and Edward in one of his odd moods. But a jolly gathering for the most part. Until the murder of course.'

'Now, James,' said Stuart. 'Do you think you could moderate the flippancy this week, for the sake of the family at least. I'm sure … Sorry, I didn't catch your name, dear?'

He's looking at me so it must be me he's calling 'dear', Judy thought, unsure whether that meant he was implying she was much younger or much older than him. 'Judy,' she said.

'You don't want Judy getting the wrong impression,' said Stuart.

'I'm not really sure what impression I'm supposed to have about all this,' Judy said honestly. Stuart was obviously not giving up his possession of the armchair, so she located a footstool and perched on it. 'Should we really be drinking and making merry?' she asked. 'It's not even been a full year since Edward was killed. In this house.'

'Apparently it's exactly what we should be doing,' said Helena, drily.

'We found this when we got here.' Stuart passed James an A4 piece of card. 'It was propped up on the mantlepiece.'

'It's good quality card and the same font as the invites,' said Dinah. 'So it's likely it's from Edward's solicitor too.'

James read it out loud.

Welcome All

May you all enjoy the hospitality available to you at Bracestone House.

Mr and Mrs Linden have been retained to be at your service and to fulfil your every need – within reason!

An itinerary of activities has been arranged, Mrs Linden will inform you of the details.

Relax and get into the festive spirit in the memory of and with the full blessing of Edward Luddenham.

A few house rules apply:

1. *You are all invited guests, so please respect each other and try to get along*
2. *You have each been asked to bring and share a story. When, where and in what order you tell them is up to you. But the stories must be told!*
3. *If you are interested in the contents of Mr Luddenham's will then you are required to stay until Christmas Eve*
4. *Qr pxughuw wklv bhdu sohdvh*

Wi-Fi code: DEF123

'What on earth was that bit at the end before the Wi-Fi code?' asked Judy.

James passed the sheet to her.

'Oh I see. Some sort of cipher. Have you cracked it yet?' she asked.

10

'Maybe it's the name of Edward's killer,' said James with a smirk.

'Left on the mantelpiece, rather than handed over to the police?' said Helena, missing his sarcasm. 'It'll be something trivial like "Merry Christmas Folks!" Dad was fond of Dickens, maybe it's the Tiny Tim quote from the end of *A Christmas Carol*, "God bless us every one."' She shuddered. 'I never liked that story.'

'Guilty conscience?' asked James.

Helena glared at him.

'Now, now, remember golden rule number one,' said Stuart. 'Be nice.'

'It's not anything like that,' said Judy. She'd taken a pen and a notebook out of her handbag. 'It's a transposition code. Each of the letters of the alphabet have been substituted with another one. They can be quite tricky, but this one is fairly straightforward since we've been given the key.'

'What key?' asked Helena. 'And what does it say?'

Judy slipped her notebook into her bag, slightly disconcerted that she had been right about having to play games this week. 'I think it only fair that we each work it out for ourselves,' she said. 'Now as I seem to be the only one without a drink, I'm going to take Edward at his word and see what else his drinks cabinet has to offer.'

When she had returned with a large glass of Malbec, Stuart was back in the armchair, so she settled on the footstool again and stretched out her legs.

'Lovely shoes,' said Dinah, gesturing to Judy's red patent leathers.

'Thank you,' replied Judy.

'Although,' said Helena with a concerned face. 'I think for Mrs Linden's sake outdoor shoes really should be left in the hall.' She indicated her own sheepskin-clad feet.

'When I've had a chance to unpack,' said Judy politely, 'I will do just that.' She took a long drink of her wine. This was going

11

to be quite a week, but she was oddly looking forward to it. So far her fellow guests were providing enough interest to keep her curiosity piqued.

'Who else are we expecting?' she asked.

'Edward's granddaughter, Rose, and my son, Barney, are arriving tomorrow,' Stuart said. 'Neither of them can get here any earlier. Barney's off on a shoot for his latest project – a folk horror film! And Rose is a teacher. End of term bell doesn't ring until lunchtime tomorrow. Damn young to be teaching in a high school if you ask me. And physics of all subjects. Imagine, James: fifteen-year-old boys being taught gravity and friction and whatever else they do at O level these days by a girl still in her twenties.'

James, who had been to refill his glass, did not respond. He had pulled aside one of the velvet curtains and was apparently more interested in the darkening view through the window.

'Young woman,' said Judy.

'Beg your pardon,' said Stuart.

'If she's in her twenties, the term you're after is "young woman" and unless she's teaching in a museum, she'll be following the GCSE syllabus. O levels left school shortly after I did.'

Stuart peered at her. He said, 'Hmm,' and leaned back in his chair.

'Another arrival,' said, James, turning away from the window. 'A taxi's just pulled up. Looks like we'll be seven for dinner.'

★ ★ ★

The table was set with crisp white linen, red and green place settings and highly polished silver and cut glass. Mrs Linden had just cleared away the plates on which she had served a starter of crayfish salad. Linden, a tall man with a stoop and thinning hair had appeared an hour earlier to ring the dinner bell. He had greeted each of the guests with a silent nod as they made their way into the dining room and stood sentinel by the door as they ate.

'Well that was splendid,' said James. As much to break the silence as to actually commend the first course which had been adequate but not quite up to Mrs Linden's usual standard, he thought. Dinah had asked if there was a vegetarian option. 'Not that I am one, a vegetarian that is. But shellfish …' She gave a little shudder. Her dish had been swiftly removed and returned with the crayfish scraped off the lettuce leaves. Helena had explained to anyone who was interested that she and Jon were mainly vegan but ate seafood, 'with Jon being Icelandic' she added in explanation. 'It's a holistic diet,' she said. 'We eat what feels right at any given time.'

'Same as me then,' said James, who had pushed his salad leaves aside.

Judy had come down for dinner in a dark purple jersey dress and coordinating mule slippers. Her clothes, James noted, had an understated elegance that might make a casual observer think she was unaware of how well they suited her. He suspected she wasn't. A small smile played on her lips now. Amused at the unsubtlety of Mrs Linden or by her fellow guests? Perhaps it was her way of coping with the pomposity of Stuart Yorke with an 'e', who was regaling her and Jon with a description of an extravagant seafood buffet he'd once encountered at a private London club. James had forgotten until now how unbearable the man could be. Dinah appeared distracted. At a loss perhaps without her crocheted creature in her hands. But really, he suspected, whatever everyone's other thoughts and musings, they were all mainly waiting for the most recently arrived guest to explain why she was there.

She had gone straight up to her room when she arrived and when she came down to take her seat at the table had simply said, 'Hi, I'm Sara Slade. I'm a private detective. Nice to meet you all.'

The crayfish had arrived, Dinah's lettuce had been scraped and returned. Mrs Linden had bobbed in and out and her husband had waited at the door. It wasn't until now, with the plates cleared and the staff out of the room that Stuart, predictably taking the lead, cleared his throat and asked, 'Why exactly are you here, Miss Slade?'

Sara leaned back in her chair. She was a slim, athletic woman, with dark grey hair cut in what James believed was called a pixie crop. She wore black woollen trousers and a fitted paisley shirt. Her silver jewellery was simple, but included a stud in her nose, which James was delighted to think must be particularly irritating to Stuart.

'I was invited,' she said. Her voice was low and had a trace of an accent. Possibly Scottish, or just south of the border. 'As I believe we all were, to enjoy the hospitality of the late Edward Luddenham on the anniversary of his untimely death.'

'And to work out whodunnit?' James asked, toying with his empty wine glass.

'The police certainly haven't had any luck so far,' said Sara. 'Plenty of suspects ... or at least a houseful of people with opportunity,' she avoided their eyes, 'but also with alibis. No murder weapon. An open back door with a mess of footprints in the yard that only muddied the investigation. I used to be a police detective myself, I can understand their frustration.' She spread out her hands. 'The killer, it would seem, is still ... out there. Are none of you curious to know what happened? No one worried he or she might strike again?'

'How did you know Edward?' asked Dinah, whose focus seemed to have returned to the room, although she chose to ignore Sara's question.

Sara tilted her head as if choosing how much to tell. 'He was a client. He had engaged my agency's services in the past.'

'I saw you last year,' James said putting his wine glass down firmly. That was what had been niggling at him. 'You were in the village down the road on Christmas Eve. Talking to Edward outside the Cross and Lamb. I was driving through on my way up here. I pipped my horn, but neither of you looked up. I even mentioned you to the police when they interviewed me.'

'The police were, and continue to be, aware of my involvement with the case.'

'Are you saying,' said Stuart. 'That you were investigating Edward's murder, before he was killed?'

'As I said, Edward, Mr Luddenham, was a client. I cannot break the confidentially of my contract.'

'Lamb shanks, mashed potatoes and a side of winter greens,' Mrs Linden announced as her husband held open the door and she pushed a hostess trolley towards the table. She handed round warmed plates and then set the dishes down in the centre of the table. There's extra potato for them that don't eat sheep.'

Helena sighed as she and Jon faced their double-potato laden plates.

While they made their way through the main course, James steered the conversation on to one of the requirements of their invitations. They had all been asked to bring a story of 'mystery and murder'.

'Does it have to be both?' mused Dinah. 'And does it have to be true?'

'Who would ever know if it wasn't?' said Sara.

'Well I've got one,' said Stuart, 'and I wouldn't mind being first up to the crease. Get it out of the way. It's a true story and Ned is in it.'

'Edward was involved in a murder before he was murdered?' asked Dinah.

'All will be revealed after dinner,' said Stuart.

15

A SLIPPERY SLOPE

They reconvened in the study with three dining chairs carried through to supplement the seating. James and Stuart helped themselves to whisky, Helena and Jon were sharing a bottle of wine they had opened during the meal, and Judy and Sara had both accepted Mrs Linden's offer of a cup of tea. Dinah had presented the housekeeper with a crumpled sachet from the depths of her pocket, 'Hot chocolate,' she said. 'All hot milk, no water if you don't mind?'

Stuart decided to stand by the fireplace, one arm resting on the mantel. It seemed a fitting storytelling pose, but as everyone else took their time getting settled his left knee started to ache and he began to wish he'd reclaimed the comfy armchair.

'I like to think of myself as an honest man,' he began at last, shifting his weight onto his right knee, which responded with a niggling pain. 'But I am aware that in the story I am about to tell, I confess to … Well, if not dishonesty, then at least the withholding of some truth.' He eyed his audience warily.

James was watching him with a sardonic expression. Judy had raised one of her splendid eyebrows. Dinah was counting stitches and the 'Beige Twins', as Stuart liked to think of Jon and Helena, were snuggling up to each other in a way that he felt was a touch too intimate for such a gathering.

He cleared his throat. 'The reason for my, let's call it reticence, to share something that only I knew about this case – a murder investigation – will hopefully become clear. Although as the case was never fully resolved it has bothered me occasionally,' he laughed nervously and tugged at the knot of his tie which seemed suddenly uncomfortable. 'I do at heart believe in justice being served. However, sometimes, well, I'll let you all be as it were, the judge ...'

'Ned and I knew each other since we were at school,' he began. 'Kept in touch – as you do – no matter what life threw at us. Every January without fail we went skiing together. Both loved the sport and the mountains. Gave us time to refresh our batteries away from whatever hell or paradise we left at home. A different world of which we never spoke. Sport, history, books, films, music, all eager points of discussion during our two weeks away. But just as he never expected me to talk about whom I had left at home in my then bachelor flat in Bermondsey – I was, as it were, "between wives" – so I never quizzed him on his personal or business affairs either. Although I couldn't help but be aware of his financial success and the extent to which he was expanding his father's small business into an empire.' Stuart shifted from one foot to the other, and leaned for comfort against the wall. 'And he had no doubt already some inkling that having abandoned a career in finance and switched to law, only a couple of years after passing my bar exam I was regretting my change of career.'

'Did you stick with it?' interrupted Dinah. 'Law?'

'Alas no, I found it too restricting in the end.'

'So what did you do instead?' she asked.

'Bit of everything really, you know,' said Stuart with a well-practised vagueness. 'In business, out of business. Several businesses in fact. I could bore you with the details, but I am trying to tell a story.

'This year's trip promised to be slightly different,' he continued, 'in that there would be three of us. Ned was bringing along someone from that other world. Which to be honest I wasn't too pleased about. Ned and I had a comfortable way of rubbing along together. Both of similar competency on the slopes, both with a fondness for good food and wine après-ski. This year he'd invited along a work colleague, although as Ned owned the business, I suppose it would be more accurate to call him an employee. A young food technologist who'd been behind Luddenham Food's highly successful frozen desserts range the previous summer. Those concoctions of cream and custard and fruit that tasted freshly homemade even if they'd been in the freezer for six months. Inviting him along was possibly a form of reward or maybe he was testing him out to see if he was upper-management material.

'This Ben Galip seemed a decent enough chap. Slight in build with longish dark hair that he seemed happy to hide behind. Ned warned me in advance that he wasn't the most chatty of chaps. And he did keep himself to himself for most of the journey there. "Just get him talking about the chemical composition of synthetic cream," Ned had said, "there'll be no stopping him." I decided to give that particular conversational gambit a miss.

'Ned had booked everything as usual. I always left the details up to him. He could be guaranteed to find the best hotels and chalets. The best deals on ski passes and travel. I just packed my bags and joined him and Ben at the airport.

'Our destination was Andermatt in the Swiss Alps. Ned, true to form, had found us a gem. The luxury Hotel Oberof on the edge of the resort with 'boutique' chalets in the grounds. Owned by a Midwestern American who had fulfilled his dream of returning to his family's Germanic roots. Russell Stouber was smaller than I'd imagined and quietly spoken, which just goes to show you shouldn't always presume. He greeted us personally on arrival and took us down to our cabin – "Chalet Gentian" – which nestled below snow-capped mountains among a cluster of evergreens. The other two cabins, at a decent distance apart were all also occupied, we were told. As guests of the hotel, we were free to take advantage of everything the hotel had to offer while being afforded the privacy of separate accommodation. The chalet was cosy for three but we each had our own bedroom and shared a large central area with a log fire, fur-blanket-draped sofas and a magnificent view of the mountains beyond. There was a small kitchen where, Mr Stouber informed us, we could if we wished make our own meals rather than acquaint ourselves with the five-star restaurant at the hotel. Or, for a small extra charge, our designated chalet girl, Hedy, could cook for us. She would be along that evening to introduce herself and to take note of any special requirements.

'"I would recommend," Stouber said, "that you request some of her spiced biscuits. A family recipe and not to be missed."'

'"Ten out of ten once again, Ned," I said as I filled our tumblers. After unpacking, the three of us were relaxing in the lounge of the chalet with measures of the Glencormac I'd bought in Duty Free. I'm all for Apfel schnapps and what have you but there's nothing better for making you feel at home than a decent Scotch.

'"The off-piste is notorious round here," Ned said. "Are you up for it, Stuart?" He was joking of course. I'm a competent skier but I know my limits. Like Ned, I planned to stay on some of the less demanding slopes. Ben, however, it turned out, was no novice. Of course he wasn't one to blow his own trumpet, but with coaxing from Ned he admitted that he had skied for his school.

'I refrained from asking what type of school took part in skiing championships and accepted him at his word. "What exactly does a food technologist do?" I asked instead as I nursed my second whisky.

"'It's basically chemistry," said Ben, "but working with food ingredients. Exploring what can be catalysed or blended to produce specific successful results."

"'Such as Luddenham's Frozen Fresh," said Ned, raising his glass. His toast was interrupted by a knock on the door and the arrival of Hedy. A young woman with a creamy complexion and thick auburn hair, pulled back into a long plait. She carried with her a basket and asked if "*die Herren*" would like her to make a light supper.

'Snow was falling steadily outside and while the delights of the hotel restaurant were only a few hundred metres away we hadn't made a reservation, and the comparable delights of the warm chalet and the remainder of the whisky were right here.

'Ben settled it by saying that he would very much like to have a home-cooked meal on our first night. This pleased Hedy who from her basket produced a small cardboard box. "*Paprika-Plätzchen*," she said. "Cookies. Spicy and not sweet. *Mein* own recipe handed down from my beloved Italian grandmother. But," she wagged her finger at us, "not to be eaten until your supper plates are empty." She gave a cheeky smile and disappeared into the kitchen.

"'Lovely," said Ned. I wasn't sure whether he meant the prospect of biscuits or the undeniable charms of the young woman.

'We awoke the next morning to clear blue skies, glittering snow and the prospect of a full day's skiing. Last night's schnitzel supper had been delicious, but we still tucked in heartily to the cold platter of meats and cheeses that Hedy had left for us. There also remained just one of her biscuits, which Ned and Ben graciously allowed me to have. They were truly remarkable.

Delicately spiced with a moreish cheesiness and a soft bite. I resolved to order a box for every day of our stay and perhaps a few extra to take home as gifts. Having Hedy at our service really was the cherry on the cake.' Stuart paused and narrowed his eyes at Judy and Dinah. 'If that's not politically incorrect.' He suspected from their expressions that it was at least borderline.

'But to continue. Ben too had been impressed with the biscuits; I refuse to fall for the Americanism of "cookies". As we made our way to the ski slope, he was in intense discussion with Ned about possibly adding biscuit dough to the Freshly Frozen range. "I'm going to ask her for the recipe," he said. "I'm sure it can't actually be secret. I could probably work out the ingredients myself – there's paprika obviously but some cheese too I'm sure, maybe horseradish? I might ask her to bake some in the chalet, to see exactly how she gets that texture." I admit I was suspicious of his interest and wondered how much Hedy's generous smile and twinkling blue eyes were part of his desire to spend time with her.

'All thoughts of biscuits and indeed chalet girls were forgotten in the glorious morning on the slopes. Ben had somewhat understated his prowess. Nervous and clumsy on terra firma, he was transformed on the snow into a creature of confident grace. By one o'clock we were all famished and in need of lunch. We descended on a bar that despite its cluttered decor of hunting trophies, rifles and drinking horns, was according to Ned highly recommended and rumoured to be a favourite among the minor royals.

'The barman was darkly hirsute and grunted rather than spoke. He wore a grey T-shirt with stains under the armpits. As he slammed our plates of toasted cheese and ham baguettes on the table, I got the impression he had ambitions beyond serving sandwiches in one of Switzerland's top ski resorts. "Do you have any black pepper," I asked. He gave me a glare befitting of a Michelin chef who'd served foie gras and been asked for ketchup.

"'Nein,'" he spat. For a charged moment I thought he might actually spit, but he was hailed by a customer at the bar, so they instead were treated to his foul-tempered visage.

"'A bit rude,'" I said, taking a bite of my baguette.

"'Part of the place's charm,'" said Ned with a sly grin. "Nothing like a bit of contempt from the serving classes to make their supposed social superiors feel like they're somewhere special." It was those sorts of comments that reminded me that despite his wealth Ned's origins had been anything but privileged. As Ned and I tucked into our lunches, Ben prodded at his unenthusiastically.

"'Not what you fancy?'" I asked. He shrugged, then as if to change the subject, pointed up at the stuffed head of an elk gurning down at us from the wall.

"'Wouldn't want to come across one of them on the mountain. Though I'm pretty certain they're not local to …'"

'A sudden bellow of "Stinks!" caused Ben and everyone else in the bar to fall silent. It was followed by the presence beside our table of a tall man in a loud yellow ski jacket. Designer goggles perched on his thick blond hair. Ben jumped to his feet and looked ready to flee for the door but was prevented by an enveloping half embrace from the yellow jacket and a vigorous thumping on his back. "Stinks!" the man bellowed again into Ben's ear, as if on the off chance he hadn't heard him the first time. "Can't believe it, mate. It's been too long." Behind the man stood an equally blonde woman in matching goggles, her garish jacket sky blue rather than yellow, with gold stars at the shoulders and cuffs.

'The man grasped Ben's shoulders and roughly held him out at arm's length.

"'Where've you been? Locked up in a lab somewhere with

your lotions and potions?" He didn't wait for Ben to reply but thrust out a meaty hand to Ned and myself, his cuff slipping back to reveal a particularly ugly and possibly antique gold wristwatch.

'"Charlie Sarns," he said. "Old school friend of Stinks. This is the missus, Pip," he gestured half-heartedly to his companion. "Keeping tabs on me as always." He rolled his eyes in what I presume was intended as comic exasperation. The woman didn't change her expression; she had perhaps seen and heard it all before.

'"Order us a couple of butties from the bar will you, darling?" Charlie said. "The usual with extra gherkins. And a large glass of decent Pinot, none of that German mouthwash."

'He sat down at our table without waiting to be invited. Ben was back in his seat but seemed to have shrunk into himself. All the confidence he had gained from his skiing now drained away. We introduced ourselves and Ned asked some polite questions about Charlie and his wife. He was "big in futures", Pip was a linguist, a salacious wink, "or at least until the babies start arriving. God help us." Pip returned with his wine and a cola. Charlie took a sip from his glass and winced. "That dirty-faced barman has pulled a fast one, Pips. Take it back and this time watch him pour it from the bottle."

'An uncomfortable hour ensued with Ben, whom Charlie insisted on calling Stinks no matter how often we used his actual name, retreating further into himself. Charlie and Pip, it transpired, were staying in one of the other Hotel Oberof chalets.

'"Have you met the delicious Hedy Berger yet?" asked Charlie. Pip glowered at the girl's name. "Quite the treat, isn't she?" he continued. He gestured to the surly barman who was wiping down the counter. "Hard to believe that's her hubby. Still, needs must I suppose. Not much choice round here, unless you run off with one of the guests." He winked at his wife, who studiously turned away.

'In a blatant attempt to steer the conversation in a different direction, Pip Sarns began to discuss the delights of the hotel's restaurant.

'"We've booked for Wednesday evening," she said. "Have you?"

'We shook our heads and admitted ignorance about what Wednesday night might involve.

'She pulled a regretful face. "You may have missed the boat. I imagine it will be oversubscribed. A shame as it promises to be pretty special. Beau Dascer." she said. Then, realising that the name meant nothing to us, she added, "The internationally acclaimed, possibly Michelin-starred chef, though I can't quite remember exactly what it said in the blurb. He's creating one of his special 'table d'hôte' menus. A twelve-course tasting board, including his signature '*Escargot en beurre flambé*'."

'"Man's a genius," interrupted Charlie. "Can't have you chaps missing out. I'll have a word with Stouber. Knew him back when he owned a single motel in Minnesota and was looking for European investors. I'm sure he can squeeze you on our table. More's the merrier and Stink's never been a big eater, have you, old man?" He nudged Ben sharply with his elbow. "Be like school dinners all over again, Stinks. Always a riot."

'If I wasn't much mistaken, Ben looked as though he might be about to cry.

'On our walk back to the ski lift, having left Pip and Charlie in the bar, where the latter was unashamedly chatting up a young waitress, Ben was even quieter than usual. Suddenly as we passed a kiosk advertising snowboarding lessons, Ben kicked out viciously at a plastic penguin wearing sunglasses, sending it flying. Swearing under his breath, he retrieved it and placed it back in its place, patting its smooth black head, as if in apology.

'"Bloody Charles Sarns," he said slouching along with his

hands in his pockets, as we continued home. "Of all the idiots to turn up and ruin everything."

'"He was rather … loud," I said.

'"Loud?" Ben came to a sudden halt. His normally placid brown eyes burning with dark fire. "That's not the half of it. Made my life hell at school. I wasn't the only one, but I was his favourite punch bag. Dubbed me 'Stinks' in the first term of first year. Said it was because I loved chemistry so much, but he knew it would catch on and would become a name to taunt me with. Soon it was all anyone called me, even the masters, who adored Charlie the golden boy. At the end of fifth form we had one of those ridiculous 'yearbooks'. Sarns's photo was of him in his rugger top, a smear of bloodied mud on his cheek and the caption 'Most Likely to Win at Life'. Mine made me look about twelve and was labelled 'Ben "Stinks" Galip, Most Likely to Blow Up the School'. Sarns got hold of my copy and crossed out the last three words. Hilarious." Ben kicked out again, this time at thin air. "Now he's rewritten history and we're best buddies. He even wants us to ski together. He can't bear to think anyone could be better than him. Well it's not happening. I'm going out on my own tomorrow at the crack of dawn. Good luck to him if he tries to find me."'

★ ★ ★

'The next morning another glorious day of skiing dawned. Ben – true to his word – had left before either Ned or I awoke. We set off together, planning to try out one of the trickier slopes today but when we were almost at the lifts, I realised I'd left my gloves in the chalet. Ned said he would wait for me before heading up, so I hurried back. When I reached Chalet Gentian, Hedy was on the porch, struggling to unlock the door. When she saw me, she smiled with relief. She really was a very bonny young woman and this morning was sporting a

25

blue neckerchief almost the same cornflower blue as her eyes. Ahem, I digress.

'"This is the wrong key," she exclaimed. "It is happening again. The Oberhof housekeeper, she is *eine Dummkopf*! She confuses the keys. She gives me the key to the restroom not the storehouse. And now this is not the key for your chalet." She dangled a small key with a blue tag attached. "The housekeeper, she says they are each their own colour, but all the time she is changing the colours. Who is to know!" She shrugged. "But it is OK. You are here, Mr Yorker."

'I resisted correcting her pronunciation; it was close enough.'

Stuart paused. Had the craft-shop woman sniggered? Her face appeared serene now, no sign of mockery, so he continued.

'I let her into the chalet and expected her to go straight to the kitchen and start on the cleaning but instead she slumped into one of the dining chairs and put her head in her hands.

'"Come on," I said. "It's not that bad. We won't mind if you just give the place a quick once-over to make up for some of the time you've lost." She lifted up her face; her eyes were damp and her cheeks flushed.

'"It is more than the key," she said. She tilted her head. "Do you sometimes find life just a bit too hard, Mr Yorker?"

'I hesitated. In truth, no I didn't. At that point, even allowing for my recent divorce and my doubts about my career, life had been pretty fair to me one way and another. Even if I had any complaints, it would have seemed petty to bring them up when I was staying at a luxury ski resort. Instead I asked if her problem was with the hotel.

'She shook her head. "Work is good. Even with the idiot housekeeper. At work I am able to spend time with lovely English men who are polite and grateful and – aha!" She rummaged in her bag and produced a familiar cardboard box. "And who appreciate my cookies."

'At home not so much, I suspected, remembering the ill-natured barman whom Charlie claimed was Hedy's husband.

'As if reading my mind, she said. "*Mein Mann, er ist*, he is often …" she searched for the right word, "difficult. *Ja*, difficult. But here I am at work and I will make your chalet sweet and clean. Also of course I will see you all later at *Abendessen*."

'"At supper?" I asked. I wasn't certain about our plans for this evening. As ever, I had left the details to Ned.

'"Mr Sarns in *das Chalet Edelweiss*. He has invited you all for dinner, *nein*? I am to cook a special Alpine feast for you all. It pleases me very much. Mr Sarns is a kind and charming man. Yes?"'

★ ★ ★

'Ben was adamant that he would not be dining chez Sarns.

'"Not tonight nor any night." He had successfully avoided Charlie on the slopes all day and had looked horrified when Ned confirmed that we were all three invited to supper at Chalet Edelweiss.

'"I'll make myself a sandwich, or finish off this morning's croissants," said Ben. "I'll be fine."

'"Hedy will be there," I said.

'Ben looked away.

'"And she's cooking a special Swiss …"

'"No," said Ben firmly. "Those school lunchtimes Sarns recalled so fondly?"

'*Such a riot!* Sarns had said yesterday.

'Ben shook his head, his mouth working but no words coming out. Eventually he said. "I've had problems, with eating, with food ever since." He looked down at his feet in their striped socks. "Especially in social situations. It's partly why I followed the career path I did." He smiled ruefully. "My attempt to rationalise the whole process of eating. It's got better over the years but I still … I can't. I'm not going through all that again."

'That evening, sitting around the dining table in the Sarnses' chalet, it was clear that Ben's decision not to come had been wise. In his absence Charlie regaled us with tales of the many japes and pranks he and his school and later university friends had revelled in. The majority of the school years ones, involving sneezing powder, slugs and clingfilm, had Ben, or boys that sounded like him, as their victim. Ned and I had debated turning down the invitation, but Ben had insisted that we go, especially as Hedy would have put in so much effort.

'I have to admit that I, as much as my companions, was not immune to Hedy's charms. She was a good fifteen years my junior and I did not flatter myself, entirely, that she would find a man of my age attractive. Still, we had all seen her husband ... And I should add,' he smoothed his hands over his bald pate. 'This was the early nineties and I was sporting a full head of hair. However it became increasingly obvious that while she was attentive to us all, there was a particular chemistry between her and our host Charlie. Not the blatant flirting in which he had engaged with the waitress at the bar. This was something altogether more serious, showing itself as much in what they didn't say or do. There were no fluttering eyelashes or dimpled cheeks directed at him and he didn't taunt her with double entendres that she would only half-understand. Instead there were smouldering glances and low-voiced exchanges. Late on in the evening, I emerged from the bathroom into the hallway to see him with his hand on her behind and her eyes closed in apparent ecstasy.

'Ahem,' Stuart cleared his throat, 'My story appears to be wandering into a very different genre, one that I am not in the least qualified to tell.'

Judy chuckled and Dinah said, 'You old devil! Don't hold back on the juicy details.' Stuart adjusted his tie again; that woman had an annoying ability to make him feel uncomfortable. He continued regardless.

'Back at the dining table, Mrs Sarns was not oblivious to what was happening. Daggers in her eyes each time Hedy squeezed past the table with a laden dish and ice in her voice when she finally said, "*Danke*, Hedy. That was delicious. You may go now. I can serve up the *Apfeltorte* and coffee. I'm sure Herr Berger is eagerly awaiting your return."'

★ ★ ★

'Ben had agreed to ski with Ned and me the next day. The weather was a bit grim, so we had a leisurely breakfast and Ben and I played a game of chess, before heading out shortly after eleven. As we set off, I gave Ben a potted description of our evening and he said he wasn't at all surprised.

'"Sarns was always a 'player'. Even at school. Breaking hearts and goodness knows what else. There was even a rumour about him and one of the PE teachers. Nothing ever proven of course. Poor Pip, that's one leopard who will never change his spots."

'As we passed Chalet Edelweiss, we witnessed an extraordinary commotion. Charlie and Pip Sarns were standing on the porch with the hotel owner, Russell Stouber. Pip was shouting and gesticulating. Charlie had his hands in his pockets, looking disconsolately at his feet. Stouber was making placatory gestures, but above Pip's shouting was the wailing of Hedy Berger, who was leaning against the railings of the porch, sobbing into her hands.

'Ned stepped forward. It was really none of our business, but he clearly felt that someone needed to take charge of the situation and that was always Ned's speciality. Pip stopped shouting as he approached. Hedy looked up and ran at him, flinging her arms around his waist and begging him to save her.

'*From what?* I wondered, drawn to the drama despite myself.

'"What seems to be the problem?" asked Ned, untangling the young woman from his middle. He was addressing Mr Stouber, but Pip spoke up before he could.

"'Charlie's watch, which belonged to his grandfather and is of extreme sentimental – not to mention monetary – value, has been stolen. He couldn't find it this morning before we left to use the hotel spa. We were in a rush to leave, wanting to try to get the jacuzzi to ourselves. But when we came back, he looked in all the usual places: bedside cabinet; bathroom shelves. I helped him practically turn the place upside down searching. It's nowhere to be found." She pinned Hedy with a stare that would shame a gorgon. "This young woman was here with her mop and her biscuits when we left. No one else had access. No one else could be the thief."

"'I don't understand," said Charlie, "I'm normally so careful with it. But ..." He smiled ruefully. "I did have a skinful last night. We finished off that bottle of just-opened Chablis after you guys left. There's a chance, I suppose, that I might have put it somewhere stupid. Maybe it's dropped behind the sofa or something."

"'I've looked behind the sofa," said Pip, through what sounded like gritted teeth. "And through all the pockets of all your clothes, including the ones you weren't even wearing last night."

'Mr Stouber piped up that maybe they could search the chalet again before things were taken any further.

'Pip's eyes flashed. "That woman is not to set foot in our chalet again. Mr Stouber and I think you should seriously consider her future in your establishment. If you're keen to carry out a search, why don't you start with the room she shares with that ruffian husband. See what that turns up."

'There was a gasp from Hedy, who had flushed at the reference to her husband.

"'Let's just calmly assess the facts," said Ned. "Charlie's watch is missing. Might I suggest that I help with another search of your chalet. A second pair of eyes can be useful and Charlie, could you have a good think about whether you might have put the watch somewhere different from usual? A 'safe place' that's slipped your mind perhaps?"

'"Search my room too!" said Hedy. She was standing arms and legs wide, chin defiant. "Pat me down like a TV detective Mr Stouber, if that is what is you wish."

'"There'll be no need for that," Ned said, to the obvious disappointment of Pip, who looked as though she was about to volunteer to do the body search herself. But if it will help calm the situation. Stuart, could you perhaps go along with Mr Stouber and Hedy to the Bergers' room and just take a look."

'The watch was not in Chalet Edelweiss. It was not in the Bergers' room or among Hedy's possessions or cleaning equipment. Charlie continued to insist that he must have mislaid it, although he looked increasingly concerned as it failed to materialise. A dark cloud of suspicion hung over Hedy and reluctantly Stouber agreed that she would no longer be allocated duties in the chalets.'

★ ★ ★

'That evening was the Grand Menu à la Beau Dascer. True to his word, Charlie had arranged for us to be "squeezed" in. Not at his table, but on another one with an elderly German couple. Ben agreed to come along as we wouldn't actually be sitting with the Sarnses and I suspect he wanted to demonstrate a show of bravery against Charlie's intimidation.

'He began to have second thoughts shortly before we left for the restaurant and took some persuading to come along.

'"It's a tasting menu," Ned reassured him when we finally left. "Just eat what you can. The dishes will be tiny."

'He was spot on. The food was delicious, but each of the seven courses comprised scarcely a mouthful. The highlights were a salmon mousse of which I could have happily eaten a full bowl, a handful of mussels in an Emmental sauce, the much-anticipated escargots and the dessert, a melt-in-the-mouth chocolate roulade. Ben visibly relaxed in the calm company of Herr and Frau Flistery, who had many tales to tell of their walking adventures in the mountains. He even seemed to relish the mussels, which were a bit cheesy for my liking.

'About two thirds of the way through the evening, there was a disturbance at the Sarnses' table. Charlie's vigorous tones rose and fell in counterpoint to a rapid French repost from a rotund figure in chef's whites. Ben looked at first alarmed and then amused by the fracas. He asked a waiter what the problem was and was told that one of the guests had said that he suspected the snails had been defrosted from a supermarket packet. The chef, Beau Dascer himself, had come out from the kitchen to deny the accusation.

'"But surely the customer is always right," said Ben with a half-smile, "and what's wrong with frozen food anyway?"

'The waiter shook his head. "Do not let Beau Dascer hear such heresy. You would not wish to attract his wrath."

'Dascer flung a final and very French insult at Charlie and returned to the kitchen. Charlie sat back down and the rest of the evening passed smoothly. At Ben's request we didn't linger after the meal, although the Sarnses boisterously invited us to join them in the bar for drinks. We retreated instead to the peace and quiet of our chalet.'

★ ★ ★

'It was early afternoon the following day when Ned and I heard the news. After an energetic morning, in which we'd successfully completed a slalom run, we'd opted for a leisurely lunch at the bar. Pip Sarns was in there, dressed in "civvies" rather than her skiwear, looking off-colour and reading a magazine. When Ned asked after her health, Pip scowled at him and muttered about "Greeks bearing gifts". When prompted for clarification, she explained that Hedy had left a "peace offering" of a box of cookies on their porch last night. Still ravenous after the paltry meal at the hotel, she and Charlie had wolfed the lot. She had woken in the early hours, emitting what she graphically described as "tsunami-like waves of vomit". She was blaming the biscuits. Ned began to suggest that last night's seafood might be a more likely suspect as Ben too had been suffering, but she waved him away, and turned her back on our table.

'We were just considering whether or not to have another of Yannik Berger's surprisingly good brandied hot chocolates when Russell Stouber walked in. He headed straight for Pip and clasped his hands behind his back.

'"May we please talk in private, Mrs Sarns? I have something very serious to impart."

'Pip looked up from her magazine, her expression neutral. She glanced behind at me and Ned. "Whatever it is, go ahead. I am among friends."

'Russell looked at us anxiously and Ned nodded for him to go on.

'"It's Mr Sarns," he said. "He has been in an accident. He veered off-piste and collided with a tree. I am terribly sorry, Mrs Sarns." His voice broke with what sounded like genuine sorrow, "Your husband died instantly. There was nothing anyone could do."

'Pip had been looking greenish before; she now turned white as a snowbank. If she hadn't been seated, I fear she would have fallen. She looked panicked, and then strangely calm. It was only after a few minutes had passed that she put her hand to her eyes and began to sob.'

★ ★ ★

'A tragic accident. Nothing more, it would seem. Charlie had set off down a particularly tricky slope that Ben had mentioned as being one of his favourites. It had proved technically too difficult. An eyewitness saw him swerving erratically and losing the course before heading straight for a stand of trees.

'Pip, through her very visible grief, was predictably not convinced it was an accident. When the local police arrived, as was usual when there had been an unexpected death, she had demanded that they take her concerns about Hedy seriously. She told us that she had laid out to them her conviction that she and Charlie had been deliberately poisoned by 'that girl' and the coroner would be examining Charlie's body for traces of toxins. She also told them about his "stolen" watch, which they said was surprising to hear, as he had been wearing a watch matching that description when he died. The face was broken and the hands stuck at six twenty-five.

'"But he was in the chalet at that time. I'd been awake for hours by then, intermittently vomiting, while he continued snoring," she said. "He never wore his watch at night, so how could it possibly have got broken then? I am prepared to swear he wasn't wearing it as he left. He would have told me if he had found it! It doesn't make sense."

'Neither did her claim that she and Charlie had been poisoned. If she had asked, we could have reassured her that the biscuits were unlikely to be to blame for her disturbed night. She had not been the only one taken ill. Ben had not made it to the slopes that morning. From the early hours he had been occupied in the chalet bathroom with a tsunami of his own. It was later revealed that the Flisterys, who like Ben and Pip had particularly enjoyed the moules, had also suffered. Charlie had refused to eat his mussels on the grounds that they were too garlicky. The rest of us it seemed had avoided the bullet in that particular game of seafood roulette.

'But Charlie, nevertheless, was dead.'

'You started this story with talk of murder,' said James. 'Surely you're not going to disappoint us with a mere tragic accident.'

'I've never been on a jury,' said Stuart, 'and I would never

34

want to be. But I did train in law and I remember during my studies being concerned about the fine lines between the various charges brought against someone who has in some way caused another person's demise. Murder, manslaughter – voluntary or involuntary, gross negligence, death by reckless driving, causing or allowing death by neglect and then the pleas, diminished responsibility, loss of control.' He sighed. 'So many variations on a theme. You can understand perhaps why I decided not to continue as a lawyer.

'We did indeed believe, for the rest of the afternoon and evening, that it had been a "tragic accident". None of us went quite so far as to blame Charlie's arrogance and overconfidence. Although Ben came close. Things took a more sinister turn the following day.' Stuart waggled his empty glass in James's direction 'Could you get me a refill, old chap?' James reluctantly got to his feet and obliged, topping up his own drink at the same time.

Stuart continued. 'A solemn-faced Mr Stouber visited our chalet at breakfast time and informed us that we were to present ourselves to hotel reception in the next couple of hours, and each submit to formal interviews with the murder detectives who had arrived from Zurich. Stouber confided, rather indiscreetly, that the same command had been issued to Mrs Sarns and various members of staff, including Hedy and her husband and the chef Beau Dascer. None of us were permitted to leave the resort without permission from the police.'

'How could it have been murder?' asked Judy, her smooth forehead creasing into a puzzled frown. 'Had Ben faked his sickness? Snuck up to the slopes and pushed his nemesis to his death.'

'Or was it the chef?' said James. 'Still fuming about Charlie's frozen-snails aspersion – he'd lain in wait in a snowdrift wielding a deadly length of cheese wire.'

Stuart smiled indulgently. 'There were witnesses to the event

35

and none of them saw anyone else intervene in Charlie's fatal trajectory. Also not only did Ben seem genuinely ill but he was actually upset by Charlie's death. He said that the past week had acted as a sort of catharsis. Seeing Charlie outside of the confines of school and realising that everyone else considered him a boor and bully lessened some of the personal impact on himself. He'd been at the beginning of a process of healing that spending the remainder of the week with Charlie might have completed. He claimed his death was not something he would have ever wished for.

'However, he had shown a particular interest in Hedy's special cookies. He had even acquired some of the ingredients to try to recreate them himself. And it was the biscuits, and in particular one of the ingredients, that the new investigation now put under the spotlight.'

'Hedy *did* poison the biscuits!' said Judy. 'That's a shame. I quite liked the sound of her. Using her feminine wiles to twist the men round her little finger and all the while having that dreadful husband to contend with. I was hoping she wasn't a murderer.'

Stuart shook his head. 'The coroner confirmed that Charlie had not been poisoned. He was in no doubt that the cause of death was a major chest trauma from the high-speed collision with a tree. But he was curious about Charlie's eyes.'

'His eyes?' asked Judy.

'They were bloodshot and inflamed. "Red raw" apparently. He called for the ski goggles that Charlie had been wearing to be inspected. Specks of a fine red powder were found, lodged in the seal around the lenses.'

Stuart paused and sipped his whisky, leaving his audience waiting. 'Analysis of the red residue found in the goggles, which may well have involved someone tasting a speck on their finger, revealed it to be paprika.'

'Oh no!' said Judy.

'One of the not-so-secret ingredients in Hedy's spiced biscuits and a particularly aggressive irritant when in contact with sensitive body parts such as the eyeballs.

'The forensic conclusion was that the paprika, a particularly peppery variety, was powerful enough to have temporarily blinded the man and precipitated the accident.

'This of course put Hedy once again in the spotlight. She and her husband, Yannik, were interrogated by the police, the local crew now replaced by detectives from Zurich. Hedy had access to the paprika that she used liberally in her cooking, but why would she kill "the sweet Mr Charlie who had shown her nothing but kindness?" as she said to us that evening in the hotel bar after being interviewed but not yet charged. "And of course I had my keys surrendered. How could I have played with Charlie's *Skibrille*, his googles! My poor cookies I had to leave on the step of the door." Her English was disintegrating with her distress.

'After she left, Ben and Ned agreed that she had no apparent motive to do away with Charlie, who may well have seemed a potential means of escape from her unpleasant partner. Although personally I think that would have been a case of jumping out of the pan into the fire. Mr Berger, if he suspected anything was going on between his wife and Charlie Sarns, might have ample reason to want to do him harm. But he swore he never set foot in any kitchen and declared himself 'allergic' to his wife's biscuits. Also, like Hedy since the incident with the watch, he had no means of accessing the Sarnses' chalet and contaminating the goggles.

'"Thank goodness I never set foot in that place," said Ben, whose fingerprints, along with Herr Berger's, were not found in Chalet Edelweiss. "If the police are looking for a motive, taking my revenge on Sarns through food would have been only too fitting."

'Pip Sarns was and remained the main suspect, even after the police concluded their investigation. We had all witnessed her jealousy over Hedy and knew that Charlie had a reputation for infidelity. Even more damning, a jar of paprika was found in the kitchen at Chalet Edelweiss. But it was clean of fingerprints and Pip claimed to have never seen the ingredient or indeed any of the contents of the food cupboards before.

'"Do I look," she said, her voice shaking as she recalled her humiliating treatment by the police, "like a woman who cooks?!"'

'So the case was unsolved?' asked Sara.

'By the police yes. While the paprika in the goggles was ruled to have been a probable cause of the accident, it could not be proven that it had been put there maliciously or even intentionally. Although the amount was more, in the forensics experts' opinion, than could be explained by someone just handling biscuits that contained the substance. It was impossible to prove that any of the guests or staff at the resort had deliberately tampered with the goggles. Charlie's death was officially recorded as misadventure.'

'She got away with it,' said Judy.

'You said the police didn't solve the case,' said Dinah eyeing Stuart carefully. 'I suspect you have more to tell.'

Stuart pursed his lips and stroked his goatee. 'I had no more proof at my fingertips than the police did. I did however have some information that I chose not to disclose.'

Sara whistled. 'Withholding evidence?'

'Not evidence. Just knowledge that may or may not have had some bearing on the case. But which I knew from my law training would not be enough to bring a charge against anyone.'

He cleared his throat. 'I would like to take your attention back to the watch. The one that Charlie was wearing when he died. The ugly expensive watch that had belonged to his grandfather.

Stopped dead at twenty-five past six, which confused the investigation as he was still in the chalet at that time, fast asleep according to his wife. The question is what was it doing on his wrist, when it had allegedly been stolen.'

'He must have found it,' said Dinah. 'In his sock drawer or whatever other "safe place" he'd forgotten he'd hidden it in. Too embarrassed to tell his wife after all the fuss she made.'

'That was certainly the conclusion that the police came to. The watch was one that required winding up. Again, it seemed odd that he hadn't corrected the time before he set off.'

Judy groaned. 'If you're going to tell us he was killed at half past six in the morning and his accident on the slopes was somehow faked to befuddle the investigation, then I'm sorry, Stuart, but I'm calling bull—'

'No need, Ms Monye. There is a much simpler explanation.

'On the evening before Charlie's death, I had been waiting for Ben and Ned to finish getting spruced up for the grand tasting menu experience at the hotel. I was enjoying a small whisky appetiser in the chalet lounge when I saw a figure at one of the windows. It was Hedy, beckoning me to come outside. She met me on the porch. Her eyes were red as if the crying had continued since that morning's accusations about the missing watch. Indeed, perhaps it had been amplified by the reaction of her husband to having his room searched and being told his wife was in danger of losing her job. She was holding two cardboard boxes and handed one of them to me.

'"Cookies for you and the other gentlemen," she said. "To say thank you for this morning. This box," she said with a defiant lift of her chin, "is for Mr Sarns, as he too defended my honour. I will leave them on his porch. I only hope he does not share them with that …"

'My German was good enough to know that the word she used to describe Pip was not a compliment. She turned pleading eyes to me. "I need your help," she said. "Please, Mr Yorker." She placed her soft fingers on my hand and glanced quickly over each shoulder. "There is more than just cookies in the box."

'I raised the lid. There, nestled among the spiced biscuits, lay Charlie's ugly watch. My eyes widened at the implication.

"'*Nein, nein*, Mr Yorker. I did not take the watch. What good would it be to me? I could not even sell so *ein schreckliches* thing. This I found in my cleaning bag, hidden inside a pocket. I did not place it in there. My bag was in the kitchen this morning while Herr und Frau Sarns were still in the chalet. She put it in there. She wants me to be called a thief!"

'It was a terrible accusation. However, jealousy had burned darkly in Pip Sarns' eyes and if Charlie already had a reputation for playing away, perhaps his wife had resorted to drastic action.

"'What do you want me to do?" I asked.

"'Return it," she said. "I cannot get inside the chalet, I no longer have the key. But you are their friend. Please. Put it somewhere where it could have been lost. Somewhere silly forgetful Charlie may have left it. Please, Mr Yorker."

'How could I refuse? She had been cruelly treated ...'

'You believed her?' interrupted Sara. 'Just like that, you decided on the basis of her big blue eyes and tremulous accented English, that she was telling the truth?'

Stuart shrugged. 'Perhaps I was swayed by the fact that Charlie and Pip were not the most appealing of couples and I was willing to believe the worst of them. But even if Hedy had in a moment of madness taken the watch, at least she was now trying to do the right thing and return it. So I agreed.

'I had no opportunity that night as we were late leaving the chalet, delayed by the time it took for Ned to persuade Ben that the meal would be a good idea. Not knowing of course that Ben would unfortunately be one of the guests to consume a bad mussel.

'First thing the next morning I headed over to Chalet Edelweiss with the intention of asking if I could borrow a book on German cathedrals that I had spotted on the shelves there. I had no interest in the damn buildings, but it was the only title I could recall. My intention was to get into the building and carefully drop the watch somewhere near the bookcase, perhaps behind one of the ornaments. However, as I stepped onto the porch, I heard raised voices from within. Nothing new there, I thought. Then the door was suddenly flung open and I heard Pip screech, "She's poisoned me, I tell you," as Charlie barrelled out of the door and slammed it shut behind him.

'"Stuart!" he said. "Sorry, mate, in a bit of a rush." He was dressed for the slopes, skis over his shoulder, designer goggles perched on his head.

'"Everything OK?" I asked, nodding at the closed door.

'"Not really. Pip's been throwing up half the night. Blames it on Hedy's cookies. The little minx left me a box on the doorstep last night. We were so hungry after that so-called gourmet meal that we wolfed the lot. I'm feeling absolutely fine, but Pip's laid out on the sofa like a dead duck. Look, I can't stop to chat, I'm going to catch that early bird Stinks, see what he's actually made of on the snow."

'"But …" I began as he pushed past, about to explain that Ben too was incapacitated that morning. But he was in too much of a hurry. "Your watch," I said. He stopped.

'"I found it," I said. I had to extemporise, knowing that entering the chalet while Pip was indisposed would be awkward. "Up at the spa. I popped in for a quick steam this morning and there it was under one of the benches in the changing room. You must have taken it up there with you after all. Maybe it was in your pocket." I was babbling, and he looked confused. But he grabbed the watch from me and strapped it to his wrist with just a quick glance.

41

'"Damn thing needs winding up. Thanks, Stu. I owe you one." And he was off.

'And the time it was stopped at?' James asked.

'Six twenty-five,' Stuart confirmed. 'The police were flummoxed by the watch and where it had come from, but I couldn't explain without implicating myself or Hedy. The story of me finding it at the spa wouldn't really hold up. It was only because Charlie was in such a rush that he took my explanation at face value. If he'd had time to question it, I'm sure he'd have remembered that the spa complex had already been thoroughly searched for it.' He scratched at his beard with his finger. 'But of course if he did have any doubts, they died with him on the slopes.'

'That explains the watch,' said Sara with a shrug, 'and tells us you have a certain gullibility when it comes to attractive young women.' She folded her arms. 'It doesn't prove that Pip Sarns killed her husband.'

'It certainly does not,' Stuart said. 'And I don't believe she did. Her knowledge of the culinary basics was such that I doubt she could have picked out paprika from turmeric or oregano. There were several people at the resort with a grudge against Charlie Sarns, maybe one or more of them enough to want to harm him or at least make him take a tumble on the slopes.

'But on that morning, as Charlie pushed past me in his haste to hit the slopes and perhaps humiliate Ben all over again, I noticed something that changes the story.' Stuart took a sip of his whisky and waited until he was sure he had his audience's full attention. Dinah obligingly put down her sea dragon. 'It's always bothered me somewhat,' Stuart continued, 'that Pip didn't seem to have mentioned the anomaly to the police.'

'What anomaly?' asked Judy

'Is that the right word? Perhaps I mean mistake. Charlie was in such a flap that morning leaving the lodge. His skis over one shoulder, goggles perched ready for action on his head. I almost mentioned it to him, but he was in too much of a rush. And it didn't seem to matter at the time.'

'What didn't?' asked Judy patiently.

'He and Pip had matching goggles, very distinctive, and I imagine very expensive. Wrap around with gold-coloured lenses that could do all kinds of special things in different light conditions. Which they explained to us at length when we were round there for dinner. The only difference between the pair was that Pip's had three tiny gold stickers at the edge of the black frame, which matched the design on her ski jacket. Her "lucky stars", a reference to which, on top of the many bottles of wine we had consumed, prompted an off-key Madonna impersonation that Charlie compared to a cat's dying wails. Much to Hedy's amusement as she was serving up the veal.

'The goggles on Charlie's blond thatch that morning were Pip's; I saw the little gold stars blinking in the sun.'

'Ooh!' said Judy.

Aha, so the puzzle queen hadn't seen that one coming, Stuart thought. He paused, enjoying the moment. *Is this how a pianist feels*, he mused, *as they execute an arpeggio?*

'Perhaps the grieving widow never noticed he had taken the wrong ones.' He shrugged. 'She doesn't appear to have pointed it out to the police, more concerned perhaps with how the paprika could have got in them. Unaware that while Hedy may well have 'given up her keys' – as she was so keen to prove to me by asking me to return the watch – the incompetent housekeeper in charge of them may well have been confused over which ones had been returned and when.

'Perhaps for Pip, losing Charlie was a new beginning, rather than the end of her world. And if she realised that she was in fact the intended victim of a "prank" that had turned deadly, it would be simpler and safer to look the other way.'

PUZZLES

Goose Egg

Which five characters in Stuart's story might 'confusingly', like the narrator himself, be found on a Christmas Dinner table?

Here is the Cast of Characters to jog your memory.

STUART YORKE	NED LUDDENHAM
HEDY BERGER	FRAU FLISTERY
CHARLIE SARNS	HERR FLISTERY
PIP SARNS	YANNICK BERGER
BEAU DASCER	BEN 'STINKS' GIPAL
RUSSELL STOUBER	

A Cook's Conundrum

The ingredients in Hedy's spicy biscuit recipe are listed below, but in her attempt to keep it secret she has missed out the vowels in each word and shifted the spaces. Can you sift out the right ingredients?

150 g	SV DPL NF LR
125 g	GRT DPRMS NCHS
125 g	FR DGCL DBTT R
1 tbsp	DJ NMST RD
1 tbsp	S WTP PRK
1/2 tsp	S SL TFLKS
1 tsp	GRN DBL CKPPPR
1 tbsp	SS MSDS

Final Puzzle Clue #1

One of the words in Hedy's recipe is the name of a French town that was the birthplace of a fifteenth-century Duke of Burgundy, known as Philip the _ _ _ _ .

The missing four-letter word is the clue that you need to take forward to help solve the final puzzle at the end of the book.

BENEATH THE STREETS

'To paraphrase Jane Eyre,' said Helena, looking gloomily out of the open back door into the rain-drenched garden beyond, 'it's too wet to go out, so shall we have another story?'

'Sounds more like Dr Seuss,' said Judy, topping up her coffee mug from the cafetière. 'But a good idea nonetheless.'

The Bracestone House guests were gathered in the kitchen where Mrs Linden had cooked them up 'a full Yorkshire', including local sausages, eggs from 'an old dear in the village who keeps chucks', and black pudding, 'from over the border'.

'Scotland?' asked Sara, as she tucked into a slice.

'Lancashire,' Mrs Linden replied.

It had been James's idea to breakfast in the kitchen rather than the more austere dining room. For all his teasing of her, or maybe because of it, Mrs Linden obviously had a soft spot for him and agreed to the invasion of her domain.

The farmhouse-style table was big enough to accommodate them all and the old-fashioned range and well-scrubbed wooden surfaces gave the room a homely appeal. Although Helena, standing in the doorway, her hands wafting cold damp air over her clothes, doubted she'd ever get the 'greasy spoon' smell out of her oyster-shell pink silk blouse.

'Perfect time for a story,' said James, placing his knife and fork on his emptied plate. He patted his stomach. 'It'll give us chance to recover from the first of today's feasts. Be a love, Mrs L, and put on another pot of your finest Joe.' He added a wink that no one else in the room would have considered wise.

'I've got a story from my past,' said Helena, re-joining the others at the table. 'And from the more distant past, over a hundred years ago to be exact.'

'Ooh, fabulous,' said Dinah. 'I love a historical murder. Is there a steam train in it or some bodice ripping?'

'Neither I'm afraid,' said Helena. 'There are some twenties gangsters though.'

'Perfect,' said Dinah. 'I'm going to make a start on an octopus.' She selected a mass of red yarn from the denim bag by her side along with a gold-coloured hook. 'Off you go.'

Helena began.

'I screamed so loudly that I'm surprised the walls didn't shudder.

'Toby shouted: "No, please, no! Leave us alone!"'

Helena glanced around her confused-looking audience. 'Oh. They do say start your story in the middle of the action, don't they? Perhaps that's too far in. I'll reel back a bit.

'This all happened many years ago. Long before I met Jon.' She patted her partner's knee. 'Back in the heady days of my twenties, when I thought I had my whole life planned out. Which I now realise is just a waste of a spreadsheet.

'Do you know Wethergate? Quaint market town, at the western edge of North Yorkshire. I was spending Christmas there with Toby, my fiancé of three and a bit months. We were both teachers at a sixth form college and were making the most of the holiday. We'd passed a couple of lovely days exploring the town, sampling the many bars, taking a boat trip on the river, admiring the stained glass in the minster and indulging in mulled ale and cranberry-stuffed Yorkshire puddings at the Christmas market.

'I had been looking forward to spending Christmas Eve in our hotel's award-winning restaurant, before snuggling into a comfy armchair in the tweedy but cosy lounge, sipping a Baileys or two and gazing into Toby's serious brown eyes as we discussed our wedding plans. But Toby, wanting perhaps to avoid another debate about trad church vs a marquee in a field, had instead booked a surprise. A tour of the labyrinth of underground rooms that an eighteenth-century merchant had dug out, or rather had his workers dig out for him, beneath the streets of the town.

"'Lovely,' I'd said, when he produced the tickets with a flourish. "And after we've spent a couple of hours poking around a maze of cramped, damp and probably haunted tunnels, maybe we could sign up for supper with Dracula."

'Words that would come back to – hah! – haunt me later that evening when quite frankly sitting down with a vampire would have been preferable.

"'No one knows exactly why he made the tunnels," Toby explained excitedly as we approached the tour's starting point by the old tollbooth. "There's not much information about him on the website. It's all a bit sketchy. He was a tea and cloth merchant so he may have been planning storage units, though you'd have thought it would be too damp. There was some speculation that he might have planned to let them out to wine sellers or some such. Anyway, they were abandoned in Victorian times when people, really poor people, started moving in and squatting there. Horrible conditions. Living, birthing and dying in there."

"'Dying?' I said. "So the tunnels probably *are* haunted."

'He shrugged. "Only if you believe in that sort of thing." He obviously didn't. "There are plans to open them up as community spaces and shops for local craftspeople in the future."

'Toby had done his research. I questioned why we were shelling out fifteen pounds each for a guided tour, when he could have told me everything I needed to know.

'"You're not allowed in without a guide," he insisted, "and they know tons of extra information and stories that aren't on the website. A couple of different companies run tours, but this sounded the most authentic."

'Our start time was six o'clock – just about when I'd been planning to start tucking into the restaurant's famous Marmaray anchovies, followed by a seafood Wellington, with the prospect of chestnut profiteroles for dessert. The snow that had hung heavy in the sky all afternoon was now falling, speckling the cobbled streets and creating dizzying whirls beneath the yellow glow of the street lights. A small group of people were already gathered by the 'Tunnels Tour Starts Here' sign. They looked like a bunch of reluctant carol singers: three young men in hoodies, a couple in their sixties, muffled up in thick coats, hats and scarves, and a tall, slim woman with a blonde bob, whose expensive-looking jacket, white linen with a gold trim, seemed inadequate for the weather. Our guide was easy to spot, being the one dressed in a heavy woollen cape-like coat with a deep velvet collar and a tricorne hat.

'"Is he supposed to be from *Poldark*?" I asked. "I thought that was Cornwall."

'"It was. And he isn't. That's William Higginbotham," Toby said approvingly.

'"Beg your pardon?"

'"I was telling you about him before. The tea and cloth merchant. That's who the guide's dressed up as. He looks exactly the same as the painting of him on the website. I wonder if that beard is real?"

'"Well, it matches his hair, though that doesn't look convincing either. But don't go tugging it to find out." Toby could be unpredictable at times. It was one of the things I loved about him.'

'Note the past tense,' said Dinah without looking up from the complex web of chains in her crochet-in-progress. 'I take it this tale doesn't end with "Reader, I married him …"?'

Helena smiled and continued her story.

'The black beard covered the lower half of the guide's face so thickly that I wondered if we would be able to hear him speak. But not to worry, as the minster bells chimed the hour, his voice boomed out.

'"Welcome, welcome ladies and gents, to what I promise will be an exhilarating and potentially life-changing experience."

'There was a stir among the small crowd. The phrase "life-changing" usually accompanied either a big-money win or horrible physical injuries. Not what any of us had signed up for. Not that I personally had signed up for anything, I reminded myself as the guide, who despite his garb, introduced himself as Gavin, led us down the street to a large wooden door next to an apparently abandoned shop. He unlocked and opened the door and instructed us to follow him inside and down the stairs. The way was lit by flickering wall lights. I at first took them to be gas lamps but realised they were electric, presumably set to "ye olde atmosphere" mode.

'There was a bottleneck at the foot of the stairs, where Gavin was trying to make space to address us all. Some jostling broke out among the three young men who were indiscreetly drinking from cans of beer "hidden" in their pockets. I heard a grumble from the elderly man whose wife had introduced herself, unasked, to Gavin as "Jean from Lansing, Kansas, USA and this is Malcolm. He's not a big talker." The willowy woman looked on with an expression of serene patience. She and Gavin seemed to know each other. He repeatedly glanced at her as if for approval. Was she his girlfriend? Or his boss? Either way, he seemed keen to impress her.

'"Edinburgh's vaults may have its witches," he said, "and I believe the catacombs of Paris boast an impressive display of skulls. But only the Wethergate Tunnels can offer sex and drugs and rock 'n' roll."

'Jean gave a little squeak and squeezed her husband's arm, but he appeared oblivious.

'Gavin cleared his throat. "But before we start, a brief safety warning. The ground in the tunnels is uneven, the lighting in some parts is patchy and ..." he paused, "occasionally unreliable. The rooms leading off from the corridors aren't all accessible. Some are in use by private individuals and have locked doors, others have been deemed unsafe. Please only go through the doors that I indicate. We had a catastrophic roof collapse earlier this year. The guide on duty that day is sadly no longer with us."

'This elicited a gasp from Jean. Gavin frowned and continued. "He got a job advertising golf sales. Said he never wanted to work indoors again."

'How old was Gavin? I mused. The silver streaks in the black beard and now slightly askew wig made him look middle-aged but his skin was unlined. He might only be in his early twenties.

'We followed his bulky shape down corridors lit by the flickering "antique" lamps and sporadic green safety lights, which pointed to the way out. The air was musty and chalky, but dry rather than damp and it was definitely not as cold as outside. We took left and right turns, sometimes heading further underground, sometimes rising back up, past boarded-over doorways and openings into empty spaces. Gavin mentioned points of interest along the way, including a room with a barrelled ceiling lit by a single red lamp which was allegedly used as a brothel in the late nineteenth century and "the Customs

51

House", a square room furnished with an ancient, stained sink and a tiled floor, where ten kilos of cocaine were discovered in 1956. The eyes of the young male trio lit up when Gavin announced we'd be "popping in" to the latter room for "light refreshments" on the way back. They obviously hadn't seen as I had the small kettle, jar of instant coffee and packet of digestive biscuits that awaited our return.

'As we gathered around our guide before a painted green door, he spread his arms and cloak wide in a dramatic, almost vampiric gesture. I took hold of Toby's hand, which felt surprisingly cold and clammy. "You OK?" I whispered. He nodded but his face was pale and he kept glancing at the ceiling as Gavin folded his arms back down and started to talk about William Higginbotham.

'"... the great-grandson of the original merchant of the same name. Higginbotham Junior Junior Junior, or 'the fourth', for the benefit of our American friends," he smirked at Jean and her husband, "who had continued the family trade in cloth and tea, entered the tunnels one night in 1923 and never came out again." He stroked his bushy beard and side-eyed the willowy woman. She was examining her nails, but there was the trace of a smile on her lips.

'"Less financially astute than his predecessors," Gavin continued. "William the fourth had whittled the family fortune down to a nub. Found himself in hock to too many people, including one Alf 'Snapper' Gatersby. A particularly nasty local criminal with a reputation for random acts of brutality. There's a picture of him in an old newspaper report, thickset with a head smooth as a snooker ball and dark deep-set eyes. Not someone you'd want to meet in a dark alley, or indeed, a dimly lit tunnel."

'Toby glanced quickly over his shoulder. His grip on my hand was starting to hurt.

'Gavin pressed on. "On the night in question, Christmas Eve

as it happened, William arranged a meeting with Snapper down here," he stretched out his left arm, displaying the silky lining of his cloak, "in this very room. Let's step inside."

'The "room" was square in shape. Flat slabs of stone covered the entire floor apart from the very centre, where a slab was missing, revealing the earth floor below. The walls were bare, the same rough plaster as the corridors, although holes and a channel scored along one side indicated there may have once been shelves. On the wall opposite the door there was a dark arch-shaped opening just above head height. A green safety light glowing steadily below it provided the room's only illumination.

'The air was chillier in there, making the skin of my face tingle. I rewrapped my scarf more snugly and reached for Toby's hand, but he now had both of them firmly in his pockets. The young men were lined up against one of the walls, nudging each other, as if daring one of them to misbehave. Jean was listening intently to Gavin, her head nodding in time to his words. Her husband meanwhile was scanning the room with a small smile on his face as if it reminded him of somewhere more pleasant.

'Gavin stood with his feet apart, hands clasped behind his back.

'"Young William, as he was known, though he was in his early fifties by then, had a sort of office down here," said Gavin. "Just a desk and a couple of chairs. More of a hideaway than a place of business. Somewhere he came perhaps to escape the horrors of his financial ruin up in the outside world."

'"A man cave," muttered Jean darkly, glaring up at her husband, who by the blissful expression on his face, was in a different world entirely.

'"It appears that it was Snapper's idea to meet down here. Which should surely have been a red flag for William. But he was desperate and perhaps by that point was resigned to his fate. Or, as events transpired, maybe not …"

'Jean sneezed.

'"Bless you," I said automatically.

'One of the bantering boys loudly broke wind. Had that been the dare? Nobody said a word.

'Unruffled, Gavin continued. "Snapper insisted on bringing his own security too, a local ruffian known as Slippy Pete. Notoriously handy with his fists and quick and deadly with a length of fishing wire. William agreed to the arrangement. His secretary, my own long-departed great-grandfather Oliver Judd, thought this unwise."

'"Your great-grandfather worked for the Higginbothams!" asked Jean. "Is that why you chose this career?"

'Gavin looked cross at having his flow interrupted, though really if he wanted to hold us all in his tale he maybe shouldn't have been so keen to name-drop his connections.

'"It was one of the factors," he said, smoothing the velvet collar of his cloak. Confirming my suspicion that he was in this for the costume as much as anything. "Oliver stuck by Young William even when the chips were down. And they were so far down by this point, they were subterranean." He sniggered at his own little joke, which nobody else acknowledged, except for his willowy girlfriend/boss, who merely raised her eyebrows. "There was a very strong likelihood that Young William was about to lose not only his business, but also his home, a fine Georgian mansion on Gifford Street, and leave his wife and heirs destitute."

'"And your great-grandfather out of a job," observed Jean.

'Gavin cleared his throat. "Perhaps. But with so much at risk, Young William may have felt he had no other choice but to meet Snapper on his terms. He forbade my great-grandfather from following him into the tunnels that night. Instructing him to wait outside. Which he did, on a night colder even than this one. He was standing sentinel at the same front door that

54

we came through earlier, when William entered the tunnels at quarter to five. Snapper and Slippy Pete arrived fifteen minutes later, just as the falling snow turned to a blizzard. They were given admittance by my great-grandfather, who locked the door once they had stepped through and resumed his vigil in the snow, for what he hoped wouldn't be too long." Gavin crossed his arms over his chest and dropped his head. There was silence in the room. Even the bantering boys seemed captured by the story, no doubt hoping for a violent and bloody outcome. My feet were going numb with the cold and lack of movement. I wanted to stamp them or do a little jig, but it seemed inappropriate. Only the clouds of our breath disturbed the chill air as we waited for Gavin to go on. The minutes ticked silently by.

'"And then …" snapped the willowy woman at last. "What happened next, Gavin? Aren't you going to tell us?"

'His big sister? I wondered, her tone reminding me of my own experience with inter-sibling taunts.

'Gavin lifted his head and there were sharp intakes of breath all round. In the intervening five minutes his eyes seemed to have aged, shadowed by dark crescents, his pupils were huge. His skin glistened and looked loose on his bones. His full lips were tinged with purple.

'"Over an hour later …" he intoned – yes I know that sounds overdramatic but that's exactly what he did, he *intoned*, like a funeral bell – "… my great-grandfather Oliver was half-frozen to the bone, in the icy stillness that had followed the blizzard. He'd not dared to leave his post or move more than a few inches from the door. He heard a sudden roaring sound from within the tunnel and a hammering on the wooden door. He fumbled the key with frozen fingers. As soon as the lock turned, the door was wrenched inwards and Snapper's henchman, Slippy Pete, came charging out. Before he had chance to speak, Oliver was being held up against the wall, Pete's fingers around his throat and his beaky face inches from his own."

'"Ooh, that's the spirit," Jean declared. "You've really got into your stride now, Gavin. Very good. Do go on."

'Gavin blinked as if her voice had thrown him back into the room. He took a deep breath and continued.

'"Slippy was shouting about secret tunnels, hidden exits, trapdoors. Demanding that my great-grandfather tell him how William had got out. Oliver was baffled. He tried to explain that there was no other way out. The tunnels were a closed system and this door they were standing by was the only entrance and exit."

'"Wouldn't be allowed today, would it?" Jean said. "You Brits are very keen on your Health and Safety. No fire exit. Can you imagine, Malcolm?" Her husband had wandered over to inspect the wall alcove; he nodded, but not in apparent response to her question.

'The willowy woman bent towards Jean. "But I'm afraid it is still the case. I agree it's not ideal. If there was a fire or a flood, there could be a stampede, and only one way out! I bet that wouldn't be allowed in Kansas."

'Jean's eyes widened. "Did you hear that, Malcolm? In an emergency we're to sprint for the front door."

'Was Malcolm deaf? I wondered. He did appear to have some type of hearing aid in his left ear, half hidden by the flaps of his plaid cap. Maybe he had turned it off.

'Gavin meanwhile was proving himself quite the professional. Once Jean had finished, he continued his tale.

'"Slippy wasn't having any of it. He examined the snowy ground in front of the tunnel. The unblemished surface must have satisfied him because he muttered, 'Well he didn't come out this way.' He grabbed Oliver and dragged him inside the tunnel, making him lock the door behind them, then marched him down the corridors. Remember, back than there was no electric lighting. There were oil lamps on the walls lit by William when he arrived but by now several of them were running low.

"'As the pair hurried along, they cast wild shadows high and low, and they both stumbled on the rough ground. Pete seemed uncertain of which turns to take and might not have made it back to this room without Oliver's instructions. My great-grandfather was frightened for his life, not knowing what he might find when they got here. When they arrived, Pete flung him into the room. The desk was still there, towards the back wall, on its surface a pewter water jug, a large ceramic tankard and a guttering oil lamp. The two chairs were flung aside on the floor, along with a second tankard. But Oliver barely noticed any of that at first because of the horror that lay in the centre of the floor. Alfred 'Snapper' Gatersby, sprawled on his belly, his bald head surrounded by a pool of blood. His throat had been cut."

"'That'll be why they got rid of the paving slab," Jean said helpfully. "In poor taste to have kept it. Don't you think Malcolm?" She nodded in agreement with herself without checking for her husband's response.

"'Pete told Oliver that he had been standing guard outside the closed door of the room, on the orders of Snapper, while his boss and William had their 'talk' inside. After about forty minutes he decided to make sure all was well inside. He knocked on the door and when he got no reply, opened it to the scene just described. Snapper dead on the floor and no sign of Young William. He'd scoured the room tapping the walls, even standing on the desk and holding up the waning lamp to investigate the arched opening above it, peering through to the empty room on the other side. Then he'd inspected the corridors and adjacent rooms before going to fetch Oliver.

57

'"My great-grandfather, in a state of shock, said they must call the police. It was obviously too late for an ambulance. Slippy Pete just laughed and said there was no way they were leaving this infernal maze until they found the man who had killed his boss. They spent the rest of the night methodically exploring the tunnels and rooms. Where they found locked doors, they burst them open. Crates and skeps were wrenched apart, sacks slashed, every nook and cranny prodded and investigated. All the while my great grandfather protesting that there was no secret exit, no other way out. He had in his pocket the only key to the door.

'"Finally, they gave up, and on emerging from the tunnels my great-grandfather hailed a pair of passing constables. He felt he had no choice, though he feared for what it would mean for his employer, who must surely be the main suspect. However, despite an intensive investigation by local detectives, William Higginbotham was never found. The coroner concluded that the victim had been stunned by the heavy tankard before his throat was slashed. Fingerprinting, in its infancy in the twenties, would have been of no use, as the tankard and its handle were wiped clean. Slippy Pete was questioned. But both Oliver and the two constables he'd called to the scene confirmed that there had been no blood on Pete's hands or clothing and in the absence of a knife or other weapon, no charge of murder was ever brought against him. My great-grandfather was questioned intensely but he too was eventually let go. The murder of the Snapper was never solved and to this day no one knows what happened to Young William."

'Gavin flashed a brief smile and rubbed his hands. "Moving on. If you follow me back out to the corridor, we will continue the tour to the Vaults. The very space where eighties death metal band Valhalla Calling recorded their seminal album *Drag Me Down to Hel*."

'"Hang on," said one of the youths, who had a large peace symbol on the front of his hoodie. "You mean he got away with it?"

'One of his friends looked round the room. "He escaped through there," he said, pointing up at the arched opening in the wall. His hoodie had the word SMART and a donkey on it. "Obvious, innit? He stood on the desk and went through there to the next room. Waited till the other pair were nattering away, sneaked out to the entrance and got out using his own key."

'Gavin shook his head. "There were no footsteps in the snow outside the entrance, remember. No one had left." He put up a hand to stop the lad's incoming objection. "Even if there were another way out, William couldn't have reached it. That opening does indeed lead to another room behind, but that room was blocked off at the time. The police had to dismantle a brick wall that had filled the doorway for decades. The flooring inside was fine sandy soil, undisturbed by footprints of any kind."

'"That's right," said Malcolm. The first words he had spoken. He was a large man, but his voice was soft and low. He reached to his ear and pulled out an earbud from which came the sound of distant violins and a soprano's voice.

'"Delibes," murmured the blonde woman. "Beautiful."

'Malcolm tapped the bud into silence and slipped it inside his jacket pocket.

'"My grandpa was a young constable at the time. In the North Yorkshire police for twenty years before he moved my grandma and my father and his siblings over the pond. Big fan of Eisenhower, for a while at least. He was the smallest and lightest of the officers sent to investigate that night, so he was given the task of seeing if it was possible to get through that gap. He managed it fine, sat there hunched up, swinging his legs over the edge. But there was no chance he was going to drop down the other side. Said he'd have busted his legs. So they got him back down and they demolished the bricked–up doorway instead."

"'What did he reckon happened?" asked one of the young lads, hunched inside his hoodie. "How did he think the William bloke got out?"

'Malcolm shrugged. "He was as baffled as the rest of them. There were rumours at the time about Higginbotham's wife. Apparently, she did alright for herself afterwards. Maybe William was sending her money from abroad or Scotland or wherever else he'd hidden himself. The cops all hated working that case. They were convinced the place was haunted and refused to stand on guard on their own. Some of them complained of weird smells and shadows, others, including my grandpa, heard tapping noises when no one when else was supposed to be down here. Grandpa claimed he heard a moaning sound once and thought the river was going to come flooding in. It thoroughly rattled him, that case, more than anything he encountered later on the streets of Wichita."

'The boys moved closer to the Americans.

"'Go on, Malcolm," said Joan. "Tell them the rest."

'Malcolm looked over to Gavin, who said, "Be my guest," before folding his arms over his chest. The blonde woman, standing beside him, smirked.

"'Slippy Pete was arrested for GBH not long after," continued Malcolm. "My grandpa was a sergeant by then and it was one of his last cases in England. The police knew Pete had been a lynchpin in Snapper's empire, which just before the gang leader's death, was about to be busted wide open. They had charges of murder, extortion drug dealing and everything in between waiting to throw at him. Slippy was in charge now and the gang had cleaned their act up, or at least were covering their tracks with legitimate businesses. But a zebra doesn't change its stripes. Slippy couldn't keep himself out of fights. Grandpa, who was one of the officers who interviewed him over the GBH, said Slippy was well-named. Never gave a straight answer when a roundabout one would do. But when my grandpa mentioned the brutal death of his old boss Snapper, it really shook Slippy up. He said he'd got the biggest shock of his life walking into that room. He'd never got over it and never worked out for himself what had gone wrong."

'Gavin clapped his hands sharply to bring everyone's attention back to him. "All very interesting and thank you for the additional insight. But we must press on. I promise the Vaults will not disappoint."

"'Quite a story," said Toby as we trailed at the back of the group leaving the room. He'd got some of his colour back and seemed less anxious. "Worth the price of our tickets, I reckon. A proper locked-room mystery."

"'But an unsatisfying one," I said, being a big fan of *Jonathan Creek* who always found the answer. The best part was finding out not only whodunnit but how. "Without a solution it sounds as though it might have all been made up."

"'What would be the point of that?" he asked. "And anyway," he added as the rest of our group disappeared around a corner ahead. "Malcolm confirmed it, with his story about his grandfather."

"'Maybe he's a plant," I said. "A gangland murder does make the tunnels more exciting. Otherwise it's all a bit samey down here, isn't it? If you get impressionable visitors imagining Snapper's mutilated ghost hanging around, or worse, the undead Young William stalking the corridors for his next victim …"

'At that point the corridor's flickering lights all went out. Toby yelped and clung to me like a drowning kitten. Presumably to reassure me that he would give his life to protect me.

'I pushed him off and grabbed my phone from my pocket. There was no signal showing, but the light of the screen provided some illumination. Toby started stabbing at his own phone before muttering, "It's dead. I knew I should have charged it back at the hotel."

'Our faces glowed pale in the artificial light. Toby's eyes were wide. At both ends of the corridor green emergency lights still glowed, but they added to, rather than lightened, the spooky gloom.

'"One phone will have to do," I said. "We'd better find the others."

'But when we rounded the corner where we had last seen them disappear, we were faced with another bend in the corridor, and shortly afterwards with the choice of two different tunnels. I held my finger to my lips and we both strained our ears for voices. Surely either Gavin or Jean would have something to say about the sudden darkness. But we could hear nothing.

'"We'd better head for the exit," I said.

'"But how are we going to know which twists and turns to take?" Toby asked. "Unless you left a trail of breadcrumbs." He gave a brittle laugh.

'"We follow the exit lights," I said. "That's what they're there …"

'The green lights ahead blinked out. I looked back and the one at the far end of the tunnel had gone out too.

'"I'm pretty certain that's not meant to happen," I whispered.

'"Why are you whispering?" asked Toby, before beginning to shout, "Help! Help! We need help!"'

'Humph,' said Dinah holding up her project to examine what appeared to be a pair of red tentacles, 'It's becoming clearer by the minute why that relationship didn't last.'

Helena continued her story, '"It's like the emergency corridor lights at college," I told him. "They must be connected to a central battery which has failed at the same time as the mains power outage. Maybe there's been a water leak somewhere …"

'"Water?" said Toby his voice rising a pitch. "Like floodwater? It does flood in this part of Yorkshire. I've seen it on the news. Oh my god, we're going to drown."

'I nearly slapped him.'

Dinah chortled.

'Instead I persuaded him that we should retrace our steps to what he helpfully described as "the murder room". Using the waning light of my phone we made our way back. It was such a relief to see the green painted door.

'"We'll wait in here," I said. "Gavin mentioned stopping in the Customs Room on the way back, so, presumably, they'll be heading back the same way. I'm sure they won't be long." We waited in silence. Toby either embarrassed by his bout of hysteria or too petrified to speak.

'I scanned the room with my phone light, mainly to reassure us both that no bogeymen were skulking in the corners. Despite my determination to keep calm, another person's fear can be horribly infectious. My light lingered on the arched opening on the back wall, but it offered up no help. I did a 360-degree scan and then went back over it all again.

'Something didn't look right.

'I examined the walls once more and realised that the holes and gouges where the shelves had been had disappeared. I shone the light on the floor. It was bare earth, not stone flags. We'd been too concerned with our predicament to notice when we'd walked in.

'"This isn't the murder room," I said.

'"Alright, keep your hair on. I only called it that as a joke."

'"No, I mean we're in a different room." I shone the pale light up to the arched space, which unlike the one in the murder room didn't have an emergency light beneath it, working or not. "I think we took a wrong turn and have ended up on the other side of it. In the room that was still bricked up in 1923."

'I went out into the corridor and examined the door. It was painted green but on closer inspection its smooth surface looked quite modern, unlike the worn panels of the door we'd passed through before.

'"It's fine," I said. "All we need to do is take a right outside this door, then another right and another. That should take us back to the corridor with the murder room in it."

'It didn't. The two doors in the corridor we found ourselves in were both boarded up. Toby began to shout for help again, but as before, there was no reply.

'"I don't understand," I said. "It must be a trickier layout than I thought."

'Toby made a small moaning sound. "What's not to understand? We're going to die here. No one is going to know where we are and we're going to die."

'"Don't be ridiculous," I said in my best imitation of our college's principal. It got his attention. "The lights will come back on soon. In the meantime, put your left hand on the wall and we'll retrace our steps, this time taking left turns."

'Five minutes later we were back in the room that wasn't the murder room, and I had a plan. I held up my phone light to the back wall. "I'm going up there," I said, pointing to the arched opening. "So I can look down into the other room. If the door's still open, I might be able to see out into the corridor. I'll be able to call out to the others when they pass by. Come on; I need your help."

'Toby reluctantly allowed me to clamber onto his shoulders, from where I could easily reach the ledge and climb onto it, just like Malcolm's grandfather had done, from the other side, all those years ago. The ledge was surprisingly wide. The wall between the two rooms must have been about two feet thick. There was enough space for me to wriggle myself around and sit with my feet dangling over into the other side. I understood why Malcolm's grandad hadn't wanted to drop down when he was up there facing the other way. In the dark it seemed like I was perched on the edge of an abyss. There were no sounds from the corridor beyond and the emergency light in there, like all the others, was out.

'"Shine some light back down here, please," begged Toby.

'As I twisted round with the phone clamped in my hand, its feeble beam glanced over the ceiling above me. It wasn't arched like the stone on each side. It was flat and recessed.

'And there was a trapdoor in it.'

'You opened it, I presume?' asked James.

'I tried. I expected it to be locked, but when I pushed upwards, it moved ever so slightly. It was heavy, as if something was on top of it, weighing it down. I put my shoulder to it, with all the while Toby calling "What are you doing now?!" from below. Again the trapdoor shifted, enough to convince me that with a bit more effort, I could budge it. This was years before I'd developed my mindful power kettlebells workout, but even then, I had decent upper body strength. I pressed everything into it. Forgetting the dark, the confined space, my fiancé trembling in the emptiness below. I focused and with a final heave the trapdoor flew open. From the chest up I was in a vast dark space, thick with the smell of the river overlaid with the stink of dead rodents. Something not-so-dead brushed against my hand. I dropped my phone and screamed. And Toby joined in.'

Helena gazed wide-eyed at her listeners, lost in the memory.

'Rats?' asked James.

Helena shook her head. 'No, well yes, there were rats or mice. Something small and furry with scuttling feet, definitely. But that wasn't the worst of it.' She closed her eyes at the remembered horror.

'I had to find my phone. The light had gone off when I dropped it. Toby was probably still wittering below, but I'd blanked him out. I leaned forward and gingerly put out both hands, fearing I'd touch warm fur or that my fingers would be nipped by sharp teeth. By some miracle my right hand landed on my phone,' she stopped and swallowed hard. 'The fingers of my left hand brushed against soft cloth then closed around something hard and smooth.'

She paused and swallowed. 'I moved my fingers slowly over the curved surface, found hollows, sockets. I didn't need to switch on my phone to know. I was holding a skull.'

Somebody at the table squealed.

'You'd found Young William!' said Dinah, who Helena was certain wasn't the source of the squeal.

'No,' said Helena. She took a deep breath. 'I'd found Alfred Gatersby, AKA Snapper. I didn't know that straight away of course. When I did switch on my phone, its trembling light showed only pale bones half-covered with shredded rags.

'Hours later, when the lights had come back on in the tunnels, the rest of our party had emerged from the soundproofed Vaults and we were all above ground again, I called the police. The American man, Malcolm, bless him, stayed behind in the murder room, his eyes fixed on the arched opening and the secret that it held. I think he felt some guilt about his grandad not having spotted the trapdoor when he was up there eighty years earlier.

'We stayed three more nights in Wethergate, as planned, before heading home. Ended up having a Boxing Day drink with the willowy woman. Her name was Penelope and she ran the rival tunnel tour company. She'd hoped to be able to undermine Gavin's operation but was now deflated. Gavin had already restyled his website, leading with the headline 'The ONLY tour to have UNCOVERED a skeleton and DISCOVERED the Wethergate Tunnels' HIDDEN SECRET'. She was thinking of cutting her losses and proposing a merger to Gavin, who she'd decided was "rather sweet". Perhaps my boyfriend/girlfriend thought had just been premature. It was a couple of weeks later, when I was back at work, that I had a phone call from a policewoman who wanted to update me on my "find".

'In addition to the skeleton, lying in what turned out to be the basement of an old warehouse, they had found a cupboard stashed with cans of food and bottles of beer dating from the twenties, and an old leather briefcase containing a bloodied cut-throat razor, shaving soap and a large quantity of black hair.

'Snapper had staged what had appeared to be his own murder but was in fact the killing of William Higginbotham the fourth. The gangster was about to be arrested and charged with every crime the police could slap on him. He and William were of similar build, which is why he'd picked him of all his debtors. Shortly after their subterranean meeting began, he'd knocked William unconscious with the tankard, then swapped their clothes. He shaved William's head and beard with the razor, the shaving soap and water from the jug and finished the job by cutting William's throat. He used the desk to climb up to the hole in the wall and the trapdoor, carrying his briefcase containing all the evidence of his crime.'

'Hang on, though,' said Dinah. 'William's secretary identified his body. Even with the shaved head he must have known that it wasn't his employer.'

'Or maybe he thought quickly and decided that if Slippy Pete was happy to say it was the body of Alfred Gatersby, then so was he. With one man already dead, accusing the thug who had threatened to rip his throat out of being a liar may have seemed an unwise move.'

'So Slippy Pete was in on the plan?'

'Possibly not. He certainly made no effort to find his boss. Who as you may recall, ended up rotting in a basement. Snapper had bought the warehouse from Higginbotham's father. He may have bought it knowing about the trapdoor into the tunnels, thinking it might prove useful someday. Once he got up to the basement after killing Young William, he must have known he wouldn't be able to go back down. The tunnels would be swarming with police. Judging by the supplies they subsequently found stashed there, he may have intended to lie low for a couple of days, before slipping out of the warehouse under the cover of darkness.'

'But he died in there instead. What happened?'

'That took longer for the police, the twenty-first century ones that is, to work out. A dirty rag wrapped around the remains of Snapper's hand suggests he may have cut himself when he was shaving William. Perhaps after a few days in a fetid basement the wound had turned septic. His skeleton, before I disturbed it, was laid across the trapdoor. Faint marks on the grubby floor suggested he may have crawled there, perhaps with the intention of taking his chances in the tunnels. But he'd left it too late.'

'Why didn't he go up through the warehouse as planned?' asked James.

'The door out of the basement was locked. Snapper doesn't appear to have had the key. The police found gouge marks around the lock, possibly made with a rusty metal rod found discarded nearby, which may have contributed to Snapper's infection.'

'But why was the door locked?' James persisted.

'We can only speculate. Though Malcolm did mention that Slippy Pete took over Snapper's criminal empire and raised it to greater and, superficially at least, more legitimate success. Whether his boss told him of his plan or if Slippy worked it out for himself, we will never know. But while the body of Alfred Gatersby lay undisturbed for eighty years, the floors of the warehouse above were developed and made use of – its owners over the decades apparently having no curiosity about what lay behind the locked door to the basement. It was still in use that

Christmas. Toby and I went there on the first night of our stay. A plaque above the door stated that the building had been in the hands of the same family since 1923. A noisy place, not quite my cup of tea. But Toby, who for multiple reasons became my ex-fiancé before a wedding, traditional or bohemian, could take place, loved to make shapes on the dancefloor. He was in his element there, at Slippy's: a nightclub named by the owner after his dear old great grandpa.'

PUZZLE

Goose Egg

Can you spot the names of four major tunnels in this story?

Janey's Adventure Underground

During a guided tour of the Wethergate Tunnels as part of a birthday trip away, Janey Brooks becomes separated from the rest of her group. After a couple of wrong turns she finds herself in a room with two doors: one is painted green, the other is red.

Janey hadn't been enjoying the tour much anyway. She remembers an odd coin that she found on the ground in one of the tunnels earlier and takes it out of her pocket. On one side there is a picture of a robin, on the other a holly leaf. She flips the coin, and it lands robin side up. She opens the red door and steps through to find herself in a gently descending tunnel.

After twenty-five footsteps she reaches the top of a set of stairs with thirty-six steps. At the bottom of the stairs there is a shorter tunnel. It takes her twelve footsteps to reach a locked door with a keypad. The number needed to enter the room is the square root of the steps she took to reach the top of the stairs, multiplied by the square of the steps she took from the bottom of the steps to the door, multiplied by the square root of the number of steps on the staircase.

What (4-digit) code will open the door for Janey?

Beyond the door is a dartboard and three darts. Janey must hit a double twenty, a triple seventeen and the bullseye in order for a panel in the dartboard wall to swing open.

What total three-dart score does Janey need to open the panel?

She achieves the required score and passes through the opening into almost complete darkness. Only a single blinking blue light guides her forward. She stops at the edge of an expanse of water. It might be a pond, it might be a lake – it is impossible to tell. There is a small boat moored. She steps into it, unlocks the oars and begins to row. She reaches the other side forty-seven minutes later, having crossed at an average pace of 1440 strokes per hour.

Janey is quite tired when she gets out of the boat and just wants to go back to her hotel and have a cup of tea and a slice or two of birthday cake. She follows a sign that says WAY OUT, which leads her through winding and gently ascending tunnels to a circular room.

The room has seven doors. Each door has on it the name of one of the Seven Dwarfs and a number. A small plaque explains that once she has opened a door she has to go through it and it will close behind her. One of the doors will open onto the street where Janey is staying. The remaining six all open back into the room with a red door and a green door, where Janey's adventure began.

Janey has no idea which door to choose and is really regretting wandering off from the guided tour and indeed not choosing to go skydiving on her birthday instead. Her moment of despair is broken by a crackling Tannoy announcement:

'Calling all birthday boys and girls,' calls a voice of almost hysterical jollity. 'A special clue for your special day: choose the door whose number is equal to:

the code for the keypad at the bottom of the steps

multiplied by

your successful three dart score

then minus

the number of strokes it took you to cross the lake

and add

the number of letters in the dwarf's name on the correct door.'

'Oh dear,' says Janey, 'if only I'd taken notes as I went along.'

Which of the seven doors will take Janey back out into the streets of Wethergate?

Happy 706997   Doc 607990   Grumpy 609776
Dopey 690799   Bashful 677098   Sleepy 706779
Sneezy 607998

Final Puzzle Clue #2

Make a note of the name of the dwarf in the correct answer as this is the clue that you need to take forward for the final puzzle at the end of the book.

THE MASKED CAROL SINGER

The North Yorkshire weatherscape had improved dramatically by the early afternoon. One by one the house guests drifted outside to the kitchen garden, with its beds of seasonally bare earth, but a splendid view of the moorland at the edge of which Bracestone House perched. The freshly rinsed browns and yellows of old heather gleamed expectantly in the frail sunshine, and while there was still a breeze it brought with it a tantalising hint of the not too distant sea.

James rubbed his hands together briskly. After lunch he had traded one of his usual floral shirts for a black T-shirt emblazoned with the name 'Flypaper' in an ornate script. Dinah, who often had 6Music on her radio while she worked, suspected that that he was hoping someone would ask him what it meant so that he could impress them with his knowledge of modern indie pop. But so far nobody had.

'I'm fancying a run out to Whitby in the MG,' he announced. 'I've room for three more if you don't mind a cosy ride.'

Judy, who had been inspecting a small knot garden that according to labelled white sticks would be full of herbs in summer, immediately took him up on the offer.

'I too would like to come,' said Jon. 'I am very fond of the British seaside. Not as dramatic as the Icelandic coast, no fjords or black sand or lumps of glacial ice, but of much interest nevertheless. I particularly like the seafood, those little jars and trays of ...?' he looked to Helena for help.

'Whelks and winkles,' she said, pulling a face. 'I'll leave you to them if you don't mind. I've a backlog of yoga videos on my laptop.' She twisted her head from side-to-side. 'I slept like a log last night but I'm feeling very stiff. She raised one arm above her head and leaned to the left.

'I'm glad to hear you're sleeping so well,' said Dinah. 'I imagine it must be distressing for you staying here, with the memory of what happened to your father.'

Helena paused mid-stretch. 'I did consider booking a B&B in the village instead.' She sighed and straightened up. 'Jon persuaded me that as the invitation specifies staying here, that's what we have to do. So here we are. My sleep would be more disturbed if it wasn't for some wonderful herbal pills that Jon discovered. Kelp and valerian. Taste disgusting but a couple of them and I'm out for the count.'

At that moment Sara emerged from the kitchen in leggings and a long-sleeved T-shirt.

'I'm going for a run out to the old ironstone mining works,' she said.

'They're fascinating,' said James. 'Well worth a visit. Let me know what you think.'

'Have fun,' said Dinah. 'I would don my Lycra and join you, but I've got work to do.' She patted her ever-present craft bag. 'If anyone wants me, I'll be in the conservatory.' As she turned to go, Mrs Linden emerged from an outhouse. The sleeves of her black dress were rolled up and she was carrying two freshly plucked chickens. She blew a stray feather from her arm. 'You may all do as you please, but dinner will be at seven o'clock sharp. And don't be spoiling your appetites with ice cream,' she added as she headed into the kitchen.

'I'll join you for a seaside jaunt,' said Stuart, who up until that point had been rapidly typing messages on his phone. 'Bit of sea air will be very welcome.'

'You are looking a bit peaky,' observed Dinah. 'If you don't mind me saying, you were up in the night rather a lot.'

Jon guffawed.

'Stuart Yorke with an "e"!' exclaimed James mockingly. 'Is there something you two haven't told us?'

'We have adjacent rooms,' Stuart explained patiently. 'I'm sorry if I disturbed you, Dinah. You'll have to excuse an ageing man's body.'

'Ah it was your bladder rather than the late-night phone calls keeping you up,' said Dinah, nodding.

Stuart glowered.

'Sorry,' she said, 'but for such an old house some of the walls are very thin.'

'Indeed,' said Stuart. 'Now could we please change the subject away from my bodily functions and start our excursion? I'll come in my own car though,' he added. 'I'm collecting my son, Barney, and Ned's granddaughter, Rose, from the train station later. It's worked out well them catching the same train from London. They've even got seats near each other. Barney has my boy Dash with him too.'

'You've got another son?' asked Judy.

'No,' said Stuart with a wry smile, 'better than that. Dash is a miniature schnauzer.'

★ ★ ★

The Whitby contingent returned to Bracestone House several hours later with wind-blasted cheeks, a salty tang in their hair and in Jon's case carrying several jars of assorted small shellfish. They found Sara and Dinah in close conversation on the sofa in the study.

'Is this a formal interrogation, detective, or can anyone joined in?' asked James.

The two women looked up. They held out their hands in explanation.

'Ahh,' said Judy to Dinah, 'you're teaching Sara to crochet.'

'Trying being the operative word,' said Dinah grimly. 'It's as simple as ABC but some people just can't get the hang of it.'

Sara put down her hook and a square of crochet, which to Judy's eyes didn't look too bad.

'I guess I just don't have the right type of brain,' she said.

'Me neither,' said Judy. 'It's something to do with right and left hemispheres, isn't it?'

'Creativity versus analytical ability, verbal and non-verbal,' said Stuart, joining the conversation as he entered the room. 'There's something to it no doubt, but we shouldn't restrict ourselves with labels. I for one regularly complete the *Times* crossword but have also been known to dabble with watercolours.'

'Dad, your paintings are pants,' said the tall young man who followed him through the doorway. In his late twenties, he was dressed in jeans and a jumper, with a huge rucksack on his back. His dark hair was shaved at the sides with the rest pulled back in a tufty bun. Finely sculpted facial hair framed full lips, the lower of which was pierced. His skin was a few tones darker than Stuart's, but when they stood side-by-side he was unmistakeably his son.

'This is Barney,' said his father, ignoring the boy's harsh appraisal of his artistic talents. He introduced the others.

'Have you got Helena's niece with you as well?' asked Dinah.

'She's gone straight up to her room,' said Stuart. 'Exhausted from the journey I think.'

Barney rolled his eyes. There was a rhythmic tapping sound from the corridor, as if a message was being diligently typed on a typewriter. A sturdy rectangle of silver-grey fur, with fierce eyebrows and a neatly trimmed beard, sauntered into the room, made a steady sniffing circuit, inspected everyone's legs, then sat expectantly at Sara's feet.

'You have been selected,' said Stuart, 'as "Most Likely to Share a Treat".'

Sara held out her empty palms, 'Sorry, boy, no snacks here.'

'Over here, Dash,' called Barney, holding up a biscuit. The dog abandoned Sara without a backward glance.

'Dash because of his speed?' asked Judy, raising an eyebrow.

'Short for Dashiell. Dashiell Hammett,' said Barney. 'You know, the American detective writer? Grandpa Felix loved old detective stories, Sherlock Holmes, Raymond Chandler, but Hammett was his favourite.'

Stuart nodded. 'After Barney's mother and I, well, separated a few years ago, I moved in with my father, lived with him up until his death last summer. He would ask me to read to him most evenings. When I got Dash, he became part of the routine. Sitting at my dad's feet, his grumpy face resting on his paws looking for all the world like he was listening with as much attention as Dad.'

'Well he won't be short of new stories here,' said James. 'Hope you've arrived armed with a good one, Barney.'

The boy pulled a face. 'Films and games are more my kind of thing,' he said. 'But I'll come up with something.'

★ ★ ★

For Friday night's supper Mrs Linden demonstrated the breadth of her repertoire by providing a Thai feast. In addition to Barney, the guests were joined in the dining room by Rose Luddenham, who sat opposite her aunt at the table, which was laden with plates and bowls of enticingly scented food. A slight young woman in a corduroy pinafore dress with short and shaggily cut bright crimson hair, she regaled the company with the details of her 'tortuous' journey from London.

77

'The train was jam-packed,' she said, 'and this annoying boy in the seat across the aisle spent half the time watching videos on his phone and cackling to himself and the rest of the time telling me the plot of the "amazing folk horror film" he's making.' She made a face at Barney, who stuck out his tongue. 'It's nice to be here again,' she said, looking round the room. Her eyes suddenly brimmed with tears. 'But it's so sad remembering last year.' She shot a hurt glance at her aunt and Jon. 'If I'd known plus ones were allowed, I'd have brought Devi. She was really miffed about me coming away and leaving her.'

'Jon isn't a plus one,' said Helena. 'The invite was addressed to both of us. And please don't be getting maudlin. It's not what your grandfather would have wanted.'

'Isn't it?' asked Rose with a sniff. 'Well maybe he should have included my girlfriend on the guest list then.'

James cleared his throat. 'Of course we all have mixed feelings about this gathering. Its purpose … the memories it brings back.' He wasn't the only one who darted a look at the private investigator in their midst. 'But I think Helena is right. Remember Edward's "rules". He wanted to us to enjoy ourselves.'

'Or did he want us all to drop our guard? Hoping one of us might let slip something we didn't intend to,' suggested Stuart. 'Or mention something we saw last year that we didn't realise was relevant at the time. Something that Ms Slade can scoop up.' He gave a Sara a semi-apologetic smile.

'In vino veritas,' said James, raising his glass.

'Well I'm alright then,' said Rose, clinking it with her glass of fizzy water. Before the meal Mrs Linden had reassured her that she had remembered her tastes from last year.

'Got you a whole fridge shelf of those tins of flavoured water,' she'd said.

'Aitch-2-Oh? asked Rose. 'Fantastic. Did you get Lust for Lime? That's my favourite.'

'I'll have to have a check, pet.'

Helena made a noise of exasperation as Rose slurped noisily through her paper straw. 'You do realise it's just overpriced water,' she said.

'Overpriced flavoured fizzy water,' said Rose.

'You'd be better off with a herbal tea,' said Helena. 'It's practically the same thing.'

Rose scrunched up her face in disgust. 'Except its hot and flat, so not really. Thanks anyway, Aunty Hels.'

Helena winced.

'Your aunt doesn't like being called that,' said Jon.

'Soz, I forgot,' said Rose with a sweet smile. 'Can I call you Jonsi like that cool Icelandic singer?'

'No, thank you,' said Jon, but he smiled too.

'Do you remember last year we had that sing–along round the tree?' said James.

'Of course we remember,' said Helena icily. 'It was during "Rudolf the Red–Nosed Reindeer" that I realised my father wasn't with us and hadn't been for the last hour. Half an hour later Linden found him dead on his bedroom floor.'

The uncomfortable silence that followed was eventually broken by Dinah. 'No carols this year then?' she asked. 'That's a shame as they rather form the theme of my story.'

'A proper Christmas story,' said James. 'Splendid.'

'It's not a very long one,' said Dinah. She looked at her plate laden with rice, vegetables and steamed dumplings. 'Maybe I could tell it to you between courses. I for one am going to need a rest after this, before I tackle Mrs Linden's Sticky Mango Rice Pudding.'

★ ★ ★

'This might be a true story,' Dinah began, once the plates and bowls had been cleared away, 'or it might not. That's up to you to decide. Or to care. It concerns the little–known sport of

79

competitive carolling, in which the winners are awarded golden Christmas wreaths and the losers usually leave with no more than a jar of coins or a mince pie or two if they're lucky. But on this occasion, there was far more at stake and for one participant, much more to lose.'

'The Loveday sisters lived at 21 Unity Street, a tall, narrow terraced house in a tired seaside town on the northeast coast. Tired in that its heydays of train-busting tourists, beaches confettied with toddlers, grannies, donkeys and windbreakers and the row of amusement arcades lighting up the northern sky, were a decade gone. This was the morning after, the clearing away of empty glasses, filling the recycling bin and humming Adele's "Skyfall" as a half-remembered karaoke tune.

'The sisters liked it this way. They'd never been ones for crowds or parades, though Jessie did enjoy the occasional lemon-top ice-cream and a blowy stroll along the prom and Di never missed the Teatime Classics showings at the cinema on Saturday afternoons, or indeed any film that had that lovely Hemsworth man playing Thor.'

'Aha!' interjected Jon. 'This is a story about yourself and your family, Dinah?'

'As a matter of fact, no,' said Dinah. 'My name is never shortened. Shall I continue?'

'Carry on carry on, dear Dinah. Never say Di,' said James.

She ignored his witticism and resumed her tale.

'In winter the sisters hunkered down in their well-heated home, took stock of their possessions, repairing and discarding where required, and prepared for the one event of the year for which they released their sparkle. Silk dresses were unzipped from dry-cleaning bags, sumptuous extras were bought by Pam from the butcher's and baker's and all of the rooms in the tall, narrow house were chaotically adorned from an attic trunk labelled simply "Christmas".

'A query yelled from the kitchen signalled, as it did every year, the start of the sisters' Christmas baking: "Two tablespoons of brandy in the mince pies, or one?"

'Pam's response, as she balanced precariously on a stepladder pinning one end of a paperchain to the top of the living room curtains, was, as ever, "Two of course!"

'Jessie was holding the other end of the chain as she balanced on the arm of the sofa, adding, "Don't skimp, sis, it gives them a lovely fizz." She was feeling giddy already at the thought of her twin sister's festive concoctions. She had only moved back in with her siblings three years ago but Christmases past had always been spent in this house, their family home, and the season never failed to transport her back to the innocence and joy of their childhoods.

'Half an hour later, just as the last paper cut-out snowflake was stuck to the window glass, a final gilded cardboard star hung from a wall light and one more piece of holly was placed on the mantelpiece, Di brought through a tray laden with teapot and cups and a plate of still-warm pies. "Shall I be mother?" she asked. As one the women all looked to the family photograph above the fireplace: their now deceased parents posing proudly with their daughters. Pam peered more closely, as if inspecting it for the first time.

'"For twins, you two couldn't be more unalike. You've always been the scruffy one, Jess, look at the state of your frock."

'"Can't be smart in head sense *and* dress sense," said Jessie. "Got to choose one of them." Which earned her an affectionate punch on the arm from her twin, who was wearing a trim and very clean pinny over her immaculate blouse and slacks.

'"Do you think the singers will start tonight?" Jessie asked as she sank her teeth into crisp sweet pastry, enjoying the tang of the brandy on her tongue.

'"It's the fourteenth so I should think so," replied Di. "Ooh, these pies are a bit poky. Do not consume while operating heavy machinery."

"'Does a balloon pump count?" asked Pam, who had pinned her long hair up in a bun and was focused on stretching out lengths of coloured rubber. She had dreams of filling the living room with exotic balloon animals but had never managed to progress beyond a contorted sausage dog. "I do hope we get a good turnout," she continued. "The carolling makes Christmas for me."

"'The forecast for this week isn't very festive," said Di. "Just rain, cloud and more rain."

"'Nothing deters the Delf Bay carol singers," declared Jessie rather too loudly. "They're all keen to get their practice rounds in before the Big Sing Off."

'Her twin noticed with not much surprise that Jessie had manged to consume three mince pies in a very short time.

"'Keep her away from the balloon pump, Pam," she warned. "But as for the singers I think you're right. A little bit of rain won't put most of them off. Oh no, Pam," she groaned, as her youngest sister started a hearty rendition of "God Rest Ye Merry, Gentlemen". "Can we at least wait until sundown?"

'Delf Bay had a strong musical reputation. The annual piano festival had celebrated its fiftieth year the previous spring and there had been the usual convocation of community choirs in October, with groups travelling from as far as Denmark, Slovenia and Waltham-on-Thames. Singing was part of the town's heritage, from its traditional fisherfolk's shanties to the hymns of its many churches and chapels and the prolific output of the Delf Slambase, a workshop for wannabe young rappers that met every other Saturday in a soundproofed room beneath the library. Pam was particularly enthusiastic about music in all its forms, although she drew the line at Trap and wasn't keen on Grime. She played the piano every Sunday at the Southcliff

Wesleyan chapel, where her voice rang out clear and strident, its volume rising and falling in inverse proportion to the size of the congregation.

'The town was especially renowned for its carol singers. Not the informal meandering groups found in other communities. The carollers of Delf Bay prided themselves on their quality and number. Select coteries of singers, representing the many aspects of town life, began practising in the autumn and by the middle of December when the performances launched the competitive spirit was already fierce. The culmination was the Sing Off on the pier on the twenty-third, from which only one group could emerge as the winners. The WI, of which Di was a member, held auditions, with only the six most harmonious Instituters being allowed to participate. Their main rivals were The Highlights, a collaboration between three of Delf Bay's hairdressing salons. Several pubs provided teams, although only they and the sporting fraternities, the bowling club and the junior footballers used that term. With the addition of the Lifeboat volunteers, the Parents and Toddlers playgroup and mini-choirs from four of the town's churches, there were usually ten to fifteen groups of carollers doing the rounds in the evenings leading up to the final event.

'For the last two days a bowl of coins had been sitting on the telephone table in the sisters' hallway, in anticipation of the singers and their fundraising tins. The sisters had as one resisted the lure of mobile phones, for which they claimed they had no need. Pam disapproved of telephone conversations altogether, so refused to have the landline device, a reproduction Bakelite model, moved to a more comfortable location. Jessie was the only person in the house to have regular phone calls. Every second Monday her son, Jacob, would ring from Birmingham.

'Oh yes,' said Dinah in response to a murmur from her audience. 'Jessie was a mother. A grandmother indeed in-waiting.

It had been Jacob's moving out, after three years of intermittency while he was at university, that prompted Jessie to move in with her sisters. Although she'd brought him up single-handed, she and Jacob had never been as close as she thought they should have been. Perhaps he reminded her too much of his father, perhaps he saw that recoil in her eyes, in the restraint of her love. Her sisters noted among themselves that whenever Jessie came back into the living room after her brief phone conversations with Jacob, her face looked both happier and sadder than before.

'Jessie had worried it would be a squash and a squeeze moving back in, but her sisters assured her that even though the top floor of their old family home had long since been divided off and let to "a pair of young professionals who did something in television", there was still plenty of room.

'"There might only be two bedrooms but it's not as if any of us haven't shared before," Di assured her. And Jessie had found some comfort in sharing a bedroom with her twin again. Although her sister's snoring betrayed her non-musicality and made her wish she was bunked up with Pam, whose snores and sniffles might be more melodious.

'The bowl, waiting patiently by the mostly redundant telephone, contained fifty-pence pieces, almost fifty pounds worth, collected and saved by the sisters over the preceding months. Each group of carollers received one, or two if there were more than six of them. Pam disapproved of large groups of singers.

'"Too much opportunity for 'mimers' lurking at the back," she said. Her beady eyes spurred any such slackers into lusty, albeit often tuneless, cooperation. She also railed against a growing trend for costumes. This had begun one particularly snowy Christmas when the second Delf Scouts took it upon themselves to dress in Victorian style cloaks and homemade top hats, carrying lanterns on poles. The result was very effective and the new scout hut bike shed was funded in half the time expected. Other groups followed in the wake of their success, some with more effort than others. "This is getting silly," Pam had announced, after being regaled by two sumo wrestlers, a caveman and four children dressed as wizards. "I blame the Americans and Halloween."

"'Oh but look," Jessie had said, "a darling robin." And there was indeed an additional child, barely of walking age, clad in a raggedy brown cloak over a red jumper. A paper beak obscured his nose and mouth.

"'Adorable, I agree," said Pam, "And he or she might have the voice of a singing bird, but how are we supposed to hear 'The Holly and the Ivy', through that contraption? Masked carolling shouldn't be allowed.'"

★ ★ ★

'The first carollers arrived promptly at six o'clock that evening. Four sopranos from the Bluebird Café with a couple of tenor mechanics from the garage next door, all dressed as pirates.

"'Not bad considering the eyepatches and the parrot," said Pam as they watched the singers depart after a slightly wobbly "Little Town of Bethlehem" and a more strident "O Come All Ye Faithful". "Though personally I'd deduct points for the thigh-slapping."

'Jessie fully expected that her sister would in time issue them all with scoreboards to hold up after each performance.

"'Do you remember the skinhead?" Pam asked wistfully as she closed the door and returned the coin bowl to the telephone table.

"'That was just before you moved back in," Di said to a confused-looking Jessie. "We'd invited the couple upstairs down for an eggnog on the first night of carolling. Pam opened the door to a gangling youth with a shaved head, shivering in a T-shirt and jeans. Debbie, who'd been making free with the eggnog, giggled at the sight of him, but undeterred he opened his lips and what came out ..." She pressed her hand to her chest.

"'Sheer heaven,'" Pam finished for her. "I tumbled so many coins into his scrawny palm that anyone who came after was sadly short-changed. We have never heard his like again."

'Over the following three nights the succession of singing rounds picked up pace, so the sisters, taking turns to answer the door, hardly had time to sit down between visitations.

"'Who needs a television?'" Pam declared. Her sisters murmured their agreement. Although Di, who enjoyed her regular trips to the cinema, sometimes wondered what it would be like to be a soap addict, able to vicariously live a more dramatic life.

'There were still seven days to go before Christmas, when at about 8.30 in the evening, though the wind and rain was rattling the windows, the sisters heard the familiar clearing of throats, a deep voiced "1 2 3", and the opening bars of "Good King Wenceslas". They each laid aside their various activities. The twins were laboriously unravelling an old jumper and winding it into a large ball of wool. Pam had been curled up under a blanket reading *The Pursuit of Love*. She flung down the novel and jumped to her feet, but Di beat her to the front door. The six or seven men and women outside all wore red bobble hats and matching scarves branded with an animal logo and entwined initials that showed them to be representatives of the Fox and Goose pub.

'Jessie, delayed by the giant ball of wool rolling under a table, was the last into the hall. Through her sisters' heads and shoulders she took in the sight of the singers, their rosy cheeks, the water dripping from their noses. Their voices ranged from a wobbly soprano through to a chillingly familiar baritone. She slipped quickly back into the living room. Her heart pounding, she closed her eyes, but still his voice resounded: "Bring me flesh and bring me wine." She pressed her palms against her ears but couldn't block out the knowledge that the rumours were true. He was back in town.

'She wasn't totally unprepared. Di had warned her that a woman in the Post Office queue on Monday had heard from Mandy who worked the Saturday-market fish stall, that he was back. The Delf Bay chain of gossip was already speculating that he had abandoned some poor woman down in Lincolnshire and had returned home "scouting for fresh prey". Jessie hadn't seen him for over twenty-five years. None of the family had. Not even his son, Jacob, whom he'd never met. Jessie knew she hadn't been the only woman he'd beaten and abused, and Jacob probably had half-siblings scattered across the country. She had worried through long dark nights that her failure to report what he'd done, to act when she could have, had left him free to cause more damage. But fear and protection of her son had overridden all.

'She poked her head back into the hall and peered between her sisters. He was at the edge of the group. By his side was a slight woman, her eyes downcast. As her voice rose tremulously off-key, he jostled her with his shoulder and her lips clamped closed. Did he recognise her siblings? Were they just another group of anonymous middle-aged women? Could he even have picked her out in an identity parade? She stayed hidden behind the door, just in case.

'When the carollers were gone, the sisters gathered around Jessie, reassuring her. They'd all known it was him. Pam had almost closed the door in the singers' faces. But Di, knowing at least one of the women in the group, held her back. That night in the dark bedroom, Jessie whispered her fears out loud. That he would come looking for her. Would hurt her again. Would find out about Jacob and claim him as his own.

'"He can't touch you," her sister whispered soothingly. "Not while you've got us watching your back."'

★ ★ ★

'On Friday evening Pam was hurrying past the train station after her piano practice at the chapel. The rain was unrelenting, the water seeping down the back of her coat. She paused at the sight of a large group of carol singers on the steps of the Town Hall. She changed her course towards them, admiring their persistence in the downpour, as they started, then stopped, then started again a rendition of "We Three Kings". They were a convivial-seeming mix of several groups: the hairdressers; a Girl Guide patrol dressed in brightly coloured capes, leotards and tights, and sporting glittery eye masks; the Fox and Goose pub singers; and a boisterous group of young men in animal onesies whose allegiance was unclear. Far too many costumes for her liking and she tutted at the quantity of masks. Although at least the Guides only had their eyes covered, unlike the portly Santa in the midst of the red-hatted Fox and Goose drinkers. His shiny plastic mask, with bulbous cheeks and fulsome beard, totally obscured his face. Pam shook her head in dismay; there'd be little singing going on behind that, she was sure.

'The following afternoon, Di was heading home along the promenade, after a particularly enjoyable cinema showing of *Meet Me in St Louis*. The empty benches of the long parade watched over the vast expanse of the sea. When the sky was clear the moon would silver the low waves and turn the water all the shades of indigo. But there was no moon tonight, only a grey blanket of cloud promising, or depending on your outlook, threatening to unburden itself of snow.

'Scenes of the film still played through Di's mind. Her thoughts switched to Jessie and the possible consequences of the return of the dark figure from her past. Not all of the

88

Loveday sisters were known for their caution, and she mused how, while like the sisters in the film, they had a duty to protect each other, vengeance could be a tricksy game. As if thinking of the man had made him manifest, she saw in the yellow arc of a streetlight ahead the pub carollers and a gathering of elderly folk in wheelchairs with their carers. The stillness of the night was barely broken by a beautifully harmonious "Silent Night". She glanced at the singers, noticing the man's continued presence and that one of the crew had chosen to wear a mask. A particularly crude looking Santa face, with shiny pink cheeks over a solid white beard. She shook her head and passed by without adding to the collecting tin.

'Back home, hanging up her coat she could smell evidence of a fresh flurry of baking in preparation for their forthcoming Christmas Eve soiree. As well as the couple from upstairs, Pam had invited Michael, a "friend" from the chapel whom they were all eager to meet. In the warmth of the kitchen she sampled one of the sausage rolls. 'Incredible,' she said. She didn't know how her sister did it. Such a light touch with pastry. She reached for a second one but was lightly tapped on the wrist by Pam.'

'"It's all very well being appreciative," said Pam, wagging her finger, "but don't go scoffing the lot. They're Debbie's favourite too. She'd be ever so upset if there were none left."

'"What about Michael?" Di asked. "Does he like a sausage roll?" If Pam heard a salacious tone in her voice, she affected not to notice it.

'"Michael likes good Christian singing and a strong cup of tea," she said. "Both of which he'll find in abundance here, even if we run out of pastries."

'On the evening of the twenty-third, Jessie, ever the last-minute gift buyer, was making the most of the town's 'Manic Monday' Late Night Shopping event, to buy a few final items: an automated wool-winder, a joint present for herself and her twin, which she'd ordered from the haberdasher's, and a hamper of chocolate goodies from the sweet shop for her sisters to share. A special thank you for their support over the last few weeks. Pam joined her as she hesitated outside the deli on the square, trying to remember if they had enough cheese.

"'Don't buy any more," warned Pam. "We'll have Stilton coming out of our eyes. It's a select gathering tomorrow night, we're not feeding the five thousand.' At that moment a noisy crowd rounded the corner into the square. Among their number were various recognisable carol singers, including the skipping girl guides, who, Jessie was able to inform her less worldly sister, were dressed as superheroes.

"'They'll be on their way back from the Sing Off," she said, a hint of regret in her voice. The final competition concert on the pier was something she had always attended with Jacob. There had been something special about gathering on the wooden pier above the waves, voices raised in chorus, her arm round her son. He had seemed to appreciate the occasions too and had often leaned in closer. She had half-hoped he might come home this year, if not for Christmas, then for the carol concert at least. In the circumstances, perhaps it was better, she decided, that he hadn't.

"'It will have been ram-jammed," Pam said, the term being one she reserved for any particularly crowded situation that she was grateful to be absent from. From the other side of the square by the brightly lit Christmas tree, Di waved and beckoned them over. "Some of the singers are having an impromptu follow-up concert here," she said. "A bit more space than on the pier. Do let's stay for a song or two."

'Jessie shuffled her laden bags behind her, doing her best to hide the blatantly beribboned handle of the chocolate hamper. A scoutmaster in a top hat and a sweeping cloak was trying to create some choral order among the motley ranks gathered around the tree. He had to shush The Highlights, who were giddy from their triumph at the Sing Off. Their lead – an elderly woman with rainbow highlights in her hair – wore the victory wreath around her neck.

'"We absolutely smashed it," cried Clara, the colourist from the Dyeworks, where four times a year Jessie discreetly had her roots done. Clara's enthusiasm earned a scowl from three of the nearby WI. Jessie predicted a coming battle of the descants, when the scoutmaster cleared his throat and announced "Hark, the Herald Angels Sing".

'When she spotted the red bobble-hatted singers among the crowd, her heart began to beat faster and she had to force herself not to flee. The plastic-faced Santa was there again, hat pulled tightly round his ears. As was the slight woman, about her own age, whom Jessie had seen the first time they called at the house. When the song began she seemed hesitant but as the voices rose around her, hers rose with them and she seemed to swell like a robin in his winter plumage. Her face lifted to the cloudy sky as if willing the stars to break through and shine. Of him, the man Jessie had dreaded facing again, there was no sign.

'After a third song, a rousing "Jingle Bells", one of the Fox and Goosers, a red-haired woman whose hat was decorated with a hopeful sprig of mistletoe, rattled a bucket in the sisters' direction. "Anything we collect tonight is going to the Women's Shelter in Borough," she said. "Dig deep, my lovelies, for a good cause."

'Pam had sniffed at the final song, considering it a frivolous interloper, but threw in all the coins from her purse, as did Di who, to her sister's dismay, had joined in gustily in the "dashing through the snow". As Jessie placed a five-pound note in the tub she gestured towards the woman's fellow pub singers. "Missing your baritone tonight," she said, trying to control the quaver in her voice.

'"Him!" the woman said. "Hah! He was full of himself at the pier show, practically soloing 'Ding Dong! Merrily on High', but disappeared sharpish after we'd said we were continuing here." She leaned towards Jessie. "Lovely voice, but not what you'd call the pub's favourite customer."'

★ ★ ★

'It was early on Christmas Eve when his body was found on the shingle beach. An unpleasant Advent revelation for an early morning dog walker.

"I know it's Christmas and one should never speak ill of the dead," said Pam. "But I'm going to say it: good riddance." She was addressing the small gathering in the sisters' living room. Glasses of port in their hands and the table spread with an array of pastries and other delights. Michael, a silver-haired man with a gentle smile, raised his tin of lager and nodded with approval. He had eschewed Pam's proffered cup of tea but Pam, whose cheeks were flushed in his presence, didn't seem to mind at all.

'Jessie didn't know how she should feel. The monster from her past was dead. He was gone, physically at least, though it would take longer for him to disappear entirely from her mind and memory. But she'd had an unexpected and very chatty phone call from Jacob that morning, saying how much he wished he could have come back for the carols. Maybe it wasn't too late to build bridges, to start to shuck off the past and look to the future and the new life that her grandchild would bring.

'"Penny for your thoughts, dear twinny?"

'Jessie turned to her sister. "Resolutions," she said, "for the New Year." She laughed, suddenly pointing to the centre of the room where Pam had uncharacteristically started a game of "pass the balloon", using one of her deformed creations. The couple from the flat above were contorted around a fat pink balloon that had two eyes and a curly tail stuck to it.

"'Those two are so much fun," Jessie said. "I'm glad they agreed to come tonight. Go for it, Sally," she called as the young woman used her nose to move the balloon pig over the back of her husband Tim's head.

"'Lovely couple," said Debbie, placing her arm around her twin sister's waist. "Sally's won awards for her TV documentaries. They wanted to film the carolling rounds this year, and the pier concert, with interviews and whatnot in between. I managed to dissuade them."

'Jessie rested her head on Debbie's shoulder. "Mmm yes, probably best not to risk dispelling the glamour. I saved you some of the sausage rolls by the way," she said.

"'I should think so too, after scoffing all my mince pies, before I had chance to taste my own wares," said Debbie. "It's an art, you know, baking; the results deserve to be savoured, not just devoured and forgotten."

'Jessie thought about what else might be considered an art. The art of disguise, of deception, of murder? The community of Delf Bay were in shock at such a public death on their shore. Gossip was rife and she had picked up snippets here and there. The police had their work cut out interviewing everyone who had been on the pier that night: the last place the man had been seen alive. One witness reportedly saw him alone at the far end, looking out to sea. Another claimed he hadn't been alone at all, but in the dark they had been unable to identify his companion ("A man though, I'm sure, he had a beard"). The police weren't ruling out foul play.

'This morning, looking for her slippers, Jessie had found the plastic Santa mask hidden under Debbie's bed in the twins' shared room. She'd turned it over in her hands, remembering how those cheeks had gleamed among the singing faces of the carollers. Her finger traced the whorls of the shiny white beard, then she shoved it away in the wardrobe, under an old coat. It was unlikely, she hoped, that her sister would feel the need to wear it again.

'Pam had been right when she warned her three sisters that not all the masked carollers were singers. But for one night only, one of them had been a killer.'

'There were four sisters!' exclaimed Judy.

'But of course,' said Dinah. 'Were you not keeping count?'

PUZZLES

Goose Eggs

The sisters' names – Jessie, Pam, Debbie and Di – are all shortened forms of longer names, which coincidentally are also the first names of four more famous sisters. Who were they and why is the Loveday sisters' address – Unity Street – and Pam's choice of reading material relevant?

Muddled Carols and Final Puzzle Clue #3

Several carols are mentioned in Dinah's story. Can you extract five of their titles from the scramble of letters below? But beware each of the anagrams includes one or more spare letters. These spare letters when rearranged on their own produce a festive word that also appears in the story. This word is the clue that will help you solve the final puzzle at the end of the book.

1. EMERGENT DESERT MONGREL, YAY
2. CAVO SNOGGED TWINKLES
3. IT ENLIGHTENS
4. COSY DARE VINYL ADDICTION
5. KITS WHEN GREEN

THE TELL STONE

'Dinah's story will be hard to beat for Christmas content,' said James. 'But I've possibly got the most local one. It took place on the moor that surrounds this house.'

After they left the dinner table, they resumed their evening roost around the fire in the study. Outside, while the rain had held off, there was now a howling wind. Even with the heavy curtains closed its presence could be heard and felt. The sash windows rattled and the flames in the hearth wavered.

Four more comfy chairs had been pushed and carried through from the drawing room, so only two of the hardback seats were needed.

'We'll take it in turns,' said Sara, sitting on one of them.

'Good idea,' said Stuart, directing Barney to the other.

Rose plumped herself down cross-legged on the rug in front of the fire. She was enveloped inside a huge crocheted cardigan, which had been a present from her grandfather. She'd rightly guessed it was one of Dinah's creations. 'One of my coats of many colours,' the older woman had told her happily.

James leaned forward, about to begin his story, when Stuart spoke up.

'Look, now we are all here could we perhaps address the elephant in the room?'

'I hope you're not talking about me, Mr Yorke,' said Dinah in mock-horror.

'Don't be ridiculous,' said Stuart. 'Look, this is all very cosy but we do seem to be avoiding the burning question. Which is,' he continued before anyone had chance to ask, 'why are we all here?'

'Edward invited us,' said Dinah.

'No,' said Helena, 'his solicitor Mr Brotherton did. Damned man, he's very hard to get any information out of. Father's will has been "on hold" for a year now. And while I understand that the murder investigation is still ongoing, it's ridiculous that we,' she indicated herself and Rose, 'can't at least be shown his last testimony. All I get every time I do manage to get through to the man is that there "will be news soon". The invitations and that stupid list of "rules" are the closest thing we've had to "news" so far.'

'With a big reveal on Christmas Eve,' James reminded her.

'Are you personally expecting to be a beneficiary?' asked Helena.

'Not of anything financial,' said James, 'but I did wonder if he might bequeath me some of his research notes, his papers and so on.'

Judy cleared her throat.

'Although,' James said looking at her apologetically, 'there might be others with more of a claim.' He gazed glumly into his glass for a moment, then looked up with a smile. 'Ah well, I'll just have to make do with having only one bestseller under my belt.'

'You think Grandpa's book – what was it going to be called?' said Rose. '*Northern Bad Guys* …?'

'*Notorious Northerners*,' said Judy.

'Yeah, that one. Do you think it would have made him famous?'

James shrugged. 'It had a good hook and some terrific stories. The Barnsley Gang for a start. Pulled off a series of heists, got away with close to £5 million. Two of the gang were discovered dead in a canal, the rest of them and the money never found. The true crime genre is very big right now. It might have picked up some TV interest.'

'We did some filming the summer before he died,' said Barney. 'As a try out for making the book into a film or maybe a series of shorts. He read out bits while walking round the moors and in the graveyard in the village. Trying to get the right atmosphere. I reckon it could have been really good if we'd had a chance to do it properly.'

'He was a good storyteller,' said Helena with a smile. 'Demanding that we all sit here together telling stories is very like him. And that daft puzzle at the end of his rules, which, by the way, Jon, and I have worked out now.' She raised her glass to her absent father. 'Ha, ha, Dad, very funny.'

'He once told me,' said Jon, 'that if he hadn't gone into frozen foods, he would like to have made games and puzzles.'

'And a great success he would have made of it too, I'm sure,' said James, trying to keep the impatience out of his voice. 'But shall we crack on with my story? We seem to be in agreement that it's what Edward would have wanted.'

'Is there a dog in it?' Barney looked down at Dash, whose bristly head was resting on his feet. 'One of those black hounds that stalk the moor with headlamp eyes or a giant cat that turns out to be a lost moggy standing on a rock?'

'No it's not that sort of story.'

'Shame,' said Barney. 'It would be a good night for a spooky story.' He adjusted his feet, but Dash remained attached.

'A woman wailing for a lost love?' Judy moved her arms in a Kate Bush shimmy.

James shook his head.

'A bog man?'

'A mist that brings madness?'

James slumped his shoulders in mock despair. 'All worthy subjects of stories but alas not mine. And now I think perhaps you won't want to hear it after all, lacking as it does moaning women, howling hounds or men dragged from the peat.'

'What does it have then?' asked Rose.

'A stone.'

'A magic stone?' Rose asked, her expression suggesting that for his sake and for the approval of his audience, it had better be.

James was tempted to say yes just to keep everyone's attention. But that wasn't the point of his story. 'Not actual magic,' he hedged. 'Although, perhaps we should look for magic in everyday occurrences.'

'So an everyday story about an everyday stone, then,' chuckled Stuart.

'In Iceland,' Jon volunteered, 'we have a story of a stone that is found in the nest of the wagtail in May. It is to be kept in a bloody neck scarf and put in your right ear when you wish to learn something from it. It will then tell you everything that you might want to know. It is called "the tell stone".'

Mrs Linden crossed the room, rattling a tray laden with glasses and a bottle of what she declared was a herbal rice spirit from Bangkok. She placed it on a low table by the fire. 'Talking stones sound like the devil's work to me,' she said. 'Does anyone want ice? It's not how the locals drink it mind.'

Everyone declined the option of ice.

'I'll leave you to your fairy tales then,' Mrs Linden said and left the room.

'The tell stone?' said James. 'As it happens, Jon, magical or not, that would be a fitting name, for the stone in this tale too.

'Out on the moor,' he began, 'a cairn of stones, a familiar outcrop of rock or a boundary stone could mean life or death to someone lost in mist or fog or just the heavy dark of a moonless night.' He glanced towards the rain-lashed window. 'On a night, indeed, such as this. But whereas such a stone might be ordinarily a beacon of hope, one January several years ago, not three hundred metres from where we are sitting now, a boundary stone marked a death.'

The bulb in the standard lamp flickered and Rose snuggled deeper into her cardigan. There was silence except for the purr of Dinah's crochet needle as it hooked and looped, and a soft contented snore from Dash.

'It's called Running Jinny by local folk,' said James. 'It stood for hundreds of years marking the boundary of the old deer park, one in a line of five or six. They all have names. This one, so legend goes, is named for a serving girl who killed her master. The spot where the stone stood was the furthest she reached before the devil himself grabbed her and dragged her down to hell.'

'A murder,' said Dinah, lifting her eyes from the almost-completed crocheted octopus in her lap.

'Yes, but not the one that this story's about. Running Jinny toppled over some time in the twenties and has lain mostly unobserved in the heather ever since. Tripped over occasionally by ramblers who have wandered off the path. It has words carved on it. Inscribed there over forty years ago and seen freshly chiselled by a pair of hikers who, one mist-wreathed New Year's Day morning, also discovered the body of a dead man lying across it.'

He stopped. 'Shall I be mother?' he asked. He unstoppered the bottle of Thai liquor and filled each of the small glasses. He took one for himself and passed the tray to Sara on his left.

Helena gave Rose a quizzical look as she took a glass. 'I'm not a complete teetotaller,' her niece responded. 'Just like you're not a complete vegan.'

When everyone who wanted one had a glass, James resumed his story.

'The inscribed words on the stone formed a short phrase. The hikers thought there might be more, obscured by the dead man. But when the body was finally moved by the police hours later, there was only blood on the stone beneath, the phrase complete of itself.'

'What was it?' Barney asked eagerly, accepting a bloody tale as readily as a ghostly one. 'What were the words?'

James leaned back in his chair, now certain of his audience's attention. 'As I said, it's barely three hundred yards away, up from the gate at the end of the kitchen garden, along a clear sheep trod. Why don't you go and take a look for yourself? Get it first-hand?'

'Don't be ridiculous,' said Judy. 'It's blowing a hooley out there.'

'It's not raining though,' said Rose, who had wandered over to the window and peered into the night. 'We'd need torches ...'

'Just tell us, James,' said Dinah, putting down her hook and yarn, her woolly creation gleaming ruby-like in the firelight.

James closed his eyes as if it was a struggle to recall, although the words were imprinted there as if he had seen them only yesterday.

'The man's body, his throat slit, his body naked but for shorts and a pair of running shoes, lay at an angle over one half of the stone. On the other half in a clumsy, and, as I said, apparently freshly chiselled script were five words. A poem? A prayer? A cryptic confession?'

'Which one?' asked Barney. Dash stood up, stretched, yawned and looked up at James, as if he too would like to know the answer.

James pursed his lips. 'If you're not prepared to go and take a look for yourself right now, you'll have to wait for that revelation while I tell the whole story.'

Dinah let out a snort of frustration and went back to crocheting the seemingly endless tentacles of her octopus.

James clasped his hands together. 'It was the morning of New Year's Day, 1983. A young couple were out hiking, having made an early start from the pub where they had spent the previous night. Heads sore from the celebrations, which had culminated in rounds of whisky and repeated and ingenious new verses of "On Ilkla Moor Baht'at".

'I was a cub reporter on the local *Evening Courier* at the time, so was able to get a first-hand account of what happened. The young woman said that at first she thought the prostrate shape was a sheep asleep or sickening. Her boyfriend claimed he knew what it was straight away and was half-tempted to steer them away from the path. He'd been planning a romantic marriage proposal at the summit of Crummenden Moor. The discovery of what was at the very least a seriously unwell man, was going to ruin the moment. In the event, it was more than just that moment that was spoiled. "I'll never forget it," he said. "It was brutal. Like an ancient sacrifice. A slaughter."

'By "it" he meant the face-down semi-naked body of local vet and fell-runner Bartek Janowski. Slumped over the recumbent Jinny Stone, of similar length to his body, but three times his girth. His skin touched by a delicate sheen of dew, which spangled the dark hairs on his back and legs. A savage puncture wound to the back of his neck was ruled by the coroner to have been the deathblow. Though he had other surface injuries too, including a bruise on his left cheek, which may have occurred as his body fell.

'It was one of the mountain rescue volunteers who mentioned that the words on the stone were freshly carved. He knew the boundary marker well, being a runner himself. The annual New Year's Eve Dash had taken place the previous day. Bartek Janowski himself had been one of the participants, finishing a close third. The volunteer had been a race marshal and had stood by Running Jinny for two hours, counting the runners as they passed. He swore that twenty-four hours ago the surface of the stone had been unmarked. Later evidence, reported faithfully by me in the *Courier*, confirmed that loose grains of the distinctive local gritstone had been found on the corpse.

'Bartek lived down in Salwarth, the village in the valley due south from here. Newly married and newly moved to the area, after taking up a post at the veterinary surgery in the February of the previous year. Drawn here by his love for the fells and the opportunities afforded by the choice of two local running clubs and a packed racing calendar.

'Animals great and small kept Bartek busy when he wasn't pounding the trails across the moor. His wife Charlotte took longer to fit into village life.

'"She's only shy," her neighbour Sue Stimpson told me. "She was very grateful whenever I popped round with a box of biscuits or a tub of soup. I always make too much since my husband passed. I find it hard cooking for one, although I've become a dab hand with leftovers. And since I lost Graham, I've so much spare time on my hands." Sue was a resourceful woman. I met her three times and on each occasion, she tried to give me some bottled fruit or pickle and once a pot of evil-smelling embrocation that she assured me would ease my "smoker's chest". A couple of weeks after that interview the *Courier* published her first column, "Winning at Widowhood" under the name Mrs S. T. Stimpson.

'Seven months after the Janowskis' arrival in Salwarth, Charlotte had started working as a teaching assistant at the village Primary School and became: "much perked up" (Sue Stimpson); "A stalwart of Key Stage One" (her headmistress); and "My favourite person ever" (Emily, Year 1).

'"I've never liked the moors," Charlotte Janowski said when she finally agreed to speak to me for the *Courier*. "I often shut the curtains at the back of the house, even during the day," she admitted. "If you look out on it too long it feels as though it is moving in, pressing at the edges of the village. All that heather and rock and sheep, and birds wheeling and starting and generally giving you the spooks. The only time I went for a walk up there with Bartek, I felt so alone. So vulnerable. Like I was going to be picked off at any minute. By a big bird, or a lightning bolt. Or maybe I'd fall in a bog and sink before anyone even knew I'd gone. Anything could happen up there and nobody would know."

'I paused the interview at this point, while Charlotte fetched a glass of water and a fresh wad of tissues. She moved with an almost stately grace, which I at first took for coldness. But as she carefully dabbed at her red-rimmed eyes I felt that this was a woman who bore her grief with a devastated calm, as if now the worst had finally happened, the world held no more horrors for her. She ran her fingers once through her long auburn hair and our interview resumed.

'"I was asleep when it happened. Oblivious. I knew Bartek was going out for an early run, even though we'd toasted the New Year in at midnight and he'd been racing the day before. It was Bartek's special place up there, he couldn't keep away from it. He said the emptiness, the near silence made him feel whole. He'd run in all weathers, with his club or by himself. It made him a calmer person." She paused with what I seem to remember I described as "a wistful look" in her eyes.

'"It did us both good, his running. While he was out it meant I could get on with jobs around the house that he never had the time or patience to do. Fixing leaky taps and wonky shelves, upcycling bits and pieces of old furniture, I even rebuilt part of the garden wall where it had collapsed." She showed me the callouses on her palms to prove it. "There's such a profound difference, isn't there," she said, stroking the toughened skin with her thumb, "between someone being absent and you knowing they will be back soon, and them being gone and you knowing they're never coming home."

'I spoke to Gwyn Lewis, the running club president, at Bartek's funeral. Gwyn refused to be interviewed for the paper and said any of his comments must be off record. He'd told the police everything he knew, which was mainly that Bartek was a much-valued vet.

"'He saved our rabbit's life last summer," Gwyn said. "She lost an eye but when you're a rabbit it's the ears that count, isn't it?"

'He'd also been a rising star of the running club. "He would have been men's captain this year," said Gwyn. "He and Tracy Louise could have led Salwarthdale Harriers to glorious heights."

"'Tracy Louise?" I asked, taking a sip of warm white wine and perusing the buffet.

"'Our ladies' captain. A tiny powerhouse. Close to winning the English Championships the last two years and could have got it this year I reckon."

"'Could have?"

'Gwyn shook his head. "Bartek's death, and it happening while he was out running, has been such a shock," he said. "The pair of them were quite a team." His eye twitched and he coughed as a tall, lean man in a sombre jacket over what was undeniably a tracksuit, approached. "In terms of their commitment to the club, I mean." His eyes switched to the man as he drew closer.

"'Afternoon, Tom!" He slapped the man on his shoulder. "Ian, this is Tom Adams, one of our top runners and husband of our ladies' captain. Sad day, Tom, sad day."

'I shook the man's hand. "You and the rest of the club must be pretty shaken by what's happened," I said.

"'Aye, I guess you could say shaken," Tom replied, folding his arms across his chest. "Some maybe more than most."

'Bartek's missing running top continued to mystify the police. When he set off that morning at seven thirty, he'd been seen by Sue Stimpson, who'd awoken with one of her bad coughs. She said she rarely slept past six in the morning anyway and liked to spend those early hours at her window with a cup of tea, admiring her cherry tree through the changing seasons and "watching the world go by". "He was wearing his red, white and blue jersey for definite," she said. "I would have remembered, I assure you, if his chest had been bare."'

'The words,' burst out Judy, her fingers tapping impatiently on the arm of the sofa. 'What about the words, on the boundary stone?'

'I was just getting to that,' said James. He took a sip of his Thai spirit, winced and placed the glass carefully down on the table. 'The words, freshly carved with no small effort into the ancient stone of Running Jinny were key to the case. Or at least that was the opinion of Detective Inspector Robertson, who was leading the investigation. He was an old friend of my dad's and he was encouraging of my career. We often had what I suppose you might call brainstorming sessions, over a pint or two. The contents of these informal chats, I promised not to print, or at least not until Robertson gave me the nod to do so.

'DI Robertson probably told me, a copy-hungry hack, more than he should have about an ongoing unsolved murder in the small village community where I lived and worked. But he valued my curiosity and occasional insightfulness, both of which had been of help to him before. It was in fact me who put the police on the right track with the inscription.'

'At last,' muttered Judy, 'we're getting there.'

'The main reason that the inscription was considered so crucial was that the police had very little else to go on. Bartek had no obvious enemies. He was considered to be a competent and very likeable vet, with whatever's the animal equivalent of a good bedside manner. He was respected by his running peers. There were the inevitable racing rivalries, both outside and within the club, but the Harriers' president, Gwyn, had assured the police there'd been nothing worth killing for. There was no sign of the weapon, although having put two and eight together and made a reasonable ten, the coroner had deduced that it was likely to be the same tool that had carved ...' James paused and took another sip of his drink. 'That had carved the words on the stone. Bartek wasn't an especially tall man ...' He waved away murmurs from his still frustrated audience. 'But the angle of the neck wound suggested his killer was at least six foot.

'"The killer took that running jersey for a reason," DI Robertson told me. "We've had officers and dogs scouring the moor for it, and for the weapon. They could both be at the bottom of a peat bog for all we know. The moor is riddled with enough of them. They might emerge in a couple of hundred years to puzzle archaeologists of the future. But that's of no help to us, today."

'"Perhaps they kept it as a trophy?" I suggested. "A reminder of what they had done."

'DI Robertson raised a woolly eyebrow. Have I mentioned the detective's facial hair, by the way? If not it's quite an omission. I swear the man could have been a department store Santa without any props. No props at all, he even had the rosy cheeks. Marvellous. Anyway, where was I?'

'The words on the stone?' said Judy, but with little hope in her voice.

'Ah, yes. So the police had a paltry list of suspects. Bartek's assistant at the surgery was known for spending his evenings in the pub grumbling about the workload his boss expected them to get through and muttering about how the more they overworked themselves the more mistakes they'd make. A volatile local landowner had been so angry about the route of a race that Bartek had organised the previous October that he'd shouted obscenities at the runners as they passed. And a member of Boulsby Striders whom he'd frequently pipped to the post had put in an official complaint about Bartek's "unsportsmanlike behaviour at stiles". Not only were their motives fragile, all of them had alibis for that morning.

'The investigation took an upward turn however when the truth came out about Bartek and Tracy Louise's relationship. Salwarth is a small town and Salwarthdale Harriers had its fair share of gossips. Bartek and Tracy Louise were always sharing lifts to races, and never had a spare seat for anyone else. They often ran ahead of the pack at the Wednesday night club run but were always last to get to the pub afterwards. They had regular training sessions together, reccying race routes and ticking off endless hill reps in the hours before and after work. No one else was ever invited along. This information reached the police, and while none of it was particularly damning, it suggested a possible affair, and the associated motives of passion and jealously among the people involved.

'Under pressure, Tracy Louise reluctantly admitted that she and Bartek had been more than just running buddies. A revelation that added to Charlotte Janowski's trauma and I imagine some difficult conversations in Tracy Louise's own household. In terms of being a suspect, at five foot two, she didn't really fit the bill.'

'Unless she tripped him up,' interrupted Jon, 'and stabbed him in the neck when he was on the ground.'

'The coroner ruled that out. The fatal blow happened when Bartek was vertical, with a thrust from above. Tracy Louise's husband, Tom, was of far greater interest to the police. For several years the Harriers' leading runner, he repeatedly finished behind Bartek at races, and was beaten by him, by a single vote, in the election for the new captain. Added to this now was the revelation that he was also a runner-up in love. He denied the murder of course and had an alibi. He had been at the Spinning Wheel pub with Tracy Louise and another couple from the club until half past twelve on New Year's Eve. They'd walked home, gone to bed and slept through until ten in the morning on New Year's Day. Tracy Louise's statement matched his to the letter.

'It was almost two weeks into the New Year before the killer was identified, and I must with some lack of modesty lay claim to pointing the investigators in the right direction, by working out the significance of the message on the stone.

'When I spelled it out to DI Robertson, he shook his head in disbelief and said, "Of course. It's obvious!"

'*It is when someone's just told you the answer,* I thought, but I let him take the credit when the arrest was made.'

'And are you perchance going to spell it out to us?' asked Judy. 'Because I for one ...' She was interrupted by a shout from the hall. The door to the study burst open and in strode Rose, her raincoat dripping onto the carpet, her red hair clinging to her head. 'It's raining again,' she said. She peeled off her coat, hung it on the back of a chair and hunkered down in front of the fire, holding her damp hands up to the heat of the flames.

'Where have you been?' asked Dinah.

'To see the stone,' guessed James smugly.

'To see the stone,' agreed Rose.

'And?' asked Judy. 'Did you find it?'

'I did,' she said, 'eventually.' She scowled at James. 'I took a photo of the inscription, but I can't see how it helps.' She held out her phone. 'Is it a poem? A quote from the Bible?'

Judy grabbed the phone, frowned at the screen and then read out what she saw:

GRABJOY

+ + + + + + + + +

WHILEITLASTS

+ +

x

'Is that Emily Dickinson?' asked Rose. She started to search for a matching quote on her phone.

'More likely a Brontë, surely, up here,' said Judy.

'It does sound like Emily B, or maybe Emily D,' added Dinah. 'One of her death ones?'

'Nope,' said Rose, still tapping at her screen. 'I'm not finding anything.'

'Hang on,' said Barney as he walked over to Edward Luddenham's desk. After rummaging in a drawer he produced a writing pad and a pen. 'I'll copy it out to see if that helps.'

'Meanwhile,' said James, 'shall I continue?'

'Yes,' they chorused.

'At my request, DI Robertson and I went up to look at the site of the murder together. Up on the bleak moor. Bracestone House sombre in the background but standing empty at that time. Forensics hadn't been able to remove the stone itself of course. But they'd photographed it from every angle, taken samples and impressions. Specks of Bartek's blood embedded in the cuts in the rock suggested they had been chiselled out after he was killed. And notably, there were no letters beneath his body, as if the message, such as it was, had to fit the uncovered space.

'Crouching in the heather, while I examined the stone face, I asked if blood had been found in all of the letters.

'Checking his notes Robertson said, "In most but not all. It makes sense I suppose that the blood would have worn off the tool after a while of chipping."

'"Just out of interest," I asked, "did forensics make a note of the letters that didn't have any trace of blood in them?"

'The DI looked at me. "That will require a phone call when we get down from this blasted heath. But go on." He passed me his notepad. "Write them down," he said.

'"Write what down?"

'"The letters that you are betting didn't have any trace of blood," he said.

'When the results came back, I was mostly right. The last couple of letters in the final row were blood free, it may have all worn off the chisel by then. But there were a distinct set of letters within the inscription that had no trace of blood in them at all.'

'Which ones?' said Barney.

'Hah!' said Judy. 'Have you learned nothing? He's not going to be sharing that with us straight away.'

'Actually I am,' said James, glancing at his watch. 'Because it's getting late and I've got the new Osman to finish before I can sleep soundly tonight.' He drained his glass, this time without wincing. 'Any joy, Barney?'

Barney had outlined and brightly highlighted so many different letters on his sheet of paper that it resembled the type of inspirational poster beloved by the owners of guesthouses and B&Bs.

'Are the crosses significant?' he asked.

'They are,' said James. 'Specifically the sixth one in the long row, lying directly between the letters BJ and TLA.'

'Bartek Janowski,' exclaimed Rose and Judy simultaneously.

'And Tracy Louise ...' said Dinah.

'Tracy Louise Adams,' James finished for her. 'A simple, timeless, but for an illicit affair very public, declaration of love.'

'By Bartek?' Rose asked.

'It seems most likely. But who carved those letters is possibly of less interest than who added the remaining ones.'

'To hide the message!' said Rose.

'Exactly.'

'Well, Tracy Louise might panic if she saw it,' said Jon. 'Her husband would be bound to see it on one of his runs.'

'So she kills her lover and hides his message?' asked Judy, not sounding convinced.

'As it happens,' said James. 'On the morning of the murder, Tracy and Tom were exactly where they had told the police they were. At home, in bed. As attested, by their neighbour.'

'Was he there as well?' asked Rose.

'No. But Tracy and Tom lived in one of the newer semis at the far side of the village. Shiny and neat but with, as in some parts of this old pile, very thin shared walls. The neighbour could hear, let's say, "amorous activity" on and off from just before eight till at least nine thirty. He banged on the wall but apparently only got, ahem, a louder banging back.'

'But Tracy Louise loved Bartek,' protested Rose.

'Bartek loved Tracy Louise,' said James. 'Tracy had some nice times with Bartek, but she was never going to leave Tom. Bartek didn't believe her, and perhaps with what turned out to be his final act, he had been hoping to force the issue.

'If you look carefully at Rose's photograph, his and Tracy Louise's initials are relatively neat compared to the clumsiness of the rest. He had been practising. There's a stone outhouse behind the vet's surgery where he kept an old bike that he sometimes used for home visits. Never one to miss a chance to exercise. The temporary vet who came to cover the practice found the key and had a look in there. He didn't realise the significance of what he saw on the wall. It wasn't until the assistant filled him in on some of the details of the case that he thought it might be worth mentioning it to the police. He turned up at the station three hours after I had told DI Robertson my theory about the love message. His discovery inside the shed confirmed it. Apparently random letters had been chiselled into the stone wall. In no particular order, but they were the letters that Bartek wanted to get right.'

'So, he carved his message on the fallen stone and someone found and changed it?' said Barney.

'Yes, or more rather found him as he finished it. Possibly as he sat back on his heels to admire his work. Killed as he was kneeling down, not standing as the police first thought.'

'A crime of passion,' said Dinah with some relish. 'His wife followed him up to the moors despite her hatred and fear of the place. Saw what he'd done, what it implied for their future. Picked up the discarded chisel and stabbed him ...' Dinah plunged the end of her crochet hook into the head of her octopus, 'dead.'

'Sort of,' said James. 'The killer did follow Bartek up to the moor that morning. They'd had their concerns. There had been signs. They suspected an assignation and went looking for proof. Perhaps for a confrontation. What they found was a blatant symbol of adulterous lust. Something that struck the killer to their core and drove their hand to an act of fury and vengeance.' He checked his watch again. 'Dear me, it is getting late. But I imagine there will be uproar if I pull a Scheherazade and make you wait until morning for the denouement.' He smiled and continued. 'The killer did their best to hide Bartek's message in a scrap of nonsense, then recklessly signed it and walked away.'

'Signed it!' exclaimed Barney. He looked at the piece of paper on which he'd written and embellished the letters. He had boldly encircled Bartek and Tracy Louise's initials. 'But the rest are just random words, not a name.'

James peered at the piece of paper. 'You missed a bit,' he said.

Rose snatched the piece of paper and compared it with the photograph on her phone. 'Yeah there,' she said. 'Under the words. Two vertical crosses and an x.'

'That's a signature?' asked Dinah.

'No it's a cat's face,' said James. 'More precisely, it's Sue Stimpson's ancient ginger tom, Graham, who didn't survive a routine operation under Bartek's scalpel just before Christmas.'

'I thought Graham was her husband,' said Judy.

'No. No idea what the poor man was called. He'd popped his clogs three years earlier. Left Sue devasted of course, although ...'

'Although?' asked Dinah.

'The gossip network of Salwarth, in this case primarily Tracy Louise, whose mum used to have her hair done at the same salon as Sue, filled me in on this point. Six months before his death, Mr Stimpson, a driving instructor, was caught in a compromising position with one of his pupils. It was a brief local scandal. He promised it would never happen again, Mrs Stimpson forgave him and all was rosy again in their garden. Until one tragic day in December when he fell from a step ladder and broke his neck.'

'Where was Mrs Stimpson when this happened?' asked Barney.

'*Apparently*, watching from her window with a cup of tea. Said she saw the whole thing. It would be almost comic if the man hadn't died. He was up the ladder trying to fix a string of fairy lights in the cherry tree. Graham the cat, getting on a bit but still agile, scampered up the tree in pursuit of a bird or a squirrel. Gave Mr Stimpson such a shock that he stumbled backwards and fell.'

James put his hands on his thighs as if about to get to his feet.

'That's what she said she saw and nobody was able to refute her. She wasn't so fortunate next time, however, when she went down for the murder of Bartek Janowski. And dashed her hopes of a career in local journalism.'

'She confessed?'

'Not straight away. But they didn't need a confession. When Robertson went round to question her about the inscription she tried to bluff him out. Told him and his sergeant they were welcome to search her house. So they did. They found the chisel, clumsily stashed in a utensils jar in the kitchen. Charlotte later identified it as coming from their house, though previously she'd made more use of it than her DIY-adverse husband. More damning was Bartek's running top, neatly folded in a drawer of tea towels. Stained with his blood and imbued with the very particular scent of Mrs Stimpson's special embrocation.

'You said the inscription was signed,' insisted Rose. 'Surely the face of a cat wasn't enough to convince your detective friend.'

'She signed it alright,' said James. 'Look at that last line "while it lasts". Tracy Louise's initials had no blood in them, but neither did the finally three letters. Because before she tapped them in, Susan Tamara Stimpson, a woman who had not only lost her beloved pet, but also couldn't bear infidelity to go unchecked, had wiped the chisel clean.'

PUZZLE

The New Year's Eve Dash

Fifty-two runners took part in the hilly five-mile New Year's Eve Dash, the day before Bartek Janowski was killed. They came from near and far and most, even those in fancy dress, wore the distinctive vests of their running clubs.

This included Abel, Bella, Colin and Davina.

Each of them ran for a different club, the four being the Coley Clippers, Salpit Striders, Farahill Fliers and Hylem Hurriers.

The four distinctively different club vests were red & white stripes, all green, blue and white checks and green and blue stripes.

The finishing times for the four runners were forty minutes, fifty-one minutes, fifty-eight minutes and one hour two minutes.

From the information provided below can you work out each runner's club affiliation, the colour of their vest and their finishing time? You might find it helpful to draw a grid or table on some paper to plot out your answers.

1. There was white on Davina and Abel's vests
2. The Clipper finished twenty-two minutes ahead of the slowest of the four
3. Bella neither ran for the Striders nor finished behind all of the other three
4. Abel ran either for the Striders or the Hurriers and came last
5. The Flier was the second fastest of the four runners

116

6. The runner in the red–and–white vest came in four minutes ahead of the Strider

7. Bella in her striped vest was faster than Davina but not faster than Colin

Final Puzzle Clue #4

The clue that you need to take forward for the final puzzle is either CLIPPERS, STRIDERS, FLIERS or HURRIERS – the correct one being the club whose runner finished third of the four.

THE MAN WHO MADE LISTS

'Are you alright, Mrs Monye?' Mrs Linden asked.

Judy opened her eyes and blinked slowly. She was in the kitchen, in the armchair by the fire, wrapped in a tartan blanket. Mrs Linden was standing in front of her, hands on her hips, peering at her in concern.

'Oh, I'm still here,' Judy said. Her mouth and lips were dry. 'I came down in the night and I must have fallen asleep. What time is it?'

'It's eight o'clock in the morning,' said Mrs Linden. 'You look wiped out, pet.'

Judith rubbed her eyes. 'I had a disturbed night.'

'Ah, you wouldn't be the first to not get a good night's sleep under this roof. Especially in the winter. The wind and the rain and the frost and the hail. Playing like billyo on the roof and the windows. Not to mention the creaking.'

'The creaking?' said Judy.

'Is that what kept you up? Floorboards, doors, walls, they've all got their own special tune and never in harmony. Even the nights I sleep well, it can give me bad dreams.'

'I think it was a noise that woke me,' said Judy. 'About two o'clock in the morning. Outside my bedroom window everything was black, but I could still see movement, trees and clouds blowing about. I thought I heard the noise again, this time it was definitely outside my room. I went out into the corridor and ...' She hesitated, her left hand squeezing the opposite wrist. 'I came downstairs to make a hot drink. I thought one of Helena's Sweet Dreams herbal teas might help me get back to sleep. There was an old newspaper in the fire basket, with an uncompleted crossword. I settled in the armchair with the tea – which was very soothing, lavender and chamomile I think – and lost myself in the puzzle. I'd just got a fiendishly cryptic one. I might even have said "Ha!" out loud. Then,' she swallowed again, 'the kitchen light went out.'

'Aye, it does that sometimes. Faulty bulb connection. It's working now.'

'Yes I can see,' said Judy. 'I know it sounds silly,' she continued, 'and I'm not usually so easily spooked. It must be all these stories we've been telling. I'd left my phone upstairs and I didn't know where there were any torches or candles. So I just stayed put, in this chair.'

'You'll suffer for that today,' predicted Mrs Linden. 'You'd better ask Miss Helena for some yoga exercises to loosen you up. In the meantime, shall I make you a cup of tea and a bacon butty? I'm doing one for Mr Burton anyway.'

'James is already up?'

'Aye. He's gone out the front,' said Mrs Linden. 'Having his morning cigarette.' She sniffed. 'The first of his daily ten.'

Outside, last night's storm had abated, leaving the world looking as exhausted as Judy felt. James was standing on the gravel drive, smoking and looking out towards the line of trees that hid the road from view.

'James,' said Judy.

He turned. His eyes were bloodshot, his jowls heavy. He gave a smile that seemed forced. 'Judith, how are you this morning?'

'Tired,' she said, 'and confused.'

'Really? By what?'

'When I came out of my room last night and bumped into you, on the second-floor landing.'

'Ah, yes.' His eyes tried but failed to twinkle. 'Ships in the night. Me in my T-shirt and boxers, you in your rather dashing velvet dressing gown. Could have looked quite comprising.'

'Not really,' said Judy. 'But you said you'd been to the bathroom.'

'Is that not allowed. Are you going to give me a fine, Mrs Librarian?' He laughed and tried to step past her back to the house.

'Except your bedroom is in the West Wing. I remember you saying on our first day that you had a perfect view of the old hawthorn tree on that side of the house. So why were you in the East Wing?'

'The West Wing toilet was occupied,' said James, with a touch of impatience. 'I don't know by whom. I'm too well-mannered to knock and ask. So I decided to avail myself of the other available facilities.'

'Which are between my room and the corridor leading to the West Wing,' said Judy. 'Sorry, it just seemed to me ...'

'Yes?'

'That you had come from Edward's room.'

James ground out his cigarette in the gravel and crossed his arms over his chest. 'Bingo! Or should I say Cluedo. You've got me, Mrs Monye. It was me in the master bedroom with the antique candlestick.' He dropped his arms. 'If you must know, I'm a bit particular about these things. Rather than make do with one of the shared loos, I thought why not use Edward's ensuite? A bit of privacy, I thought. Not knowing I would be encountering Nancy Drew on my way back to bed.'

'Oh, I see. Of course I should have realised. Sorry.'

'Not at all, don't worry about it. We're all a bit on edge, aren't we? But let's remember Edward's number-one house rule and just all try to get along.'

'I'll do my best,' she said as he walked off. *Though it would help*, she thought, *if people didn't make up such stupid lies*. On the day she arrived, when she'd realised that the room in which Edward had been killed was close to her own assigned bedroom, curiosity had led to her take a peek. The furniture was shrouded in white sheets. There was a splendid four-poster bed and a walk-in wardrobe. A huge fireplace with a hearth unlit for almost a year. As it had been the scene of a murder, she had taken careful note of the room and its layout. And she knew one thing for certain: there was no en suite.

★ ★ ★

'Well, that was quite the day out,' said Rose, nabbing the comfiest of the armchairs and throwing her legs over the arm. 'Well done, Grandad, or whoever else it was who planned that itinerary.'

'If I'd known,' said Judy, settling onto the sofa, 'that shooting at people and ducking behind moonrocks to avoid been shot in return was so much fun, I'd have taken it up years ago.' She was amazed that she'd been able to keep up with the others after a night of broken sleep, although she had manged to snooze in the car on the way to and from the activity centre. She now felt oddly invigorated.

'The crazy golf was fun too,' said Dinah, sitting down beside her. 'Not literally crazy, disappointingly, but enjoyable nonetheless.'

'And dinner at the pub in the village tonight,' said Stuart, rubbing his hands together.

'Do we have to pay for our own beers?' asked Barney. His father frowned. 'I was just asking,' said Barney, slumping onto one of the hard chairs.

'Everything is on Edward's tab, according to Mrs Linden,'

said James. 'He really did go to a lot of trouble to arrange all this.' He turned to Sara. 'He knew he was going to die, didn't he?'

Sara looked nervous.

'I know about the client confidentiality,' said James, 'but can't you at least shed a bit of light? To be honest, I did wonder if we were going to be spending these four days undergoing some sort of tests. Like *I'm a Celebrity* but involving peat bogs and sheep testicles instead of the more exotic kind. But we're being led to believe that Edward simply wanted us to have a nice time at his expense on the anniversary of his death. He knew it was coming.'

Sara nodded. 'Yes, he did.'

Helena gasped.

'Or at least he thought he did,' Sara hesitated.

'It's OK,' said Dinah, 'none of this will go beyond this room.'

Sara sighed. 'Edward had received what he believed to be a threat against his life. He didn't know, at the time, whether it was merely intended to frighten him, or a promise of action that would be taken. As we now know, it turned out it was the latter.'

'Frighten him? To what end?' asked Helena. 'Blackmail, extortion?'

'What's the difference?' asked Barney.

Sara pressed two fingers to her forehead and closed her eyes. 'I really, really can't say any more. For now.'

'The lady detective needs time to manipulate her grey cells,' said Stuart chirpily. The Laser Quest adventure had seemingly enlivened him too, perhaps because he had so thoroughly lain waste to his son. Barney had protested that his dad wouldn't stand a chance against him playing a video game. Stuart had picked up his son's laptop as soon as they got back, opening it and saying, 'Choose your game'. But Barney had snatched it back. 'No chance, Dad, you'll ruin my high scores.'

'Shall we have another story before we head to the pub?' asked Stuart.

'Is it my turn?' asked Judy. Perhaps getting her own tale out of the way would banish some of the unease she had felt last night, although she was still puzzled by James's behaviour.

'It can be,' said James, prodding at the burning logs in the hearth with a poker. 'Nobody else is exactly rushing forward to volunteer.'

'Right-ho,' said Judy. 'Is everyone sitting comfortably?'

'Not really,' said Stuart who was at last taking his turn in one of the hardback chairs. 'But,' he continued, 'please do begin.'

'You're probably expecting me to produce a well-thumbed library book — a Christie or a Conan Doyle — to read a tale from,' began Judy. 'After all, I've got the swollen crime fiction shelves of a large library at my disposal. But as it happens I have a more personal story to tell, as Edward was well aware. We'd been working together, or at least I had been helping him, with his *Notorious Northerners* book. He was particularly keen on tracking down information on the Limes. Do you remember them? They were all over the papers in the eighties, early nineties, Clara and Jerry?'

'The Humberside Bonnie and Clyde,' said James. 'Famously elusive, but they were caught on camera once, in silhouette on the Humber Bridge, wearing trilbies and sunglasses, him holding a gun. Made for some great double-page spreads, even if it did glamorise their crimes.'

'That was them,' said Judy. 'We found some clippings about a particularly brutal killing spree that they'd tried to cover up as burglaries, while neglecting to actually steal anything. It reminded me of an experience I'd had myself a few years earlier, so of course I told Edward all about it.'

Judy adjusted herself on the sofa, ensuring she was a good distance from Dinah's crochet hook, which she tended to wield like a miniature sabre when she was excited.

'I should begin by saying that murder — other than the

fictional or historical – is not usually on the bill at the library. In fact other than the theft of books – which of course is of itself heinous – it's a bit of an actual crime desert. We had a streaker once, quite a shy one though; he covered his front bits up with a copy of *The Da Vinci Code*. Another time Martin had to call up to the archives for back-up to help him remove a man who was writing on the walls of the children's library in crayon. They weren't bad words, but they were strange enough to disturb Martin and he's a goth so not easily shaken. We've never had a murder. Not on site at least. But a few years back I was asked to help solve one. Ah, that's perked you up at the back,' she said, nodding towards Barney, who had put away his phone. Dinah too had paused mid treble-crochet and put down her latest amigurumi creation.

Judy continued. 'This story begins on a cold December morning. I mainly work in Local History, but staff shortages mean I often, as on that day, do shifts in General Lending. One of those days behind the issue desk when I wished I'd taken up blacksmithing or kippering or some occupation where you're guaranteed a source of heat and have no choice but to take your cardi off at the door. The library building is Victorian and the main desk is at the centre of the Great Round Room. It's the original reading room, lined with wooden shelves and topped with a glass dome that produces plenty of light and singular acoustics. Warm, however, it is not. That particular morning among the echoing coughs and sniffles of readers huddled at the long tables that are laid out like spokes, I was deep inside three layers of woollens. I was just considering wrapping my outdoors scarf round my neck when up walked Ted Fairchild. Seeing his face grinning at me over the counter was like being transported back in time.

'We'd both started at the council in the same week. Me in the library, relaunching my working life once my boys were both at high school, and him, twelve or so years younger, in his first post-uni job in the building conservation department. After a general induction tour with a group that included the chief exec's new secretary and a rather hoity-toity planning inspector, five of us went for a coffee in the canteen and it became a regular thing. Over the years we careered our own paths through the council hierarchy, slowly upwards, frustratingly sideways, or in one case down and out (the hoity but, as it turned out, easily corruptible planner). Each Tuesday morning we took our coffee break together in the canteen. Catching up on in-house gossip (mainly about the planning inspector) and attempting the *Times* crossword, a task I completed more quickly on my own the rest of the week.

'Ted left the council after five years to join a consultancy and our friendship, such as it was, wasn't strong enough to keep going. But here he was, so many years later, slapping his broad palms on the library counter and whispering, "Got time for a coffee, Judy?" as if he'd never been away. He hadn't changed. Well, of course he had. None of us can actually hold back the years, no matter what the cosmetic industry tries to sell us. But that's what you say, isn't it, when you instantly recognise someone you haven't seen for a long time, even though you've both gone through a lot of life in between? He was forty now and leaner, his face tending to the craggy, none of that round boyishness he'd carried through his twenties. He had a new sharpness and was altogether less comfortable looking than I remembered. Still smartly turned out, though. Crew neck sweater under a dark grey jacket and proper trousers, not jeans.'

Judy avoided looking at denim-clad James at this point.

'I was due a break so I signalled to my colleague Eric that I was off and took Ted through to the public café. They have better coffee in there than the instant on offer in the staff room, and a reliable range of flapjacks. The space, which echoes the circle of the reading room, was decked out for the season, with tinsel, greenery and festive bunting made by the Crafty Readers

Club. A low murmur of Christmas songs was playing on a loop, just too quiet to be able to clearly make out a Wham! from a Wizzard.

'I ordered my usual mocha. Ted just had a black coffee, I think. Though we did share a cherry and walnut slab. To the faint soundtrack of festive hits he began to relate what he'd been through over the past year and I gained some understanding of the pain evident in his eyes. Six months ago he'd lost his grandfather, who had brought him and his brother up ever since their parents died in a car accident when the boys were still in primary school. Just three weeks ago his brother had drowned in a tragic accident. I knew about the death of his grandfather, Geoffrey Fairchild. It had been in all the papers: "Retired Headmaster Stabbed in Bungled Burglary". It caused quite a stir, especially as the culprits still hadn't been caught.'

'I remember that one,' James said. 'I covered it for the *Daily Argus*. Wasn't it pinned on a drugs gang? The police knew who they were but didn't have enough to send them down?'

'Apparently so,' said Judy. 'The only thing stolen was a Meissen shepherdess. Worth a fortune. It was found on a needle-strewn mantelpiece in a drug raid in Leeds a few weeks later, clean of prints and no one confessing to how it had got there.' She paused. 'But Ted was focused on his brother's death to begin with.

'"You remember Damien?" Ted asked. As he spoke his dead brother's name, his fingers started tapping a rhythm on the leg of the table. A memory surfaced of a round face, blond curls and eyes of a fierce dark blue that matched Ted's.

'"He joined us a couple of times for quiz nights," I said. "Over at the Crown and Anchor." An intense young man, who had scant interest in his little brother's work colleagues, but a treasure trove of a mind when it came to trivia. We'd won the quiz every time he was on our team.

'Ted nodded miserably. "Not everyone got him. He was a bit of a loner. But he was one of the good guys. He was devastated when Gramps was killed. We all were but Damien had no one else he was close to. I've got my wife, Suzy. She's been a rockstar. Damien was on his own. It didn't help that he was the one who found Gramps that day. It must have been such a shock. He became, well, a bit obsessed."

'"In what way?" I asked.

'Ted leaned across the table and beckoned me to do the same.

'"What connects real ales, paint colours and obscure song titles?" One of his feet was tapping now, his knee gently knocking the table.

'I didn't know what to say. "Are you OK?" seemed too pointed.

'"Come on Judy, you were always the cryptic crossword queen. I know how frustrated you got when me and the gang tried to help, and you were second only to Damien when it came to general knowledge. Our very own council Mastermind."

'"It's a puzzle?" I asked.

'"I think so. And I think the answer could point to who killed Gramps. And maybe explain why Damien ended up dead too."

'"What happened?" I asked.

'He took a deep breath. "Damien was out for his usual long Sunday morning walk along the river that flows past the bottom of Gramps's garden. He'd been living at the house since the funeral." He shrugged. "Bit creepy I thought, with it being where he'd found a dead body. But it was where Damien wanted to be. It was raining heavily, had been non-stop since Friday night. But he had all the top waterproof gear and he wasn't one to be put off by a bit of wet." Ted took a sip of his coffee. "Nobody knew he was missing till his body washed up by a weir on the Monday afternoon. It was ruled an accident. He'd got too close to the edge of the riverbank. May have even tried to cross the submerged stepping stones. But I don't know." He fixed me with his eyes which had regained some of their former spark. "It doesn't seem right. Him dying so soon after Gramps. Especially as he had spent the past couple of months telling anyone who'd listen that he knew who Gramps's killer was and that he had 'physical evidence'."

'I sipped at my mocha, which was disappointingly lukewarm. "And what has that to do with, what was it, beers and paint?"

'In reply Ted reached into the inside pocket of his jacket. He pulled out a fat leather-bound notebook and handed it to me. At first glance it appeared very old but on closer inspection I recognised it as the type sold in fancy stationery shops. Imitating an old book with raised bands on the spine, scrolled gilt corner protectors and an embossed fleur-de-lys. Where the binding was scratched it was clearly not real leather and the corner protectors were plastic.

"'Open it," Ted urged.

'His brother's full name, Damien Fairchild, was inscribed on the first page. I began to flick through, expecting a diary and feeling uncomfortable prying into a dead man's inner thoughts. But instead of daily entries there was just page after page of lists.

'I looked up, needing an explanation.

"'Damien has made lists all his life," Ted said. "He started with scraps of paper in a shoebox when he was a kid, then filled notebook after notebook. Favourite *Beano* characters; Top Ten Top Trump sports cars; Most Deadly Dinosaurs. The usual boyhood obsessions. This book was his most recent. It's over two thirds full. They're not dated so there's no saying which ones were definitely added after Gramps died. But he was killed in June and one of the lists about twenty or so before the end is Top Twenty-one Manchester City Goals of the Twenty-first Century, and it includes one of the many they scored at the

FA Cup final in May. So we can probably discount any pages before that one."

"'Discount them in terms of what?" I asked, part of my brain still working over the beer, paint, obscure songs conundrum.

"'Damien said he had hidden the proof of who killed Gramps. I asked him why he couldn't just take whatever it was to the police. He said it wasn't enough on its own and he didn't trust them to deal with it properly. He alone, apparently, knew how to nail the killer with it. It didn't make any sense. He wouldn't say what the proof was or where he'd hidden it, only that the answer was in his latest book of lists. He waved it in my face and the faces of everyone else he told. Took it with him wherever he went. Even had it on him when he died."

'I turned the book over in my hands. "This went in the river with him?"

"'Like I said, he had top-notch wet weather gear. That was in a dry bag in his rucksack along with his phone and keys." Ted chewed at his lower lip before continuing. "I'm worried that maybe on the day of his 'accident' someone tried to get the book off him and that's how he ended up in the river."

"'The same 'someone' who killed your grandfather?"

"'It would make sense, wouldn't it? He went on about his proof so much. It was like he was advertising the fact that the book held a clue. As if he wanted to draw the killer out, you know. Make them try and steal it. Maybe it worked, but not as he planned."

"'And 'they', if they exist, didn't get the book."

"'No. So we can still find the answer hidden in it. Hopefully before the killer finds the evidence and tries to destroy it."

"'We?" I asked. "You and Suzy?" Though I'd already guessed where this was leading.

'He groaned. "We've have been trying for days. Ever since the police returned Damien's rucksack. There must be over a hundred lists in there, and at least twenty since the Man City goals one. I've read every single list and there's nothing obvious. There's no 'People I Think Killed My Grandfather' or 'Motives for Murder' or 'Poirot Stories that are Just Like Gramps's Death'.

"'Those connections I asked you about." He took the book from me and flicked through the pages. "See some of the lists have symbols drawn next to them? There's this one from near the beginning called 'Real Ales?' with a symbol of a hook and two from after the Man City Goals one, including the very last entry, look." He stabbed at the page with his finger "'(Im)possible Paint Colours for Study' and this earlier one 'Non-Hit Wonders'. Both have the same symbol next to their titles. I think it's supposed to be a shepherdess's crook, like the one the stolen figurine was holding. Each symbol is drawn in the same colour ink, so they might have been added at the same time."

"'As a clue?" I asked.

'He shrugged his shoulders. "All I've come up with so far is the name Tom."

"'Tom?"

"'Yeah, Old Tom beer, a paint colour called Tom Cat Grey and a song title, 'Go Easy Major Tom'." He groaned again. 'I know several Toms, but none of them have any connection to Gramps and without a surname it's not much use anyway."

'I wasn't convinced that "Tom" was the answer. Surely there had to be more to it than just a badly hidden first name. I began to read through the most recently added lists, hoping for a flash of inspiration, already drawn into the puzzle as Ted had known I would be.

"'You're my best bet, Judy. I need to know what Damien thought he knew." He clasped his hands together as if making a fierce prayer. "Then we can find that proof and show it to the police. I've more faith in them than Damien had. We need to find it before anyone else does. The house is going on the market soon. If whoever killed him has heard about hidden evidence, they might come back. Gramps always had good locks on all the doors and windows, but even so."

"'If the house was so secure how did they get in the first time?"

"'Bloody Colin!" Ted exclaimed, so loudly that the woman at the next table spilled her coffee.

"'Who's Colin?" I asked.

"'The gardener," Ted replied, only slightly lowering his volume. The woman glared at him as she mopped up her spilled drink with a napkin. Ted carried on regardless.

"'He was supposedly working in the kitchen garden the whole afternoon, with a clear view of the back door. Which he left unlocked because he kept popping in to use the loo.

"'Gramps was killed in his study. The police narrowed down the time of the murder to between twenty past two and four o'clock when Damien found him. Our solicitor, Andrew Wetherby, arrived at one and left at two. Had a word with Colin on his way out. He left by the back door because from Gramps's study window he'd spotted Mrs Wilson, a neighbour, marching up the drive with a tin foil tray and he didn't want to get cornered by her. She delivered her lasagne and talked at Gramps on the doorstep for about twenty minutes but wasn't invited in. Gramps was very strict about who he'd allow in the house after Granny died. It was family only, with an exception for Andrew, who's basically family." He grimaced. "He's Suzy's dad."

"'So the neighbour was the last person to see him alive?"

"'Other than the killer, yes. Mrs Wilson heard Gramps lock the door firmly as she left. Damien arrived at four o'clock. The front door was locked and bolted from the inside, but the back door was ajar and Colin was snoozing in a deckchair. Damien shook him awake and he swore he'd just that second closed his eyes. But the man's a drinker, he might have been asleep all afternoon." Ted sank his head into his hands.

'I took the opportunity to check my watch. I was only supposed to take twenty minutes for my break and I'd already run over. There was unlikely to be a rush on at that time of day and Eric was very capable, but I didn't want to take advantage.

'"Was Colin a suspect?" I asked, putting my purse in my bag and generally trying to indicate that I needed to get back to work.

'"The police questioned him endlessly. Even when they made the link to the drugs gang, they thought he might at least be an accomplice, but they couldn't pin anything on him. There were no rogue fingerprints in the study and no sign of the weapon. If Colin was involved, maybe Damien's hidden evidence will be enough to send him down." He grabbed my wrist, his voice fervent. "Please, Judy, you have to help me."

'I took the book home with me and over the weekend, in between washing football kits, cooking and trying to convince my husband and kids that yes of course they had my full attention, I studied the lists and tried to find a pattern.

'I typed some of them up on the computer, rearranging them in columns, highlighting letters, looking for hidden words in the initial letters. It felt hopeless. I was like a Bletchley Park cryptologist with a book full of cipher code but no key.

'On Sunday morning, while Michael was at the swimming pool with the boys, I thought I had a breakthrough. I'd decided to focus on the three lists marked by what definitely looked like a shepherdess's crook, although I'd already dismissed Ted's "Tom" theory.

'It took me half an hour to spot the pattern, by which point I'd decided that at least half the items in those lists had been made up by Damien, and another hour to work through my discovery. I'd lined up the three lists side by side on my computer and noticed that several entries in each of them included animal names, including Daft Badger beer, an unpleasant sounding paint shade called Flayed Possum Pink and a song with the improbable title "Hit Me Up Purple Tiger". I deleted all the animal elements and then looked at what was left. I removed all the personal names (including the Toms), the names of colours, geographical features and jobs (the delicious sounding Turquoise Lake Porter contained all three).

'It took me slightly longer and a few missteps to work out that I could group and then delete the synonyms for 'head', 'fat', 'struck or hit' and 'feeling good'. This removed among others Round Nut Stout, Happy Yellow and a song called 'Vibing Beat'. I was left with about twenty seemingly unconnected words. Had it all been a colossal waste of time? Like trimming a hedge to the point where there was nothing left but a handful of twigs. I experimentally set aside the many personal pronouns and conjunctions. When I rearranged what was left I laughed out loud, although I knew Ted would be disappointed with what I'd found.

'"Don't Be Daft, Wouldn't Make Things This Easy' – is that it?" The word disappointed didn't really cover it. Ted was incredulous. Possibly furious. Though over the phone it was hard to tell. "That's the message? He said he had evidence. What the hell was he playing at? He taunted us with that book. All for a silly joke."

'Taunted seemed an odd word. But then the whole situation was beyond what I would usually consider normal. While I was intrigued by the puzzle I'd been set, part of me was doubting that Damien's lists were really hiding the name of his grandfather's killer. I was chuffed that I'd managed to crack one code, but revealing a message from beyond the grave gave me an uneasy feeling. Who exactly, I wondered, had Damien intended his message for?

'"There must be something else in there," Ted said. "Damien could be an idiot sometimes, but he can't have been making the whole thing up. That wasn't his style."

'I explained that I couldn't give any more time to it this weekend. He said he'd come and pick the book up from the library this week and rang off.

'I went for my usual Sunday evening table tennis session with Eric and some other friends from work. My mind wasn't really on the game though. The sense of urgency (or was it fear?) in Ted's tone had worried me. Walking home from the community centre after saying my goodbyes I thought I saw a figure slip behind the trees that bordered the recreation ground. It was a breezy night and I managed to convince myself it was just the shadow of the swaying branches. That the tapping I heard as I walked home was again just the trees being bothered by the wind, not footsteps echoing mine. But I made sure the doors and windows were securely locked before Michael and I went to bed. I hadn't told him about Ted and had been vague about the puzzle. Michael could be, still is quick to jealousy. I didn't want to admit that a man from my past had been the cause of my distraction this weekend. While he was cleaning his teeth in the bathroom I peeped out of the window to see if a strange figure lurked under the streetlight, as they always do in thrillers. But the pool of light was broken only by the slink of next door's cat.

'I was woken the next morning by my ringing phone. It was Ted.

'"There's been a break-in at the house," he said. "I knew they'd come back. They've pulled the place apart. Nothing's been taken as far as I can tell. I think they were looking for the book. Or the supposed 'proof'. I'm more convinced than ever now that they killed Damien to try to get it."

'I remembered my unease last night, the flickering shadows, the tapping sounds, how I'd flinched when the black cat strode boldly beneath the streetlight. Was Ted in danger? Would I be if I continued to help him? I murmured something noncommittal, after telling Michael it was someone from work.

'"It's Damien's funeral on Wednesday morning," Ted said. "Nine-thirty. I want you to come. And I want you to bring the book."'

'I was working a late shift on Wednesday as it happened, not starting until half one. Curiosity won over my anxiety. As soon as Michael was off to work I chose my most sombre outfit, put the book of lists in my handbag and drove to the crematorium.

'The building was sleek and modern. Its pale wooden walls and elegant white and green flower arrangements only added to the starkness of the occasion. Before the ceremony, Ted introduced me to a group of people that included Damien's former sixth-form tutor (who was called Tom!) and Colin the now ex-gardener. Ted told them I was the new 'custodian' of Damien's lists which the family were donating in their entirety to the library. This was news to me.

'Ted read a brief but heartfelt elegy to his brother. I tried not to fidget during the short service although I had a strong desire to keep checking over my shoulder, unable to shake off a sense of discomfort. Ted had been so insistent that I bring the book but hadn't wanted to take it from me when I arrived. The family solicitor, Andrew Wetherby, also got up to speak. He wore a shiny dark green suit, with a white shirt and a wide black tie adorned with an ornate pin. His grey curls and beard were long and unruly, giving his appearance a manic edge. He read a brief poem from the screen of his smart phone and recalled how through his long-standing friendship with Geoffrey Fairchild and his honorary membership of the family through his daughter's marriage to Ted, he was privileged to have memories of watching Damien grow from "a serene baby" into a "unique

135

and very special young man". Another tap on his phone and a slide show of photographs appeared on the wall behind him.

'The wake was back at the house, where Ted and his wife had cleared away the chaos and debris of the recent burglary. The sitting room was large enough to accommodate everyone and a buffet was available in the adjoining dining room. While I was trying to decide between the olive tapenade bruschetta and cod goujons, and before I plumped for both, I noticed Colin walking purposefully over to the nearby drinks table. He wiped his sleeve across his wide forehead before cracking open a can of beer, whose black and white label declared it to be called Daft Badger' – a real beer after all! I introduced myself and gave my condolences. Colin shrugged.

"'I'm here because it's what his grandad would have wanted," he said, taking a long draught. "Me and Damo never really got on."

'I was tempted to ask if that was because he called him Damo.

"'We were at school together," Colin continued, already eyeing up a second beer. "Same year, but we were never what you'd call mates. Damo fancied himself a cut above the rest of us. Kept himself apart and used words he didn't expect us plebs to understand. I nearly didn't take the gardening job when it came up. Expecting Damo would look down at me, working for his grandad. But he was away at college and hardly came home so it wasn't too bad." He reached for another can with one hand while simultaneously crushing the empty one in the other. "The old man was a proper gent. Said his garden had only truly blossomed once I'd got my hands on it. Talked a lot about leaving me a 'sizeable bequest' in his will, but nothing came of that in the end. All I got was six months wages and the tools I'd worked with for years." He poured more beer down his throat, then emitted a small belch. "'Scuse me. You know what I don't understand? How the buggers managed to slip past me."

'He narrowed his eyes, perhaps picking up on something from my expression. "I know everyone says I was asleep. But when Damo got there, I swear I'd barely closed my eyes. I'd started digging over the beds when the solicitor bloke left. He had *The Archers* starting up on his phone, a proper addict like my mum had been, bless her soul. He'd missed it the night before and wanted to catch up on the whole exploding dairy storyline. I told him I wouldn't give him any spoilers, being a bit of a fan myself for Mam's sake, and he hurried off with his phone to his ear. I don't wear a watch when I'm working, but that's how I knew it was just after two when I started digging over the beds. Thought I'd done a good hour's work when I sat myself down, but Damo found his grandad at four, so it was more like two hours. No wonder I was knackered.'

'"It must have been a shock. Damien shaking you awake."

'"I wasn't asleep." His lips clenched. 'Like I said, I'd only just closed my eyes. He said something typically Damo about 'honey herbs' and some woman called Sybil. Wasn't she in *Fawlty Towers*? He was always doing that, saying random things."

'Cerberus, the sleeping guard-dog sedated by a sybil, I thought, remembering Damien's list of Multi-headed Mythological Beasts. Not random at all.

'"I was just getting out of my chair," Colin continued, "when Damo came charging back out of the house saying Mr Fairchild had been stabbed. He phoned for an ambulance, but it was too late."

'"And the police never caught the monsters."

'I turned at the woman's voice. She was petite and blonde and had a tight grip on Ted's arm.

'"Judy, meet Suzy," said Ted. He looked exhausted, his black suit doing his already pale skin no favours.

'"You're Ted's librarian friend," the woman said with what I swear was a purr. "He says you're the cleverest person he knows."

She seemed amused by this. Out of the corner of my eye I watched Colin sidle away, two more cans of beer clutched to his chest.

"'Suzy's a doctor. An oncologist in fact," Ted said. "So technically, Suzy, my love, you are most probably the cleverest person I know." His wife nudged him in the ribs. He scowled as if it had been more painful than playful. "But there's clever and there's *clever*,' he continued, 'and so far Judy's the only one of us to make sense of anything from Damien's lists."

'I was still feeling uneasy, and Ted announcing that I was the key to tracking down the killer didn't help.

"'Ah, the curious book of lists!" Andrew Wetherby had joined us and introduced himself with a firm handshake, adding, "Suzy's Dad."

"'Ted tells me he's tasked you with finding a secret code in Damien's book that will tell us who killed Geoffrey." He looked sceptical, either at the likelihood of there being such a code or of the chances of a middle-aged librarian working it out.

"'The lists make for a fascinating read," I said cautiously. "Damien had very wide interests."

"'And yet, a rather narrow way of approaching them. Reductive, don't you think, turning everything into lists?" The solicitor's smile was condescending and revealed a shred of lettuce caught in his teeth.

"'It depends," I said, suddenly compelled to defend Damien. "It was his way of making sense of the world. And some of the lists are very witty, perceptive even." I was thinking of Damien's Twenty Synonyms for Members of the Legal Profession, which were inventive but perhaps intentionally intended to cause offence.

"'Really? Maybe I could have a flick through. If you have it on you of course?" His eyes slid to my handbag. Had Ted told him I'd brought it with me today?

"'Not now, Daddy," said Suzy. "We're at Damien's wake for goodness' sake."

"'Of course, of course. A time and a place. We mustn't be guilty ourselves of reducing Damien's memory to an idiosyncratic collection." He took off his glasses and produced a monogrammed handkerchief from his pocket to wipe them with. "I seem to spend half my life at funerals at the moment. Comes with the age and the job I suppose. I was at a funeral when poor Geoffrey was attacked, as it happens, Judith. If I hadn't had to rush off to the church when I did I might have still been there when the damn burglars showed up. Ted phoned me while I was at the wake. Beyond tragic to hear about the death of one man while surrounded by the grieving family of another."

"'You must have been one of the last people to see him alive?"

"Indeed. Although Jennifer Wilson was heading up the drive as I left. I nipped out the back to avoid her. Pleasant enough woman but such a chatterbox." He leaned forward conspiratorially. "I think she considered Geoffrey a bit of a catch. Trying to seduce the old bugger with hot dinners and iced buns. He was a harder nut to crack than that, but you can't blame her for trying."

"'Is she here today?" I asked, glancing around the small assembly of people.

"'No, she's on her honeymoon." Andrew tucked his handkerchief back in his pocket. "Geoffrey wasn't the only one treated to her baked goods. The landlord of the Black Bull found her steak and kidney pies too good to resist. They got married last week."

'I made my excuses and went outside for some fresh air. The front entrance opened out to a driveway bisecting shaggy lawns that were showing evidence of Colin's absence. I walked round to the back of the house where the garden descended in a series of cultivated terraces to the river. I was admiring the stark beauty of a silver birch perched on one of the upper terraces, when Ted appeared at my side.

'The harsh December sunlight accentuated the hollows under his eyes, the rigidity of his jaw.

'"This must be awful, for you," I said. "Have you been sleeping? Eating properly?" There might only be twelve years between us, but his wretchedness brought out my maternal side.

'"Oh don't worry about me," he said impatiently. "I'll never get over losing Damien. And no I'm not getting enough sleep. But mainly I'm furious and, to be honest with you, Judy, frightened." He dragged his hair back with his fingers, revealing a pronounced widow's peak that made his appearance even more ghoulish. "First Gramps, then Damien. What if I'm next?" His eyes were wide with fear. He grabbed my wrist with his clammy hand. "You did bring the book with you? Like I asked?"

'"Yes," I said. I patted my handbag.

'"Good, good." He lowered his voice. 'It's like I said before. What if Damien deliberately let it be known that his book contained proof of who killed Gramps? To draw the killer out."

'"You really think Damien was using the book as bait? To make the killer do what, confront him? Confess? Make a blunder and unmask themself?"

'"Yes, yes. All or at least some of that."

'I remembered my anxiety on Sunday night. The feeling that I was being followed.

'"So here we are," I said. "In the house in which your grandfather was killed, and you've asked me to carry the book. The bait. Are you trying to copy Damien's trap? Because," I gestured towards the houseful of mourners, "that did not end well."

'Ted was silent. A breeze ruffled the sleeves of my black chiffon blouse and sent a shiver down my spine. I made my mind up.

"'I don't want to be part of this anymore." I pulled the book out of my bag and threw it to Ted. He lunged for it but missed and it fell splayed on the ground.

'We both bent to pick it up, but I held out my hand.

"'Wait." The jolt as the book hit the ground had dislodged something. An ear of clear plastic stuck out from between the binding and the spine of the book. Using my fingers like tweezers, I slowly pulled out the hidden object. My mind was already racing ahead: clear plastic bag = white powder = drugs gang. But instead the bag that emerged contained what appeared to be a small dagger.

"'What the hell?" whispered Ted.

'I held up the bag so we both had a good view. The metal blade, about four inches long, narrowed to an ornate handle embossed with lettering. Both the blade and handle were stained a rusty red.

"'It's a letter opener,' I said.

'Ted seemed to sway. "That's blood, isn't it? My grandfather's blood."

"'The murder weapon?" I said. "This was Damien's proof?"'

'The lettering on the handle was clear in spite of the dried blood, three ornately inscribed letters that looked somehow familiar, 'A B W'.

"'Andrew," Ted said hoarsely.

'I remembered the solicitor's monogrammed handkerchief, the fancy tie pin.

"'He's got his initials on everything," Ted said.

"'But why would Andrew kill you grandfather? They were old friends."

"'Why would anyone kill him?" He blinked rapidly. "Maybe they fell out. An old grievance perhaps, or money. There was some argy-bargy between them about Gramps's will a while back. Gramps had this ridiculous idea about leaving half his

141

estate to the gardener! I never took it seriously, but Andrew was dead set against it. Suzy and I don't the need the money of course, ha, not with her wages. But Andrew wouldn't want to see any of our share siphoned off.' He smoothed back his hair again. "Tricky one for him, I suppose. Conflict of interest and all that."

'"You think he resorted to murder to stop it happening?"

'"Maybe, I don't know." His eyes were shining now. "People have killed for less." He gave a hiccupping laugh. "To think of all the time we wasted trying to decode Damien's lists. It was all just a joke. The evidence actually was inside the book." He laughed again and the sound verged on hysterical.

'I wasn't so sure about his dismissal of the lists. I'd kept on reading them in the days leading up to the funeral. Playing with their meanings and wondering about the hand-drawn symbols randomly scattered throughout. One page in particular had given me pause for thought. I hadn't shared what I'd found with Ted and now didn't seem like the best time.

'Ted clapped his palms together. "I'm going to tell Andrew that we've found Damien's hidden proof. If he is the killer," his voice shook. "Then he'll have to act, he'll try to get it from me. He'll be exposed and I'll make him confess."

'"But if you think he might have killed Damien as well …."' I began, unconvinced by his wild plan. "Wouldn't it be safer just to take the knife to the police?"

'"No," said Ted. "Andrew knows his way around the legal system. He'd get away with it somehow. Damien must have known that. No, I'm going to make him confess. It's what Damien wanted. A confession. And I'm going to get it."

'He grabbed the book and the plastic bag from my hands and dashed back into the house.

'I couldn't see him or Andrew in the throng of people in either the lounge or dining room. Suzy was in a corner talking to an older couple. There was no sign of Colin the ex-gardener, his post at the drinks table being taken up by three young women sobbing over a shared bottle of white wine. The only other person I recognised in the room was the minister who had conducted the funeral service. He seemed as good an authority figure as any.

'He appeared bemused when I said I needed him to come with me. But when I added that I was concerned for Ted's safety he clasped my hand, said he understood completely and agreed to help me find him. We went back outside. At the top of the terraced garden the vicar questioned one of the pall bearers who was admiring the view.

'"Saw him heading down towards the river, couple of minutes ago," he said. "And that solicitor bloke heading in the same direction not far behind."

'The minister and I hurried through the garden. The steps between each terrace were slippery and slowed us down. Before we reached the bottom level I spotted Ted down by the river, where a low fence guarded against the drop to the water below. To his right was a jetty where a boat laden with what looked like blankets was moored, bobbing on the fast-flowing current. Andrew Wetherby appeared from behind a clump of tall holly bushes on the lowest terrace and marched towards Ted. As the minister and I drew closer, our view was obstructed by the bushes, but we heard a querying shout from Andrew. Then Ted spoke, his words cutting clearly through the cold air.

'"Your knife, my grandfather's blood. It doesn't look good, Andrew."

'The minister touched my arm and put his finger to his lips. Together we crept forward silently until we could see both men through a gap between the branches of the holly.

'They were standing by the fence. Ted was clutching the book of lists in one hand and held the plastic bag containing the paper knife in the other.

"'Is this why you demanded I come down here?" asked Andrew. "Yes, that's my knife. I gave it to your grandfather years ago. I've no use for such things anymore." His voice sounded tired. "Geoffrey didn't have any interest in texts or emails. He kept an old-fashioned desk. Inkwells, fountain pens. He took a fancy to my old letter opener. Said having his oldest friend's initials on it made it all the more special." He pressed his palms together pleadingly. "I didn't kill him, Ted. You know I didn't. I was at the mayor's funeral and wake the whole time."

"'Ah, but were you?" taunted Ted, his legs doing a little jig, dangerously close to the edge of the bank. "Who have you got to witness you leaving the house? Colin the gardener? Ha!"

"'It wouldn't be difficult to make the old sot believe it was two o'clock, by playing the *Archers* theme tune on your phone," he sneered. "Maybe you did go to the mayor's funeral where there were lots of convenient witnesses. Not difficult to slip away from such a crowd and not be missed. You could have been up here by say, quarter to three to carry out your treacherous deed. You tricked Colin into thinking it was two o'clock when you left, the time just before Mrs Wilson saw my grandfather alive. You knew she'd been there because Gramps told you. But what if it was actually nearer three and Colin had indeed just closed his peepers when Damien turned up at four."

"'You really have given this some thought, haven't you, young man?" Andrew stepped closer to Ted.

'I tensed, conflicted over what to do. I looked to the vicar and he shook his head.

"'You've concocted a fantastical, but frankly untenable tale." Andrew continued. He put out a hand as if to touch Ted's arm but then withdrew it. "Ted, I know you've got a problem. Suzy's told me."

"'All lies," Ted spat. He danced away, manoeuvring Andrew closer to the low fence.

'"If you insist," said Andrew. "Look, it's good that you've found what may well turn out to be the murder weapon." He patted the air in front of him in a placatory manner. "Let's take it to the police. They can check it for fingerprints."

'Ted stared up at the bag as if in confusion and muttered something that from my listening post sounded like " ... been careful about that." Then, more clearly, "Damien didn't think the knife would be enough though, did he? He wasn't certain there would be any incriminating fingerprints. The ones on the blade perhaps belonging to Gramps, from when he grabbed the knife and hurled it into some recess of his study, unfindable by his killer." He fixed his eyes on Andrew again. "He needed to be certain. He needed me to confess."

'Andrew's mouth fell open in shock. The minister's grasp on my arm tightened.

'"But there'll be no need for that," Ted continued. "After your body's been dragged from the water I'll tell the police exactly what happened. How you confessed everything to me. How you cried 'I did it for you and Suzy' before throwing yourself to your death." As he lunged towards Andrew, the minister and I hurtled from the bushes with warlike cries of "Nooo!"

'Ted turned at the sound. Andrew flung himself at his legs and felled him to the ground. Ted writhed and before Andrew could pin him down he half sat up and hurled the bag containing the knife over the fence to the river below.

'And that was basically that,' Judy said. 'Ted never did confess, but the police found the bloodied handkerchief that he'd wrapped round the knife handle and he hadn't been as careful as he'd hoped. As well as Geoffrey Fairchild's prints on the blade, they retrieved a partial thumbprint that was a match with Ted's.'

'How did they do that if he threw it into the river?' asked Rose.

Judy smiled, glad that someone had been paying attention.

'It turns out Colin was having one of his legendary snoozes in that rowing boat full of blankets. He got up to see what all the fuss was about after hearing Ted shout his name. He was standing on some rocks just below the bank when the plastic bag came flying. With a reflex he didn't know he had, he managed to grab it before it hit the water.'

'Ted killed his grandfather?' asked Barney, shocked.

'Sadly, yes. Ted's "problem", which Andrew alluded to and which was also known about by the minister and Mr Fairchild, was a serious cocaine habit. He'd tried to get clean a few times with no success. His grandfather warned him that if he didn't get permanently clean he was going to disinherit him and leave his half of his legacy to Colin. It may just have been an empty threat. But it scared Ted who was relying on his inheritance to eventually pay off his growing debts. He entered the house sometime between about half past two and four o'clock while Colin was indeed sleeping off his lunch-time beer outside. He had a fatal argument with his grandfather and fled clutching the most valuable object in the room – a Meissen shepherdess. The gifting of which to his dealer gave him some temporary relief.'

'Did Damien suspect his brother or did he think the letter opener was evidence against the solicitor?'

'We'll probably never know for certain. But I think Ted was right. Damien couldn't be certain that the fingerprints on the knife belonged to the murderer. He wanted to face the killer of his beloved grandfather and ask them why they did it, maybe force a confession and convince them to hand themselves in. Which is why he spread the story of his book of lists holding the proof. Whether Ted was there the day his brother "fell" into the river is something else we'll never know.'

'And Ted approached you,' said Dinah. 'Hoping you would help him find the evidence before anyone else did.'

'Yes, I didn't know whether to be flattered or annoyed at

being used like that,' admitted Judy. 'When he realised that the knife was the hidden "proof", he saw his chance to make everyone think Andrew was the killer.'

'But you said you'd found something else in the lists,' interrupted Rose. 'Something you weren't in a hurry to share with Ted.'

Judy took out her phone. 'One of the lists was marked with a symbol that I thought at the time was a badly drawn fleur-de-lys. Although with hindsight I realised it was a stylised knife. I took pictures of all the lists with symbols, including that one.' She tapped on the screen and passed it to Rose.

'Moons of Saturn in Reverse Order of Interest,' the younger woman read out. 'There's Erriapus at the top (never heard of it) and Titan − I know that one − at the bottom.' She stared at the phone for a few seconds and then passed it to Barney. It did a circuit of the room before returning to Judy, leaving puzzled faces and shaking heads in its wake.

'What have the moons of Saturn got to do with Ted being a murderer, no matter what the order of interest?' asked James.

'The order is the key,' Judy said. She swiped the phone screen and passed it to him. 'Damien specified in reverse order. Here's the list again but this time ordered from bottom to top.

'So Titan at the top,' said James. He began to read out the other names but gave up and handed it to Dinah. She glanced at it, shook her head and was about to pass it on.

'Oh wait,' she said. 'I can see it. You have to read the initial letters going down the list. Oh dear.'

'Indeed,' said Judy. 'It appears Damien may have suspected his brother was a killer all along.'

PUZZLES

Mini Puzzle

According to NASA, Saturn has 146 moons in its orbit. Here are the names of the eleven that Damien chose to include in his list 'of interest'. Can you put them in an order that makes their initial letters spell out the message that had troubled Judy?

RHEA	SKRYMIR	MIMAS	EGGTHER
ANTHE	CALYPSO	TITAN	SKATHI
ERRIAPUS	DIONE	ENCELADUS	

A Question of Connection and Final Puzzle Clue #5

The twenty words below can be rearranged into five groups of four, each group consisting of words connected because they belong together in a list.

HERCULES	TRIANGLE	BARNACLE	CROW
CRANE	MARQUEE	OCTAGON	JAY
ACOUSTIC	RHOMBUS	CIRCLE	KRILL
CRAB	OTHER	LOBSTER	SQUARE
PHOENIX	PYRAMID	SCORPION	WREN

For example, if tiger, lion, lynx and puma were among the words they could be grouped together as they all belong to the list 'Big Cats'.

Some of the words may appear to belong to more than one list, but in the end there can only be five groups of four.

Once you have chosen which words to group together, you need to work out the fourteen-letter name of the list that the group of four which includes 'Hercules' belong to.

This is the clue you will need to take forward for the Final Puzzle.

SOME LIKE IT HOT

As they walked down to the Cross and Lamb in the village that evening, snow began to fall.

'Maybe we'll have a white Christmas after all,' said Dinah, who before they set off had enveloped herself in an enormous black fake-fur cape.

'We could all end up stuck here and not able to get home,' said Judy, sounding almost wistful.

'Don't say that,' said Rose. 'Devi will kill me if I'm not back for Christmas Eve.' She was missing her partner more than she'd known she could. Somehow Devi would have made this whole weird thing, staying at Grandpa's house, sharing it with strangers, trying to be jolly when she just felt sad, so much more bearable.

'She can't kill you if you're not there,' observed James.

'We might stay on,' said Helena. She and Jon were walking down the dark road as one, his long beige coat slung over both their shoulders. 'Depending on how things pan out.'

'How much dosh you get off Grandpa, you mean,' said Rose. She knew she shouldn't be snarky, but her aunt was so transparent.

'Darling, do I have to remind you? The question of my father's legacy is more than just about the money.'

'How is the search for a location for your wellness centre going?' asked Sara.

Helena looked at her sharply. 'He told you about that?'

Sara stuck her hands in the pockets of her down jacket. 'In the course of my investigation some private family details needed to be shared.'

'We are looking at options,' said Jon. 'Helena's father may have told you that he had some ... reservations about our business plan. But I've made several changes to it since then. It can't be denied that Bracestone House ticks many of our boxes.'

'Will Mrs Linden be giving people head massages while Linden whips them with birch twigs?' asked Rose.

'You really have no idea what we mean by Holistic Wellness do you Rose?'

Rose shrugged and skipped ahead to join Barney and Dash. It really was too easy to wind up Aunty Hels.

The Cross and Lamb prided itself on its traditional décor of dark wood, polished brass and gloomy landscape paintings, its real ales and fine wines and its hearty pub fare. There were no complaints from the Bracestone guests and despite the earlier antagonisms, by the time the meal was finished there was a feeling of general contentment among the replete diners in the small back room that had been reserved for their use.

'Anyone for another drink?' asked Stuart. They had already shared several bottles of wine but now most of the glasses were empty.

'We could do shots,' said Barney. 'Tequila or Baby Guinness? That would liven things up.'

'Do you really think this place does shots?' asked Rose scathingly. 'Have you seen the horse brasses?' She had to admit to herself though that watching this lot throwing back tequilas would have been hilarious.

'They've got spirits, so they can do shots,' said Barney.

'No shots,' said Stuart. 'We're here under Ned's name, and we should respect that. Although,' he paused and chuckled, 'he wasn't one to turn down a party back in the day.'

'I wouldn't say no to a pint of the IPA,' said James, getting to his feet. The others called out their orders and Stuart and James headed for the bar.

He had been denied his shots, but Barney's face was already flushed from the wine, of which he'd had more than his fair share. He leaned forward and placed both of his palms on the table. Rose held her breath, wondering what he might be about to say or suggest in his father's absence.

'I know none of us are officially suspects in Mr Luddenham's murder,' he said. 'But do you think the police are keeping an eye on us?' The rest of the table looked at him blankly.

'What do you mean? asked Rose.

'Well, I've definitely been followed,' said Barney. 'A couple of times, in fact. The last time was around Halloween. They were smart with it, like professionals.'

'Was one of then wearing a *Scream* mask?' asked Rose, unable to resist the urge to tease him. She raised her hands like claws and contorted her face. 'Was Ghostface out to get you?'

'I'm serious,' said Barney sulkily.

'Did anyone else get a series of odd phone calls round about May?' asked Judy. 'Just silence on the other end of the phone?'

Everyone shook their heads.

'Oh,' she said. 'Just me.' She let out a deep sigh. 'It was probably just a wrong number.'

'You don't need to worry, Judy, you weren't even here last year,' said Rose.

'Or was she?' said Barney. 'Dun-dun-derrr!'

'Talking of "them" keeping an eye on us, isn't that why you're here, Sara?' asked Helena, turning to the private detective.

'More effective than having someone tailing us or bugging our phones.'

Sara looked shocked but before she had chance to reply, Stuart and James returned.

Stuart distributed the glasses with a show of largess, until Barney reminded him and everyone else that the drinks like the rest of the evening were on the tab of Edward's estate.

Rose took a sip from her half pint of cider. 'Shall I tell a story?' she asked. 'You'll like it, Aunty Helena, it's about the benefits of wellbeingness. Sort of.'

Her aunt gave a small smile and leaned in to Jon.

'Do you think staying for the length of a story is wise?' asked Judy. She was still nursing half a glass of red wine from dinner and had turned down the offer of another drink. Through the many-paned windows they could all see the snow was falling thick and fast.

'It'll blow over soon,' said James. 'We've got torches. Better a walk home though freshly fallen snow than battling through a blizzard.'

Judy shrugged and raised her glass in assent.

'Story time it is then,' said Rose. 'This is about something really weird that happened to me and Devi. It was a couple of years ago, but it still gives me the shivers.

'Grandpa had transferred a very generous early Christmas present into my bank account and I'd decided to spend it on a special treat. A long weekend in the Scottish Highlands with my best beloved. Staying in the luxurious if over-tartaned Ballycastle Hotel with not only log fires, four-poster beds and festive feasts every night in the baronial hall but also an amazing wood-fired sauna and ice bath set-up in the grounds with views of the loch and the mountains behind.

'The sauna was just a plain wooden hut from the outside, but on the inside it was utter bliss.

'Devi was suitably impressed. "Rose, you are a legitimate genius," she said as she ladled water from the bucket at her feet and tossed it on the heated ceramic stones. "Only you could have convinced me that sitting in our swimming cossies in the middle of Scotland in December could feel this good. Thank you, my lovely."

'"You're welcome," I said, inhaling the hot woody scent. "I can't disagree. This heat is truly glorious."

'"You think this is hot, ladies? You have no idea."

'The sombre voice came from a man sitting in the corner near the door. He and a younger man had entered the sauna shortly after us. One of the disadvantages of the set-up was that we couldn't have the place to ourselves, well not unless we were prepared, or able, to pay the extortionate Exclusive Premium price. The two men shared such similar looks, a prominent nose, lowered brow and cropped dark hair, that I presumed they were father and son. The younger man's muttered "Dad, don't" confirmed it.

'"They need to be told, Douglas." The man's dark eyes looked Devi and I over as he continued. "Only the true believers will be saved. The rest of yous are doomed to the fires of hell."

'"Lovely,' said Devi under her breath. "Nothing like a sprinkle of homophobia to warm your cockles."

'"Don't take it personally," said the sporty-looking woman with grey hair who, along with her husband, as silver-haired but less fit and toned, was sitting between us and the two men. She introduced herself as Lucy.

'"It's nothing to do with your sexuality, is it Pastor Lachlan? Graeme and I have had it all explained to us. It's not about who or what you're into," she assured us. Her voice had an un-Scottish lilt, from somewhere in northeast England I thought.

'"The church promises redemption for all those who truly believe and repent," the pastor said. "Whatever their sins."

'"Maybe we do believe," I said boldly, not particularly enjoying my and Devi's relationship being discussed by strangers. Especially as we were all scantily clad in swimwear, which in Lucy's case was a very flattering bikini. We were all, even the pastor, wearing pointed green felt caps. The sauna supervisor, Ben, had explained when we arrived that the hats helped to keep your head cool in the sauna and warm in the cold baths. That may have been in the case, but it was a comical sight. We looked like Christmas elves on a mini-break.

'Devi had whispered that the whole thing about their supposed purpose was bull. "It's just the hotel staff taking the mickey. They're probably taking secret pictures to make into Christmas cards."'

'"Maybe you do believe." The pastor's eyes gleamed. "But it's not me you have to convince."

'Devi threw another ladle of water on the hot stones and the resulting cloud of steam briefly obliterated him from our view.

'There was a grunt and a quick blast of cooler air as the hut door was pushed open and closed again. When the steam cleared, the two men were gone.

'"They really need to do something about the door," said Lucy. "It needs to be a tight fit, but you shouldn't have to barge it open."

'"Do you fancy trying the cold baths yet?" I asked Devi. A quick dip outside in one of the six metal bathtubs filled with icy cold water, was the necessary yin to the sauna heat's yang.

'"Mmm, not yet," she replied. "I don't want to get out until I'm unbearably hot to the point of self-combustion." She took a long draught from her water bottle. It was metallic pink and patterned with flamingos, an early Christmas present from me, which I was cross to see she had already dinted.

'"Snap," said Lucy, raising her own matching but unblemished bottle. I decided not to comment, Devi's clumsiness being pretty much her only flaw.

'I recalled the doom-laden words of the pastor.

'"You've heard his spiel before then, Lucy?" I asked.

'"The pair of them were at the table next to ours at supper last night," she said. "And joined me and Graeme uninvited for lunch today, claiming there was nowhere else to sit. Not the cheeriest dining companions we've ever had."

'"Certainly weren't," confirmed Graeme. "Fire, brimstone and damnation over my smoked salmon and Chardonnay was not pleasant. And when he wasn't condemning us all he was complaining."

'"About the food?" I asked. It hadn't been great last night. Lots of it, but pretty bland. At lunchtime I'd wished I'd just saved some bread and cheese from breakfast. I'd been pre-warned by poor reviews on TripAdvisor, but as Grandpa was paying for the whole thing it felt ungrateful to grumble.

'"He was complaining about everything," Lucy said. "It was his son's idea to come here. A birthday treat for his father, but a misjudged one I fear."

'"Part of Lachlan's grumble was that he had to have a medical check this morning," Graeme explained, "before he was allowed to use the sauna. Got a bit of a previous history of fainting in hot climates when he was ministering in North Africa. He swears he's fine and that the whole procedure was a waste of time. Claimed he was allergic to having his blood pressure checked!"

'"Is that a thing?" asked Devi.

'"A potentially bad reaction to the latex in the cuff apparently," said Lucy. "Though I was a nurse for forty years and never came across it. Happened to him once in Lagos, he said and nearly finished him off. Anyway, Ben, who oversees all that as well as maintaining this place, gave him the all-clear and even Lachlan, after some persuasion from his son, had to admit that a robust health and safety procedure wasn't a bad thing."

'"That poor boy," said Graeme. 'His father gives him a rough ride. The lad can't do right for doing wrong. His dad has him running around like some kind of lackey. Couldn't see our Ben putting up with that, could you, Luce?"

"'Oh, never," replied Lucy. "He's the reason were here," she said, sotto voce. "It's a bit above our usual budget, but with him being a member of staff, he got us a special Mum-and-Dad discount."

'I felt I should explain that we were also only here because of my grandpa's generosity, but at that moment the door was barged open with such force that it almost shook the walls. Lachlan and Douglas came in, fresh from the cold baths, the former's bare skin pink and glistening, while his son showed no evidence of having taken a dip. Had he just stood in the snow and watched?

"'That door needs planing," muttered the pastor. "And why've they got it opening inwards? Ridiculous design. They should get the sauna laddie on to it." At that moment the laddie himself, Ben, whose actual title according to his badge was Health and Wellbeing Facilitator, entered the hut bearing a plate of orange slices. He obviously had a knack of opening the door that didn't involve brute force.

"'It's important to keep hydrated," he reminded us. "Drink plenty of water and help yourself to these. There's also a jug of fresh orange and mango juice on the table outside."

"'And very good it is too," said Lachlan smacking his lips. "The tastiest thing I've sampled since we got here."

'Lucy rolled her eyes as if to say, at last he's found something not to complain about.

'But then he added, "A wee bit oversweet though, maybe less mango next time, young man."

"'Of course, sir. I'll see what I can do."

"'Shall we go for a cool off?" I asked. And this time Devi agreed.

'We put on the flip-flops that we had stashed in the small

airlock area between the door to the sauna and the external door of the hut. Outside, Ben was rearranging the jugs of juice and water.

"'Adjusting the sweetness, to appease the pastor," guessed Devi. "A bit obsequious don't you think?" she whispered, though Ben had moved out of earshot.

"'I expect he's embarrassed in front of his parents."

"''Cos they're in their skimps?" said Devi.

"'I doubt it. Lucy looks amazing in that bikini. I mean just embarrassment at having a dissatisfied customer. Though Lachlan seems to be appreciating the sauna and wellbeing side of things at least."

'We scampered across the snow, past the piles of ready-chopped wood to the tin baths. Mind over matter, I reminded myself. Just do it. I climbed in, hardly registering the cold and sank immediately up to my neck.

"'Aaaargh!" It was brutal but exhilarating. I checked my breathing, making sure it was steady and I wasn't gasping. Devi meanwhile was prevaricating, dipping in first one hand and then the other.

"'Hurry up," I said. "I'll be getting out any minute." I didn't dare submerge my head but tilted it back better to appreciate the indigo sky, dimpled with stars.

"'Alright. Alright."

'She stepped in and squealed. As soon as she had both legs in she splashed her arms and jumped immediately back out again. "Come on, Ms Masochist," she said, rubbing at her bare skin. "Let's get hot again."

'My feet were bone-achingly cold on the scamper back while the rest of my body was singing. In the airlock we pushed and pushed at the sauna door. My teeth started chattering.

"'Bloomin' thing," cursed Devi. She banged on the door. The moon-like face of Douglas, the pastor's son, filled the small window. Devi pushed the door again and this time, assisted by Douglas pulling on the other side, it flew open.

'I settled back on the bench next to Lucy, who had shifted up closer to the coals. Every inch of my skin was tingling with the contrast between the cold and the heat.

'"I'm looking forward to dinner," said Lucy. 'I hope the venison is on again. "Graeme particularly enjoyed it last night. But I let myself be distracted by the haggis."

'"Too chewy," grumbled Lachlan, though no one had asked for his opinion.

'"The haggis?" I asked. I'd thought it over-salted, the accompanying vegetables boiled to mush.

'"The venison," he spat. "The amount this place is costing you think the food at least would be up to scratch. I will be having words before we leave."

'"I'm sure you will," muttered Devi.

'"There's just no pleasing some people," said Lucy huffily.

'"The vegetables were overcooked and they only serve the wine in decanters because it's watered down," piped up Douglas. "Isn't that right, Dad?" he added, so eager to please.

'But his father just responded with a "h'mf!"

'"The pineapple upside-down pudding was delicious," I said.

'"Filth," muttered Lachlan. A comment which reduced the rest of us to temporary silence.

'"Another dip?" Devi asked. She sounded keener than before so although I wasn't quite warmed through from last time I agreed. As we flip-flopped our way over the now well-worn path in the snow I realised Douglas was following. As Devi and I stepped into the water, this time both submerging our bodies completely, Douglas stepped gingerly into his tub. He knelt upright in the water, which must have been painful for his knees, and for a horrible moment I thought he was going to start praying.

'Instead he said, "Dad brought me up all on his own. Mum died when I was three. He has a loyal congregation and is respected in our town. He doesn't mean to frighten people."

'It sounded more like a character reference than a son's praise for his dad. He avoided looking at us as he spoke. When he'd finished he dipped his hands one at a time in the water.

'Devi sighed. "Just do it," she said, now a cold-tub veteran. "The longer you take, the worse it will be."

'"She's right." Ben's voice came out of the dark. He stepped into the soft glow of the fairy lights and began checking the temperature monitors in the empty tubs. Close on his heels were Graeme and Lachlan, the latter stopping to sample the refilled jug of juice. Lucy trailed behind, clutching an inflatable pillow, her water bottle and a phone all in the same shade of pink. She was smiling at her phone, which she must have retrieved from the changing room lockers, along with the pillow. She tapped at the screen before putting the phone down on the juice table and joining us at the tubs.

'*Oh, lovely*, I thought, *we're all going to have baths together, this isn't weird at all*. Lachlan, who was particularly red in the face, seemed to be meditating in front of his tub.

'I was ready to get out but wanted to see the pastor's approach to the cold water. He made a huffing noise, scratched furiously at his neck and belly, then, as I'd anticipated, practically threw himself into the water. He completely submerged his head and body, bursting back through the surface like an angry seal.

'"Do you think that's wise?" cautioned Lucy, who was sitting serenely in her tub. "You don't want to induce a dizzy turn. If it gets in your ears, the cold water can really throw your balance." She nestled back on to her pink pillow. "Graeme and I do a lot of open-water swimming." she said to me. "It was how we met, forty years ago, breaking the ice together one morning on the upper reaches of the Tees." She leaned closer over the edge of the bath. "It was Graeme who gave me the confidence to swim in my skin. You know, in the nuddy."

'I glanced over at Ben, who had just turned away.

"'Shame we can't all just strip off in here," Lucy shot a cheeky glance at Lachlan, who was lying back in his tub, only his head above the water. "Though it might be uncomfortable for some." I presumed she meant Lachlan, though I imagined Ben might not be too happy at the suggestion either. Bad enough seeing your parents scampering about in their skimpies, never mind having to hear about them skinny dipping. Or maybe they were a skinny-dipping family.

"'We're swimming the length of Coniston next year for my seventieth birthday," said Graeme.

"'Do you think that's wise?" said Lachlan, mimicking Lucy's previous tone.

'There was an embarrassed silence broken by the splashing of water as Devi and I both clambered out of our tubs and raced for the sauna. We were joined shortly afterwards by Graeme and Lucy. Lucy tripped on her way in, dropping her water bottle.

"'Ooh, the cold does get to my hands," she said, flexing her fingers. She shoved the door shut and scrambled for her bottle on the floor. I resisted asking if it had been damaged, though noticed Devi moving her fingers to cover up the dent on hers.

"'Father and son started having a bit of a barney after you left," Lucy said when she'd got herself settled on the bench again. "Douglas was very put out when Lachlan suggested that they cut their losses and leave tomorrow instead of staying until Sunday. Ben may have saved the day by immediately offering them both complimentary massages tomorrow afternoon. For such a hard man, the pastor does seem to enjoy a bit of pampering. It was a smart move on Ben's part. Might be enough to make up for the pastor's discontent with the food."

"'You must be very proud of your son," I said.

161

'"What? Oh yes. Yes, we are. This place has been the making of him, hasn't it, Graeme?"

'Her husband nodded but looked wary.

'"It's alright, Graeme, these two will understand. He's not had the easiest of times, our Ben. Struggled at school. Didn't go to university like a lot of his friends did. Couldn't hold down a job and ended up running with a bad crowd. Bit of a rollercoaster. But he finally got through a college course and he's landed on his feet here. Found his calling if you like, and the chance to carve out a very nice career for himself."

'We all sat in silence for a while enjoying the heat and, if I were honest, the absence of Lachlan and Douglas. Devi was leaning back against the wall, her eyes closed.

'"Are you OK, Devi?" I asked.

'"Mmmm, I'm fine, hot but fine. Just a few more minutes though, then I'll be ready for another cold dip."

'Graeme cleared his throat and then coughed and coughed again.

'"Sorry," he said. "Caught a bit of a frog." He looked for his water bottle. "I must have left my water outside." He coughed again. "Can I have a swig of yours, Lucy?"

'She lifted up her bottle but then frowned. "Sorry, love, it's empty. I forgot to refill it before we came back in."

'Graeme stood up, pressing his fist to his chest, trying to suppress the coughing.

'"You can have some of mine," I said holding up my bottle.

'"Better not," he said. "What with Covid and whatnot. I'll pop out and get mine." He reached for the door handle and gave a hard tug. "Blast this damned door," he said. He pulled again but it still wouldn't budge. His coughing was now causing his whole body to shudder.

'"Stay calm," said Lucy in what I imagined was the voice

she'd used as a nurse to soothe her patients. "Sit back down and take some deep breaths."

"'I'll get it open," I said. "In the meantime, please do have some of my water." This time Graeme took my proffered bottle and after a couple of swigs his coughing subsided. But no matter how hard I pulled at the door, it wouldn't budge.

"'Lachlan and Douglas will be along soon, I'm sure. Or Ben. He can't be far away. We just need to stay calm," said Lucy.

'There was a low moan behind me. I glanced back. Devi did not look well. Her face was very pink and her breathing hard and ragged.

"'What's the matter?" I asked.

"'I'll be fine," she said. "I'm feeling a bit dizzy and sick, that's all. I could do with getting out of here." Her breathing sharpened. "I've run out of water too. Could you try again with the door?" There was the beginning of panic now in her eyes.

'I tugged and tugged at the door, but it just wouldn't budge. How could it be so stuck?

'Behind me I could hear Devi gasping like a fish out of water. Graeme started coughing again.

"'Get a grip," his wife hissed. I glanced down at her fingers gripping the edge of the slatted seat. Even she was losing her calm.

'Suddenly Douglas's face loomed in the window, as pale and gleaming as before, but this time on the outside looking in.

"'Thank goodness," I said.

'He drew back quickly as if running away, then I realised what he was about to do and I stepped back. There was a thud as Douglas's full weight hit the door. A pause and on his second attempt it flew open.

"'Oh, thank the Lord," said Graeme. Lucy and I helped Devi to her feet and out of the door. It was only then that I became aware of Douglas's distress.

'He was waving one hand in the direction of the cold baths. We all turned to look. The moon spotlit the central tub and the shape that was lying still in the water.

'"My dad," Douglas shouted. "My dad. I think he's dead!"

'We all rushed over. Lachlan lay motionless, his eyes open and staring at the cloudless sky.

'"CPR," I said, looking to Lucy. "You might be able to save him." Lucy seemed frozen, terrified at the sight.

'"Let me through, let me through." It was Ben. He plunged his arms into the water and tried to lift the pastor. With mine and Graeme's help we pulled his lifeless body out and laid him on the snow. I ran to the changing rooms to get my phone to call an ambulance, while Ben began to press Lachlan's chest.

'When I returned with the news that an ambulance was on its way, Ben was on his feet.

'He looked exhausted. "It's too late," he said. "He's gone. If only I'd got here sooner but someone reported seeing a woman up on the east tower acting like she intended to jump. There was no sign of her when I arrived, but I had to check."

'Douglas let out a wail. "I only left him for a few minutes to use the loo. When I came back he was shuddering, his face all red, and then he just went still. It's your fault!" he shouted, rounding on Ben. 'You said he was fit enough to use the sauna and ice baths. But he wasn't, was he! And you weren't even here to watch out for him. You with your stupid Facilitating Goodness or whatever title. You killed him!"

'We started shivering while we were waiting for the ambulance to arrive, although we'd all put on the robes we'd stored in the lockers. Lucy and Graeme said they were going back to change in their hotel room and Devi and I decided to do the same. Realising I'd left my towel in the sauna hut, I went back in to retrieve it. The air was still warm in there, but I got chills thinking of those horrible moments when we'd felt so trapped. I picked up my towel and spotted Devi's water bottle on the floor. It was heavier than I expected and made a sloshing sound as if half full of liquid. But she'd said she was out of water. I opened it to check inside. It smelled odd, like those sickly cocktails we'd had on our friend Alice's hen night. Had Devi been secretly quaffing pina coladas in the sauna? No wonder she came over all funny. Then I realised the bottle was smooth all the way round, with no big dint in the side. It was Lucy's. She was the secret drinker. That's why she didn't want to share her bottle even when her poor husband was having a coughing fit.

'As I was about to leave I had a final check that nothing else had been left behind. Something on the floor by the door caught my eye. A piece of wood, pale like the chopped logs outside. It was a wedge shape, like something you'd use to keep open a door. Or to jam one shut.

'"The ambulance is here," called Devi. I slipped the piece of wood into the pocket of my robe, still puzzling over it, and went to join her outside. We watched as Lachlan's body was laid on a stretcher and carried away.

'That evening I sat in the lounge in one of the winged armchairs by the fire waiting for Devi to come down from our room. Douglas had gone in the ambulance with his father. I'd spotted Ben talking to one of the paramedics before they left but hadn't seen him since. Two policemen had been in the lobby a few moments earlier, trying to calm down the increasingly agitated hotel manager.

'Lucy and Graeme were sitting in a window seat, their faces tense. Graeme was talking urgently, Lucy shaking her head. Graeme saw me looking and nodded tersely. I was certain they must be talking about Ben and the chances that he would lose his job and possibly fall back into his old ways. I felt I should say something. Lucy looked at me sharply as I approached and then down at her hands.

165

'"How are you both doing?" I asked, which I realised was a stupid question as they both looked so dreadful. "It's all so horrible," I continued. "Seeing the pastor like that, then Douglas's outburst. How this might reflect on Ben. And now the police are here."

'"It's a horrendous situation," said Graeme. "But responsibility comes with consequences. We all have to learn that."

'He turned to stare into the darkness outside. I was shocked at his response; maybe that was why the air was tense between him and Lucy.

'"I picked this up," I said, taking the flamingo-patterned bottle out of my bag and handing it to Lucy. She grabbed it from me and I flushed. I could hardly say that I wasn't going to reveal her drinking secret. I hoped she might see reassurance in my eyes, but she was refusing to look at me. I said something banally comforting and returned to the armchair by the fire.

'I tried to pass the time reading a brochure for the hotel, thinking it unlikely we would want to sample either the delights of the Highland dancing in the ballroom or the mixology demonstration in the cocktail bar this evening. It was hard to think of anything other than the dead body of the pastor and his son's traumatised response. I put the magazine down and looked over at the window seat. Lucy and Graeme had gone.

'"Hey!" Devi tapped me on my shoulder. "Sorry I've been a while. I got waylaid talking to Ben." She sat down in the armchair opposite. "He's been called in to the manager's office, to speak to the cops."

'"That sounds bad," I said.

'"I dunno," she said. "Maybe, maybe not." She leaned forward, cupping her chin in her hand like a dark da Vinci cherub. "Anaphylactic shock," she said. "That's what Lachlan died of. Or so the paramedic reckoned. His mouth and throat were all swollen and he was covered in hives on his neck and back."

'"His latex allergy?"

'She shrugged. "They won't know till after the autopsy, but they think it was something he ate. The paramedic told Ben people who are allergic to rubber can have a bad reaction to other things as well."

'"Mangoes?" I asked. "Oranges?" I thought of the glassfuls of chilled fruit juice Lachlan had downed.

'"That's exactly what I asked," said Devi. "But no. Bananas are bad apparently, and the pollen of some trees. But more often pineapple."

'I remembered Lachlan's surprising response to the idea of a pineapple upside-down pudding: "Filth." Had he reacted to it badly before? In which case surely he wouldn't have eaten any last night.

'"That fruit juice at the sauna. Did you try it?" I asked.

'"Yeah it was supposedly just orange and mango, but Lachlan was right, it was too sweet. A bit icky really."

'"Like a pina colada?" I asked.

'"Yeah that's it, but without the saving grace of coconut and rum."

'"So just the pineapple," I said. Her mouth fell open.

'I put my hand in my pocket and pulled out the wedge of wood I'd found on the sauna floor. Could it really have been what had jammed the door so tightly shut? But the door of the sauna opened inwards. If this had been wedging it, it must have been placed there by someone inside the hut. I remembered Lucy dropping her bottle, fumbling on the floor near the bottom of the door.

'As I got to my feet, Graeme walked into the room accompanied by a red-haired younger man in chef's whites. They embraced, then the man headed for the dining room and Graeme came over to us.

'"I need to talk to the police," I said. I held out the wedge of wood as if in explanation.

'He shook his head. "There's no need," he said. "Lucy's in there with them now. Excuse me," he said and sat down heavily in the chair I'd just vacated.

'He sighed heavily. "Another bad review would have been the end for Ben," he said. "For our Ben," he added gesturing in the direction of the dining room where the red-haired man had gone.

'"Your Ben!" said Devi as we both had the same realisation, that the couples use of 'our Ben' had been more than just a northern way of speaking.

'"You called him that to distinguish him from Wellbeing Ben," I said.

'Graeme nodded. "*Our* Ben stepped up when the head chef was sacked. He's been trying to improve the quality of the food," he continued. "But it'll take time. The kitchen is understaffed and he's never had so much responsibility before. Lucy says she just wanted to distract the pastor, give him something else to think about other than complaining about the food. She thought he'd just come out in painful hives and blame it on overdoing things in the sauna. It was a ridiculous idea with tragic consequences." He rubbed his forehead. "She's wracked with guilt about the other Ben being blamed. After all, he's somebody's son too. I don't know what the police will make of it. I'm sure she meant well."

'"Meant well?" I said, aghast. "She knew he might have a potentially fatal allergy to pineapple juice, so she laced his drink with it?"

'Graeme shrugged. "Lucy knows about allergies from being a nurse. She says such an extreme reaction is very rare. She didn't mean to kill him."

'I thought of Lucy's face as she watched Devi struggling for breath and her own husband doubled-over coughing when we were trapped in the sauna. A wooden wedge keeping the door jammed, stopping us from going outside and possibly finding the pastor still alive. By the time Douglas got us out it was too late. And Ben had been called back to the hotel for a reported emergency; had that been the message I saw Lucy tapping on her phone?

'I remembered that peculiar twist of her mouth as Lachlan derided the food at the hotel, and said he was going to "have words". Would it have been enough to just distract him, to hope that he would forget about his intended complaints and bad review? Enough to protect her son?'

Rose looked around the room at her grandfather's invited guests. 'What might any of us be prepared to do to protect the ones we love?' she asked. 'Graeme believed his wife meant well. But as the pastor himself might have warned us, the path paved with good intentions only leads to one place. And it's "hot, hot, hot".'

PUZZLE

Goldilocks and the Four Bears

Goldilocks had been warned about the woods, about the cottages that nestled in them and about helping yourself to chairs, porridge and beds when there might be bears about. Her great-great-great grandmother had a bad experience once and the family didn't want history to repeat itself. Goldilocks had half-listened to the warnings, but her mind must have been on something else because today she found herself in in the deep dark woods inside a sweet cottage that had a sign outside saying 'House of the Four Bears'. She stood before the kitchen table contemplating four bowls of porridge and wondering which one to eat.

The residents of the cottage were Daddy Bear, Mummy Bear, Little Zak Bear and Baby Mia Bear.

One of the bowls was made of blue glass, one of striped ceramic, one of silver metal and another of painted wood.

Each bear liked one additional ingredient in their porridge, with each of them choosing a different one from sugar, cream, fresh berries and raisins.

The temperatures of each of the four bowls of porridge were 15°C, 20°C, 28°C and 35°C.

From the clues provided below, can you work out the temperature of the porridge in each bowl, which bear each bowl belonged to and the single ingredient each liked to add. You might find it helpful to draw a grid or table on some paper to plot out your answers.

1. The ceramic bowl contains the hottest porridge.
2 Daddy Bear never eats cream.
3. Toddler Zak Bear likes his porridge to be fifteen degrees cooler than his sister's.
4. Both Mummy Bear and Baby Mia Bear like fruit in their porridge.
5. The bear who likes fresh berries in their porridge, hand-carved their bowl in a woodwork class.
6. The sugar drenched porridge is in a glass bowl.
7. The second hottest porridge contains fresh fruit.

Final Puzzle Clue #6

Goldilocks came from a family who adored porridge and for her the perfect temperature of the oaty goodness was the same as her great grandmother's, who being a woman of her time, still measured in Fahrenheit, her favoured temperature being 68°F.

The clue that you need to take forward for the final puzzle is either DADDY, MUMMY, ZAK or MIA – the correct one being the bear whose porridge Goldilocks decided was just right.

SNOW GOOSE

Bracestone House was late to rise the next morning. The trek home from the pub through drifted snow had turned into quite an expedition and it was past midnight before they were all safely tucked up in their beds.

As each of the guests pulled open their bedroom curtains that morning they had been greeted by a scene blanketed with snow, with more still promised in the laden sky.

'A winter wonderland,' said Dinah, looking out of the window of the study where they had all gathered after a leisurely breakfast.

'You won't be saying that when you're trying to dig your car out on Christmas Eve,' grumbled Stuart.

'I'm staying in the village for Christmas actually,' Dinah said. 'House and cat-sitting for a friend. Whatever the weather when we leave, I'll make it down that hill.'

'Alright for some,' said Rose gloomily. 'What if all the trains are cancelled and the roads are blocked?'

'We'll just have to have a cosy Christmas here all together,' said Helena with a strained smile. She was by the desk, with several of the drawers open.

'Great,' said Rose. 'With Lurch and Mrs Lurch for company. Is it just me or do they give everyone the creeps? She keeps shuffling in and out like something from a cuckoo clock and he looms by doors like he's on guard at Buckingham Palace.'

'Don't be so rude,' said Helena, though her mouth twitched.

'I do find his constant silence unsettling,' admitted Dinah. 'I tried to quiz him about the workings of the boiler this morning. The hot water always seems to run out just when I want a bath. After a series of grunted affirmatives and negatives he finally said, "You'll have to ask the missus about that." A whole sentence. It felt like a victory.'

'Why are they even still here?' asked Rose. 'Grandpa's been dead a whole year.'

'All part of his masterplan, I'm sure,' said Helena.

Rose headed over to the sofa as Helena turned back to the desk drawers.

'Looking for something?' asked Sara, coming over to join her. She had tried to keep her voice light, but Helena still took offence.

'I'm not hunting for a lost will if that's what you're implying,' she said, then let out a sharp sigh. 'I know you're just doing the job my father paid you for. But it doesn't make it any easier for those of us still grieving, you know.'

Sara stepped back. She was about to leave Helena to it when the other woman said, 'I was actually looking for some family photos.' She gestured to the panelled walls of the study on which were dotted a selection of framed maps and engravings. 'There are none on display, but Dad was always snapping away with his camera.' She pointed to a small pile of photographs on the top of the desk. 'These are all I've found so far.' She spread them out. A couple were in colour, including one of a loose gathering of people under a banner that read 'North Yorks Lit & Sci Soc Centenary 1913–2013. Among the group were Edward in a suit and James resplendent in a flowery shirt. But they were mostly black and white. Quite arty, Sara thought, no traditional family snaps. 'Your father fancied himself as a photographer,' she said.

Helena shrugged. She picked up two of the pictures. 'These must have been taken just after he bought this place. This one of the hawthorn trees has still got the tumbledown old wall behind it that Dad had rebuilt straight away. And this one ...' she said passing Sara an image of the front of Bracestone House, its windows and doorway etched with light and shadow, 'You can just about see the flowery curtains in the front parlour. They were thrown out as soon as he moved in.'

'Replaced by some heavy damask that I had the joy of replacing with a much more suitable William Morris linen the year before last,' said Dinah, joining them and taking the photo from Sara's fingers. She squinted. 'Is that Linden in the background? I almost didn't recognise him. Goodness, life here has aged him.'

'Time takes its toll on us all,' said Sara, examining a photo of Edward himself looking straight at the camera. 'Although age suited your father. He has a definite touch of Harrison Ford about him in this one.'

'Do you think so?' said Helena. 'Hmm, I think it's the hat.' After a pause she added, 'If he shared his looks with anyone, it was my brother Tristan.'

'His accident must have been a terrible shock to the family,' Sara said gently, remembering what she had been told about the man's tragic death.

'It was so needless.' There was anger as well as pain in Helena's voice. 'He wasn't even supposed to be going climbing that day.' She wrenched open another drawer and stared at its contents: a pencil sharpener and a scattering of paperclips. 'The two of us were supposed to be meeting in Harvey Nicks to choose a present for Mum's birthday. I cancelled at the last minute. I had a headache and couldn't face the crowds. He went climbing instead.'

'You can't blame ...' began Sara.

'Oh but I do,' said Helena, shoving the drawer shut with such force that some of the photos slipped off the desk.

As she gathered up the pictures, Helena asked, 'Do you think any of us are in danger being here?'

'Who from?' asked Sara, watching Dinah as she returned to her chair and began rummaging in her bag of wool. The woman's mass of black hair looked particularly wild this morning, with a pair of crochet hooks struggling to hold it up in a bun.

Helena glanced over at the other guests and said in a low voice, 'My father was brutally murdered here by an unknown assailant. Someone who managed to get into the house without being seen or ...' She rubbed at her arms and dropped her voice to a whisper. 'Or who was already here.'

'One of last year's Christmas guests you mean?' asked Sara, also sotto voce.

'Maybe,' said Helena. 'The police seemed to think it possible, the way they interrogated us all.'

'Do you think anyone here is capable of murder?

'How would I know?' said Helena. 'Isn't that more your bag? What does a murderer look like, act like? I've watched enough crime dramas to know they aren't all Jack from *The Shining.*'

'Your father invited us all here, or at least his solicitor did on his behalf,' said Sara carefully. 'I don't think either of them would intentionally put any of us in danger.'

'Dad might,' said Helena, 'if he thought it would get the right result. What Jon said earlier about Dad and games. He liked playing them, but he always wanted to be in charge and wasn't above changing the rules to suit himself.'

The fire, thanks to some gentle coaxing from James, was once again roaring.

'Come on then,' he said, taking a seat. 'Who's got a yarn suitable for a snowbound day?'

'I have a story that might fit the bill,' said Sara, joining Rose on the sofa. 'Or rather a case I suppose, from when I was a detective inspector in the Northumbria police."

'Ooh, I do love a police procedural,' said Dinah, picking up her latest creation, which she had announced would be a unicorn when it was finished. Although, Sara thought, it seemed to have the neck of a swan.

'I'll try to keep out the boring details of police legwork,' she said.

'Good plan,' said Dinah, trying to untangle a particularly knotted skein of white wool. 'More Starsky and Hutch, less "It was later the same Wednesday when I apprehended the gentleman" court report.'

'I'll see what I can do,' said Sara.

'It was the end of February, six years ago, when almost every part of the country was deluged by snow. Trains delayed, roads at a standstill, schools closed and, when the blizzards stopped, a calm hush all over the land. Most people stayed indoors, but the adventurous wrapped up and ventured out to enjoy it. Christmas card scenes of sledges and bobble hats, snowball fights and carrot-nosed snowpeople. As a police officer, perhaps inevitably, not everything I witnessed that fortnight was quite so festive.

'She was found in a snowdrift, against a ruined castle wall, by a family out for a morning walk. A young woman, with short dark hair, an olive complexion, delicate hands with the nails painted a deep pink. The varnish was unchipped, applied when she still had hopes and plans. Every death on my job was a tragedy but some touched me more than others. No identification on her, only a train ticket from Edinburgh to London, a journey that for some reason she had broken in a small town in Northumberland. Nobody at either end claimed her or reported her missing. We called her Snow Goose, after the silver bird on a necklace she wore. And because my more poetic sergeant, DS Morris, said she was like a bird passing through, not intending to stop. Alighting briefly to take a breath and have a brew. He was young and keen and went on to become a Detective Chief Inspector, so perhaps his fancifulness proved to be a strength in the end.

'I'd arrived shortly after eleven in the morning with Morris. The gritters had been out so our journey from North Tyneside to the town of Engleby, just off the A1, hadn't been too delayed. The castle ruins, consisting of an impressive façade, with little remaining behind, lay on the edge of town. A local uniformed constable called Sally Greenwood led us to the site, where the CSO was just finishing up. The girl appeared to have been strangled and there was no evidence of a sexual assault but we would have to wait for confirmation from forensics. Her clothes gave little away, although the coat was by a French brand and the slogan on her T-shirt, under a fine knit jumper, read *fille solo* – 'single girl'.

'No one had been reported missing locally and none of the officers who knew the town recognised her. Door-to-door enquiries produced little result, other than that a young woman had been seen in the centre of the town the previous day fitting her description – below average height, sturdily built, short dark hair.

'News filtered slowly around the town that a body had been found, so although the officers were discreet with their enquiries it soon became clear that the girl we were asking about had been found dead.

'The owner of the Bluebird Café in the market square said that a young woman had been in at about 9.30 in the morning, their first customer of the day. She'd ordered coffee and, after studying the menu intently, crumpets with butter and jam. Very softly spoken with a "foreign accent", the café owner said. "French maybe? In fact, yes, definitely French. She said "*Merci!*" when I brought the crumpets over." He grinned broadly, proud of his not-forgotten schoolboy French. But dropped his smile immediately when he remembered the reason for the enquiry. He thought she may have had a small rucksack with her, and she paid with cash, he said. "Bit unusual these days, it's mostly cards and phone apps, especially with the young 'uns.'

'Mid-afternoon, a woman in a long skirt and all-enveloping woollen shawl turned up at the station. She was recognised by PC Greenwood as Maya, the *Big Issue* seller who came to Engleby on market days to sell the magazine. She was originally from Syria, she explained, apologising for her English, which to be honest was more clearly understandable than DS Morris, who, despite his lyricism, was prone to mumbling. She wanted us to know that she had seen the girl yesterday afternoon. "The French girl," she said.

'"You're sure she was French?" I asked.

'"Certainly," she said. "I lived in France for three years before I came to England. She was French." She shrugged. "Maybe Swiss or Belgian but she was speaking fluently in French to her friend."

'This was the first we had heard of a friend.

'"Was the friend French too, then?" I asked.

'Maya frowned. "He looked familiar, maybe he is local. He was not so clear to hear. He rushed his words but what I heard, yes, he too was speaking French."

'"What were they talking about?" I asked.

'"He was angry. That was more with this you understand." She crossed her arms and lowered her head. "His body language. The girl said she was sorry – *désolée*. She talked about *ma mère*, her mother. She spoke so quickly, I am sorry that was all I heard. The boy snapped back at her. It was a phrase I have heard in French before as well as in English. It was: *Rentrez chez vous*." She looked at me straight. "It means 'go home'."

'This was the first proper lead we'd had but her description of the boy wasn't particularly helpful. Tall, lanky, anorak with the hood up and jeans, and, Maya thought, expensive trainers. That could describe most of the teenage boys in Engleby and nearby Morpeth, even the ones who couldn't really afford the trainers.

'The train ticket suggested Snow Goose had travelled to Edinburgh from London King's Cross a week before. It was an open return. She must have used it to get back from Edinburgh, breaking her journey at Morpeth and for some reason then travelling – by bus? On foot? Surely not in this weather – the additional couple of miles to Engleby.

'The police in Edinburgh had so far had not had any reports of a missing woman. I sent Morris over to Morpeth to check the CCTV footage from and around the train station to confirm when she had arrived and what luggage if any she had with her. Surely a trip to Edinburgh required at least a small rucksack? I also asked him to look out for any sign of her being accompanied or followed by a "tall, lanky boy".

'By six o'clock we had a preliminary coroner's report. Death was confirmed to be by strangulation, with the time of death narrowed down to the previous evening. Morris had rung from Morpeth with the news that the CCTV cameras had for once come up trumps – Snow Goose had got off the Edinburgh to London train yesterday morning at nine o'clock. She had been alone and carrying a small light-coloured rucksack. There had been no sign of anybody following her.

'"So where were you, Snow Goose?" I asked the sad pale photograph stuck on the incident room wall, "between your coffee and crumpets and your final journey towards the castle ruins. And where had you been intending to spend the night?" I asked PC Greenwood to ring round guesthouses and hostels in the area. The young woman had bought a £200 train ticket so maybe wasn't short of money. "And the hotels too," I added.

"Ask about any single female guests who didn't turn up last night."

'But none of the places had a no-show for a guest that fitted our victim's description.

"'Maybe she really was just passing through, our *oie des neiges*," said Morris, when he had returned from Morpeth hugging two warm parcels of fish and chips that he'd picked up at the Engleby chippy. "The last train to London from Morpeth is quite late. She could have been hoping to catch it." Although his words were even less clear than usual, thanks to a mouthful of vinegary chips, I agreed he might have a point.

'As I was finishing off my fish supper and checking the exact times of the East Coast trains, the desk sergeant came through and announced that a Mr Adrian Middleton wanted to speak to us.

"'He's a solicitor," the desk sergeant said. "Got an office on Main Street. Did the conveyancing when I bought my flat, I'd recommend … Ahem, sorry Ma'am, I'll send him through to the interview room shall I?"

'Mr Middleton was very apologetic. In his early forties, lean in a smart dark grey suit, hair trimmed close to his skull to make up for his receding hairline, he had nervous fingers, constantly twitching at his cuffs or a non-existent loose thread on his trousers. He'd had a long, busy day – his associate had been on a course in Newcastle leaving him to "answer the phone as well as everything else". He had no idea about what he called "the excitement" in town today until he'd arrived home – "a mews terrace in the nice end of town" – and switched on the TV. There had been a short report on the local news about the discovery of the body of a young woman, whose death was being treated as suspicious and who may have been French.

"'To be honest," he said, "and in my profession, I'd be unwise not to be, when she didn't turn up yesterday at four o'clock I was relieved. It's been a difficult time for everyone." He flicked angrily at the fabric on his right thigh. "I thought maybe she had been a time waster after all. Got cold feet at the last moment and decided against it. It's a long way to come isn't it unless you're certain it'll work out?"

"'Could I just ask you to back up a bit please, Mr Middleton?" I said. "Are you saying that you think the young woman may have been someone who had an appointment with you?"

"'Yes, that's right. She'd insisted on a meeting at four p.m. which quite frankly is later than I usually like. I prefer to get meetings with clients out of the way in the morning and in the afternoons …"

'I held up my hand to indicate that I'd rather he waited until I'd asked my questions.

"'Could you tell us her name and the nature of her business with you?"

'He took a deep breath. "Yes of course, sorry. It's just all been such a mess and this really isn't going to help matters at all."

'I raised an eyebrow.

"'Sorry, sorry, yes of course." He tugged at each of his cuffs in turn. "A young woman is dead. It's an absolute tragedy. And it would appear by your interest, most likely a crime. Oh dear. So." He steepled his fingers together. "Where to begin?"'

'He's quite a character, your Mr Middleton,' Dinah said drily. 'Could be straight out of Dickens.'

'Well you meet all sorts, don't you,' said Sara. 'He was certainly not short of words, just not the ones we were interested in.

"'Her name?" I prompted the solicitor.

"'Ah yes, Gabrielle Lapierre."

"'She's French?"

"'Yes. At least her father is. However, she claimed … and I must point out that this is of the nature of a confidential discussion." He looked at me and Morris nervously.

181

"'I can't guarantee that anything pertinent to the case won't be made public," I said. "A young woman has been murdered. We need to find out who did it and ensure that the perpetrator is caught so they cannot kill again.'"

There was a sudden snigger from Dinah. 'Sorry,' she said. 'It's just the word perpetrator. Always makes me giggle. Carry on, you're doing great.'

Sara scowled but continued where she had left off.

"'Catching the killer, of course," said Mr Middleton. "An absolute priority, of course. Ahem, the young woman, Gabrielle Lapierre claimed that her mother was Marie Hunter née Engleby.'"

'He looked at me as if expecting the name to mean something. When I didn't respond he continued.

"'Marie Hunter lived here in Engleby, until she died five years ago, after a brief battle with cancer. It was a horrible shock to her husband, Phillip, and their two boys, Joe and Matthew.'"

"'How old are the boys?" I asked.

"'Erm, late teens, seventeen and nineteen, I think. No, twenty. Marie was a devoted mother and as I say it was a terrible shock. Her own parents live locally too, Lionel and Catherine Engelby. As the surname suggests, Lionel's family have lived here for generations. Catherine Engelby's parents were the Stocktons, who formerly owned the Manor House. Fancy hotel now but the family made a small fortune from the sale of the estate, though they hung on to the castle ruins.'"

"'And Gabrielle?" I prompted.

"'Well, you'll see, this is all relevant. In her will, most of Marie's property and possessions etc. passed to her husband but she also allocated a substantial sum, part of her own legacy from her Engleby grandparents, to be divided, in her words, 'equally among my children'. To be received by each of them when they reach the age of twenty-one.'"

182

"'So her two sons would be coming into that soon."

"'Yes," said Mr Middleton. "Their father, Phillip, thinks it's too soon and I'm inclined to agree. The eldest, Joe, is a bit of a hothead. He's been taking a gap year for the last two years. Phil wants him to go to university. He got the grades alright, but Joe has other as yet to be specified plans. His father's worried he's waiting to receive a chunk of his mum's bequest and then he'll be off to London to waste it on wild living, motorbikes and whatever else the youth of today get up to."

"'But Gabrielle claimed she was also a child of Marie?" I enquired, trying to keep on topic.

"'Yes, threw a complete spanner in the works. Phil got a letter from her three months ago. She was living near Poitiers with her French grandparents. Her father had died recently and going through his papers she claims to have made a startling discovery. Her father had told her that her mother had died shortly after Gabrielle was born. All she had known of her was that she was English and that her surname 'Engleby' was the same as the name of the place where she'd been born and was allegedly buried. Among her father's correspondence she found letters from her mother that she had never been shown. One from fifteen years ago asking if she could meet Gabrielle and one from five years ago, written when Marie was dying. In that letter, she said that although she had been unable to acknowledge Gabrielle in her lifetime she had never forgotten her and had made provision for her in her will.

'Her grandparents professed to know nothing. They had never met Marie. They only knew that their son Fabien had loved her deeply. He was an academic and had met Marie while he was on a sabbatical, lecturing in Manchester. He had returned to France with a baby and the tragic news that her mother had died of complications after the birth. They'd taken him at his word. As had Gabrielle.

'"When she discovered a possible alternative story, she decided to come to England," I said. "To claim her bequest?"

'"She said that she wanted to meet her family, to find out more about her mother. And, after I confirmed that Marie had died, only five years ago, she expressed her desire to visit her grave. I should stress that she did not know the size of the legacy that was due to her if she could prove she was Marie's daughter."

'"You were in communication with her?"

'"Yes, by email. Phil had come to me in quite a state when he received her letter," Mr Middleton shook his head. "Can you imagine? To be suddenly told your wife had a child that she had never mentioned?"

'"He had no idea?" Morris sounded sceptical.

'"She told him that she'd had a late miscarriage while she was a student. Mentioned a fellow student, a one-night stand. She hadn't told her parents. The family are practising Catholics, they wouldn't have taken it well. But the news that she had given birth to a daughter, who she had then abandoned in France, was a bolt from the blue. Marie was Lionel and Catherine Engleby's only child. Lionel's a fit old dog, mid-seventies but still plays squash. His wife, however, is not so well. Started with signs of dementia shortly after Marie died and she's grown considerably worse since. Poor woman." He shook his head. "Poor Lionel."

'There was a lot to work through, but I still needed to find out where our Snow Goose, Gabrielle Lapierre, had been all day yesterday.

'"Gabrielle had an appointment with you at four?"

'"Yes. I offered to be the intermediary between her and the family. Lionel and Phil were both keen to keep this from the boys for as long as possible and Lionel didn't want Catherine to be bothered with it until it was actually proven that this girl wasn't a fake. It would be far too confusing for her. I agreed to a meeting with Gabrielle and asked her to bring any evidence that she was who she said she was. She had her birth certificate with Marie Engleby named as her mother, place of birth Manchester. Where, as it happens, Marie was at university about twenty-five years ago. She also said she had a photograph of Marie taken with her father when they were in their twenties. Lionel and Phil wanted more than that. They insisted that her claim would not be taken seriously until her relationship with Marie was confirmed by a DNA test. I'm not keen on those tests myself. They can open up all kinds of unexpected cans of worms. But I had to abide by the family's instructions. She would have taken the test in my office yesterday if she had turned up. Perhaps the fact that she didn't is proof that she was a hoaxer after all."

'"Did she definitely not arrive? Maybe she was late and you'd already gone home?"

'Mr Middleton shook his head. "I was with my accountant for an hour before that and we overran somewhat, by about ten minutes. My associate was working in the outer office. She said nobody had shown up in the meantime. I had some paperwork to catch up on so stayed at my desk till about quarter to six before locking up and walking home. She definitely failed to meet our appointment."

'"In her emails, did Gabrielle indicate whether she intended to visit anyone else in Engleby, or whether she planned to stay overnight?"

'Mr Middleton shook his head. As he had nothing more to give us I sent him on his way but told him I would probably be in touch again.'

Sara paused then tapped her lips with her fingers as if she'd lost her thread.

'So now you knew who she was,' said Dinah, helpfully. 'You'd have several new avenues of enquiry to follow ...'

'That's right,' said Sara. 'We did.' Her momentary vagueness shaken off, she continued. 'It was early evening, but I was able to contact the police department in Poitiers and send them a photograph of our victim. An officer there promised to make enquiries and contact Gabrielle's family. Although I stressed that, as yet, we didn't have a positive identification. I asked PC Greenwood to search for Gabrielle's social media accounts, in the hope that she might turn up a photo or names of the young woman's friends in London, Edinburgh or the North East. Meanwhile, DS Morris and I were going to head out into the night.

'The untouched snow on the ground was as crisp and white as meringue, although it had turned to sludgy caramel on the roads. As we drove out to visit Phil Hunter we passed pristine fields and hedges capped with mounds of white. Shortly before the turning for the lane to the Hunters' house we passed a squat grey church, the gravestones in the burial ground shrouded with snow. Was that the graveyard where Marie Engleby was buried? I wondered if her daughter had fulfilled her wish to see her mother's grave. Her father had lied about when Marie died, but perhaps it had been a comfort that this part of his account at least was true.

'The evening sky was bulbous grey, threatening another downfall. I wished I'd booked rooms at the pub in town, or a hotel in Morpeth. We might have a tricky drive back to Newcastle tonight, and a worse one getting out here again tomorrow.

'Phil Hunter had sounded impatient on the phone, as if the death of a young woman, even one who claimed to be his wife's daughter, was yet another inconvenience he could do without. He agreed to speak to us however, and welcomed us warmly enough into his home. A handsome man in his early fifties with hazel-brown eyes and no sign yet of grey in his ash-blond hair. He was walking stiffly, a hamstring injury, he said, incurred playing squash with his father-in-law. The house was detached with gardens all around and a view across fields to distant low hills. Way off to the east lay the sea.

'I complimented Phil on the location.

'"That was all Marie," he said. "She grew up in Engleby. It was her idea for us to move here. I'm a Sunderland lad myself but I fell in love with the place. And it was good for her to be near her parents." He sat down, rubbing his forehead with the palm of his hand. "Her death shattered us all, but it's taken a particular toll on her mother. For me, for the boys even, time has begun its healing, but not for Catherine. Even now she can't accept that Marie is gone."

'"Which is why you and Mr Engleby decided not to tell her about Gabrielle?"

'"Yes," he said. "We thought it best to wait until we knew for certain. When we got the results from the DNA test. I suppose now we'll never ..." He cocked his head at a sound from the hallway. "Joe?" he called.

'"What?" a boy's voice replied.

'"Have you had some tea?"

'"Yeah. Had a burger at Lola's." Feet thumped up the stairs.

'Phil went to the door and shouted into the hall, "Take your boots off in the house. How many times do I have to tell you?"

'At that moment my phone buzzed. A text from PC Greenwood back at the station, who had come up with some interesting finds in her trawl of Gabrielle Lapierre's social media. I slipped my phone back into my pocket.

'As Phil came back to his chair there was a series of thuds from the hallway. I imagined a pair of boots being flung down the stairs.

'"Boys eh?" he said. "That's my eldest, Joe. He's a good lad but it's a difficult age."

'"Just turned twenty?" I said.

'He looked surprised, then nodded. "Middleton told you.

187

Joe's had what he insists is just an extended gap year. He's off to uni in September with any luck."

"'And shortly afterwards he'll be inheriting his legacy from his mum?" Morris said.

'Phil looked up sharply. "Middleton gave you all the details then?"

"'Only what was relevant to Gabrielle's journey to the UK," I said. "He wasn't being indiscreet. This is a murder investigation."

"'Is it definitely her?" he asked, his voice softening.

"'We think so. We've found photographs of her online, which match up. But we're waiting for one of her family to come over from France to make a positive ID."

'Loud music began to rumble from overhead.

"'Your sons don't know about Gabrielle?" Morris asked.

"'No. It didn't seem wise. On the one hand they might be excited to know they have a sister. But there would be a lot of questions about why she lived in France, who her father was, why Marie abandoned her. Questions that quite frankly I don't have the answers to. And now that the girl's dead, maybe we'll never know. I suppose I'll have to tell them about her now. They've probably already heard about the killing. Their social media will be rife with speculation."

"I'm sorry," I said, "but could I ask where the three of you were yesterday between about four o'clock and midnight?"

'He looked affronted but then said "I was here. I run my own business from an office in the house. It was Thursday wasn't it, so Matty will have had drama club after college. He's at the sixth form in Morpeth. Think I heard him come in shortly after six. We ate together about seven. Just a shop-bought pizza. Watched some telly together, one of those panel shows. He was off to his room before the ten o'clock news. I had a whisky and then bed."

"'And Joe?" asked Morris. The music overhead had grown steadily louder, drum and bass if I had to hazard a guess.

'Phil spread out his hands. "He's twenty years old. I no longer apparently have the right to check up on his whereabouts twenty-four hours a day. At a guess I would say he was round at his girlfriend's house. Nice girl, Lola, lives on the estate at the bottom of town. Didn't hear him come in but he was here for breakfast. If you can call shuffling into the kitchen and pouring cereal straight into your mouth from the packet, breakfast."

'"A young woman, who we believe was Gabrielle, was seen talking to a tall dark-haired boy in the town centre yesterday afternoon at about three o'clock." I said. "Might that have been …?"

'There were noises outside, a scuffling sound. A loud "Ow, get off!"

'"Boys," Phil shouted getting to his feet, wincing at the pain in his hamstring. He wrenched open the door. "Both of you in here now."

'Two young men slunk through the door. They were both tall like their father, but with darker hair. The one I presumed to be the younger was rubbing his arm. The other was smirking, taunting his brother, though his expression changed when he saw me and Morris. We were in plainclothes but Morris's notebook, and in fact his entire bearing, were a giveaway.

'"Is this about that dead woman?" Joe asked. Even from where I was sitting I could smell the fragrant odour of weed emanating from him. His brother hung back, less confident.

'I stood up. "Joe and Matty, is it?" I asked. Matty nodded, Joe shrugged one shoulder.

'"DI Slade," I said. "Pleased to meet you both." I focused on Matty. "*Parlez-vous français, Matthieu?*"

He blushed scarlet and his brother started laughing, prodding him with his elbow as Matty batted him away. "Get off me, you dingo!"

'"Boys!" their father thundered. "What's going on, Inspector?"

"'Matthieu is Matty's poncey online name," mocked Joe, answering for me. "It's what he calls himself on Facebook. Saddo."

'Matty wrapped his arms around his body and stared at his feet.

"'Matthew's aptitude for languages is nothing to be ashamed of," said Phil. "If you'd applied yourself in the same way, Joe, you might not have had to abandon modern languages before you even got to GCSE."

"'You don't speak French then, Joe?" asked Morris.

"'No," he said. "I speak street, innit." He made some unintelligible symbol with his hands. This time it was Matty's turn to laugh, though he sounded more nervous than his cocky brother.

"'As you appear to already know, the body of a young woman was found this morning," I said. "I'd like to ask you a few questions, Matthew, that may help our investigation," I said. "Joe, do you think you and Detective Sergeant Morris could go and make us all a cup of tea?"

'The older boy's mouth gaped.

"'Do as the detective says, Joseph. Or there'll be no allowance this week." When his son still didn't move, Phil added, "Chop chop, lad, this is serious."

'When Morris and Joe had left the room, Matty joined his father on the sofa. He clasped his hands between his knees suddenly looking much younger than his seventeen years.

"'Are you studying languages at college?" I asked.

'He nodded.

"'French and Spanish," his father elaborated. "Along with English lit. And he did a Russian summer school last August."

"'Is that why Gabrielle Lapierre contacted you, Matty, rather than Joe?" I asked. Now it was Phil's turn to gape. "Because you use a French name on Facebook?"

190

'He nodded, still mute. But then, before his father had a chance to speak first, he blurted, "Is it her? Is it Gabrielle who's dead?"

"'I'm afraid it looks that way," I replied. "One of our team was checking online to see if Gabrielle had any friends in the UK. She spotted the name Matthieu Hunter and realised it was you. Had you been messaging each other?"

"'A bit," he said, glancing nervously at his dad, who was biting his lip in an effort not to interrupt. "She said that her mum came from Engleby and she was going to come over and visit. She was going to see a pen-pal in Edinburgh first and call in on the way back".

"'Did she say what her mum's name was?"

"'No, she didn't. Not then." He clamped his mouth shut.

"'But when you met in town yesterday afternoon. She told you then?"

"'You met with Gabrielle?" asked Phil, unable to stay silent.

"'I didn't know who she was, Dad. I thought she was just some French girl. She looked pretty in her profile pic but that was all. She messaged to say she was in Engleby. Drama was cancelled 'cos Mr Betterby was ill, and I'm free last two periods on a Thursday, so I got the earlier bus. She met me at the stop." Tears filled his eyes. "She looked just like Mum, Dad. She really did."

"'What did she say to you?" Phil asked.

"'That she'd been to the church to see her mum's grave, our mum's grave. That she'd spoken to Granny and Grandpa ..."

"'She did what!" Phil grabbed his son by the shoulders. "How dare she! Had you told her where they lived?"

'Matty wriggled out of his father's hands. "No, of course not. Why would I? She said Granny thought she was Mum and even though they were going to make her do a DNA test she knew for certain she was my sister."

'Phil looked too furious to answer.

'"Have the Englebys been in touch about this?" I asked, though it was clear from his reaction that it was the first he'd heard of it.

'He shook his head. "I really wish they didn't have to be involved at all. That blasted girl!"

'It was too late to visit the elderly couple; Phil assured me they would both be asleep by now. It would have to wait until the morning, although I suspected Phil would speak to Lionel before I had chance to.

'I had one final question to put to Matty, before Morris and Joe returned with the cups of tea that had only been an excuse to get the older boy out of the room. "Did you tell Joe?" I asked. "About your new sister?"

'"Of course not," said Matty. "He'd have gone bananas."'

★ ★ ★

'We were back in Engelby first thing the next morning, the snow having held off. When I'd picked Morris up in Gosforth he was holding a Tupperware with freshly made bacon butties in it. There's a reason he was my favourite sidekick.

'Our first call was to Lionel and Catherine Engleby at their house, the old rectory, which lay in its own walled garden, set on a hillside looking down on the church below. Their son-in-law was already there.

'"I felt I should prepare them," he said, defensively.

'"Phil's a damn sight more considerate than that young woman the other day. Just turning up on our driveway," said Lionel. "Unforgivable, giving Catherine such a shock. She's still in bed, by the way. I don't want her disturbed."

'"I was hoping we would be able to speak with her," I said. "The young woman was killed on Thursday evening. You and your wife were among the last people to talk to her."

'"We'll see," he said warily.

'He had the bearing of a military man, although that may have been a generational thing. Stiff upper lip and all that. Deep-set brown eyes that could have been warm if they hadn't been so full of anger. He had a good thatch of white hair and a matching moustache and was wearing what my mum would call "the full Marks and Sparks for the Older Man" – beige slacks, a crew neck navy sweater over a checked shirt and slip-on shoes.'

'Nice details,' murmured Dinah.

'I'm a detective,' said Sara. 'It's my job to be observant.'

'Although Lionel was in no mood to talk, he did give us the bare facts of what had happened on Thursday. Just after lunch, which when pushed he was able to define more precisely as "two o'clockish", he and his wife were both in the garden doing jobs.

'"More to keep Catherine busy, really. There wasn't much we could do in all that snow." Lionel had left Catherine clearing away twigs and weeds from around the snowdrops while he went round the back of the house with a refuse bag of dead leaves for the compost heap. When he came back his wife was standing in the driveway talking to a young woman.

'"Never set eyes on her before." His mouth twitched. "I won't deny she had a look of Marie about her. She was pretty, dark-haired, with strong features and her eyes … Well, it doesn't matter now, does it?" His shoulders slumped and he lost some of his defensiveness. "Catherine was chatting away to her as if she'd known her all her life, which indeed she thought she had. 'There you are,' she said when she saw me. 'I've told Marie she can give you a hand moving that old bench. She agrees you shouldn't try and lift it on your own.'

'"I was livid. I realised who the girl was. She had no right turning up and trying to worm her way into our lives. I told her that we had arranged for everything to be done through the solicitor. This of course instantly confused Catherine, who

193

thought I was talking about old Jeremy Edwards who passed away years ago. The young woman said that while a DNA test might prove who she was by science, she already knew now she had met us in the flesh that she was the daughter of Marie Engleby. She said she'd been to the church to see Marie's grave. Catherine got agitated at that of course. She has moments of lucidity where reality and the world in her head collide. I could see it was happening then.

'"Catherine asked, 'Did your father send you?', pointing her trowel at the girl.

'"The girl said her father was dead, which just made Catherine even more distressed. I said I was going to show 'our visitor' the old bench that needed moving and led the girl away. Once we were out of earshot I told her in no uncertain terms that she was to get off our property. I didn't want to see her again until the whole thing had been sorted via the proper legal channels. She left after that, but not before I'd found out from her that it was the priest down at St Cyril's who'd told her where we lived. He'd helped her find Marie's grave. I only hope she was discreet about why she was interested. A Catholic man of the cloth who takes confessions should know how to keep mum, but even so. We don't need the whole town knowing our business."

'I reminded him that the town was currently the scene of a murder in which his family name was inextricably tangled. Keeping quiet about Gabrielle's claimed identity might not be an option.

'"Do you believe she was Marie's daughter?" Morris asked him.

'Lionel blinked and looked away. He cleared his throat. "Does it matter now?" he asked. "I suppose the DNA test could be carried out post-mortem, but as the question of the inheritance is now moot I don't really see how it would help anyone."

'As Morris and I headed to the church to track down the

priest I wondered how many people in the town knew about Gabrielle's claim to be an Engelby. There was the solicitor of course, Lionel, Phil and Matthew. Matthew claimed not to have told his volatile brother Joe, but I wasn't convinced he couldn't have found out. And Joe had no alibi for Thursday afternoon and evening. Lionel also had no solid alibi for the hours after he last saw Gabrielle. He'd told us that at some point in the afternoon while he was making a pot of tea, Catherine had one of her wandering episodes. It had taken him almost an hour to find her.

'"She was in the burial ground," he said. "Kneeling in the snow, covering Marie's grave with the weeds she'd pulled up from the garden. I got her home alright, but it had been a very wearing day for both of us. We were in bed, me reading and her in restless sleep, by eight."'

'We entered the graveyard of St Cyril's through a carved lychgate and were following the path to the main door of the church when a figure in a black cassock emerged from the shadows of a large yew tree. An elderly priest, leaning on a wooden walking stick.

'"You'll be the police detectives," he said. "I'm Father Terry." He shook his head slowly. "Terrible business with that young woman. When I heard about it on the news this morning I thought maybe I'd better come and find you. But here you are finding me first."

'"You have some information for us?" I asked, wanting him to give his version of what had happened.

'"I saw her yesterday morning," he said. "At least I presume it was her from the description. She was poking around among the graves. For a local history project, I think she said. Although from her accent I knew she wasn't from this side of the sea, never mind the Tyne. We chatted a bit about the town, the castle and of course this church and its graveyard."

"'Was she interested in any particular graves?" I asked.

"'Englebys," Father Terry said. "The family the town is named after or vice versa, depending whose version of history you believe. We don't have any of the original ancestors, but I showed her some of the more recent ones, by which I mean Victorian and onwards."

"'Including Marie Engleby's?" asked Morris.

"'Ah yes poor Marie. She did seem particularly affected by that one. Knelt by the stone and traced the name and date with her fingers. Perhaps it was the deceased's age that distressed her. She was only forty-five."

"'And was she interested in any of the living Englebys?"

"'The stone says: 'Beloved daughter of Lionel and Catherine'. She enquired about them and I pointed her in the direction of the old rectory. Perhaps I should have given Lionel some warning."

"'Warning?" I asked.

"'In consideration for his wife. She gets very confused. A visitor from foreign parts turning up could be quite a shock."

"'Especially if she resembled their dead daughter," I said.

'The priest frowned, leaning with both hands on his stick. "Do you think she did? I suppose superficially … Is she a distant relative perhaps?"

'I said that we were waiting for a positive identification of the woman before we made any statement about her connection to the village.

"'Catherine came down to the church yesterday afternoon," I said.

'Father Terry cocked his head. "Really? Oh dear. I hope she found her way back up the hill," he said.

"'Lionel fetched her," I said. "So you didn't see or speak to either of them?"

'The priest shook his head. "I was in my study all afternoon, preparing my sermon for Sunday. It was to be on Jesus' temptations in the desert. But in the light of this recent tragedy I may have to start again."

'I asked about his whereabouts on Thursday night. He had led Evensong until seven, then after an hour of personal prayer and contemplation in the chapel had retired to bed. "I've got the bungalow next door," he said. "Not as grand as the old rectory, but handy and cheaper to heat I suppose."'

★ ★ ★

'Back at the station, over a cheese and onion pie from the local bakery (I swore I would be back on veggies and salad once the case was over), Morris, PC Greenwood and I reviewed what we knew so far.

'"The question is," I said, facing a clean patch of the whiteboard, marker pen in hand, "who had most to lose from Gabrielle's sudden appearance in the town?"

'"The Hunter boys, Joe and Matt," said Morris. "If it was proven they had a sister, their inheritance from their mother would be divided by three not two."

'"And their inheritance from their grandparents," said PC Greenwood as I started to write. Morris and I turned to look at her. "Marie was Lionel and Catherine's only child. When they die, everything – including Catherine's wealth and landholdings from her Stockton family – including the ruins of Engleby Castle, would all go to Marie's children."

'I whistled. "No wonder they were keen on the DNA test."

'I wrote the boys' names on the board. Neither of them had alibis that would hold up in court, but we needed something more solid before we could make a charge. I paused for a moment and wrote "DNA test" on the board. "A test could prove that Marie was Lionel and Catherine's grandchild, a half-sibling to Philip's sons. But as Adrian Middleton had pointed

197

out, DNA tests often uncovered unexpected things. Did anyone else have any reason to worry about the results?"

'"The solicitor?" asked Morris. "He knew all about it. Maybe a test would reveal something he wasn't comfortable about."

'He would certainly know everyone's business in the town. Maybe their secrets too.

'Mr Middleton, however, was not in his office. A young woman who introduced herself as his associate explained that he'd had to travel up to Durham to deal with a tricky conveyancing issue. "A couple are getting cold feet," she said. "It would be a big sale. He's hoping to put their minds at rest."

'"When are you expecting him back?" I asked.

'"Oh he'll be home for his tea as usual," she said. Then she blushed and added, "I'm his fiancée as well as his associate." She showed us the modest ring on her left hand. "We were planning to have the ceremony in the grounds of the castle. Got permission from the family and everything." She pulled a face. "I've gone off the idea now."

'The woman's mention of the castle made me think we should perhaps take another look there while we were waiting for Mr Middleton's return. Although a thorough search of the area had been carried out, it was possible that something had been missed. But more than that I felt the need to look again at the place where our Snow Goose had ended her journey.

'The frost-dappled stone walls sparkled in the winter sun, giving some idea of the castle's former glory. The snow on the ground was churned up by the boots of police officers and by townspeople who had come to lay flowers by the wall where Gabrielle had been found. A woman wrapped in a tartan blanket was crouched by a pile of the plastic wrapped bouquets. She turned as we approached and stood up. Tears misted her pale grey eyes.

'I introduced myself and DS Morris. She nodded as if she, like Father Terry earlier, had already worked out who we were.

'"It wasn't Marie, was it?" she said, and I knew this must be Lionel's wife, Catherine. She held a small teddy bear in one hand, either taken from the ground or brought as another offering. "I know that really. I just wanted so much to hold my darling daughter one more time. To see her face peaceful and not in pain. The girl who came to our house, she had the same beautiful eyes. That aquamarine blue that Marie inherited from her father. I used to tell him his eyes were the colour of a stormy sea that I'd be happily shipwrecked in. I was so naughty, but it was true." She began to croon, "Drowning in his eyes …"

'"Shall we get you home?" I asked, touching her arm gently.

'"Good idea," she said, her song forgotten. "We can have scones. I wanted Marie to come in for scones, but Lionel said she had to help him with that stupid old bench. I could tell she'd rather have stayed. Oops!" Catherine's foot slipped on the icy ground and she grabbed my arm to steady herself.

'"Dear me! It's these silly shoes. I should be wearing my wellington boots. I slipped on the path at St Cyril's too. But he caught me quick as a flash, like I was a baby bird tumbling from a nest, I said. I told him I thought Lionel might have scared her away. That he wanted to test her. Make sure she's an Engleby. But she went away and maybe we've lost her for ever."

'"And what did he say?" I asked, treading carefully with my words as much as with my feet in the snow.

'"He said he'd find her. He'd make sure she didn't fly away."'

★ ★ ★

'DS Morris and I found Father Terry kneeling in prayer in one of the pews at St Cyril's.

'Who takes a priest's confession, I wondered? You'd have to find another priest I suppose, or speak to God directly, as Father Terry appeared to be doing now. He'd heard us, I was sure, but he continued with his prayers for a few more minutes. We waited. Eventually he crossed himself and got to his feet.

'"Was it the DNA test?" I asked. "When Catherine told you about it in the graveyard. You were worried about what the results might show."

'I could tell by the grip of his hand on the back of the pew, knuckles white, that he was struggling. I tried not to think about what else those firm hands of this not-so-frail old man were capable of.

'"A test would prove that Gabrielle was Marie's daughter," I continued. "But the comparison with Lionel's DNA would reveal that he was not Marie's father."

'The priest straightened his back. "So, Lionel's wife had an affair forty odd years ago," he said. "And you're suggesting Marie was the result? It would be a shock to the family of course, but it wouldn't tell you the name of Marie's biological father."

'"Unless of course the test revealed other information," I said. "Such as the names of people who had done similar tests, and whom Gabrielle and by extension Marie might be related to." I'd remembered Adrian Middleton's comment about the 'can of worms' a DNA test can open up and had done some research into what details might be shared.

'"Obviously such information isn't lost to us," I continued. "Even though Gabrielle is dead, we can still test her DNA."

'Father Terry stared into the distance, then lost what remained of his bravado and hung his head. "My brother," he said. "My stupid egotistical brother. Thought he had Norse ancestry." He looked up with a contemptuous expression. "A woman once told him he had the brow of a Viking, whatever that means." The priest's blue eyes stirred with a hint of the stormy seas that Catherine had so recently recalled.

'"Gabrielle's test might have come back with your brother's name on it as a potential relative. The truth being that he was her great uncle, and Joe and Matty's too. Your grandchildren all three, not Englebys at all. Rather than risk the scandal, you killed Gabrielle, thinking that no one would care about her claim to be an Engleby if she was dead."

"'It was an accident,' he said, though he sounded uncertain. "I found her looking up at the castle as if already anticipating her inheritance. I just wanted to scare her off, send her scuttling back to France. But she was adamant that she would take the test and if it proved positive she would come back to her mother's home. I grabbed her shoulders. She tried to shake me off. Then she started screaming. I had to make her shut up. She struggled for a while. Then she went limp." He stopped, his eyes glazed, his hand on the pew back twitching. "I didn't mean to kill her," he said.

"'That,' I said, reaching for my handcuffs, "will be for a judge and a jury to decide.'"

PUZZLE

Missing Birds

In each case, work out the two words from the initial letters and definitions given below, then fill in the name of the bird that can come after the first word and before the second to give the name of a person or thing.

C (patron saint of travellers) _____ H (a soft head-covering)

S (backless seat) _____ T (human digits)

H (offer a helping one) _____ W (direction)

S (a fir tree) _____ B (raised dots)

B (Asian city's former name) _____ T (to record sound)

Final Puzzle Clue #7

One of the missing birds is found in the name of a band who were at number one in the UK Singles Chart for four weeks in the 1970s. The name of that bird is the one that you need to take forward to the final puzzle.

THE BIG CHIP

'I had a brush with the law myself last year,' said Stuart, after Sara had finished her story and fended off enquiries about why she had left the force. 'Purely as an innocent bystander,' he continued, 'but I ended up bizarrely in the middle of the action. A nasty business with criminal gangs and guns, which was quite out of character for Seahaven, I assure you.'

'Was that when a woman went missing and it escalated into a big shoot out?' asked Barney. 'All my old school mates were going crazy on socials. It was when I was on that circus skills course. I missed the whole thing,' he added, jealously.

'Dreadful business,' said Stuart. It was unclear whether he meant the crime or his son's juggling ambitions. 'A nasty piece of work masterminded it all, but the police pretty much wrapped it up. I was there when they made the arrests. It was most unsettling.'

'I remember reading about it,' said James. 'It was curious. There seemed to be some major gaps in the police investigation that were never really explained. As if they had some help with the case. A gang insider perhaps, or a private detective,' he glanced up at Sara, 'if the police still use such things.'

'Like Holmes and Scotland Yard, you mean,' said Dinah who had dropped a loop and was staring at her handiwork with a furrowed brow. 'If they do I bet the cops insist on taking the credit.' There was a grumbling from by her feet where Dash was sprawled asleep, his legs twitching as if running in a dream.

'It's alright, boy,' she said, stroking his flank. 'Sorry. I really shouldn't have popped that piece of Stilton in with your kibbles this morning.'

Dash gave a sleepy yelp in response, his nose quivering as if he'd caught a new scent in the room.

★ ★ ★

'Her coat was the golden blonde of a freshly cooked muffin. Brown eyes like patches of mud you wanted to throw yourself into. She wore a pink bow on her head, at an angle that suggested it was a joke.

'She sidled up to me at the park bench where I was inspecting a discarded burrito. I gave her a look that said, "not for sharing". She lay down, started chewing on a raggy toy she'd carried over, and waited.

'When I'd finished eating, I sniffed her over. New to the block. A salty odour that took me back to a trip to the beach, mingled with dead rat. I gave her the nod.

'"I've got a problem," she woofed. "Word on the street, Dash, is that you're the answer." Her voice was husky. Not like an actual husky – that would be a whine. This was deep and smoky.

'This wasn't the first time. Not saying I had a reputation, but there wasn't a hound on this block, or the next, who didn't know who'd really cracked the ransacked dustbins case.

'"Got mixed up with a bad boy?" I asked. "Short of readies? Lost your stick?" She sneered at the last, as well she might. But I had no time for fools.

'She nodded up to the path where a short man in an overcoat two sizes too big was sharing words with my master, Stu. Stu's willingness to converse with total strangers while I explored the grass and trees was fundamental to our relationship.

'"He's never taken me walkies before," the dame said.

'I winced at the puppyish expression. Some dogs need to grow up. Or at least expand their vocabulary.

'"That's my mistress, Sheila's job," she continued. "Every morning she drives us down to the shore. Safer than our neighbourhood for both of us. We live the other side of town."

'Now she had my interest. There were rumours about the South Side. About the state of the parks, the brazenness of the street mogs. She didn't smell like a fighter. But you can't always tell.

'"So what's special about today?"

'"Sheila's disappeared."

'"Betsy! Hey, girl." The man who'd been talking to Stu hurled something in a high arc over our heads to the grass beyond. My new acquaintance didn't think twice before running after it.

'Now me, I'm not a ball or stick fetcher. I've done it of course. To please Stu. But his heart's rarely in it. We know each other's limits.

'Betsy returned the ball to the man, who showed no further interest in it. So she ran back to the bench.

'"Tell me what happened," I said. "And tell it slow." I cocked my leg against the bench. "I don't want to miss any details."

'Sheila had disappeared in the night while Betsy was sleeping heavily after a special treat that had arrived the day before through the letterbox. Sheila had read out the message: "For a good girl, from a good friend."

'"And she gave it to you straight away?"

'"Yes." Her big brown eyes shifted away.

'"Did she?"

'"No. I had to eat all my tea first and then do some, you know ..." She lowered his voice. "Tricks ... Nothing special.

She gave up on trying to make me walk on my back legs years ago. Just the usual 'high five, lie down, roll over'. Worth it. Juiciest bit of meat I've had in a long time."

"'And then you had a snooze?"

"'After our last walk round the block. The most important reconnaissance of the day.

"'Then you slept?"

"'Like a pup. Big time."

"'And when you woke up?"

"'She was gone. Not in her night bed, not on any of her day beds. Big mess in the food room. Upside down things, spilled things, broken things. Like a puppy had been let loose in there. Sheila wouldn't like that, she's a tidy lady."

"'Can you be more specific about the upset things."

'She stared at me uncomprehending. "Just things."

'Oh for a collie or a poodle!

"'And your raggy," I nodded at the bunch of fabric, under her right paw. "That was in your bed?"

"'No, it was on the floor, next to an upside-down thing, a sharp thing and a sticky puddle that smelled of Sheila, but didn't taste good."

"'Like how your raggy smells now?" I said, giving it a sniff.

"'Just like that." She slumped down with her nose in the rag.

'I was getting somewhere. But it was taking time. I needed an informant with a lot more eloquence and a little more distance from the case. I knew an Alsatian who owed me a favour. It was time to call it in.

'Lance lived in my 'hood, two streets away. We kept a respectful distance, not peeing on each other's bins. But I'd saved him from certain humiliation last month when he was cornered by a pair of over-cocky chihuahuas. And yes I know that's a tautology; I've yet to meet an under-cocky one. Lance was bright, but more importantly he was a regular visitor to the South Side. His master smooched over there once a week to get supplies.

'"Bickies?" I'd asked.

'Lance had shrugged his impressive shoulders and stretched out his back legs like the yoga mama that Barney watches on the big screen.

'"Human bickies, maybe," he said.

'I had the perfect opportunity to talk to Lance on that evening's last walk. The streets were dark, the pavements cold. Up above in the trees bright lights twinkled and swayed but down at nose level there were only shadows and the slink of midnight-black mogs lurking in gateways. Lance was on the grassy patch next to the railings that surrounded a play park. I'm not a big reader but I understood the sign on the gate, a miserable looking hound mostly hidden by a huge red cross.

'So we weren't allowed in the park, but on a sunny day this side of the bars was a good place to watch the little people running and swinging and hitting each other. On that cold winter night the park was silent except for the rusty creak of a chain caught by the breeze.

'"What's up, Lance?" I asked, after the necessary sniffing was completed.

'"Not a lot," he said. His master was leaning against the railings, mumbling into his small screen, his head covered by the hood of his coat. "He's not been so good. Stinky stomach. Been stuck in the house for days." He sniffed the air, which had a tang of overflowing bins to it. "Good to be back out."

'"Not been to the South Side lately then?" I asked. I had a wary eye on Stu who was standing at a considerable distance from Lance's master.

'"Negative," said Lance. He watched the knee tapping of his master who had finished his mumbling and put his screen back in his pocket. "Could be heading there tonight though."

'I told him what I needed. He said he'd do what he could.

'A missing human dame. Possible dark goings on in the South Side. This case needed some urgency, but my paws were tied. I had to hope Betsy's new dog walker was a man of habit. I had some questions for her and I couldn't just hang around the park all day waiting for her to turn up.

'The sun was shining on me the next morning. Not literally. It hadn't done that for weeks. But the sunshine of fate was beaming in my favour. When Stu and I reached the park, ready for our usual couple of circuits, Betsy and the man were there too. Stu and the man nodded at each other and fell into step. I followed them for a while hoping I might get some intel. But their talk was all about the match and how Dianaldi would be gone by next season. I knew from experience that this would be of no help whatsoever.

'Betsy had lost her pink bow. She looked crestfallen when I strolled over.

'"Where's my raggy?" she asked. "You said you were only borrowing it." She shook her cute behind. She was over fond of that wiggling manoeuvre, but I couldn't hear anyone complaining.

'"Calm down, lady. It's in safe jaws." I didn't tell her I'd passed it to Lance to help him with the assignment I'd given him. Some things need to stay on the need to know.

'"Got a question for you, Bets, so listen up. The note that came with your special treat. What did Sheila do with it?"

'Betsy looked confused then said, "It was in the food room when I woke up. On one of the not upside-down things – the table! The message and the bag were both there."

'"The bag it arrived in?"

'"Yes, that one," her soft brown eyes gleamed. "She doesn't usually leave any mess and she'd missed a bit too. It was still in the bag. But good girls don't go on tables." Her look was coy, like she wanted me to protest that maybe she was a bad girl after all. I didn't cop for it. Now wasn't the time for foolishness.

"'When Bonehead came round," she added, "he picked it up and sniffed it. But he didn't put it in the bin either. He wrapped it up and put it in his pocket." Betsy followed her tail round in a circle, first one way then the other. Maybe it helped her thinking. "Bet he was saving it for a snack. One of those humans who eat dog treats. So unfair."

"'Wait a minute. Bonehead?"

"'That's his name," she said, looking over to the pond where Stu and the man had stopped to watch the ducks. "That's what Sheila calls him. Her other two friends turned up too. They asked, 'Where's Sheila?' and Bonehead said, 'On her holidays. I'm looking after the mutt.'"

"'Hang on, doll," I said. "She's on her holidays?"

"'No!" barked Betsy, so loud Stu and Bonehead looked over to see if there was a problem. We both wagged our tails effusively to show we were being friends.

"'Sheila doesn't do holidays," Betsy said. "She is waiting for the Big Day. She talked about it all the time. Me and her are going to go away to live the high life, for ever. But until then holidays are off the table. Like a good girl," she added, spinning round after her tail again.

'I believed her. And holidays didn't explain the puddle of blood that the raggy had lain in, the meat treat which I suspected had been doped and the mess that Sheila had left behind in her kitchen.

'When Betsy had finished spinning, I asked her what had happened next.

"'They did shouting and bad words," she said. "Then Bonehead told them to get out and leave it to him. He'd see them later down the Duck. So they left."

'Down the duck? At the pond? As good a meeting place as any, I supposed. "What are the other two called?" I asked.

"'Sheila sometimes calls one of them a bad shouty name, but also Duggy and sometimes, maybe when he's been good, Dogbreath. The other one is called Sis.'"

"'With names like that, are you sure they're not Border terriers?'"

"'Nope. Definitely humans.'"

"'Still, Bonehead, Duggy Dogbreath and Sis. Not much to go on.'"

"'Duggy and Sis usually come round together,' Betsy added. "If Duggy comes round on his own, Sheila calls him Sausage.'"

★ ★ ★

'Lancelot wasn't at the park railings that evening. I wasn't too concerned; he and his owner had been known to linger in the darker reaches of the South Side for days. I hoped he'd be back soon though. Betsy hadn't complained but I don't think Bonehead was giving her the care she was used to. A master or mistress going missing was a dog's worst nightmare. Sometimes they'd just "popped out to the shops" but the wait for their return could feel like an eternity. In Betsy's case it was starting to look like a "gone for good".

'I felt for her. This was no time to get dizzy about a dame. But for dog's sake, I couldn't let this case go.

'And the sunbeams of fortune kept shining on my fur. The next day was market day. Standing in line at the fishy stall, I tried not to drool, hoping the fish man would remember to keep the skins on Stu's fillets. Stu always gave them to me as a treat. I spotted Lance sniffing around a bin, off his lead as usual. His owner was on the street corner, laughing and jostling with two other hooded youths. I gave a low grumble. Stu was too busy ordering fishy goodness to notice but Lance perked up his ears and ambled over. He didn't have Betsy's raggy on him, but he did have some news.

'He'd met a half-blind stray in the den where he and his master had been lying low for the last couple of days.

'"Name of Dex," he said, "when anyone can remember. Rangy, underfed, lost an eye and most of one ear in a fight. Reckons he's part poodle but no one knows which part. Fancies himself as some sort of Dogfather. Him and his mobster gang hang out at the back of Macavity's Grill by the river. You know it?"

'Of course I didn't know it. What I knew about the South Side could be written on a kibble. But after Lance described it, I reckoned I could find it by its smell.

'"Dex says there's been some talk. Human talk. About a big job going down. Marbles and sparklers."

'"Quit the fluff talk, Lance," I said.

'He jerked his head at the group of youths. "It's what they call them. I dunno what they are. Special human toys? Someone called the Big Chip was putting together a big deal. It was all set to roll this weekend, but someone's squealed, the Big Chip's vamoosed, the Malone Brothers aren't happy and the whole thing's sliding down the pan."

'I had no idea what he was talking about. Sadly, neither did Lance. But he'd given Dex a sniff on the bloodied chewy toy. Dex said he knew the smell. Reckoned it belonged to a woman who was a new late-night regular at the grill. Has the same order every time - sausage and chips with curry sauce. Eats it looking over the river then throws them her leftovers. Dex reckoned she'd even called him a good boy once. "Sorry about the chewy," Lance added as his master whistled him over. "Dex kept it as payment for his services."

'That evening after tea, curled up at the feet of Stu's old man, Grandpa Felix, listening to Stu re-read a favourite bit of Chandler, I thought over my options. They could be counted on the toe pads of one paw. I could do nothing and have to avoid

Betsy and the park for the rest of my life or I could mosey down to the South Side and check the situation out for myself.

'Stu was reading the bit about the story being a man's adventure in search of a hidden truth. I knew what came next and repeated my version in my head: "It would be no adventure, if it did not happen to a dog fit for adventure." I knew in that moment, I was going to have to do the one thing a good boy should never do, but a dog fit for adventure must. I was going to have to run away.'

★ ★ ★

'I risked being shown for a fool. I could have done with a pig's ear to chew it over on. But when my chance came, I had to take it. Stu was in the mood for a stroll that evening, taking the long route past the play park and up the hill to the bench that looks down over the town.

'As he settled on the seat to admire the view, he unclipped my lead to let me have a good sniff around the undergrowth. There was a familiar buzzing noise and he pulled his small screen from his pocket. Started chatting to his friend Ned. It was now or never. I let my sniffs take me inch by inch away from the bench, into the shadows away from the bright lights of the town. Once I was sure he wouldn't be able to see me if he turned around, I ran.

'Locating the South Side was a doddle. The air begins to change just after the mini roundabout. More food shops, smellier cars, humans gathered in groups and leaning on walls. It wasn't them I had to worry about. Every slink of movement in an alleyway made me freeze. If I came across a gang of street mogs I stood as much chance as a snowball on a barbecue.

'Macavity's Grill was down a maze of backstreets. The "river" out the back was little more than a ditch. The surface of the stale, still water punctured by lumps of metal and food containers. Two dogs were hanging around the open back door, wrangling over a bone. One of them had a scar where his right eye should be. Dex. I hung back. I reckon Lance had got everything worth getting out of that dog. He wasn't who I was here to see.

'I can stay relaxed and motionless for hours in the right surroundings, but on that patch of scrub by the stinking water I was on high alert for the next hour, my legs twitching like an upturned beetle's, only fewer of them. Maybe she wouldn't show tonight. I've eaten the same food every night for four years, but humans like to ring the changes. Then Dex's ears perked up and he relinquished the bone. The other dog lost interest in it too. I picked up on their anticipation, my nose quivering.

'She slipped round the corner to the back of the building like a bad girl with a stolen slipper. Tray of, if my nose didn't deceive me, sausage, chips and curry sauce clutched to her chest. She headed straight for me, or at least for her viewpoint by the river. I slunk beneath the sharp branches of something shrubby. I fancied a chip but not until I knew what was going on. As she stood there slowly eating her food, she tapped one ear and started talking. I wriggled forward and looked out; there was no one standing next to her no one on the other riverbank. She was talking to herself? I listened in anyway.

'"It's only for a couple more days. Just till they've shown their true colours. Yup, yup it's definitely one of them. Someone's been disrupting our deliveries, intercepting orders. The Goldwater job last month was a disaster. Half a mil's worth of baubles disappeared between here and Zeebrugge. It must have been an inside job. One of them is in cahoots with the Malones." She paused to finish the battered sausage. I couldn't make nose nor tail of what she was saying, but I made sure to take in every word. "Mmm, I know, but if it looks like I've been nabbed or worse, the traitor is going to get antsy. They'll make a mistake.

Give themselves away. Just hang in there, while I lie low, keep the rows and columns adding up.

'"I don't know what I'd do without you and your bean counting. Give my Betsy darling a cuddle from me if you see her. Byee."

'Human toys astound me. With no small screen in sight, Sheila had been able to communicate with her chum, and thanks to my incredible skills of concealment and subterfuge, also with me. She gave a sigh, removed the last chip from the tray. "Here you go, doggie," she said and dropped it in front of my nose. I froze, my cover blown, but as she walked away apparently unconcerned by my eavesdropping, I relaxed and snaffled up the chip. She strode over to Dex and presented him with the remainder of the curry sauce before disappearing back round to the street.

'I made sure Dex and his pal were occupied with their noses in the tray and shot off in hot pursuit. I almost missed her but just caught sight of her stepping into a building a few doors down. Upstairs was all darkness, but the downstairs window was brightly lit, the surface splattered with images of dogs of various sizes and breeds surrounded by bubbles and flowers. I sniffed the air. My whole body contracted inside my fur. Flashes of memory, of being dunked in foul-smelling water, scrubbed with a hard brush, blown at by a roaring machine. Then the final humiliation, trussed with my jaw bound while a buzzing device sheared my body and prinked at my beard and eyebrows. The torture chamber that Stu called the poodle parlour on the one and only time he'd, in his words, "forked out forty bloody quid for a haircut".

'I watched the lights above the parlour come on then go off. She wouldn't be stirring till the morning. I decided to check out the neighbourhood. On the next block, after passing an exciting five minutes perusing a blocked drain and another ten trying to prise out what I'm certain was a piece of pie crust from under the corner of a bin, I picked up a familiar scent. Betsy. She had definitely wiggled her way down here. And not too long ago. I followed the trail a couple of blocks to another dark, dank street and a closed door. There were no lights in the windows but there were sounds, voices and music from within. A sign swinging above the door showed a man with a dead duck over one shoulder.

'The door swung open, light and laughter spilling onto the street along with a man who cursed as his feet danced to avoid falling over me. Before the door had chance to shut, I shimmied inside.

'I found Betsy asleep on the floor next to an occupied table. By her head was a bowl with a skim of liquid in the bottom. I sniffed. I should have known. No wonder Betsy had eaten that doped meat without a second thought. This dame had a taste for liquor. I tested it with my tongue: brown ale. Grandpa Felix's favourite tipple.

'I hunkered down beside her, hoping two dogs would be as invisible as one. She gave a loud unladylike snore. No one at the table took any notice. They were focused on their own business. Bonehead was talking intensely to a small man in a flat cap, with sharp features and a nose that twitched like a hungry rat's. The other two men at the table were listening but not speaking. I sensed their tension, their feet tapping the floor as if getting ready to run.

'The flat-cap rat man put up his hand.

'"Listen, if the Big Chip is missing it's nothing to do with me or my brother. That's not how we operate." He shrugged his narrow shoulders. "As to whether we've had any tip offs," his nose twitched, "or insights, shall we say, into Big Chip's operations … Well, all's fair in love and international jewellery theft, eh?"

'There was a ripple of chuckles around the table. Bonehead didn't join in. Betsy stirred from her slumber. She clocked me, looked at her bowl and back at me. She showed no remorse, unfolded her limbs and executed a stretch that would have put an alley mog to shame.

'"What's going on, Bets?" I asked.

'"Bonehead's come to say his goodbyes," she said with an elastic yawn that showcased her sharp white teeth. "He's been packing his bags. Looks like he's going on his holidays." She frowned. "He's asking people about Sheila. But she isn't on holidays, is she?"

'"No," I said. "I'm certain she's not."

'The mood at the table was still hostile, bodies tense, faces grim, a proper Chihuahua stand-off.

'"Maybe you should ask lover boy where she is," said one of the men, raising his lip in a sneer.

'"What are you talking about?" said Bonehead.

'"Come on," said the rat man. "Are you the only one in town other than her sister who doesn't know about Big Chip and Duggy? Or maybe her sister did find out the pair of them were getting jiggy behind her back and, zip ..." He drew his finger across his throat. "... put an end to it. She's not a woman I'd mess about with."

'"Thought I'd warned you about messing about with women, Mickey Malone?" A red-haired woman swathed in voluminous shiny fabric sprinkled with dots, approached the table. "Only when they've invited you to, remember?"

'"Yes, Mel," he said with a yellow-toothed grin. He lifted his glass to his lips, but the woman swiped it from his hand.

'"Time's up, lads." She began to gather up the other glasses, most of them still sloshing with liquid. "I told you to sup up half an hour ago. I can't afford to have the cops sniffing round. After-hours drinking is the last thing they'll be nailing me with."

'"Give us me lager back, Mel," said one of the men. "There's only a mouthful left."

'"Well, Betsy can have it. Can't you, my favourite puppy girl?" Mel poured the golden liquid into the bowl "Aww, look, she's made a friend. What's your name, champ?"

'The men all peered over in my direction. Bonehead screwed up his features as if trying to remember where he'd seen me before. I couldn't afford to be recognised. He might report my location to Stu. I couldn't be dragged back home, not until I found out how tomorrow was going to play out.

'I scampered for the door and scratched urgently at the wood.

'Mel followed me and let me out.

'"Thanks for not peeing on my floor," she called after me as I made my escape. "If only all the gents were so considerate. Would save me a fortune in bleach."'

★ ★ ★

'I spent a cold, sleepless night in a doorway opposite the poodle parlour. I tried not to think about my warm, comfortable bed, or about how worried Stu and Grandpa Felix would be. I was a dog fit for adventure. I was sure they would understand. I staved off hunger by gnawing at a meat-covered bone I'd found abandoned in some bushes. The sauce was spiky, like ants nipping at my tongue. But it did the trick and saw me through until morning.

'The street was busy and the sun was high in the sky, freed from its usual cloud blankies, when a figure bundled in a long white padded coat, face obscured by enormous dark glasses and a wide brimmed hat over odd-looking long blonde hair emerged from the door of the poodle parlour. I sniffed the air as she passed by – Eau de Curry Sauce. It was Sheila. I waited a few minutes then tailed her down the street.

'When Sheila stopped at a crossroads, busy with traffic, I hung back. My attention was caught by a piece of paper pinned to a tree. Like I've said, I'm not much of a reader but there was no mistaking the picture. It was me. Taken last summer when I won Second Best Waggiest Tail at the Seahaven Gala. I was wearing my rosette and everything. I looked like a total bozo. Of all the pictures to choose! It meant my time was limited. I needed to get off the street before some do-gooder snatched me up and carried me home. I bet Stu was offering a big reward.

'I'd lost sight of Sheila. Had she crossed the road? Turned left or right?

'Nose to the ground, I followed a faint trail, dodging the cars and ignoring the honking horns. There she was, a long way down the road. That coat easily spottable. She turned down a side street. I raced to catch up. The street was empty, at the end were a pair of tall locked gates, with a smaller gate open to one side. A sign on the wall displayed two fishes, just like the fish van on the market. Intrigued, I stepped into the yard. Four large trucks were parked up in front of a tall building with no windows but a large doorway. Most of the opening was covered by a pull-down door, except for a narrow strip at the bottom. Was there another way in or had Sheila snuck under here? I slunk down to my belly and shuffled under.

'Inside was even colder than outside, a vast room filled with crates stacked in towers, but a distinct lack of fish smells and no scent of Sheila. I trotted past the odourless stacks, claws tap tapping on the hard floor.

'"What's that noise?" asked a woman's voice I didn't recognise.

'"It'll be water dripping," said another voice. I was sure it was Bonehead. "You know what this place is like. It'd be condemned if your sister ever let the inspectors in. So, come on Susie, what's this meeting about? Have you got news on Sheila?"

'"Me?" said the woman. "You were one who told us to come here."

'I'd reached the end of the crates and peered round. In a wide, cleared area stood three people: Bonehead, a woman, a man who I guessed must be Duggy, and Sis, and lounging against the crates to my right, Betsy, nonchalantly licking her parts.

'Behind the people was parked a small yellow truck with a device at the front loaded with boxes and behind that a staircase, with those metal stairs that hurt unsuspecting paws. It reached halfway up the wall to another floor and a row of rooms with doors and windows. The railing in front of the rooms was hung with a banner decorated with happy smiling fish.

'Bonehead spread his hands. "You DM'd me," he said. "Said it was urgent. So here I am."

'Sis shook her head.

'"It wasn't us, mate," said Duggy. He looked around nervously.

'"What you so worried about, Duggy?" asked Bonehead, crossing his arms over his chest. "Not been holding out on me and Susie have you? Got anything you'd like to tell us?"

'"What? No! I'm just concerned, like you and Susie are, obviously. She's her sister. She's been beside herself, haven't you, love?"

'"Have I?" asked Sis, her voice dry as an empty water bowl.

'"I'm leaving town," announced Bonehead. "The Malones say they're not involved but it doesn't feel safe after what happened to Sheila."

'Duggy stepped forward. His paws, I mean hands, were trembling. "What has happened to her?" he asked. "What have you done to her?"

'"Shouldn't we be asking you that, Dogbreath?" taunted Bonehead.

'"Guys," said Sis. "Stop with all the feather ruffling." She was looking at Duggy with an odd expression on her face.

'*Uh oh*, I thought. *The dirty dog's been rumbled.*

'But she turned back to Bonehead.

"'We've got to make a decision, the three of us. Are we going ahead with the shipment tomorrow? I think we should. It's what Sheila would have wanted.'

"'Past tense?' said Bonehead. 'Interesting.'

"'Well she's not here, is she,' said Duggy, his voice rising in pitch. 'If she'd been kidnapped we'd have had a ransom note by now. Unless ...' His voice lowered again. 'Unless they've already made their demands and you're holding out on us. Leaving her to their mercy so you can take control.'

"'Ha!' said Sis. 'As if he could take up the reins of anything more complicated than a hobby horse.'

'Bonehead glared at her. 'Is that what this is?' he asked. 'You've got into bed with the Malones? Figuratively of course.' A quick side glance at Duggy.

'I couldn't believe that through all of this Betsy had continued to clean herself. I gave one of my low grumbles, often imperceptible to humans, especially when I was trying to draw attention to an empty food bowl. Betsy looked up, legs akimbo. I shook my head, a warning not to yelp or otherwise give my presence away. She slowly got on to her paws and meandered in my direction, sniffing at the crates as if that was all that was on her mind.

"'You think I'd betray my own sister?' scoffed Sis. 'Is that why you're going to do a runner? Scared that me and the Malone brothers will bump you off next?'

"'You're lying!' said Duggy loudly.

'There was a creak from the floor above but none of them seemed to notice.

"'You killed her, Susie, admit it,' said Duggy. 'You found out we were having a ... well that I was ... You're just using the Malones as a bluff.'

'Bonehead started to laugh. 'So it's true! You and Sheila. Blimey. Playing with fire at both ends there, mate.'

'Sis opened her mouth to speak but stopped at the sound of slow handclapping. From behind the little yellow truck stepped the rat man Mickey Malone and another man who looked so identically rodent-like that he must be his brother.

'"Bonehead," said Mickey, "nice to see you again so soon. "Duggy and Susie, what a pleasure. Very convenient, this little gathering. Saves me and Markey making individual visitations." His brother smirked and cracked his knuckles, the only human ability I'll admit to being jealous of.

'Duggy stepped forward with a firmness that I suspect was braver than he felt. "Susie was just about to tell us all about your little arrangement," he said. "A low blow taking out our Queen Bee. You better not have harmed her."

'"Us? Harm the Big Chip? As if we'd dare," said Mickey.

'"As if," said his brother.

'"Where is she?' asked Bonehead.

'"You tell me," said Mickey. "Buenos Aires? Abu Dhabi? Or wherever else international jewel thieves hide out when they've been rumbled."

'"Penzance," said Markey.

'Mickey looked at his brother.

'"It's where I'd go, is all." Markey looked at the ground and shuffled his feet. "It's got a lido," he muttered.

'"Not that where she is matters," said Mickey. "She's jumped ship and your leaking vessel is in need of a new captain." He sniffed. "Would keep you on as crew but you're all useless." He nodded to his brother. Markey reached his hand into his jacket.

'It was now or never. I looked at Betsy and she blinked.

'She was one brave dame. I'd silently signalled my plan to her, and she knew the part she had to play. I had faith that she'd play it well.

'On my nod she shot towards the Malone brothers with what my retired greyhound acquaintance Bill would describe as the speed and focus of a rabbit from a trap. Her jaw clamped around Markey's ankle. He dropped the gun that he'd pulled from his jacket.

"'Get it off, Mickey, get it off!" The harder he shook his leg the tighter Betsy dug in. His brother bent and clasped his hands around Betsy's slender neck.

"'Leave it, Betsy. Good girl, leave it now!" Sheila's voice rang loud and clear from the balcony above.

'Betsy unclamped her jaw, Mickey released her neck and she gambolled over to the bottom of the stairs where she stopped and gazed up at her mistress. There was devotion in her eyes, but I couldn't blame her not wanting to actually climb those vicious stairs.

'Sheila, free now of the hat, glasses and fake hair, leaned with her hands on the balcony railing, her padded coat like a cape of snow, and took in the scene below.

"'What a mess," she said.

"'Sheils!" cried Duggy.

"'Not now, Sausage," she replied.

'Sis hissed something at him.

"'And stop that, Susie, he's not worth it. None of you are," she sighed. "So come on, we're all here, even you pair of idiots." She gestured to the brothers. "Someone has been undermining me at every turn. Trying to knock down the business that's taken me years to build up. I've been doing my best to keep it going but there's a traitor among you. Someone who knew the details of shipments, logistics and how to package up a crate of tiaras and watches so it looks like a box of frozen fish. It had to be one of you three, Bonehead, Duggy, Sis." Her gaze switched back to the Malone brothers. "Maybe you could enlighten me, Mickey?"

"'Maybe," said Mickey, who was not too subtly edging his way over to the discarded gun. "Or maybe me and Markey could just take all four of you out. The mutt as well for good measure.

222

Make it look like an internees ... an internice ... a domestic dispute," he finished. "Take all the loot for ourselves."

'He was getting too close to the piece for my liking. They might all hate each other but at least they were all alive. I intended to keep it that way.

'As Mickey lowered his hand, I dashed from my hiding place snatched the gun in my jaws and made off with it back into the safety of the stacks.

'"Another mutt," shouted Mickey. "What is this, *101 Dalmatians?*"

'The cheek. A Dalmatian wouldn't have my wits or Betsy's bravery. They're all spots and no pyjamas, as Grandpa Felix might have said.

'"So come on then, who was it?" cried Sheila.

'I moseyed back round for a better view, the gun still firmly in my jaw, ready to run with it if need be.

'Sheila was leaning over the railing.

'"You?" She pointed at Bonehead. "The classic deputy, outwardly faithful but secretly scheming. You, Sis? Driven by jealousy? If I could do the dirty on you then why not kick me right back where it hurts. Or you, Duggy?" She cackled. "All that pillow talk. Did it go to your head? Make you think you could be more than just a tiny chip?"

'"Wrong, wrong and wrong." A new voice from up on the balcony. A figure stepped from the shadows. Red curls, a huge blue dress, this time covered with zig zags like a sky full of lightning.

'"Mel!" Five voices spoke from the floor at once. It was the dispenser of happy juice from the Dead Duck.

'"Mel, am I glad to see you," said Sheila. She looked down at the upturned faces. "Now we'll get some answers. I needed ears on the ground during my absence. Betsy darling would have done it for me if she could, wouldn't you, sweetheart? You three thought you were so discreet. Having meetings in our usual room at the Duck and Gun, even inviting the Malones along last night. Nice move, Bonehead. But who better than Mel, your favourite landlady and the company's bookkeeper, to keep tabs on you all for me."

'"Mel does the books?" said Sis.

'"Who did you think did them?" said Sheila. "I've got a bucket full of skills but maths ain't one. So come on, Mel." She turned to the redhead. "Spill the beans. Which of my nearest and dearest is a double-dealing dirty traitor?"

'Mel smiled. "I am, sweetheart."

'She stepped forward. I couldn't get a good view of her because of Sheila's massive padded coat. Directly below, Betsy began barking and running round in circles.

'I saw Mel thrust out her arm. Was it a gesture of apology or … Sheila screamed, tipped backwards over the railing and tumbled, falling like a heavy object from a great height, to the floor.

'I didn't need to be a St Bernard to diagnose that even with the strongest brandy she wouldn't be getting up again. She had just missed Betsy, who was now circling her mistress, whimpering. Poor hound, doped and abandoned by her favourite human, a small part in a duplicitous plan. Then agreeing to my own cunning idea, to stop a gunfight while simultaneously drawing out her mistress. Would she ever forgive me for the part I'd played? Only time would tell.

'Meanwhile I still had the shooter in my mouth and at some point somebody was going to remember that.

'As if reading my mind, Mickey Malone locked his eyes with mine. *Time for a sharp exit*, I thought, but then …

'"Dash! Where the hell have you been?"

'It was Stu. And not just Stu, but Lance and his behooded owner as well as two strangers also with dogs on leads. Behind them a man and a woman in blue uniforms with silver badges on their hats. Hurrah, the cavalry!

'I dropped the gun and the woman with the badge picked it up gingerly as if it was a particularly nasty bag of waste.

'"What the Dickens?" said Stu, looking round the room.

'"We'll take it from here, sir," said the man with the badge, pressing a button on a black brick, making it hiss. "Major incident at the Fancy Fish warehouse," he said. "Ignore previous message regarding missing dog. Back-up required."

'The Malone brothers looked at each other, then, in opposite directions, scarpered. The other three had joined Betsy by Sheila's broken body. I looked up at the balcony. No red hair, no voluminous dress. The woman had vanished.

'"Were you dognapped?" Stu said, ruffling my beard in the way that I must admit I quite like. "I've had half the neighbourhood out. Mr Bigglesworth" – he pointed to Lance's owner – "has been particularly helpful. Someone reported a sighting of you by the crossing. By sighting I mean they nearly ran you over. I persuaded these two officers to join in the hunt and, well, here we are. Though exactly where we are," he looked around the room at the stacks of boxes, the dead body, "I'm not really sure."

'The brothers didn't manage to run far. They were caught and brought to justice, their fingerprints still on the only slightly damp gun. Duggy, Bonehead and Susie ended up behind bars too. In their horror at seeing Sheila – friend, lover, sister - fall to her death, they hadn't thought to run away from the warehouse filled with evidence of their crimes.

'They never caught the red-haired barmaid-come-bookkeeper-come-wannabe criminal gang leader. She's probably in, where did the Malones say, Buenos Aires, Abu Dhabi or Penzance. Stu's often said he fancied a holiday in Cornwall. Maybe we could have a trip there some time. He could do the things that humans do on holiday and I could just carry on doing what I always do, and doing it well.'

PUZZLE

Goose Egg

The 'C-A-T' word wasn't mentioned in Dash's tale, but did you spot the names of five fictional felines hidden in the story?

Lost in Translation

No human could understand the complex communications between dogs, comprising as they do not only sounds but smells and gestures. The language used in the conversation below might seem similarly indecipherable. But once you've figured out the pattern it will all start to make perfect sense.

Two strangers, Sally and Alan, have arranged an assignation on a bench overlooking a duck pond. In the drizzling rain they sit beneath their umbrellas and speak without looking at each other. A passer-by from a distance might think he was hearing the babbling and cackling of the waterfowl, but in fact important information is being exchanged.

Can you translate their conversation?

'fNjc rwfbthf rfp sdvck,' said Sally.
'fTh nsv sshjnf np fth srjghtfpv,' Alan replied.
Satisfied that he was not an imposter, Sally continued. 'fHbv vyp tbrpvgh fth ykf'?
'pN,' he replied. 'tBv tj sj fsbf hwjt fth sfjshf.'
Susie looked out at the pond. 'hWhjc sfjshf?' she asked.
'J dff tj pt b tgjbn hdpgfjs tb fth mbqvbrjv.'

'wHp mb J dsvpppsf pt tgf tj kbbc?' she asked.

'tJvs kbs mhj rfp tj ynjcfl,' said Alan, who was actually working for the other side.

Final Puzzle Clue #8

From their conversation Sally learns that the object she is after is in a water-filled place. The name of that place is the word you need to take forward to the Final Puzzle.

THE LADS OF CHRISTMAS

By the time darkness descended once again on the snow-covered Yorkshire moor, the guests at Bracestone House had all but used up the possibilities of entertainment at their disposal.

Sara had been for what she described afterwards as an exhilarating run. Rose had spent most of the day talking to Devi on her phone. Barney had been engrossed in his laptop, occasionally leaving it to rummage among the shelves of the study 'looking for inspiration'. Judy and Dinah had gone for a walk with Dash, who seemed filled with a particular energy and curiosity. More than once they almost lost him in a snowdrift. James and Stuart also went for a 'walk' but their breath on their return indicated that they had not got much further than the Cross and Lamb.

'I would have come with you if I'd known,' said Jon.

'We had our meditation and Kundalini to do,' Helena said. 'The atmosphere in this house is not doing our chakras any good at all.'

'Where did you two meet?' asked Judy.

'At an Art of Zen boot camp,' Helena said.

'It was love at first half-lotus,' said Jon. The couple shared a knowing smile.

The fire was as ever crackling in the study hearth. The velvet curtains were pulled shut. The main lights were off, with just three table lamps dispelling the gloom.

'It's certainly been a relaxing day,' said Judy.

'That's one word for it,' said Rose, who was lying on the hearth rug flicking listlessly through her phone.

Barney yawned. 'I actually had a very productive time ...'

A clattering sound from the chimney made them all start. Rose jumped up from the rug moments before sparks flew from the logs.

'That will be Meat Hook,' said Jon, as Barney batted at the fallen embers with a piece of kindling. 'He is hoping to get his hands on Mrs Linden's rump steak.' There was another clatter above the fireplace. One of the table lamps flickered.

'Who's Meat Hook?' asked Barney.

'One of the Yule Lads,' said Jon. He looked round at the attentive faces. 'Do you not know the tradition?' All but Helena shook their heads.

'Prepare to learn then,' said Jon. 'I have a story about them for you. And as is fitting for the purpose, it is a story with death and dark deeds at its heart.'

'In Iceland,' he began, 'on each of the thirteen days leading up to Christmas, children leave a shoe on a windowsill. Each night one of the Yule Lads pays a visit and leaves candy for the children who have been good and a potato for those who have been bad.'

'Like Father Christmas?' asked Rose. 'I mean not that I, you know, still believe ... but it sounds sort of the same.'

'Like that,' said Jon. 'Only there are thirteen of them and they each have names reflecting aspects of their personality.'

'Aww, that sounds sweet,' said Rose.

'No,' said Jon. 'Not sweet at all. At least not originally. These creatures were descended from trolls. Their mother was a witch who boiled bad children alive. There was also the cat, who savaged any child who was not wearing at least one new item of clothing.'

'A bit harsh,' said Judy.

Jon shrugged. 'In a land where the winters are hard and long, it was perhaps a warning that all new knitwear needed to be completed before the coldest weather set in. The aforementioned Meat Hook and another of the Yule Lads called Candle Beggar were both out to steal from those who were careless or wasteful with scant resources.

'It was, as it is today, 22 December. The depths of winter. Only four hours of daylight in our small town of Múlafjörður in Northeast Iceland. But that morning inside our house was warm and comfortable. We were clad in our thick woollen jumpers and the kitchen smelled sweetly of the smoked lamb stew that my mother was preparing for that evening's meal. A snowstorm had been raging all night and by ten o'clock was only just beginning to abate. My sister Salka, who at thirteen probably wished she had someone older to play with than her little brother, was helping me build a complicated bridge with construction blocks on the kitchen floor. Our mother was tired of us getting under her feet.

'"The snow has stopped," she said at last. "Put on your coats and boots. Make the most of the light. But don't go beyond the town limits. There will be snowfall again before dusk."

'The streets outside were white. Snow drifted on each side, flattened hard where vehicles had driven and people had walked. Salka and I, bundled in our outerwear, hats and gloves muffling our senses, made our way to the park.

'It was not a day for playing on the swings or roundabout. But there was a flat area that was perfect for building a snowman or having a snowball fight. Our way took us through the centre of our town, where two roads cross. There was a small square there with benches, beds planted with flowers in the summer and a statue of Arnulf Thorsson in his Icelandic national team kit. He was a local man who became a professional footballer and in 1958 had been on the national team when they first hoped to qualify for the World Cup. He spent the whole campaign on the substitute bench, but he was a local hero. Especially after he came home and began coaching the town's youth team. He had trained all the children in the town, a handful of whom went on to play professionally in Iceland and abroad. His family now owned a hotel overlooking the fjord and his grandson Sigurdór was a rising star in North Iceland politics. In the New Year the newly built sports centre adjoining the High School was to be opened and honoured with his name.

'Arnulf, his grey stone figure proudly facing towards the sea, looked different today. It wasn't just the snow decorating his hair and shoulders. Somebody had tied a woollen scarf around his neck. I laughed and pointed.

"'Look, Salka," I said. "Someone has made Arnulf into a snowman."

'The scarf was scarlet in colour and it looked familiar. Although everyone wore scarves in Múlafjörður at that time of year.

'Salka stopped walking at the same time as me. Both staring not at Arnulf in his jaunty knitwear but at the shape lying close to the plinth that he stood on. A body, bundled in heavy clothing, eyes open but unseeing, a lump of black lava rock on the bloodied snow by their head. We did not need to draw any closer to identify who he was. It was the figure we had watched for, half-dreading, half-excited, the previous evening, deceived by shadows passing the house and the wind rattling the window frames. Although this morning, evidence of his visit was there in the shape of the liquorice candy he had left in our shoes.

"'Gluggagægir," we both whispered. The Yule Lad, whose name means "Window Peeper".

"He's dead," said Salka. "Gluggagægir is dead."

'Window Peeper had long been my least favourite of the Yule Lads. From 21st December onwards he would creep through town looking through windows and peepholes. Sometimes at night you would hear him sniffing outside. Although that could be the Yule Lad who followed him, Door Sniffer trying to smell out tasty food. Or Bowl Licker, who snuffled for neglected dishes of food on bedroom floors. On many December nights I shrank beneath my blankets, convinced every creak or sigh was Bowl Licker. Scared to leave any inch of me outside the covers in case he caught me with the rasp of his tongue.'

'Sorry to interrupt,' said Stuart, whose expression was smug rather than apologetic. 'But these are just fairy tales told to children. Impressive ones no doubt. But you can't surely be telling us that you and your sister actually found one of these troll creatures dead in your town square?'

Jon nodded. 'I would not ever dismiss concepts from folklore or legend as "just" fairy tales. These figures exist in our cultures, in our lives and minds, for a reason. But yes, I understand your question. The answer is that much like Santa Claus, over the Christmas period, each of the lads are 'brought to life' by people in costume, who would appear on the appropriate days in stores or gas stations or village halls. In Múlafjörður each afternoon from 14 December, one of the Yule Lads would station himself in the foyer of the community theatre with a sack of candy to distribute. It was always obvious to us who was beneath the costume, despite the wigs and beards and rouged cheeks. Each year the same resident of the town tended to take up the same role. Our own father had played Gully Gawk, the milk stealer, for several years. Although his new job at the ferry terminal in a neighbouring fjord meant he had been unable to take part this fateful year.

'Each of the Lads wore a variation on cross-garter stockings, woollen breeches and braided jackets with a scarf and a droopy cap. Each would style their false whiskers differently, some even with plaits. And each had their own prop – a pot or a spoon, sausages or milk pail, depending on their character. Gluggagægir wears metal-rimmed spectacles and often carries an empty wooden window frame to peep through. This was nowhere to be seen, that afternoon, though he was easily identifiable by the glasses through which his eyes blindly stared.

'Salka and I were not alone with this dreadful scene for long. Minutes later several men appeared, alerted by a dog walker who had been the first to witness it and who, unlike us, had not been frozen with horror and had gone for assistance. We were roughly pulled away by Olaf Bjarnsson (this year's Bowl Licker, not in his costume) though we lingered unobserved at the edge of the crowd.'

'It must have been very distressing,' said Judy. 'For everyone but particularly for you as such young children.'

"I think it was,' said Jon. 'I heard Salka shouting in her sleep over the following nights and I myself had frightening dreams, nightmares that in Icelandic we call *martrod* after the monstrous spirit Mara who sits heavy on the chest of sleepers. We both needed a way of dealing with what we had seen. I think that is why we determined to become detectives and solve the murder ourselves.'

'Like the Famous Five or the Secret Seven,' said Dinah.

'More like the Tenacious Two,' said Helena with an affectionate smile. She had obviously heard this story before.

'You needed a dog,' said Barney. 'All the best child detectives had dogs.' At his feet Dash growled appreciatively.

'When the news spread, as it very quickly did in such a small town, even one whose doors and windows were closed and shuttered against the weather, the family at the Foss Hotel on the fjord were deeply worried. Hinrik Hakonsson, the youngest son of the hotel owner and grandson of the football hero Arnulf Thorsson, was this year's Window Peeper. He had been a last-minute replacement. The eighty-year-old man who had occupied the role for the previous twenty years had taken to his bed with a severe bout of flu only a week before. The old man was small and frail. Slim Hinrik, who was also not blessed with great height, was considered the best option for the costume.

'At the news that Gluggagægir had been found dead in the square, Hinrik's mother Lila rushed to the scene. We were still there when she appeared, striding over the snowy ground to where our local chief of police, Bjarni, and the doctor Sarna Olafsdottir, who had also just arrived, stood by the body. Bjarni, a kind though not particularly fast-thinking man, I think it's fair to say, ushered Lila forward to identify the body. She wailed at the sight of the lifeless heap but then on stepping nearing threw her arms in the air as if in prayer.

'"It is not Hinrik," she declared. "This poor creature is not my son."

'Bjarni, who it seems had also reached this conclusion, nodded, but he and the doctor, who had pronounced the victim to be indeed dead, both had very confused looks upon their faces. We heard Lila asking someone when they had last seen Hinrik. It was a friend of her son.

'"When he'd finished in the theatre he came round to entertain my little ones in his costume," he said. "He stayed for some beers. Several in fact. It was much later," he added. "Maybe seven o'clock in the evening, and dark outside, snowing heavily, when Hinrik left. Still in his Yule Lad suit."

'Bjarni had joined them and was making notes in his pocketbook.

'"I saw him," said a man who was holding back a golden Labrador, straining at its leash to try to reach the body beneath the statue. "It was eight p.m. or thereabouts, round the corner from here on Oldugata. I was taking Miski for her evening walk, battling with the weather. I saw the Yule Lad reeling from side to side and peering into windows. I laughed and waved but he flicked his hand at me and continued his stumbling inspection of the houses. I thought perhaps he was just acting typical for his role but yes, maybe he was intoxicated."

'"Was it definitely Hinrik?" asked Bjarni.

'The man's face contorted in thought, then he shrugged and gestured to the costumed body. "It was Gluggagægir."'

★ ★ ★

'So who was the dead man and where was Lila's son?' asked Judy.

'Two crucial questions,' said Jon. 'Neither of which were answered quickly. The area was cordoned off and nobody was allowed to approach the body which had been covered up by the doctor. Nobody from the town other than Hinrik was known to be missing. Some of the older residents crossed themselves, fearing Gluggagægir himself had been killed and the wrath of his ogress mother might be brought down on the town. Several children cried at the prospect of one of the Yule Lads being dead.'

'Surely no one would actually believe that,' said Stuart.

Jon shrugged. 'It is perhaps more palatable than the alternative. Accepting that someone had murdered a fellow human being. Although the consequences of killing a child of the ogress Gyla might have a worse outcome.

'We would have lingered longer to find out more, but our mother found us. Descending on us like the ogress herself and all but dragging us home by our ears. She said that Father would be furious when he returned that evening. I couldn't understand why. It's not as if we had done anything wrong. With hindsight I suppose she was frightened. As were the rest of the townsfolk when word spread about what had happened. A body that remained unidentified but, judging by the interest of the police, had not met a natural end. And as Lila confirmed that her son had not returned home last night, there was also a missing person, whose clothes had mysteriously ended up on the dead body.

'Salka and I were confined to our home while the townsfolk, and in particular our mother, feared that a killer was roaming the streets. It was only when our father returned that evening,

235

his shift at the ferry terminal over until after the holiday, that we heard that Hinrik had been found.

'"Alive and well and freshly scrubbed from a long hot bath," we heard Father say to our mother from our usual listening post, playing on the Atari game in the television room that adjoined the kitchen. "And with quite a tale to tell if Bjarni is to be believed."

'Our father and Bjarni had been at school together. It was not too surprising that they had spoken about the turn of events. "Hinrik claims that as he, in his words, 'strolled home' from Olaf's house, something happened that caused him to lose consciousness. Considering his drunken state, not an unusual one for him, this may have been anything from a fall to him walking into a tree. He has no idea where exactly this happened. He awoke, he said, in one of the sheds up behind the old stables on the way to the hotel. In his underwear and covered with a horse blanket. He presumed he'd had an accident that had involved losing both his clothes and his sense of direction. His head was sore, which he put down to the beer. He wrapped himself in the blanket and ran home – through the snow! In his stockinged feet. Not wanting his mother and father to see him in such a condition, he had slipped through the back of the hotel up to his rooms, run himself a hot bath and then taken to the comfort of his bed. His mother found him there this afternoon when she went in to find a piece of clothing that might help the police dogs in their search for him!"

'This was thrilling news to me and Salka. Hinrik was notorious for his drunkenness, which had on occasion resulted in him spending the night in the police station cell. We were of an age when we found such behaviour shocking and frightening, to see an adult so out of control, and yet it was also amusing to watch Hinrik fall over and shout ridiculous things. He was I suppose in some ways considered the town clown. He was certainly an embarrassment to his high-profile family, particularly his elder brother Sigurdór, the budding politician. While his family must have been relieved by his return, answers were needed about what had happened in the night. He was not allowed to wallow in his comfy bed and was quickly hauled to the police station, which consisted of a small annexe beside the Town Hall. There he was initially questioned by Bjarni and his assistant Anya, but was then locked in a cell to wait interrogation by detectives from Akureyri, whose arrival was expected imminently.

"'Bjarni also shared some interesting information about the victim," Father continued. "They still don't know who it is and obviously it's not Hinrik. But …" He paused and glanced at the open doorway to the TV room. Salka and I hastily pretended to be engrossed in our game. Not convinced, Father stepped forward and closed the door firmly. Whatever he said next was spoken too quietly for us to hear.

'A murder in a town of 350 people was big news. I know that if you browse your TV channels or your streaming services you will most likely come across a snowy scene, dark pine trees, a detective in a handknitted jumper. It might seem that murders are happening all the time in the far north. But of course, that is no more a reality now than it was in the eighties of my childhood.

'The two murder detectives from Akureyri, the largest town in the north of Iceland, arrived early the next morning. They were put up at the Central Hotel. A small function room and side kitchen of the hotel was also assigned to them as their base of operations once they had inspected the police station's facilities and declared them inadequate.

'These details were relayed by my mother's friend, Inga Snorrisdottir. She was a cleaner at the hotel and not known for her discretion. While she and our mother gossiped in the kitchen, they were oblivious to me and Salka listening in as we half-heartedly moved the controls of our video game, not wanting to miss a word of what was being said.

'I was desperate to meet the detectives and to see inside their headquarters where they would be interrogating witnesses and examining evidence. I felt Salka and I should be invited there. We had after all found the body. But other than a few questions asked of us by Bjarni at the time, nobody had wanted our opinions on the events. I had told Bjarni that there were no footprints even close to the body so he must have been killed before the snow had started falling again. Salka had piped up that the scarf on the statue wasn't Window Peeper's.

'"His scarf is grey with white snowflakes at each end, like snow caught on a windowpane. The one on the statue was scarlet. It might have been Sausage Swiper's or Meat Hook's, their scarves are both red."

'I wanted to kick her. She should have told me that before she told Bjarni. Of course, she was right. I was cross that I hadn't noticed myself.

'"Perhaps there was a mix up in the costume box," Bjarni said, although he sounded uncertain. "I'll let the detective know, they can follow it up."

'"Anything else?" he asked. We shook our heads and were dismissed. But I did know something else, or had an inkling anyway. I was angry with Salka for not telling me about the scarf. I held on jealously to the one thing I had observed that she had not. I did not want it sent to the detectives to follow up. If they missed something so obvious, then maybe they weren't so clever after all. I would impress them with my own superior detecting skills.'

Jon paused and looked at his audience, 'Forgive me. I was ten years old. I thought I knew everything and the fact that I might be hindering rather than helping the investigation did not enter my mind.

'Once we had decided to become detectives, Salka and

I set to work. I found an old exercise book and we spent a whole morning drawing up what we knew so far. As we still did not know who the victim was, coming up with suspects and motives was difficult. Hinrik was being held as the most likely perpetrator. But if he had killed someone why would he then dress them in his own distinctive Yule Lad costume.

'The rock by the victim's head was likely to be the murder weapon, although the police thought he may not have been killed where he was found. "There was blood," we'd heard our father say, "but not enough of it." I had my own theory about the rock and I decided to share it with Salka at least.

'"Everyone thinks the rock came from the flower beds in the square," I said. We'd both noted the lumps of lava that edged one of the beds were jumbled and several were out of place. They were a decorative novelty in our town, which lay several miles from any lava fields. "But did you see," I said, "that if you tried to rebuild the edging, there would not be a space for that rock?"

'"Are you sure?" she asked.

'I nodded vigorously. Salka could beat me at most video games. But in a few years time I was to outclass her in a new game that I came to excel in. By the time I finished high school I was the *Tetris* champion of my year. Even at the age of ten, I had a particular skill for jigsaws and any game that involved fitting shapes together. I was convinced that the rock that lay beside the dead person's head did not come from the square's flower beds.

'Mother wanted us to stay indoors. But we argued that we needed some exercise otherwise the computer games would melt our brains. Father agreed that, under the circumstances, we were unlikely to be in danger. But we were only to stay in town and not wander too far along the fjord or beyond the town edges.

'The snow had settled soft and deep, compacted where people and vehicles had passed. Ideal for our bikes, BMXs that

239

we had been given the Christmas before. Second-hand but still the most exciting presents we'd ever received. Salka was worried she was going to soon outgrow hers, but I was smug with the knowledge that when she did, it would be mine. We wrapped up warm with our sturdiest boots on our feet and set off. Our plan was to check gardens for missing lava rocks.

'A task that was near impossible because of the thick blanket of snow. But we had a secondary purpose: we were also heading towards the Foss Hotel. Hinrik's nephew, Alex, was in my class at school. He seemed, in the absence of any adults wanting to tell us anything, our best source of information. As we passed the last of the houses on the road and reached the old stables just before the hotel we saw a stranger, a man in a long overcoat and heavy-rimmed spectacles wearing a woollen knitted hat in the greens and yellows of the aurora.

'One of the detectives, I guessed. He'd be looking for footprints and other clues. The man took out a tape measure from his pocket and began to measure something on the ground. He spotted us approaching and put up his hand. "Please do not come any nearer, children. This is a potential crime scene. We don't want evidence to be destroyed."

I nodded over to the shed behind the barn. "Is that where Hinrik slept last night?" I asked. I knew I sounded cheeky, but I was hoping he would just think I was being a nosey kid, not a rival detective. He wasn't fooled however, and asked us to leave. As we turned to go my rear wheel skidded and I landed painfully on the hard ground, my bicycle half in a ditch. As I dragged it back out, I saw something angular under a tangle of dead twigs and branches. I reached down and pulled it out.

'"What have you got there, lad?" called the detective, marching over.

'I gaped at the familiar object in my hand. "It's Gluggagægir's window," I said. I turned to Salka, unable to hide my excitement.

I had little time to revel in my find, however, as it was snatched from me by the detective.

'"Thank you, boy. That could be very helpful but as I said, you two need to get on your way."

'Which we did but with a new piece of information to add to our notes. Hinrik may have ended up in the shed without his costume. But he had ditched his prop only a few metres before he got there.

'Alex looked surprised to see us. We weren't exactly friends at school. He was one of the cool kids who always had the best toys and games. I could tell by the way he looked at our bikes that he wasn't impressed by them. That didn't matter. That wasn't why we were there. I started by asking him if he wanted to come for a ride. He glanced at our bikes again and sniffed as if he wouldn't be seen dead in their company, but then admitted that he was supposed to stay at home until "things get sorted with Uncle Hinrik".

'"Have they not let him go yet?" I asked. "Surely they must know that he didn't kill anyone."

'Alex shrugged. "You'd think so. But now they've said the dead person was a woman. And someone saw my uncle have a big row with a woman in the centre of town just as it was getting dark."

'I almost fell off my bike. I heard Salka whisper "I knew it" under her breath. I scowled at her, convinced she'd known nothing of the sort.

'"A woman?" I said. "Who?"

'"When Aunt Lila was in Bjarni's office, a man came in. He said he was worried the murdered woman might be someone he knew. Bjarni made my aunt leave but she saw him take the man over to the hotel to speak to the detectives.

'"Who was he?" asked Salka.

'Alex looked as though he wasn't going to tell us, wanting to keep the upper hand, but he couldn't resist.

'"It was Einar, the farmer."

'"Grumpy Einar?" asked Salka, and Alex actually smiled.

'"He is so grumpy," he agreed. "Living up there all by himself with only his sheep and that halfwit Leifur helping him. No wonder."

'We cycled off heading back to town but before we reached the turning for our street Salka stopped. "We need to go up to Einar's farm," she said. "If we can find out who the dead woman is we can start our list of suspects."

'"Einar won't tell us," I said. Not adding that I was scared of the farmer. He'd once caught me and some friends climbing on the stalls in one of his old barns. He'd chased us out swinging an iron bar over his head and transformed from a grumpy man into Thor wielding his hammer at the mountain-trolls.

'"Einar won't tell us," Salka said, "but I know a half-wit boy who will."

'"Did you really know the dead person was a woman?" I asked, as we pedalled to the edge of town.

'"Not for definite," she said. "But did you not notice her hands? They were tiny."

'The hill up to the farm was long and steep. We both had to get off our bikes and push up the rough track, following the ruts that must have been made by Einar's truck that morning. I was relieved to see that his vehicle wasn't in the yard when we reached it. I followed Salka cautiously round the back of the farmhouse, checking quickly that there were no groups of lava rocks. I needn't have bothered. The only items decorating the yard were rusting pieces of farm machinery and a thankfully empty dog kennel. Music from a transistor radio could be heard coming from the barn that I had been chased from the year before. As we approached, we could hear a tuneless whistling accompanying a jaunty pop song.

'"Hi, Leifur," shouted Salka.

'A gangly boy who I recognised from the school year above my sister's emerged from behind a sheep stall.

'"Salka," he said, his pale cheeks turning a rosier red than any Yule Lad's. I began to get an idea of Salka's scheme.

'Sure enough, she had managed to dispense with her usual cynical aura and now adopted a peculiar sweet expression that I had never seen on her face before. It was odd to see even though I knew why she was doing it.

'"Are you working all on your own?" she asked.

'Leifur nodded. "Einar's gone into town," he said, adding. "On business."

'"What's he like to work for?" she asked. Her fingers were tapping on the wooden strut of the stall.

'"He's alright," said Leifur. "I'm only here weekends and holidays, but he pays OK. I'm getting a bonus in the New Year if lambing goes well. I, I was thinking of trying out the cinema in Egilstadir. I, we, could get the bus if you fancy it." He couldn't look her in the eye.

'"Maybe," she said. "Depends on the film." She looked him up and down as if pricing him for market. "And the company." If he'd blushed any harder he would have turned into a beetroot.

'Salka pretended not to notice his discomfort.

'"Does Einar ever go to the cinema?" she asked. "With a lady friend?"

'"What do you mean?" Leifur was suddenly wary.

'"Everyone knows he's a grumpy old sheep farmer who's lived on his own for ever,' Salka said. "But I thought maybe he might have a special friend. Someone who comes over for supper sometimes?"

'Leifur laughed. "Supper? After work we sometimes have a bite together before I head home. Tough bread and dried fish. Cheese if I'm lucky. And as for the state of his kitchen! He wouldn't be inviting anyone over for supper." He frowned though as if he wanted to say more.

'Salka drew closer. Her dark hair was squashed flat beneath her hat, her nose shiny and rosy from the cold. She was wearing a big grey anorak and mittens with holes in. Leifur was gazing at her as if she was the goddess Freyja herself.

'"But he's maybe had a visitor lately?" she asked. "A relative perhaps, his sister or grandmother?"

'Leifur shook his head. "He says he doesn't have any family since his parents died and he inherited the farm. That's why he took me on. It's hard to farm when you are just one person. I think Einar is lonely." Leifur looked guilty, as if he had betrayed a secret, but Salka's sweet and fascinated expression encouraged him to continue. "The woman who came by the day before yesterday. I have never seen her before.'

'Could this be the dead woman? I had to stop myself showing my excitement.

'"They were familiar," Leifur continued. "Holding hands." He looked at Salka's raggedy mittens fondly before his eyes darted away.

'"She was here on Wednesday, on the twenty-first?" she asked.

'He nodded. "She appeared in the yard at lunchtime, just before the storm blew in. Brown and grey plaits and a rucksack on her back. Must have walked but I don't know where from. Maybe she came in on the bus. Einar looked pleased to see her but she started crying and he was wringing his hands together. I kept out of the way. They weren't exactly arguing but they weren't agreeing with each other either. I heard her say, 'No Einar. It's for me to tell. No one else. I can't let it happen.'

'"I slunk into the kitchen and pretended to be washing my hands at the sink by the window. They carried on like that for a bit, talking, then they suddenly hugged. So tightly like they would never let go. Then she pushed him off. She was shaking her head as she turned and walked away. Einar started to follow her, but she called back to him over her shoulder, and he turned and trudged back to the house. He didn't speak to me about her though I was here for the rest of the day."

"'Interesting," said Salka. "Come on, Jon. We need to get home."

"'Wait," said Leifur. "What about the cinema? In January after the lambing is over? They might have the new Star Wars film at last. Would you like to watch it? With me?"

'She smiled at him. "OK," she said, and left the barn.

"'There's no way Mum and Dad are going to let you go on the bus to Egilstadir with Leifur," I said.

"I know," she said, climbing onto her bike. "What a shame."

'My sister's cunning astounded me. I could only jump on my own bike and follow in her wake.

'When we got back into town we should have headed straight for home. The light was fading and Mum would soon be worrying. But Salka suggested a detour past "the scene of the crime" as she insisted on calling it.

'A man was sitting on the bench next to Arnulf's statue, huddled in a thick woollen jacket. He was staring at a plastic flower, a red rose on a long stalk clenched in his hands. Salka stopped her bike.

"'It's Maggi," she whispered. I had recognised him too. He taught us both science at school. He knew lots about his subject and was really passionate about it, but he was so quiet and mild-mannered he often failed to capture his students' interest. As we watched, Maggi stood up and placed the flower next to the plinth where only yesterday a body had been found.

"'He doesn't look very happy," I said. This time I was determined to lead the investigation. "Good afternoon, Maggi," I said. In Iceland we call our teachers by their first names, so although his name was Magnus Bjarnsson, like everyone else in the town we just called him Maggi.

'"Jon, hi," he said with a tired half-smile. "And is it Salka?" I was glad he'd recognised me more confidently. Science was one of my favourite subjects and I tried hard in his lessons, unlike others, such as Alex, who messed about and took advantage of his placid nature.

'"It's very sad," I said. "What happened yesterday."

'"A tragedy," he said shaking his head. He took a deep breath. "She was my sister."

'Salka and I exchanged quick glances. I suddenly felt out of my depth. It was one thing to be talking in the abstract about a dreadful crime. But to be faced by someone so close to the victim. I suddenly felt ashamed that we had taken such an interest. Maggi however seemed keen to talk to us, unaware of course that we had been investigating his sister's death.

'"I haven't seen her since we were both in our twenties," he said. "Thirty whole years gone, when we could have talked and laughed and shared our opinions on the world, argued even, as siblings do." That sad smile again. "And now we never can. The police think she was intending to come and see me. But she never arrived at my house."

'"Thirty years is a long time," I said, imagining how it would be if I never saw Salka again until she was an old lady of forty-three, probably with children of her own.

'"What was her name?" Salka asked. A good question, I wished I'd thought of it.

'"Hildur," he replied. "She was older than me by a couple of years, but we were very close growing up. Like you two, playing together, riding our bicycles. We were both shy, but we always had fun together, even after she left school and started work at the bank."

'"Then she moved away," Salka said.

'Maggi sighed, so deeply his shoulders rose and fell. "Never fall in love, children," he said. "Don't give your heart. No one can be trusted with it." He looked up at the grey statue. "Or with your life."

'Had someone broken Maggi's heart? I thought of Leifur looking so pathetically after Salka as we left the barn. If I knew him better I might have gone back to the farm and warned him not to throw his heart at her as she had no plans to catch it.

"'Did Hildur leave because she fell in love?" Salka asked. There she was again, asking all the good questions!

"'She was in love, yes,' said Maggi. "Then she left town to start a new life down in the south.' The way he said the final word suggested that the south was somewhere that no sane person would ever go. "She broke my heart and Einar's too."

"'She broke Einar's heart?" I blurted.

'Maggi nodded. "They were sweethearts since their schooldays. Everyone, myself included, thought they would marry and work the farm together. Einar's parents were old and he was already doing most of the work. Hildur would be his helpmeet and she would stay here in Múlafjordur for ever with the people who loved her most. But suddenly out of the blue she announced she was leaving. One morning she packed her bags and was gone. The sun high in the sky, turning her hazel eyes to harvest gold. It was the last time I ever saw her as she stepped into the car and they drove away."

"'They?" I asked, before Salka had chance.

"'Never fall in love.' Maggi repeated. "Hildur left that day for a new life, with Finnur, Einar's younger brother."'

★ ★ ★

"'We should have told him," I said to Salka as we pedalled home in the descending dark, knowing Mum would be furious at our late return. "About Einar and the woman talking and hugging in his farmyard. It must have been Hildur."

"'No," said Salka. "That might have made him angry with Einar and we don't know yet what he has told the police."

'I didn't see how we ever could find that out. But later, over a supper of Plokkfiskur, my favourite fish and potato stew, which I have promised to recreate for Helena may times' – his eyes twinkled at his partner, who grimaced – 'I had an idea. Our investigations hadn't been completely fruitless. If we wrote down everything we had found out. About the lava stone in the wrong place and about Hildur visiting Einar. We could take our information to the police. Einar may already have told them about his visitor, but we had some detail from Leifur about what the pair had said to each other. We could also tell them what Maggi had said to us just as we were about to cycle off. He had got to his feet and glared up at the stony face of Arnulf Thorsson.

"'My sister hated that statue," he said. "It was erected the year after Arnulf died. I was in my final year at school and Hildur had just started work. About a month after it was unveiled it was defaced. A long streak of red paint daubed on his body as if thrown from a pot. Nobody ever owned up or was found out. But I knew it was Hildur. She had drips of the paint on her coat. I washed them off with turpentine. I did not want her to be found out."

"'Why did she do it?" I asked.

"'She had her reasons," he said. His face was dark and closed to any more questions.'

★ ★ ★

'The detectives were not overkeen to see us the next morning. It was Christmas Eve and I expect they were hoping to finish up the case and get back to Akureyri before the day was over. A man about Maggi's age came out of the interview room as we waited to go in.

'"Don't leave town, Finnur," one of the detectives called after him. So Einar's brother was here too. Had he come to Múlafjordur with Hildur? Did Einar know he was here?

'We were directed to seats at the table opposite the two detectives. The younger one with the glasses said, "Hmmm, you two again." The older one had a trim grey beard and looked like my grandfather, but without the warmth of his eyes.

'"Come on then, kids, tell us what you've got," he barked.

'Salka and I both started talking at once and the detective put up his hand for us to stop.

'"One at a time please if we are to make any sense of it. You, lad, what were you saying about the lava rocks?"

'I explained that the lava rock next to Hildur's head wasn't from the square. "Somebody's garden will be missing a rock," I said. The two detectives looked at each other and the younger one took off his glasses and rubbed the bridge of his nose.

'Undeterred, I continued. "She was killed somewhere else, maybe near the shed where Hinrik fell asleep. And the murderer dressed her as Window Peeper and took her to the square with the rock and tied the red scarf that wasn't Window Peeper's on the statue." I stopped to breathe and had a sudden image of the statue streaked with red paint as Maggi had described it. Before I had chance to mention it Salka had started her account of our visit to Einar's farm and what Leifur had told us.

'"You are right," said the older detective, smoothing his beard with his fingers. "Hildur was not killed near the statue. We have just issued a press release to that effect, in the hope that someone in the town will have noticed her body being moved there. However the intensity of the storm that night means that few people were out of their homes."

'"Except Hinrik," said Salka.

'"Hmm yes, we have released Hinrik," the younger detective said, tapping the table irritably with his pen. "A woman has

249

come forward to say that it was she who was shouting at him in the street, because he had given her sweet angel child a potato instead of candy. But he is still a person of interest."

"'Did Finnur come here looking for Hildur?" I asked. "Was he here before the snow started?"

'Both detectives frowned. The bearded one said, 'I'm not sure we can disclose that at this stage." Then he relented and revealed that Finnur claimed that his car had been stuck in the snow on the high pass above town overnight and he had been forced to walk down yesterday.

"'Now, was there anything else?" He shuffled his papers.

'As he had told us about Finnur, I told him about Hildur hating the statue of Arnulf Thorsson, Hinrick's grandfather. This was news to them, I could tell. The bearded one leaned forward.

"'Arnulf was a famous local footballer?" he said.

'We both nodded.

"'Isn't there a new sports centre being opened in his name?" asked the younger one.

"'Yes," I said. "Behind the school. With an all-weather football pitch and everything."

"'Why did she hate the statue?"

"'I don't know," I said. "You'd have to ask Maggi."

"'We could ask Maggi," Salka said as we walked home. The air was warmer today and there was a steady drip drip as snow melted from the trees.

"'He didn't want to talk about it yesterday," I said.

"'No, but we could give him the news that Finnur is here. I bet he doesn't know yet."

'Reluctantly I followed her up the street past the post office and the playground to Maggi's house, the last one in the row before the road turned a bend to follow the fjord round to the Foss Hotel. We had ridden past here yesterday when all the gardens had been deep under snow. But today as we walked towards Maggi's front door I saw what had been hidden then.

'"Salka, look."

'The thawing of the snow revealed the tips of the bare branches of the shrubs in the garden and on either side of the short path leading up to the house the tops of a line of lava rocks. On the left they were neat and orderly but on the right, near the front door, there was a gap like a missing tooth.

'Before we had chance to decide what to do, the door opened and there was our science teacher standing on the step with a mug of coffee in his hand.

'"Hello again," he said. "Can I help you?"

'We were closer to the street than his house. I glanced back but there was nobody else about. I imagined Hinrik stumbling home drunk. Maggi seeing him from his doorstep, round about where he was standing now.

'"We were just wondering," said Salka, her voice not quite as steady and confident as usual, "if you knew why Hildur had come back to Múlafjordur."

'Maggi frowned. "What business is it of yours?" he said. "I told you, I didn't see her, so how would I know?"

'"It's a good question, though."

'The harsh voice from behind made us both jump. It was Finnur. Younger than his brother Einar, and looking more city smart, but with the same fierce expression and a mean sneer on his lips. He stepped round us and walked towards Maggi.

'"Hildur left our apartment in Reykjavík four days ago, with no explanation," he snarled. "By the time I figured she'd come here it was too late for me to get through the pass, thanks to that blasted storm. When I finally arrived, I was told she is dead. They arrested some drunk idiot then let him go. Now my brother Einar is nowhere to be found. Tell me, Maggi. Why did my wife come back to Múlafjordur?"

'The two men glared at each other, apparently forgetting we were there. We hung back but continued to listen.

'"Are you saying, Finnur Sigurdsson, that you of all people do not know? You and Hildur have shared thirty years together. You must know why she left here. Is it not also the reason she came back?"

'Finnur stepped closer to Maggi. We couldn't see his face, but Maggi's looked relaxed, as if he'd planned this conversation in advance.

'"She read in the newspaper about the new sports centre," said Finnur in a low voice. "She was not happy about it. Or about Arnulf's grandson trying to make political capital out of his famous relative."

'Maggi nodded. "It would be painful for her."

'"More painful perhaps for Arnulf's family," said Finnur. "For his children, all of them, the manager of the fancy hotel, the politician in Akureyri, even for the sad drunk who lost his costume. It could be damaging, even, if she came back. If she told everyone what happened."

'"She didn't want to go, thirty years ago. But she felt then that it would be safer to leave than speak out," said Maggi.

'"She wanted to leave," insisted Finnur.

'"Did she?" asked Maggi. "She loved Einar and then suddenly she left with you. She was too afraid to speak out then. Too ashamed. Is that why she agreed to go with you? Was it that or have her secret revealed?"

'I could hardly breathe or dare to swallow. The two men with their eyes locked seemed to be both lost in the secrets of their past.

'There was a sudden roaring like an aeroplane taking off and Einar appeared, hurdling Maggi's garden wall like a man half his age and barrelling into his brother. Both falling to the ground, they wrestled, Einar trying to pin Finnur down, Finnur trying to throw him off. Within a few minutes Einar's rage or energy was spent and he rolled away, cursing loudly.

'Finnur clambered to his feet, spitting with fury.

'"You killed her," Finnur said pointing to his brother. "You've spent three decades so twisted with resentment and jealousy that when she came back and told you about her childhood, what had happened, you couldn't stand it. So you killed her."

'Einar shook his head. "I never stopped loving her. Even after she left with you, with no explanation. Refusing to speak to me or see me when I came looking for her. She came back this week to tell me the truth. She came to my farm, to the home that should have been hers and mine, and told me what you did. How you threatened to tell her family and the whole town your version of the story of what happened between her and that disgusting football coach. You told her I would stop loving her, that I would be repulsed by her and she believed you. She came back here to make amends. Furious that he was going to be honoured with the new sports centre in the grounds of the school. What she told me only made me love her more. You thought you'd finally lost her. You followed her here and you killed her."

'He caught his breath and, his anger raised once more, he lunged at Finnur again.

'"Stop," said Maggi in the strident tone I had heard him use only once before, when Alex had been about to dangle another boy out of the first-floor physics lab window.

'The brothers turned to look at him.

'"Stop," he repeated. Though the word was more of a sigh. His coffee cup hung limply in his hand.

'"You killed her," said Salka. She looked so small stepping into the space between the three men that I rushed forward, thinking I could protect her if I was by her side. She grasped my hand and squeezed it. "You killed her, Maggi," she repeated, pointing at the gap in the lava stones. "You were angry because she was going to tell everyone about Arnulf. You wanted it to stay a secret."

"'Did he hurt you too, Maggi?" Einar's voice was calm now. "You were on the junior football team when he was still the coach. I remember Hildur used to come to matches and cheer you on, help out with the refreshments. You would have been, what, seven or eight? Hildur was not yet in her teens. I never liked Arnulf, for all that the town adulated him. When she became a teenager did his interest turn to you? She mustn't have known. I don't think she would have left if she had."

'At the time, I only partly understand what they were talking about, but it was enough to make me feel sick in my stomach. Salka was squeezing my hand so hard I thought I might cry. But it was Maggi who began to sob. Sinking to his haunches and holding his head in his hands.'

Jon sighed. 'The detectives got what they wanted. They were home with their families for Christmas. But such a sad, sad tale when all was told.

'After leaving Einar's farm on Tuesday afternoon, with the storm sweeping into town, Hildur had visited her brother. At first overjoyed to see her, he had become scared when she declared she was going to tell the police about what Arnulf had done to her as a child. She had always regretted not having spoken up while Arnulf was alive, knowing there was a risk that he might be abusing another child. Not knowing that he was, and that the child was her little brother.

'Maggi couldn't bear for everyone to know. He and Hildur had argued as the storm raged. She had stepped outside, saying she was going to the police station. He grabbed her, trying to stop her. She lurched away, tripped and fell, her head hitting one of the sharp pieces of lava at the side of the garden path. As Maggi stood in horror by his sister's dead body, Hinrik had stumbled past, blind drunk, half-falling into the road, in his Yule Lad costume. Terrified that he had witnessed what had happened, Maggi lifted his sister's body into his house and went after Hinrik.

'He found the semi-conscious Hinrik in a ditch near the stables. He'd bundled him into the shed and stripped him of his clothes. Under the cover of the storm he had placed Hildur, now with the costume of Window Peeper over her own clothes, in the boot of his car and driven into town. He had parked behind the church, waited until he was sure no one else was around and carried her body and the treacherous rock to the foot of the statue. As a final touch, he had clambered up and tied his own blood-red scarf around Arnulf Thorsson's stone neck, a symbol of the paint once thrown by his sister.'

'So he did want the truth to come out?' said Judy quietly.

'Perhaps,' said Jon. 'Although he might not have fully realised that himself. He must have been so conflicted, wanting justice to be done, yet burdened by his own shame over what had been done to him and his sister. Shame he had no need to feel.

'And as a result of the revelations, Hildur got her wish. The sports centre opened the following spring, with the hefty financial support of Arnulf's family, but without his name above the door. His grandson Sigurdór, the newly appointed deputy leader of the Akureyri Town Council, declined the offer to officiate at the opening ceremony. Instead the ribbon across the door of the brand new Múlafjörður Sports Centre was cut by two grinning representatives of the town's boys and girls football teams.'

PUZZLE

Christmas Day Chaos

On Christmas morning, there was no snow on Fleetfoot Street, only a drizzling rain and a cold wind that swayed the branches of the trees and sent the year's-end leaves in scurrying eddies across the pavement. Inside five of the houses on the street, five children woke up, each eager to unwrap the presents that had been left in a stocking at the end of their bed or under the Christmas tree downstairs.

But oh no! There has been a mix-up at Santa's sorting office (or possibly at the wrapping party at number 37 the previous afternoon, which was attended by all of the parents). Only one of the Fleetfoot Street children received the present they had been hoping for – the other four presents each went to the wrong child.

Can you unmuddle the mix-up by decoding the clues below, linking up the correct present with the child who had wished for it and working out which child has already received the right present?

Hamza wanted a toy Antipodean bird, the same colour as his knitted flamingo.
He received a special cut of steak, containing some computer memory.

Jenny confusingly wished for MACYS TEESHIRT.
She suspected something was missing when she opened a WND P TRCRTPS.

Musical Luka wrote to Santa asking for: A French paperclip.
He opened a box cryptically labelled 'Educational gift: Pasteur, for example, who precedes an adjustment, reportedly'.

Roxy really, really wanted: A clockwork 'three-horned lizard'.
She confusingly unwrapped A MEEK STUD PUFFIN.

Felix requested a game invented in 1943, whose name loses its last two letters in the US.
He puzzlingly received a DVD box set of four series of a game show hosted by Richard Madeley.

Final Puzzle Clue #9

The name of the child who received the present they asked for, is the word you need for the final puzzle.

DEATH ON
THE BIGBUS EXPRESS

'I was thinking about your story, Jon,' said Dinah at breakfast the next day. 'You grew up to be a Wellness Mentor, but did your sister with her obvious talents in detection join the police?'

'No,' said Jon; he seemed worried Dinah might be mocking him. 'She moved to Sweden and teaches forensic science at the University in Malmö.'

'Ooh, forensics,' said Mrs Linden as she cleared away their empty plates. 'Now there's a subject. You all have your stories of murder and mystery. Well, I'll have you know, I have one too.'

'Really, Mrs Linden?' said James. 'Well let's hear it then. Some of us are venturing into Scarborough later for a bit of last-minute Christmas shopping, now that the roads have been cleared. But I'm sure we've got time for an extra story.'

'Definitely,' said Sara. 'It would go well with the coffee and these delicious brownies. Thank you, Mrs Linden.'

'My pleasure, pet. Well, if you're sure. I'll just pop another pot of coffee on and hang up my pinny. Then if you don't mind me uprooting you, Miss Helena, I'll take that comfy chair by the window, and I'll tell you as much as I can remember.'

'Will your husband be joining us?' asked Judy when Mrs Linden was settled.

The housekeeper shook her head. 'Linden doesn't think murder is an appropriate subject for stories.'

'Well there's decades of publishing to prove him wrong,' said Judy, but then, remembering how sad she'd felt after hearing Sara's and Jon's stories, added, 'but I suppose he has a point.'

Mrs Linden wafted her hand. 'Oh, don't mind him,' she said. "He also thinks stories shouldn't be about war, love, money, politics, friendship, marriages good or bad, troubled childhoods, happy childhoods or cakes.'

'What kind of books does he like?' asked James. 'I could give him a signed copy of mine if he fancies a spot of scandal.'

'He wouldn't touch it,' said Mrs Linden. 'Too much sex.' She pondered for a moment. 'He's very fond of a book I got him for his birthday a few years back about birdsong, and there's another he picked up at a village jumble sale about a man who lived alone on a Scottish island for ten years. He usually has one or the other on his bedside table.' She smoothed down her skirts. 'He's already had the bare bones of this tale anyway. I told him all about it at the time. When I finished he asked me how much of it I'd made up and what was I thinking anyway, trying to get from Yorkshire to Devon in the middle of winter. He'd warned me beforehand it would be a tricky journey, though he hadn't guessed there'd be a murder on board.'

'Is this a railway mystery?' asked Dinah. 'Like Poirot on the Orient Express, or that one where a woman witnesses a killing through a train window?'

'Not quite,' said Mrs Linden.

'The ten-pound ticket seemed like a bargain when I bought it. Three hundred miles on a luxury coach. Linden dropped me at the bus station in York at seven in the morning. With a quick changeover in Bristol, I expected to be at my sister's house near Exeter in time for tea. Linden was invited too of course. We'd

259

been at Bracestone House for four years then. Mr Luddenham took us on shortly after he bought the place in 2013, and we'd always worked over Christmas and then taken our holiday in the quiet of January. But this year Mr Luddenham was away for all of December and he'd said we were free to take a couple of weeks off.

'The thought of spending Christmas with Jenny and her family filled me with joy. Linden, not so much. To be honest, I can't say for certain he's ever been 'filled with joy'. He's fond of Jenny of course and he tolerates the children. But he insisted someone had to stay and look after the house. I told him that four hundred years of stone and mortar weren't going to crumble just because a man past his prime wasn't patrolling its corridors. He wouldn't listen though. Said he'd be perfectly fine on his own with the radio and his pack of playing cards. If that man can be said to have a hobby it is endless games of solitaire.

'So off I toddled on the morning of the fourteenth, with my suitcase and my travel-on bag with a bit of knitting, a seaside romance, a flask and enough butties and toffees to see me through without having to pay service-station prices. The weather was looking … interesting as the coach pulled out of York and headed for the A1. Snowflakes like miniature doilies were falling but melting before they hit the ground.

'By the time we pulled into Bristol I had done some knitting, read most of my book and had a nap – it had been such an early start. The falling doilies had by now matted into curtains of white. I made use of the station's facilities then boarded the second bus for the final leg of the journey with some trepidation, not encouraged by the driver's cheery "I'd say Exeter's ambitious in this weather, but we'll see what we can do, me lover" as I showed him my ticket.

'I found a seat and settled in for the next two and half hours, pleased with myself for having if not enjoyed then at least endured the journey so far. The coach was almost identical to the one from York. The BigBus Express had been described in the advert in the *Gazette* as 'the ultimate in luxury intercity travel'. As the bus pulled out of Bristol, and eventually joined the M5, only to come to an immediate halt, I considered how far an advert could stretch the truth without it technically being a lie. 'Luxury' is in the mind of the beholder, I suppose, but, with my body squashed into a narrow seat with limited leg room, next to a bald man who kept muttering to himself and smelled of roast chicken, my mind was failing to behold any luxury at all. A tiny speaker above our heads was playing a series of what I presumed were festive tunes just too quietly and tinnily to make them out. As for the onboard toilets, well we won't go there just yet. I certainly hadn't for the previous five hours.

'My seating companion had boarded the bus carrying a cardboard box that I recognised as one that cats and other pets were carried in to the vets. I must have looked surprised, as the man had said "I take her everywhere with me" before depositing the box on the overhead rack. As soon as he sat down, he had produced a sheaf of papers, a packet of crisps, the source of the smell, and started his muttering.

'Every seat on the coach was full. Across the aisle a young Asian woman wearing headphones was leafing through a magazine. Next to her a young man with a flop of auburn fringe was already fast asleep, his nose pointing to the ceiling like the funnel of a ship.

'The young woman smiled at me and I smiled back across the bulk of my neighbour. Sorry, 'bulk' sounds judgemental, doesn't it? After all, I'm no skinny Minnie myself. But he was a large man. Jowly too, tremors rippling his skin as he shook his head while he mumbled, apparently reading out loud from his wad of paper. At one point he said, "I must say I am partial to a cockatoo," to which I couldn't help but respond, "I beg your pardon?"

'He removed his reading glasses and blinked. "I do apologise, my dear. It's these damned lines. I have to get them word perfect. I'm treading the boards tomorrow night and I can't let my audience down."

'An actor, of course. It was clear in the way he spoke, making the most of every letter of every word, his vowels like plums. He was rather loud. I noticed several of our neighbours turning to stare. He gave a little wave. I suppose if you're an actor the whole world is your audience.

'"Is it Shakespeare?" I asked. Did Shakespeare write about cockatoos? I'd seen an outdoor production of *A Midsummer Night's Dream* at Whitby Abbey once. Hadn't the man with the donkey head sung a song about birds that sounded a bit rude?

'"Alas no, madam," the man replied. "Although the Bard is well within my range. I've done my time as Polonius behind the arras, and Henry V once, in full armour, when I was at school. But 'tis the season for panto and my turn to be a dame." He thrust out a large pink hand. "William DeMarco, aka Widow Twinkle. Appearing for fourteen nights and ten matinees at the Chamberhouse, Exeter. Though you may recognise me from the telly."

'I didn't but I didn't like to tell him. I introduced myself and said, "A panto, lovely. Is it *Aladdin*?"

'He shook his head. "Bit more leftfield, my love. They like to play with tradition at the Chamberhouse. This year it's *Ooh, What a Lovely Beanstalk*. I'm Jack's mother, who sends her son off to market with the family's golden retriever and kicks up a fuss when he comes back with an energy drink and a packet of magic Hula Hoops."

'The bus, which had been travelling smoothly for about half an hour, came to an abrupt stop, throwing us all forward.

'"For goodness' sake," shouted a woman behind us. The

young woman across the aisle looked up from her magazine and the man next to her was jolted from his sleep.

"'Sorry, folks,' the driver's voice crackled through the speaker. "Bit of a queue ahead. Brake lights as far as I can see through this whiteout. Might be a tad stop-start for the next few miles, hours, decades of eternity."

"'This is ridiculous." The shouty woman stormed up the aisle with a waft of exotic perfume. I wrinkled my nose.

"'Vetiver and damask roses," said William.

'I thought he was reading from his script again, but he was watching the woman as she marched to the front of the bus. I could hear her voice as she argued with the bus driver. Another man's voice joined in, asking her to "keep it down". She returned ten minutes later, clearly still unhappy.

"'Is it looking bad?" I ventured.

'She gave me a look that could have withered a rubber plant. "It's not looking like anything other than an over-decorated Christmas cake. Snow everywhere, cars dotted about haphazardly, nothing moving. The couple from the car in front have got out and are taking photographs."

"'It was forecast to be bad," said the floppy-haired young man with a cavernous yawn. He stretched out his arms, showing off a T-shirt that read: "Don't Rush Me, I'm a Geologist".

"'And yet you boarded the bus," said the woman. She was wearing a beautiful woollen suit. You would have loved it, Miss Garnett. I think they call it Welsh tapestry?'

'Splendid,' said Dinah, nodding. 'Tapestry from Wales, very nice.'

'All greens and purples,' Mrs Linden continued. 'Made me think of the moors at heather time. And a dark purple silk blouse which must have helped stop the wool from itching.

'The boy stared at the woman, obviously not as impressed as I was by her outfit.

'"Train strike," he said. "Gotta get home to see the folks though, haven't I? It'll be worth it for Mum's cooking."

'"Are you expecting her to do all your laundry too?" asked the woman casting a critical eye over his grubby T-shirt and jeans.

'"I'm a third-year geology student," he said with a smirk. "I'm perfectly capable of using a washing machine."

'"Can and will aren't the same thing, are they?"

'The bus jolted again as we started to move slowly forward. The woman grabbed hold of the back of William's seat. William flinched. The woman patted the jacket of her immaculate suit and returned to her own seat directly behind the young people. I heard her speaking to the man next to her: "I tried my best, Brian, but there's mountains even this woman can't move." She laughed shrilly. William winced at the sound.

'Her heavy perfume lingered in the air. I have to say it was preferable to the smell of William's crisps.

'The geology student caught my eye and said cheerily, "Hi, I'm Josh."

'"Sabrina," I replied.'

There were gasps around the Bracestone House kitchen.

'What a lovely name,' said Dinah.

'Thank you,' said Mrs Linden, 'although I'd be grateful if we kept to formalities here. I was named after a well-endowed actress of the fifties. It was a source of embarrassment in my younger days. Although I like to think I've grown into it now.'

Barney nudged Rose sharply, but she refused to catch his eye.

'Now, where was I? Oh yes. Now that Josh was awake he began to take an interest in his fellow passengers, particularly the young woman in the seat next to him. She still had her headphones on. Her head was bowed over her magazine, and she tapped her lip with the end of a pencil as she studied a crossword puzzle.

"'Are you stuck?" asked Josh, twisting his body to get a better look.

'She raised her head and removed her headphones.

"'I'm Josh," he said with what had no doubt proved in the past to be a winning smile. "I'm great at crosswords."

"'Thank you," she said. "But I'm doing fine."

"'Hmm, you've only got a couple though. Are you sure two down is right? 'A beautiful Italian woman, but is she a plant?' Shouldn't that be Sophia Loren?"

"'No," she said. "That's too many letters and the answer is only one word."

"'Oh yeah, you might be right. I'm Josh," he said again.

"'I heard," she said. He was watching her, waiting. She put down her pencil. "I'm Fen."

"'I bet you are," he said.

'She scowled. "Fen," she repeated. "It's Mandarin. It's pronounced like 'fun' but spelled F-E-N."

"'Ah, OK. Shall I call you Fen to rhyme with hen then?"

"'No, thank you," she said and, replacing her headphones, went back to her puzzle.

'Josh turned to stare out of the window, but I guessed he wouldn't be able to keep it up for long. The view was of never-ending white as we crept along.

'I rummaged in my bag for my knitting.

"'Hope you don't mind," I said to William. "It's socks on a circular needle so I should be able to keep my elbows to myself."

"'Knit away, dear heart, knit away." He seemed distracted, his eyes wandering from his script, no longer reading it out loud.

"'Did you say you were onstage tomorrow night?" I asked as I checked my stitches and began the knit two purl two rib where I had left off. It was the second of a pair and I hoped to get them finished in time to give them to Jenny's husband on Christmas Day.

'I'm sure you'll understand, Miss Garnett,' Mrs Linden said. 'The demands on a craftswoman at this time of year.'

'Indeed,' said Dinah, who was wrestling with yet another leg of her unicorn, which to Mrs Linden's eye looked no nearer completion.

She continued her story.

'William sighed. "Final dress rehearsal tomorrow afternoon and then the opening performance at seven o'clock sharp. I should stress, Sabrina, that it's very unusual for me to be so ill-prepared for a role. When I was on the *Street* ..."

'"You were in *Coronation Street*?"

'A dismissive shake of his head. "*Jubilee Street*, a sitcom on one of the digital channels. I played an accident-prone ornithologist. Olivier compared my performance to a young Gielgud."

'"Laurence Olivier?" I asked.

'"Did you just drop a stitch?" he replied.

'I hadn't, but by the time I'd made sure he was explaining why he was learning his lines so late.

'"The Chamberhouse Theatre panto has had the same dame for twenty years. Never missed a performance. He was all set for this year. They've been in rehearsal for months. Then just like that," he snapped his fingers, "he's come down with something awful, paralysed with pain. Bed-bound, the poor man. There was an understudy of course. Never called up in twenty years, he was not only taken by surprise, but the local rag revealed that he was about to be named in a historic scandal. Not sure of the details but the upshot is they needed a new dame." He paused to scratch his nose. "As it happened, I'd bumped into the original dame and his agent, Becky, a few days before he took ill. She put a word in for me at the Chamberhouse. Convinced them I was the man for the job. They sent me the scripts and here I am. Next stop the London Palladium."

'"Nah, mate," piped up a voice from behind us. "Next stop's

266

Taunton." I looked through the gap between the seats. The man behind us was nearly falling into the aisle at his own joke.

'"Had you planned to come by train?" I asked William, remembering Josh's reference to the rail strike.

'He shook his head. "My contract, for reasons known only to the Chamberhouse treasurer, doesn't run to travel expenses. Archie has, however, promised me decent digs in a B&B. He said he can almost guarantee I won't have to share with the man playing the policeman and the cat."

'"Excuse me!" The wool-suit woman's shrill voice cut through everyone's conversations. I twisted round to look. She was tapping Fen sharply on her shoulder. "Would you mind turning your music down please?" She was speaking very slowly even though she had heard Fen speaking perfect English. "Your headphones aren't doing a very good job. The constant buzzing is very irritating and really rather inconsiderate."

'Fen removed her headphones and showed the woman the end of the lead that had been tucked in her pocket. It wasn't connected to anything. "I'm not listening to music," she said. "I'm just wearing these to block out," she gestured around her, "the noise."

'"It's the Christmas tunes," said the man sitting behind me. He pointed at the overhead speakers. "I love me a bit of Mariah." He was waving a plastic water bottle that I was fairly sure wasn't actually filled with water and seemed about to join in the chorus, when Miss Carey's Christmas list was interrupted by the driver announcing that we would shortly be stopping for a twenty-minute comfort break.

'The stop at the services was welcomed by all. We poured off the coach like ants in search of sugar. All except for a man in a suit and tie occupying the seat behind the driver, who was still working away at his laptop. Oblivious to us all getting off the bus he continued jabbing furiously at his keyboard while simultaneously hissing into his phone. "She won't win," he said. "She's got to learn

267

there will be consequences." I thought of suggesting that a bit of fresh air might do him good but decided against it.

'There were a few groans from some passengers who had been hoping for a grander stop. The driver had chosen one of the smaller services which offered only a basic burger and coffee outlet and toilet facilities so limited that the queue for the ladies snaked out of the door.

'I found myself waiting alongside the woman in the wool suit and I couldn't help but compliment her on it.

'"Thank you, sweetheart. It's a Fianucci. From his AW12 collection, but a classic. I'll probably still be wearing it next year. Your scarf is pretty."

'It was my turquoise cashmere. My only cashmere. A gift from a previous employer and a personal favourite. I thanked her, introduced myself and began to explain why I was travelling to Exeter. She showed no interest at all and instead launched into the details of every stage of her journey since leaving Wimbledon that morning.

'Her name was Annabel Lang. "Author and agent to the stars," she said, giving a throaty laugh. "First and foremost of whom is my husband, Brian. You might recognise him. Drummer with Harlekini. Big hair, spandex? No? They almost broke into the Top Forty in 1985. Having quite the revival actually off the back of my memoir *Life with a Rock God*. We've been extremely busy. Got a big book signing in Exeter tomorrow. If we ever get there, that is."

'It was a much cheerier, relieved and refreshed group of passengers that reboarded the bus. The evening was drawing in, with heavy clouds threatening more snow but the driver seemed more chipper too. "Only eighty more miles of snow-covered motorway and the Met Office is warning of storms and power outages," he said. "What could possibly go wrong?"

'William was resealing the lid of his pet carrier when I got to my seat.

'"Is she OK?" I asked. Hoping he'd taken her for a walk around. I hadn't seen him outside at all.

'"Fine, fine," he said. "The perfect travelling companion."

'Annabel was already back in her seat. Pouring herself a cup of black coffee from a sleek silver flask. "You might be prepared to pay extortionate service-station prices," she said to her husband, who was sipping from a takeaway cup. He had tired droopy eyes and slumped shoulders, far from my idea of a rock god. "But I'm not frittering away my royalties on bilgewater." Annabel inhaled the aroma of her drink, which did in fact smell better than the instant in my own flask.

'"Ah, robusta," she said, "the essence of Italy."

'"Prefer a bit of pizza meself," said the man behind me. He belched. "What I wouldn't give for a lovely slice of pepperoni and pineapple right now. Ow." He tapped at his chest.

'"Are you OK?" asked Fen, who had just returned to her seat.

'"Fine, love, just the old ticker." He rummaged in his pocket, found a small tube and tipped it into his mouth. "Be right as rain in a jiffy. Takes more than a hot-pizza fantasy to knock Lenny Wilde down."

'"Lenny Wilde?" said Annabel. "*The* Lenny Wilde?"

'"Depends which one you're after," he said.

'"Brian, Brian it's Lenny Wilde from The Wilde Ones."

'Her husband blinked his big soft eyes. "We played with you guys in Berlin, 1986," he said. "Brian," he added. "Drummer with Harlekini."

'Lenny nodded. "Crazy times." He sniffed. "Lived up to my name back then."

'"You certainly did," said Annabel, "as I've described vividly in my memoir."

'Lenny's eyes narrowed. "That right? Don't remember all the details myself."

'"No?" said Annabel. "Just as well some of us do."

"'Did someone say pepperoni? No spicy food onboard please," said the driver, who was walking down the aisle peering in the luggage racks and under the seats, presumably checking for hidden curries before we set off. "And madam, hot drinks are only allowed in a cup with a lid."

'Stony faced, Annabel tightened the lid on her flask and drained her coffee cup.

'Josh, who was drinking from an enormous plastic mug, said, "No worries mate. No hot beverages here." He pointed to his mug. "Cold and creamy protein shake. Almonds, oats." He produced a sachet from his pocket. "I can mix you one up if you like. Just add water."

'But the driver had moved back towards the front of the bus. He stopped and stared down the stairs that led to the toilet. "I suppose I'd better ..." He disappeared for a few minutes and re-emerged looking slightly queasy. "Could be worse," he said, as he hurried back to his seat.

'We made slow progress as the bus journeyed through the blanketed landscape of North Devon. We eventually pulled into Taunton, where most of the passengers disembarked.

'My sock was progressing nicely, but William was still fidgeting with his script, occasionally closing his eyes and tipping back his head as if in prayer.

"'Are you worried about tomorrow night?" I asked.

"'No, no, not at all. It's just ..." He paused. "It's not so much remembering the lines, the double entendres, the jokes," he explained. "It's the delivery, it's the, the ..."

"'Timing," said Lenny Wilde behind us, sticking his head through the gap between the seats.

'William made a noise close to a growl and the man's head retreated sharply.

'William remained silent for a few minutes, then said, "You have to be certain that the audience is laughing with you, not at you."

'"But you're the pantomime dame," I said. "Aren't they supposed to laugh at you?"

'"To believe that, Sabrina, is I'm afraid to misunderstand the nature of the dame. Comedic, yes, but not an object of ridicule. The purpose of the dame is not to be mocked …"

'"Oh yes it is!" piped up the voice behind us. "I'm behind you," Lenny added unnecessarily.

'"As I was saying," continued William, "it is a much-misunderstood role." He returned to his script.

'Across the aisle, Josh had renewed his attempts to "help" Fen with her crossword. "Ten across," he read. "A vixen's hand covering, found in woodland in summer. Eight letters … I know, I know! Suncream."

'Fen flipped her magazine shut. The front cover had a picture of a microscope under the title *Forensics Today*.

'I was about to ask her if she was a medical student when Brian called out, "Hang on a minute. I knew we'd made an unscheduled move back there. This isn't the M5."

'We all peered out of the windows. Nothing but fields of white with trees and bushes like cotton-wool lollipops lit by the rising moon. It was difficult to tell exactly where we were, but the narrowness of the road and lack of multiple lanes indicated that we had indeed left the motorway.

'The speakers crackled with an incoming message from the driver. "A route adjustment update, ladies and gents. There was a hold-up coming that would have us stuck till halfway into next week. I've recalibrated the satnav and we're taking a bit of a back road. We will be rejoining the motorway in about five miles, well ahead of the crowd. Just a couple of lefts and rights. Did I mention I used to be a rally driver? Ha ha." There was a click and the festive tunes resumed. Was that Wham!? Never mind 'Last Christmas', I was just hoping we'd all get to our destinations in time to celebrate this year's.

'The bus was crawling along. William appeared to be snoozing. I carried on with my knitting. Across the aisle, Fen reopened her magazine. Ten minutes later I heard Josh say, "Cobalt? Cerulean, Aquamarine? No too many letters, it's only meant to be seven. 'A kind of blue on a mid-March day, if 1 September is lost'. What does that even mean? And what's that at the end? 'It's a gas'?"

'"It's what people said in the old days,' Brian offered helpfully from behind. "When they thought something was funny or cool."

'Fen filled in the letters.

'"Really?" said Josh, peering at her answer. "Are you sure?"

'The bus jiggled as if the surface of the road had become uneven. Something scraped against the window, making me shrink back.

'"What, what?" It had woken William.

'"What the heck?" said Brian. "Is he taking us down a dirt track?"

'The bus swayed from side-to-side, sped up, then slowed, then my stomach lurched as I felt the whole vehicle slide. The view from the window was a kaleidoscope of black and white as the bus tilted, righted and with a final lurch that sent my wool, William's script and a multitude of other objects flying through the air, plunged downwards at the front and stopped.

'There was a silence that seemed to go on for ever but was broken by a scream from a woman with a blonde bob sitting in front of Fen. I leaned over William to see if she was hurt. In her lap there was a great big ball of mangy fur. Two glassy eyes glared above bared teeth.

'"Mirabelle," cried William. He pushed me aside, staggered across the sloping aisle and scooped up the cat.

'As he held her, I realised that the eyes weren't just glassy. They were glass. Mirabelle was a stuffed cat. However, whether

William's cat in a box was alive or dead wasn't top of everyone's minds right now as we all checked for injuries and damaged or lost possessions.

'The driver pulled himself up the aisle, grasping the seat backs as he went, apologising along the way. "Don't know what happened," he said. "Something ran across the road. I swerved to miss it …"

'"You swerved?" yelled Annabel. "On an ice-covered road you swerved to miss what, a deer? A weasel? Why didn't you just drive over it, you imbecile?" William hugged Mirabelle closer to his chest.

'"You could have killed us all," continued Annabel. "I'll have you struck off. You'll never drive a public bus again."

'William placed Mirabelle on his seat. He doubled over. "I think I'm going to be sick," he said and staggered down to the toilet, slamming the door behind him.

'"Great," said Annabel. "That's exactly what we need!"'

'The bus was stuck. One by one we put on coats, scarves and hats and went out to take a look. The vehicle was tilted forward, its nose jammed in a ditch — it wasn't getting out of that hole in a hurry.

'"Not to panic anyone," said the driver, "but I've tried phoning HQ and I've got no signal. Anyone else got any?" Nobody had. I took a look around. The road was little more than a lane. The coach was skewed across it. Bare trees lined either side, their branches almost meeting in an arc above. Beyond them only fields of snow and slowly rising hills.

'"We need to get back in the bus," I said, my teeth chattering. "We'll freeze to death out here."

'Back on board, even with the door shut it didn't seem much warmer. Even though most of the seats had been empty since Taunton, we all gravitated, as much as the sloping floor would allow, to our former spots. Even Fen, who seemed particularly shaken by the experience and had allowed Josh to put his denim jacket over her shoulders while we were outside. The suited man with the laptop from the front of the bus joined us; he was holding my rogue ball of wool and Annabel's flask.

'"Do these belong to any of you?" he asked. "They must have rolled under the seats."

'Annabel grabbed her flask with a curt thank you. "Hot coffee, a cure for everything." She sat down on her lopsided seat and poured herself a generous cup, resealed the lid and took a sip. "That's better," she said.

'I remembered my toffees, found them in the bottom of my bag and handed them round. Lenny Wilde offered me a swig from his "water" bottle in return. I declined but William took a nip. He was clutching Mirabelle to his chest. He still looked nauseous.

'The woman whose lap Mirabelle had landed on had recovered her composure and asked, "How long is it since she passed?"

'"Thirty years next April," said William. He looked at the animal fondly. "I stuffed her myself. It's my day job, taxidermy. Started as a hobby, but between acting jobs it pays the bills."

'Annabel was looking at him oddly. "Have we met before?" she asked.

'"I'm sure I would have remembered," he said drily.

'"Maybe it was in another life," said Lenny, who was looking despondently at his almost empty bottle.

'"An actor?" Annabel said.

'William nodded. "William DeMarco at your service."

'"Have I ever represented you, auditioned you? Bumped into you at one of those luvvies' bashes?"

'"Absolutely not," said William.

'"Ever been a rock god?" she tried.

'"No," said William. "Maybe I just have one of those faces."

'It was the beginning of a long night. The driver, whose name was Arnold, assured us that when we didn't turn up in Exeter on time the police would be alerted and someone would come looking for us. Failing that, someone might drive along the road. "I've put out warning triangles front and back, just in case." Until then we had to just wait it out. He found some emergency blankets stashed in the luggage area and we each took a couple for our makeshift beds.

'One by one we fell into some sort of sleep. The tilt of the bus made it hard to get comfortable, although before darkness fell we had spread out among the available seats and I was using my scarf to soften my pillow. I could hear Fen and Josh whispering together. Was this the start of a romance?

'Then I heard Josh saying, "Twelve across — there's a spelling mistake. 'A final draught, sew up and secure'. That's not how you spell draft, unless it means a windy one. So the second bit might be about the sails on boats. No, I know sewing patterns, you might draft them. We should ask Sabrina. She's the crafty one."

"'Shut up," said Fen, "and go to sleep."

'Morning, when it came, was dull and grey, but at least the snow had stopped falling.

'Two men in hiking gear, who had so far kept themselves to themselves at the back of the bus, said they were going to set off walking to try to find help. No one tried to stop them.

'Fen rubbed the sleep from her eyes, looked out of the window and shivered. Reluctantly she began to descend the steps to the toilet.

"'Just go outside," said Josh, with one of his enormous yawns.

"'It's too cold," said Fen. "I'll hold my breath. I was the champion underwater swimmer at my school. I can do this." Almost immediately she came back up the steps. "The door is locked. Who's in there?"

'I looked around our makeshift camp. Arnold the driver was at the front, gazing bleakly out of the windscreen. William was still asleep, clutching Mirabelle like a teddy bear. The early morning sun showed a red fuzz on his cheeks and chin.

'Lenny was outside, relieving himself against a tree.

'"It'll be Annabel," said Brian. "She had an upset tum in the night. Don't think she wanted to risk venturing outside."

'"Maybe I will just find a bush in a field," said Fen.

'"I'll join you," said Josh.

'"Eww," she said. "I don't think so."

'Half an hour later, Annabel had still not emerged.

'"Do you think you'd better check on her, Brian?" asked the woman with the blonde bob, who was called Miriam and was a paediatric nurse. She'd told us she only had two days, holiday and would have to head back to Bristol tomorrow morning.

'Brian reluctantly trudged over to the stairs, climbed down and knocked on the door.

'"Open up, Bel, there's a queue." There was no response. He banged again. "No joke, hun, getting worried about you here. Just squeak to let me know you're OK." He put his ear to the door then looked up at our faces peering down.

'"I don't think she's OK," he said.

'Lenny was all for kicking the door down. "It wouldn't be the first time," he said, rolling up his sleeves. "It's been a while though."

'Fortunately his skills weren't required. Arnold rummaged around in the big box under his seat and found the emergency key for the toilet. He held it out and we all stood back. Reluctantly, Brian took it from him, went down the stairs and unlocked and tugged opened the door. A smell rolled out that was so horrific we all recoiled. William had still been sleeping until now but sat bolt upright. "What the hell is that?"

'"It's Annabel," said Brian. He knelt and pressed his fingers to her wrist, searching for a pulse. He shook his head. "She's dead."

'"If only we'd found her before the hiking men left," said Josh as we all stood outside the bus in the snow. "They could have fetched an ambulance."

'Brian had refused to leave Annabel's body in the toilet filth. He had wrapped her in blankets and he and Arnold had carried her outside and laid her on the ground.

'"Too late for an ambulance," said Fen. "We need the police."

'"What?" said Arnold. "Ah, no, come on. I brought the coach to a standstill though a controlled slide. Nothing criminal about that. Driving on an icy road and avoiding a ferret or possibly a hedgehog. No need to bring the law into it."

'"Not to investigate the crash," said Fen.

'"Controlled slide," repeated Arnold.

'"Semantics for now," said Fen. "Though it is possible that if we hadn't … stopped. Annabel might still be alive."

'"So you're saying I killed her?" said Arnold. The rest of us gathered round.

'"I am saying," said Fen, "that somebody killed her."

'It was like someone had popped an icicle down the back of my jumper.

'"You're joking, Fen," said Josh, though his voice was unsteady.

'"This is no time for comedy, young lady," said Brian, standing beside the blanketed body of his dead wife. "How can she have been murdered? I mean, there's only us here."

'We all glanced at our fellow passengers in horror and dismay.

'Miriam, the paediatric nurse, was kneeling by the body. "Her skin is red and swollen, lips blue." She leaned in closer and sniffed. "Had she recently eaten garlic?" she asked Brian.

'"She'd eaten nothing for twenty-four hours," he said. "It was one of her fasting days. All she had was black coffee." He looked round apologetically. "She can get a bit edgy when she's hungry."

"'Was she nauseous in the night?" asked Fen. Brian nodded. "Any other symptoms?"

"'Only the upset stomach. And she had to get up a couple of times to walk up and down. She had chronic pins and needles in her arms and legs, and then cramps so bad she couldn't move. No wonder, squashed up on these seats."

"'I don't think it was the seats," said Fen.

"'Hey," said Josh. "Are you a detective?"

"'No," said Fen. "Psychology student with a minor in forensics. Looks like a classic case of arsenic poisoning to me."

"'What!" spluttered William. "In this day and age?"

"'Does sound a bit Victorian," said Brian. "Didn't they get it from flypaper back in the day and poison their victims slowly over weeks? Harlekini almost had a hit with a song called 'What's Your Poison?' You might remember it?"

'Nobody did.

'Fen continued. "It's more subtle when administered over time. Harder to detect. But in the right dose it can be a quick weapon. For a killer who doesn't want to waste time, or perhaps an opportunity."

"'But who carries lethal doses of arsenic around with them?" I asked, wishing I was back home with Linden, feet up on a pouffe, my beloved bringing me a plate of buttered crumpets and a pot of tea. A fantasy, but a comfort, nonetheless.

"'It could have been any one of us," said Fen matter-of-factly. "We were all in close proximity to the victim." She looked at Brian, at Lenny, at Arnold the driver. Even at me. "She was an unpleasant woman. I didn't like her. She basically told Josh he was a slob. Maybe he did it. Maybe it was all of us."

'We were standing almost in a circle. It was like a grim version of that kiddie's game, Wink Murder. I didn't dare catch anyone's eye in case I was next. Lenny threw his empty drinks bottle into the centre.

'"Maybe we're all done for," he said. He pressed his hand to his stomach. "I've been feeling a bit gippy. Are we going to start dropping like flies?"

'Everyone moved imperceptibly further apart, widening the circle.

'"Talking of which," said Arnold, "where's the flypaper?" He seemed the most relaxed of us all. Perhaps murder was an occupational hazard of an intercity coach driver. "'No flies on us' was once considered for the BigBus slogan, you know. But somebody up high said we couldn't get away with it. Because sometimes there are flies."

'Ignoring his diversion, Fen said, "The question of where the arsenic came from is a good one. I don't think this killer used flypaper."

'The temperature seemed to have dropped several degrees. William and I both still had blankets over our shoulders. I hugged mine tighter.

'"Where is Annabel's flask now?" asked Fen. "If she consumed nothing else all day, that must be where the poison was."

'Josh and Brian volunteered to go back into the bus, but despite a thorough search they failed to find the flask.

'"It could be anywhere out there," said Arnold, indicating the surrounding fields and trees. "Thrown in a drift, probably. That's what I would have done if I was the killer. Not that I am."

'"Guilty till proved innocent," said Lenny. "I had that on a T-shirt once." He was still rubbing his stomach.

'"When the coach crashed—" began Fen.

'"A controlled slide with the vehicle brought to a safe stationary position," interrupted Arnold.

'"In a ditch," countered Fen, continuing, "When the coach slid into the ditch, Annabel's flask rolled the length of the bus.

279

There was half an hour of chaos after the crash when anyone could have accessed it. It was eventually returned by you." She pointed at the man in the suit.

'All eyes were fixed on the businessman who had been silent up to now, clutching his laptop in much the same way as William clutched Mirabelle.

'"You were very angry about something a woman had done," I said. "When we stopped at the service station." I remembered his red face, his fingers jabbing his keyboard. "You said there would be consequences."

'"And you and Annabel had a bit of chat," the driver remembered. "When she came down to complain. I could see you reflected in the mirror. You told her to keep the noise down and then ended up having an intense discussion. You both looked so stressed out I thought you were going to gang up on me."

'"Alright, alright," said the man. "Yes, we spoke, but it was the first time I'd ever met the woman. I didn't even know her name until she'd died. And I didn't tamper with her flask." He blew out through his lips. "I was angry, am still angry, because my ex-wife is trying to fleece me for every penny I own. This suit, this laptop, my ticket on this wretched bus taking me back to live with my parents. They're all I've got."

'"So why was Annabel talking to you?" asked Josh.

'The man glanced at Brian. "She wanted some advice."

'"What kind of advice?" Brian asked warily.

'"On how to get the most from divorcing her husband. She overheard me talking to my lawyer about how Gemma was going to get everything. She wanted me to tell her all my ex's tricks. For future reference, she said. Sorry, mate."

'"I don't think it was you," said Fen. "Unless you and Brian concocted between you a 'Strangers on a Bus' scenario and he is going to do away with Gemma later. No, the poison is the key. When the coach crashed or slid," she eyed Arnold warily, "into this ditch, it did rather let the cat out of the bag." She looked pointedly at Mirabelle.

'Fen then produced the *Forensics Today* magazine she had been reading yesterday. "I finished the crossword." She turned to Josh. "And no, I'm sorry, Josh, the answer to the final clue, 'Biblical smiter sent by God, sounds like a fun guy', was not Thundering Joker. I moved on to an interesting article about historical poisons. Until the eighties, apparently, arsenic was commonly used as a means of preserving stuffed animals. You said you've been in the business for many years, William."

'"A second string to my bow," said William, though he looked concerned.

'I looked down at Annabel's body, which had been wracked by paralysing cramps in the night.

'"The other dame," I said to William. "The one you stepped in to replace. You met him and his agent a few days before he fell ill. Did you go for a drink, a meal?" William was edging towards the front end of the coach. He stumbled on the icy snow. As he steadied himself, his grip on Mirabelle loosened and Annabel's silver flask fell to the floor.

'Lenny laughed. "Your pussy's let you down there."

'William tottered backwards. "Nobody laughs at William DeMarco," he cried. "They laugh *with* me, not *at* me." He turned and started to run.

'We followed him out, knowing he wouldn't get far. He didn't even try. When he reached the ditch he began to clamber up the sloping side of the bus. "They laughed at me at school," he gasped, panting as he climbed. "When I was Willy Cromer. Annabel called me Ginger Willy." He mounted the roof on his hands and knees and paused for breath. "We were fourteen. I made her a Valentine's card with a poem in it. I signed it with an X, but she knew it was me. She stood on the desk in our form room. Vetiver and damask roses, the perfume she pinched from her mother." Tears streamed down his cheeks, catching on his red five-o'clock shadow. "She read out my poem and turned it into a joke, turned me into a joke. Well, she's not laughing now, is she?"

'He stood up, wobbling precariously, his blanket spread out behind him like a cloak. He held Mirabelle up high.

'"If we are marked to die," he began, "we are enough, to do our country loss; and if to live, The fewer men, the greater share of honour. You can rely on me to keep the British end up."

'"Well, he started off quite nicely with the Shakespeare. From Henry V's 'St Crispin's Day' I think," said Brian. "But that last bit was more bawd than Bard."

'"Tell him his pranks have been too broad to bear with," William continued.

'"Ah he's moved on to *Hamlet*," said Brian. 'Quite appropriate, really."

'"And that your grace has screened and stood between, Much heat and him," William cried. He paused. "Did you hear about the bra factory? It went bust!"

'He was still at it when the police arrived, preceded by a snow plough.

'"Looking for a double entendre, officer?" William called from his height. "Come over here, I'll slip a quick one in."'

There was a shocked silence in the kitchen, broken by a snort from Barney and a raucous guffaw from James.

'Mrs Linden,' said Dinah, 'I didn't know you had it in you.'

'As the bishop said to the actress ...' Mrs Linden replied.

PUZZLES

Goose eggs

Five clues from Fen's cryptic crossword are included in the story. Unlike Josh, did you get any of the answers right? Here they are again. And remember the puzzle was in a copy of *Forensics Today*.

1. Beautiful Italian woman, but is she a plant? (10)
2. A kind of blue on a mid-March day, if 1 September is lost. It's a gas. (7)
3. A vixen's hand covering, found in woodland in summer (8)
4. Biblical smiter sent by God, sounds like a fun guy (10, 5)
5. A final draught, sew up and secure (7)

A Puzzle of Two Cities

The BigBus Express company has routes all over the UK, including between the pairs of cities described below.

Can you name the two cities in each case? The distance between the two has been given as an extra clue.

1. The 'intrusive igneous rock comprising chiefly quartz and feldspar' city, which lies 440 driving miles north of the burial place of the last Plantagenet king.
2. A city represented by two metal birds with sprigs of seaweed in their beaks 145 miles away as the crow flies from a city that was the birthplace of an actor and director, who named his 2021 Oscar-winning film after it.

3. The home of a bridge built in 1906, which is one of only six working transporter bridges in the world, lying 130 driving miles from the UK city that claims to have more bridges than Venice and a longer shoreline, around its lakes, than Jersey.
4. The UK's first UNESCO City of Music, which lies 415 driving miles from the city that William the Conqueror's Domesday Book was originally named after.
5. The BigBus Express Company PLC has recently expanded its operations into international travel with the creation of BigPlane.com. Continuing its tradition of providing intercity travel, it has just launched its route between these two cities: an English cathedral city home to Dragon Hall, Strangers' Hall and a street called Tombland and one of the UK's newest cities, 3,685 miles away, whose local newspaper is the 'Penguin News'.

Final Puzzle Clue #10

The clue that you need to take forward is the name of the city among those in your answers that lies 275 miles south of Bracestone House, which itself stands in the middle of the North York Moors.

IT'S ELEMENTAL

'What are you doing?' Rose's face appeared so suddenly in his camera lens that Barney almost dropped his phone.

'Don't do that,' he said. 'You've spoiled it now.'

'Spoiled what?' asked Rose, turning to the low garden wall that Barney's phone had been focused on.

Barney sighed. 'There was a crow on there. I was filming it.'

'Why?' Rose rubbed at her nose. 'It's literally freezing out here and you haven't even got a coat on.'

'Who are you, my mum?' Barney asked, annoyed that she could rile him so easily. 'It was really dramatic,' he continued, determined to avoid an actual argument. 'Black crow, melting snow.'

'Is this for your folk horror film?' she asked.

Barney looked away. 'I've sort of shelved that one for now,' he said. He slipped his phone into his jeans pocket.

'Can you even make a film just on your phone?' Rose asked.

'You can on this beauty,' he replied, tapping his pocket. 'I do all the editing once it's loaded on my laptop. I showed some of the stuff I filmed with your grandad last year to Helena and Dinah. They said it looked really professional.'

'How kind of them,' said Rose teasingly. 'So if it's not a folk horror, what is it?'

'It's a bit too soon to talk about it,' he said evasively.

'Aw, come on. I've seen you mooching around the house, filming people without them knowing. Which by the way is probably illegal. What's going on?'

Barney shoved his hands in his jeans pockets. She wasn't going to like it, but she wasn't going to stop badgering him about it, he could tell.

'It's just, us all being here and the place having such a cool atmosphere … it's a really good opportunity to maybe capture something unique.'

'Unique?' she said, folding her arms over chest. She was wearing the huge crocheted cardigan again, which he thought, along with her shaggy dyed hair, made her look like a puffed-up tropical bird.

'OK, so I know Edward was your grandad and the whole thing over his death is a bit sensitive.'

'Sensitive? He was bludgeoned to death and the police still haven't found his killer.'

'Exactly,' said Barney. 'So I'm doing some filming in the house where it happened, which might help …'

'You're turning my grandpa's death into a true crime documentary?' she interrupted.

'Sort of.'

She glared at him with eyes that now seemed more like those of a bird of prey.

'I mean, I know I'd have to get the family's — that is, yours and Helena's — permission. But!' He raised his hand to stall her protest. 'It might help find his killer.'

'How?' asked Rose.

'Your grandad hired Sara to investigate and she was invited here to snoop on us this week. So either he thought one of us was out to get him or his solicitor thinks one of us did it. Either way, my footage could provide some crucial evidence.'

'And has it?'

He looked down at the patchy snow by his feet. 'Not yet.'

'You really shouldn't be filming people without their knowledge,' said Rose.

'Yeah, you already said. And I had that lecture at length from my dad, yesterday. And from James. Though I think that's because he was worried I'd got an unflattering angle of him. He was in the front parlour, crouched over one of the settees scrabbling behind the cushions. Those jeans he wears are really tight.'

'What was he doing?'

'Said he'd lost his phone. But I dunno, I think he and your Aunt Helena have been trying to find "the lost will".'

'It's not lost,' said Rose. 'It's just not been read yet.'

'But your grandad might have kept a copy in the house. Maybe they want to get a read of it before tomorrow.'

'Hmmm, Aunty Hels has been a bit antsy. When she'd had too much wine the other night she told me that this time last year Jon said if they didn't find somewhere for their precious centre in the next twelve months, they'd have to try in Iceland instead. He reckons it would be easier over there and the tourists would love it. She loves puffins and hot tubs, but she doesn't think she could survive the winters. Especially if Jon tried to make her take up Nordic skiing.'

'He's not camera shy,' said Barney. 'He fancies himself as a bit of a silver-fox model.'

They both laughed.

'I got some excellent shots of Linden the other day,' Barney continued, glad that Rose no longer looked like she wanted to peck him to death. 'You know how he lurks in the shadows all the time?'

'I know, right! I mean, what is he doing?'

Barney shrugged. 'I don't know, but Mrs L went bananas.'

'She caught you filming him?'

'Yeah. She accused me of "mocking a defenceless old man"' –
he made an attempt at a Geordie accent – 'then stood next to
me as she made me delete the whole piece.' He huffed. 'She was
proper scary. I reckon if I hadn't wiped it there and then she'd
have confiscated my phone.'

'But you saved a back-up, right?'

'Yeah, of course. I'm not a complete noob.'

★ ★ ★

'I can't believe it's our last night,' said Judy, after their final
evening meal. 'It's come round so fast.'

'The big reveal tomorrow,' said Stuart from the depths of his
favourite armchair by the fire.

'Are we out of stories?' James looked around the room.
'Barney, we haven't heard from you yet.'

Barney, who had been at the desk, hunched over his laptop,
looked up guiltily. 'What have I done now?' he asked defensively.

'It's what you haven't done,' said Stuart. 'Do you have a story
to contribute?'

'Oh, that.' Barney closed down his computer. 'Well, unlike
most of you clumsy lot, I haven't stumbled across any dead bodies
in my life so far.' He grimaced. 'But that doesn't mean I haven't
got a story. I did some rummaging through the books in here the
other day.' He walked over to one of the shelves. 'Here's the one.'
He pulled out a leather-bound volume and read out the title: '*True
Tales of Mystery and Wonder*. It's pretty ancient, from the twenties
or something. Most of the stories are a bit dense and worthy but
there's one that's not too bad. I could read it if you like.'

'What's the alternative?' asked Stuart drily. 'Endless and
pointless speculation about Edward's will?'

'Go on, Barney, read your story,' said Helena. 'At the very
least it will take our minds off tomorrow.'

'OK, but I need to sit in the big chair by the fire,' he said.

'And let's switch off the lights and just have a single candle illuminating my face. This story needs some atmosphere.'

Stuart obligingly got to his feet and let Barney take the chair. 'You'll be demanding a pipe next,' he said as he slumped onto the sofa.

Barney made himself comfortable, the candle was lit on the mantelpiece and all the other lights were extinguished. 'You're right, I could do with a pipe,' he said. He tilted his chin in a dramatic pose and stroked his short beard. 'And maybe a glass of brandy.'

'You'll do as you are, son,' said Stuart. 'Come on, get on with it.'

Barney opened the book at a page he had previously marked with a train ticket, and started to read:

'The new century had barely begun when my Great Uncle Monty departed this world and I became the owner of Dampford Hall on the edge of the Dark Peak. My first sight of my inheritance was on an appropriately dank and misty morning. I had taken the train to Buxton the day before and spent the night at a simple but amenable inn. The landlord's son took me onwards in his cart at first light. I had scarce any luggage, having left London with only a single change of clothing, my notebooks and a photograph of my parents taken a few years before they both passed. Death was on my mind as we crested a small hill and looked down on the dark gables of Dampford Hall.

'My arrival was expected. The impressive front door was opened by Uncle Monty's manservant, Rhodes, who led me into the tiled hallway where the rest of the small body of staff were assembled. He introduced me to Mrs Durham the housekeeper; Cook, who apparently had no name of her own; the gardener, a sturdy man of middle age called Young Joe; and Bessie, a sweet-faced child who looked barely old enough to be out of school and bore the burdensome title of Maid of All. Only Cook smiled. As she bobbed her welcome, she said, "There's eggs and ham ready when you are, sir."

'I was unaccustomed to being "sirred". The past ten years had not been kind to my parents or to me. Even their death in a railway accident the previous year had not prompted my mother's uncle to extend a familial hand or a modicum of financial support. I had worked my fingers to the bone to fill my pantry and keep a roof over my head.'

'Sounds like a good lad,' said Stuart, with a knowing look at his son. 'Sorry, sorry, do go on.'

'… a roof over my head,' repeated Barney. 'When I was notified two weeks ago not only of Uncle Monty's death but also of his bequest that left his entire estate to me, I felt both relief and anger at the delay in his generosity. The solicitor in Buxton had muttered platitudes about Montague Archer not being a believer in handouts or mollycoddling. "He earned his success the hard way," he said, glowering across his desk at me in my best and only jacket, worn thin at the elbows and cuffs. "He believed that rising singlehandedly above life's tribulations was the proper test of a man. But," and he appraised me with eyes that found me wanting, "he had to leave his worldly goods to someone. As he was not a believer in charity or political organisations, he reluctantly elected yourself, the only child of his niece, the last of his family, as his sole heir." I gritted my teeth, determined that my good fortune would not be tainted by the spirit in which it had been bequeathed.

'Rhodes showed me to my rooms, a spacious suite overlooking extensive and well-maintained lawns. I left my small canvas bag, dwarfed by the opulent soft furnishings and heavy furniture, and went in search of the promised breakfast. Once I was replete, Rhodes led me from the dining room to the study – "Your Great Uncle's favourite room," he said – where a welcoming fire blazed in the hearth.

'With the staff all flitted away back to their own domain ("ring the bell if anything further is required, sir") I sank into an armchair by the fire and felt overwhelmingly at peace. The chair was comfortable, the fire warming, my belly full. My feet in their many-times-darned socks luxuriated in the thick pile of the oriental rug. There was a silence to which I was unaccustomed. In my previous lodgings, an attic room in a Smithfield terrace, there had been constant clomping of feet on the stairs, voices calling from without and within, street hawkers ringing bells, dogs barking. Here there was only the soft crackle of the flames and my own contented humming of a song from my childhood that had seemed lost but now, unbidden, returned.

'My contentment continued through a day of pleasant exploration and discovery. Arraying myself in a fine greatcoat, a bowler and an ivory-topped cane, found in a cloakroom off the entrance hall, I undertook a tour of the gardens around the house and admired my estate's furthest reaches from the vantage point of the terrace. After a lunch of venison and roasted plums (I complimented Cook on her skills and she thanked me for being "a gentleman that shows his gratitude"), the weather had turned inclement. I decided to stay indoors and roam the corridors and rooms of the house. Several had been closed off with sheets covering the furniture, but I found with delight bedrooms hung with Chinese wallpaper, several well-equipped bathrooms, and a small ballroom complete with chandeliers. At the end of my tour I entered the Long Gallery, where instead of a line of noble ancestors my self-made great uncle had hung paintings of horses and hunting dogs that he had presumably once owned and a rather grim study of the steel manufactory in Sheffield that had been the original source of his wealth.

'The only fly in the ointment of an otherwise enjoyable day was an incident that happened shortly after dinner. Though "incident" would have seemed, at the time, too strong a word.

After another delicious repast from Cook's repertoire, this time a steak and kidney pie served with roast potatoes and greens, I returned to the study, planning to read one of the many volumes from its shelves. As I opened the door, I noticed an unpleasant smell. On entering the room I was met by a miasma of smoke and to my horror saw that a coal had leapt from the hearth and was merrily burning a hole in the pink and gold tufts of the rug. I rushed forward and began stamping on the flames. A move I instantly regretted as the red-hot coal burned through the sole of one of my borrowed slippers. My cries alerted Rhodes and Mrs Durham who came to my aid, armed with a soda siphon and a carpet beater.

'I spent an uncomfortable night, in spite of my plump pillows and Egyptian cotton sheets, my foot wincing whenever I shifted position. But morning broke through my window full of promise. I collected Merrylegs from the stable and rode out in the unexpected sunshine to explore my terrain. So became the pattern of my days for the next week. I was pleased with all I saw. Both house and grounds appeared in good repair. Although a slate slipped from the stable roof one afternoon, spooking Merrylegs so badly I was almost thrown. I suffered the second injury of my stay the following day when my bedroom casement slammed shut on my fingers when I was adjusting the catch. On such a still windless night too.

'On the sixth day after I had taken possession of the hall, I encountered a stranger by the knot garden. Surly faced, leaning on a spade, he stared at me for several moments before standing upright and doffing his cap.

'"And you are?" I asked.

'"Abel Jackson," he said, then adding gruffly, "sir." I had become in such a short time used to automatic deference that what I may only weeks ago have accepted as normal behaviour, I now considered bordering on insolence.

'"Where's Young Joe?" I asked.

'"Taken ill, with a fever ... sir." He scratched behind his ear. "Rhodes is my Dad's brother's son. He asked me to fill in, till Joe's back on his feet, like. That alright with you, sir?"

'I didn't see that I had any choice.

'Two days later, over my usual breakfast of eggs, ham, marmalade on toast and a very fine coffee, Rhodes informed me that Young Joe had sadly passed away from his illness.

'"It must have been a fearsome fever," I said. He had seemed in such robust health on the occasions I had seen him at work. Although I'd barely known the man, it added a fourth death to my register. One more, I thought gloomily, and I would have a full hand.

'I dearly wished I had not given space in my mind to such a dark notion when the very next day I was told by a placid-faced Mrs Durham that Bessie, the "Maid of All" had passed in the night.

'"I did not even know she was ill," I said, pushing aside my coffee cup. "Is there some sickness or malady at loose in this house?" Were we all likely to succumb? I gazed with a queasiness in my stomach at the glistening eggs on my plate.

'I was not to worry on that account, my housekeeper assured me. The maid's illness was not of the physical kind. Little Bessie's departure from this world had been by her own hand, with the aid of a rope slung from the rafters in her attic room.

'Dear reader, from the distance of the page to your mind, your thoughts to me are clear. The catalogue of injuries and deaths were mounting, I should cut my losses and leave this fateful place. Pack up a few items I'd already noted to be of value and arrange for the sale of the building and land through the solicitor.

'Indeed, if I had left Dampford Hall that day with my pockets empty and my bag containing only the shirt and breeches I had carried there, I would today be a happier man.

'Why did I stay? The new gardener notwithstanding, the remaining staff treated me with a warmth and respect that I had not encountered since the loss of my parents. I had not wanted for friends in London, but they had on the whole been mere acquaintances, with families of their own to take up their time, or drinking companions who outside of the conviviality of the tavern offered little in the way of true company.

'At Dampford Hall, in spite of the recent unsettling occurrences, I felt accepted, even needed. I felt at home. In addition, I had developed a growing interest and feeling of connection with Uncle Monty's study and the contents of its bookshelves.

'While his business empire had been built on the solidity of steel and its many uses, it appeared that outside of his factories and offices Montague Archer had developed an interest in the esoteric and the supernatural. One book in particular from his shelves had kept me enrapt over several evenings. Entitled *On the Nature of Elementals*, it covered all aspects of the manifestation of spirits and the fragile veil between this world and the next.

'It was reading these pages and studying the arcane symbols and devices, a glass and a bottle of port from Uncle Monty's cellars to hand, that I passed many a rainy afternoon and evening over the next few weeks. Damp chilly January had evolved into an unashamedly wet February that steadfastly refused to open its doors to the hope of spring.

'I was regularly accompanied on these occasions by a white and tan terrier by the name of Jimmy. He had belonged to Young Joe and after his owner's passing had been allowed to sleep on a rug in the corner of the kitchen fed on scraps by Cook. The first time he made his way up to my study (yes, it was mine now, I accepted it), Mrs Durham was apologetic. She scooped him up under her firm arm and promised he wouldn't be allowed to escape again. When he gave her the slip a second time and took

294

up his new favourite roost between my chair and the fire, I told her not to disturb him. Thereafter he was a regular visitor, his quiet snoring an acceptable background to my reading.

'There had been no further unpleasant occurrences since the death of Little Bessie. Her funeral at the church in Nether Dampford was poorly attended. In addition to the vicar, myself and Mrs Durham at the graveside there was only her father, a widower who trembled as his daughter's body in its plain cheap coffin was lowered into the ground, and his sister, an older woman whose clothes and hair were in disarray and who kept asking what was happening.

'It was almost a month after that sad day, a late February morning when a gale was battering the windows of the breakfast room and I was resigned to once again postponing a ride, that a deeply unnerving event occurred that brought back to me vividly all that had gone before.

'Looking out through the window at the rain-sodden patio and lawn I noticed something that resembled a discarded cloth at the edge of the terrace, just before the ground sloped down to the pond and fountain below. It had not been there, I was certain, when I had looked out on the same view from my bedroom earlier that morning. The white bundle was blotched with brown. With a growing sense of unease, I threw on my greatcoat and boots and hurried outside.

'As I drew closer it became clear that the motionless brown and white heap was streaked with red. With my heart pounding, I ran toward it, certain to my soul that my small friend Jimmy the terrier had come to harm.

'Relief flooded my body when I reached the spot. Though it was quickly replaced by curiosity and, I must admit, fear. The bundle was a white petticoat, soaking wet and dirtied with mud. The dark red streak blossoming on the wet cotton above a long rent in the fabric, I was certain, was blood.

'Mrs Durham, for whom the petticoat might have been a good fit, swore she had never seen it before. Rhodes and Cook denied knowledge of it too, the latter crossing herself while claiming she was not usually one for religion, but maybe it would help. I, for reasons that I admit included cowardice, did not ask Jackson, the hall's now permanent new gardener, if he knew of the petticoat's origin.

'After this I began to notice signs of distress and anxiety among the staff and feared that they may one by one hand in their notice, leaving me to fend for myself. The worry was beginning to affect me physically. Each morning I awoke with a headache and my digestion began to complain. Then after two days of reading alone in my study I became aware of the absence of Jimmy. Thinking he must have developed a preference for the warmth and titbits of the kitchen, I put aside *On the Nature of Elementals*, bookmarking a page about the celebrated spirit medium Leonora Piper, and went down to the kitchen. Cook said she hadn't seen Jimmy for a few days and wondered if he'd maybe run off, saying, "Animals can sense when there's something amiss in a house."

'I needed to get some answers and realised there were questions I should have asked weeks before now. Choosing Rhodes as my first source of information, I asked him what Young Joe was doing the day before he contracted his fatal fever and what was the state of mind of Bessie the Maid of All. Were she and Joe in a relationship? Did she feel she was in danger? Was she a thief perhaps afraid of being found out? To these Rhodes had basic answers. Joe was in good health until he'd nicked his thumb while deadheading the roses and a subsequent infection may have contributed to his demise. Bessie had been prone to nervous fits and had spoken of hearing noises in the night, not just outside her room but under her bed in the weeks before she took her life. I asked why I had not been told of this before.

Rhodes looked at me impassively and said that he presumed that like his former employer, I would not be interested in the mundane details of the servants' lives. Flustered, I demanded to be shown Bessie's room and to see the note that the girl had left. The latter Mrs Durham had preserved in her bureau. A simple two-line declaration:

No Oblivion this Heaven is neverending
Grief, fear or remorse notwithstanding
Only trusting Him I nobly go

'The girl had learned the basics of her lettering before she came into service, the housekeeper explained. The writing was crudely formed it was true, but the phrasing was unusual for such an uneducated child. Perhaps it was a poem she had learned at school.

'I assembled what information I had. It was sparse but I began to see an inevitability in the conclusion to which it led. There had been the unexplained displacement of objects – a rake in the garden, the hot coal from the hearth, the slate that slid from the roof, the snapping window, the bloodied petticoat. Then Bessie's final note, which, after much re-reading, I was now certain spoke less of the despair of a young woman and more of the confidence of someone who had discovered the truth of the afterlife. Great Uncle Monty may have died, but I believed his resentful spirit lingered within these walls, watching my enjoyment of his legacy and wishing to spoil it.

'I did not share my thoughts with the staff, although I felt that Cook at least might have been receptive to them. But I kept close watch, for any more signs of a hand from beyond the veil. Chapter four of *On the Nature of Elementals* described how the dead might make their presence felt. I became attuned to every unusual flicker in the fireplace, every unexplained movement of the curtains, when the windows were shut tight. I barely slept at night listening for creaks and groans from the floors, the ceiling, the doors.

'Further chapters of the now well-thumbed volume suggested that spirits whose physical manifestation was weak might engage the assistance of human agents. I thought again of the crude writing on Bessie's note. Had Uncle Monty directed the girl's unwilling hand? I pictured her attic room. The rafter from which the rope had been slung was high, beyond the reach of diminutive Bessie. Had my uncle in fact possessed another member of the household for his work? I began to watch the staff closely, particularly the gardener, Jackson. However the man never stepped indoors. He had moved into Young Joe's shack by the kitchen garden, from whose chimney a coil of smoke rose on still days. But mostly he could be found in the grounds whatever the weather, digging and weeding and smoking on his pipe.

'My vigilance eventually bore fruit but in an unexpected quarter. I had become fond of afternoon tea in the study around four o'clock. A pot of Earl Grey and a slice of Cook's rich fruit cake served by Rhodes to see me though until dinner time. One afternoon, Tuesday 4 March in the year of our Lord nineteen hundred and two, a date etched in my brain for the remainder of my life, I descended to the kitchen. It was only half past three, but my stomach was grumbling, and I fancied a sliver or two of cheese before my mid-afternoon repast.

'At the open kitchen door I stopped. Rhodes was already there, preparing my tray. I watched as he placed the pot, smaller than my usual one, next to a plate of biscuits. I was about to speak out and request that he add some slices of cheddar, when he reached up to the shelf above and removed a small brown packet. He opened it and tipped a quantity of its contents into the waiting cup.

'Suddenly all became clear. My headaches, my continued and increasing digestive cramps. I was being slowly poisoned by Uncle Monty through his agent, Rhodes. In that moment I knew I had to banish the evil from this house. My stomach griped. Had I had already ingested too much of the fatal powder? Filled with despair and fury, I summoned a strength that I feared might be the last surge of power my dying body would ever feel. I grabbed a copper pan from where it hung on the wall and swung it at my would-be murderer's head.

'He fell with a gentle thud, quickly followed by the crash and clatter of the tea tray and its contents on the tiled floor. The silence that followed was broken by a scream. I swung round still brandishing my weapon. Mrs Durham stood in the doorway, her hands to her face; over her shoulder peered Cook, who cried, "Oh my days. What have you done?"

'Mrs Durham shoved me aside and knelt by Rhodes' bloodied head. She grasped one of his limp hands.

'"Take care," I said my voice surprising me with its calmness. "There may be toxic traces on his skin. Whatever you do, don't touch that cup."

'She looked at me in horror. "What on earth are you talking about?"

'"Poison," I said. "Rhodes has been poisoning me over weeks, months." I dropped the saucepan and spread my hands looking in anger at the air around us, "Bidden by the spirit of my infernal uncle."

'"You foolish boy," said Mrs Durham, her former deference abandoned. "Rhodes is dead. You've killed him."

'"In self-defence," I protested. "It may already be too late for me." I clutched my stomach.

'"You daft bugger."

'We all looked towards the back door. Jackson the gardener scraped his boots on the step and entered the kitchen. His surly face softened as he knelt on the other side of Rhodes. "You've killed a man far worthier than you," he said. The scene would have been moving, a modern-day Pietà, if the body they were cradling was not that of what I truly believed to be a demon-possessed killer.

'"He poisoned the secateur blade that infected and that killed Young Joe," I said. "And staged Little Bessie's suicide, hanging the rope himself, writing her note. God only knows what he's done to Jimmy, dispatched him to animal heaven I don't doubt." Tears were streaming down my face now.

'"Why," asked Mrs Durham, getting to her feet and placing her hands on her hips, "would he do any of that?"

'I felt compelled to summon them to the study, to lay out my case, to share with them the knowledge of *The Nature of Elementals*, but the kitchen would have to suffice.

'"He was acting under the orders of my uncle," I explained. "Orders from beyond the grave. You have said yourselves that Montague Archer was not a compassionate man. That he was an exacting employer. What if his ghost resented not only my occupation of his house, but your continued servicing of my needs. You, Mrs Durham, Cook," I looked at the gardener who was staring in disbelief, "even you, Jackson, any of you may have been next victim of his murderous instrument."

'I looked down at the crumpled figure. "Alas, in order to save you and hopefully myself I had to silence the only person who could perhaps have told us."

'In response, Mrs Durham walked slowly across the room and rang three times on a bell beside the stove. It was connected to a wire that ran along the wall and out of a small door. The staff stairs must lie beyond, I thought. But all the staff were here.

'"Daft lad," she said softly. "That cup of tea wasn't being made for you. Rhodes was sugaring it for someone with a sweeter tooth."

'Moments later the door opened and a strange procession entered the kitchen. While I had already accepted the ghostly presence of my uncle in the house, I was not ready for the spectres that thus filed in. Led by Young Joe, his face pale and concerned, behind him Bessie, Maid of All, fresh as a daisy, not a mark showing on her slender neck and trotting at her heels, without a care in the world, the terrier Jimmy.

'The room span around me. My final death throes, I thought. Perhaps indeed I had already joined the ranks of the dead. A slap to my face delivered by Mrs Durham brought me, almost, to my senses.

'"You got most of it right," she said. "But slipped up," she looked down at the still, very definitely dead, Rhodes, "fatally at the end." She folded her arms. "Your uncle's last wish, a supplement to his will, was that you must earn your inheritance. He wanted evidence that you were worthy to be his heir. If you had run off at the first hint of trouble, the solicitor was instructed to annul your bequest. Similarly, if you had left after the sudden and suspicious deaths of your staff without trying to investigate the cause. The dognapping of Jimmy was an extra touch suggested by Cook, after you became so fond."

'"Mr Montague gave us the task of leaving a trail of clues that could, if your brain was up to it, lead you to deduce that he was the mastermind behind the scheme. He expected that you would tell either Rhodes or myself of your conclusion, at which point we would notify the solicitor who would remove all bars to your full inheritance. Instead, you let yourself be distracted by a volume of nonsense in the library that he bought as part of a job lot to fill the space."

'"But why did he need to test me at all?" I asked in despair as the full horror of the situation nudged at my unwilling mind. "I was his nephew."

'"You were the son of his hapless niece who married, for

301

love, a man who failed in every enterprise he began and left you penniless when he died," said Jackson. "He feared that too much of your father was in your blood. It would appear, tragically, that his fears had some foundation."

'Young Joe stepped forward, his face mournful, the tearful Bessie at his side. "As you can see," he said, "we are all here alive and well. There was no murder at Dampford Hall, sir, not until tonight.

'So alas, dear reader, I write this from my prison cell, a condemned man. Every word of it is true, though it stood me no good at my trial. My last night on earth, at least in my mortal shell. If the author of *On the Nature of Elementals* is to be believed I may well return and be able through the ether to warn others not to repeat my mistakes. But if there is no afterlife, if this is my last chance to speak, let me issue my warning now.

'Do not be tempted to rest in the certain knowledge that you have solved a puzzle, until you are sure you have reached the very last page.'

PUZZLE

Goose Egg

The narrator missed some of the clues laid out for him – if Abel Jackson was Rhodes' father's brother's son, they would have the same surname and Young Joe wouldn't be deadheading roses in February. Can you find the message hidden in Bessie's note that might have put him on the right track if he had spotted it?

> No Oblivion this Heaven is neverending
> Grief, fear or remorse notwithstanding
> Only trusting Him, I nobly go

An Elementary Message

Madam Lavery, a medium in a wealthy borough of London, received a spirit message while holding a séance at the home of a recently deceased Royal Society chemist. Unfortunately, the message that came through, spoken via the vocal cords of Madam Lavery, but in the voice of Sir Henry Talbot FRS, was strangely garbled.

Can you decipher it?

WEL(27)ME, MY (9)(95)(53)LY A(7)D (9)R(53)EN(110).

(53) W(53)LL (4) (35)(53)E(9), BUT W(2)N (39)(8)(92)R (8)WN (22)ME (27)M(99) WE MAY (73)L(19) (47)A(49). A S(92)R(59)I(34) T(8) ME, A MA(7) (8)(9) (21)IE(7)(6)E.

BUT, (33) (90)E AX(8)L(8)(81) A(7)D (90)E J(68)(5)(8)A (10)(23)(68) MEET (8)U(117)(53)DE OF A Z(8)(8), (16)(8) MA(39) (39)(8)(92) (4) ON T(2) PA(90) TO A

D(53)F(26)(75)NT PL(89)E.

(53)T (53)S (102)T TO(8) LA(52) TO C(1)A(7)GE (90)(85) PA(90)

I HOPE WE MEET AGAIN

Final Puzzle Clue #11

In his message Sir Henry mentions a rodent, the name of this animal is the word you need for the final puzzle, at the end of the final story.

EDWARD LUDDENHAM R.I.P.

'Murder should be simple.'

Edward Luddenham spoke solemnly to everyone assembled in the study of Bracestone House. He was sitting in what appeared to be his bedroom. His face on the computer screen grey, tired but very alive. An unknotted tie round his neck.

Barney had perched his laptop on a pile of books on the desk and hooked up a Bluetooth speaker.

'It's not that "Time Warp" nonsense, is it?' Mrs Linden had asked with a worried look at her husband standing by the door. 'I know Mr Burton is fond, but I don't think I could bear it a second time.'

'I've no idea,' said Barney. 'I only got the file half an hour ago. The solicitor bloke emailed it,' he'd added as everyone settled in their seats. 'He sent copies to all of you as well.'

'So that's what the pinging was in my handbag,' said Dinah.

'He says Mr Luddenham left detailed instructions to gather us all here on the first anniversary of his death to watch this. It's a video,' he added helpfully as he pressed a button on the keyboard and went to sit next to Rose.

'Haven't you got a remote control?' she whispered as the video started.

'No,' he hissed back.

'Murder should be simple. If it's not, walk away,' said Edward. 'If your plan is cunning, and involves luring your victim to a dangerous place they would never usually go, or persuading them to climb into a tortuous device or eat a salad made of vicious looking leaves, forget it. Or at least think again. The detectives, professional or amateur, will find the clues you have left. They will follow every twist and turn until they corner you at the end.

'I have no idea how I was killed. As I speak to you now, I am alive and well. There is no off-screen knife held to my back, no bullet heading in slow-motion to my brain. If I have drunk poison, I am not aware of it, yet. I hope whatever method my killer has chosen, it will be quick, painless, merciful, and please dear God no lingering monologue on why they had to do it. But most of all, I hope the act and the plan of which it was the culmination was fiendishly complicated. I want my murderer to be caught.

'If this film is playing and you, my friends, relatives and acquaintances, are watching it, then twelve months have passed since my death and my killer has not been caught. We can therefore assume that a certain amount of simplicity was employed. Your presence here is testament to the killer's ability to thus far elude both the police and the private investigation that Ms Slade had already begun at my request.'

Everyone in the room turned their heads to the fireplace where the elegantly clad Sara was toying with a red glass paperweight in the shape of a heart. She seemed surprised by their attention and gave a self-conscious little wave.

'I knew you would all accept my invitation for this Christmas treat. You would all have your own reasons for not being able to refuse; what may be puzzling some of you is why you were invited in the first place. *Why me?* you may well be asking, as no doubt many a murder victim has also thought, in their final moments. The answer is that regardless of the details of my last will and testament you were all invited for the same reason. I was murdered twelve months ago today, and one of you was my killer.'

There were gasps around the room and exchanged looks.

Some of those gasps sounded more authentic than others, thought Sara; some of those looks contained not only surprise but fear.

'The end of this story,' Edward continued, 'will come, if all goes to plan, with Ms Slade's disclosure of who carried out the dastardly deed. The murder itself, which I assume took place under my own roof – see the earlier rule, "Keep It Simple" – is at the heart of the story, so that only leaves me to start at the beginning.

'It was a cold November morning, the blue sky skittered with playful clouds. Air so pure and clean that I wanted to fill my lungs with it and never have to breathe anything inferior again. I was on a beach, at the edge of an obligingly idyllic teal sea laced with white foam and dotted with fishing boats. It was in that moment I knew I was going to die.

'Of course, we all know we are going to die, it is the full stop to our sentence of mortality. The exciting thing about life is that none of us know exactly how it will be punctuated. As such I did not have an exact date or timeline but standing there, my skin tingling in the autumn chill, my mind was clear at last after months of doubt and indecision. I knew not only that my days were numbered but that one of you was calculating, perhaps even counting down to the day of my demise.

'I took my daily dip; it's a hidden away cove, difficult to access and not overlooked – the perfect place for a murder, in fact. Perhaps I lie there now, my bones undiscovered. I think not, however. As I towelled myself dry and pulled on my clothes I resolved that it would be my final visit to the beach. Without looking back I climbed the rough track back to the top of the cliff and returned here to the house where I had lived for over ten years and where I was certain I would die.

'You might be asking yourselves not only how I could be certain of my fate but also why a man of my means did not take steps to prevent it. I could have upped sticks and moved to any part of the world, living incognito in Thailand, under cover in Jo'burg, in a beach shack on an island in the Caribbean. In truth, the thought of being hunted across continents wearied me. I was convinced my killer would not give up at such a minor inconvenience as me leaving this sceptred isle. But also a small part of me hoped, as we all now know, against hope, that I might outwit my nemesis. If I was going to attempt that, I might at least start with a home advantage.

'If I am to start at the very beginning, I should go back to my childhood and the wet day on a school rugger pitch when I collided with a left prop and met my new best friend. Don't panic, Stuart, I'm not pointing the finger at you. Not yet.' Edward smiled. 'Just underlining the fact that I have known some of you for much of my life. Others, Helena and Rose, for all of yours and a handful, including Ms Slade, since fairly recently. To keep my narrative, relatively, brief, I will only wind back to the day before my final North Sea dip when I received a well-wrapped parcel in the post. Underneath the cardboard and tape, cushioned inside a snug nest of polystyrene, sat a large glass snow globe. A snowy scene of course, white flakes drifted on the ground. A hawthorn tree, bare of its leaves but recognisable by its dense thorns and the unseasonal addition of white blossom. Also, a tiny metal bust of a man with his finger held to his lips. I knew him to be Harpocrates, the Greek god of silence. Between the two was a gravestone marked with my initials and two dates – the year of my birth and the year that was, at this point, winding to its end. A gravestone that suggested I had no more than seven weeks to live.

'Merely a threat, you might think, and a cowardly one at that. There was no note in the parcel. The label on the packaging indicated it had been sent directly from the manufacturer, a glass company in the Scottish Borders. I rang them immediately and was told it had been a special order. They normally refused to make single globes, their minimum order for customised items being ten, but the customer had paid extra and as their requirements were singular but fairly simple they had accepted the request.'

'A red flag, surely,' exclaimed Helena. 'Someone ordering a snow globe with a gravestone in it?'

'I asked them,' said Edward as if in reply, 'if they had been concerned by the request to include a dated tombstone.'

'Oh,' said Helena, her eyes dampening at this almost-conversation with her dead father.

'They informed me that the client had said it was a memorial to their recently deceased father.'

'No!' said Helena, jumping to her feet.

Edward smiled kindly. 'Calm down, Helena. At the moment I am merely laying out facts, not making accusations. When I asked who the client was they were understandably reluctant to betray customer confidentiality. When I convinced them I had personally been the recipient of the globe, the person on the other end of the phone said matter-of-factly that it had been posted to the same person who had placed the order, Edward Luddenham of Bracestone House. They refused, quite rightly I suppose, to tell me the name on the payment details. The police I presume could have unearthed the information. They wouldn't do so however on the whim of an old man. I was unlikely to be able to convince anyone in authority that the globe was anything more than a rather grim prank. I might have dismissed it as such myself, if the other two objects inside the globe didn't persuade me otherwise. I resolved to make a list of anyone who might also be aware of their significance and have reason to want to kill me. The list turned out to be longer than I had expected.

'I have a copy of a Baroque engraving of Harpocrates on my study wall, an academic image but one that I have probably elucidated upon when asked.'

'He did, indeed,' said James. 'It's that one.' He pointed to a small sepia image in a gilt frame, hanging on the wall between two of the bookcases. 'Spooky looking chap.'

'I deduced,' Edward continued, 'that his inclusion in the globe was a demand for my silence. As for the other item, most of you I know are aware of the story of the murder tree.

'It was told to me when I took possession of Bracestone House ten years ago. I shared the tale with Helena when she first visited and also with Rose. James and Stuart, you were interested to hear it too. James, of course, because of the local connection; and Stuart, well, you and that schnauzer of yours are always up for a good yarn. You must have mentioned it to Barney, who suggested it would make a good subject for a horror film. In case any of you are in need of a refresher, I will retell it to you now.'

Edward's face was replaced by a static image of the hawthorn tree in the garden, below the words 'The Murder Tree'. A solo fiddle scraped an eerie tune.

'I made this with him last summer,' said Barney excitedly.

The music stopped and Edward's voice began.

'One Sunday morning in June 1742, in the small church down in Salwarth, a man collapsed in the middle of the sermon. Until that moment he had been fit and well. A farmer who had been seen only the week before carrying a fat spring lamb under each arm.

'Pinned to his Sunday-best jacket was a sprig of hawthorn that his wife said had been given to him six weeks earlier by a tramp for good luck. She gave the twig to her daughter, who tied it to her hat in memory of her father. Before two months were up the girl fell ill with a sudden fever and died.

'Enough in such a small village to start rumours that the hawthorn twig, since burned by the grieving mother, must be cursed. The belief took hold, as such things are wont to do when times are hard and life is brutal and short.

'The source of the sprig was found to be the hawthorn tree that stands to this day in the grounds of Bracestone House. A mere sapling then, young and vigorous. The supposed tramp had been caught by a housemaid breaking off twigs and muttering over them words that she described as "sinful".

'The villagers demanded of the then owner of Bracestone House that he chop down the tree. He was a man of the Enlightenment, a man of reason not magic. He not only refused to cut down the tree but set his gardeners to watch it night and day. His sentinels, however, were not vigilant enough, or were perhaps open to bribery. Before long it became clear that branches and twigs had been removed.

'The next victim of the tree's "curse" was a housewife who had boasted to her less fortunate neighbours about the plentiful golden yolks supplied by her hens. When she was found dead among the scratting fowl, a sprig of hawthorn adorned her bloodstained bodice. A landowner fatally sliced by the new machinery he had tried to introduce at the expense of his farmhands, a clergyman who had preached indiscreetly against the adulterers in his congregation found dead, his mouth stuffed with feathers, and a young swineherd who had broken a local maiden's heart, drowned in his own animals' swill. Each of them had received a twig of hawthorn and before two full moons passed, had died.

'The killings trailed off over the years as the power of the story faded. It was revived somewhat in the thirties by a man who briefly lived at Bracestone House. He dabbled in the occult and thought that through the hawthorn he might be able to summon the devil. He succeeded only in killing many wild beasts, from crows to hares, and in the end himself.'

'I had thought,' said Edward, his face returning to the screen, 'that the story had reached an end too. But one final piece of information that I secured from the makers of the snow globe was that the tree inside had been fashioned by them out of a piece of hawthorn wood provided by their client. There was to be a full moon on 27 November, and after that on 27 December. My time limit was set.

'Judy,' he said. The librarian jolted in her seat. 'While you may spend your working days surrounded by books containing all manner of fact and fiction, I am a pretty certain that the story you brought to share among this select circle will have been one you told me yourself, recently. The tragedy of the boy with a compulsion to make lists. The moral of that tale not being that such a hobby is ill-advised, but rather that a promised inheritance, and in particular a perceived threat to a hoped-for beneficence, can drive an otherwise sane family member to a desperate act.'

Helena and Rose looked at each other in horror.

'My will, as it stood at the beginning of this my final year, left everything I owned to the remainder of my blood relatives. Those being my beloved daughter, Helena, and my granddaughter, Rose.

'Helena, we have not always seen eye to eye, but I would like to think our relationship has been something you will remember with love and affection. I am aware, however, that you and your Viking friend …'

Jon's head twitched, suddenly alert.

'… have been in need of both the capital and a suitable building for your, what is it again, Beingwell Centre?'

'Wellness Centre,' said Jon patiently.

'You showed me your business plan,' Edward continued. 'I picked it apart and told you to come back with something less fragile. You appeared hurt by my criticism, Helena, and accused me of being unsupportive and "too bloody conservative". Reason enough for patricide?' he asked.

Helena was staring at the screen, shaking her head, tears rolling down her cheeks.

'Rose, I invited you here rather than your mother, which I imagine caused her no end of agitation. It will be no news to you that I did not approve of my only son's choice of wife. That marriage's only saving grace was that it produced you. After Tristan's untimely death I watched as you grew into a young woman of whom he would have been ineffably proud. I had every intention of ensuring that you were provided for in my will. Have I invited you here because I think you would kill your grandfather?'

Edward leaned back in his chair and sighed. 'Or is it only that I wish to make the apology to you that you are owed and which you have refused to entertain ever since our, I am reluctant to call it a "row" as in my heart I believe it was just a terrible misunderstanding. You and Devi are currently in your room playing what I can only suppose is intended to be music. The door firmly locked, while the rest of the household are gathered around the tree in the hall singing carols. I did not include her on the invitation to this anniversary gathering, thinking to spare her another Luddenham drama.

'Your private life, my dear, is just that, private. When I made a passing comment about you being the sole hope for continuing the Luddenham line and that I hoped you wouldn't wait too long before finding a good man, it was just me being typically grandpa-ish. I hadn't anticipated your reaction. Or the embarrassment it would cause to you and Devi. Why you had chosen not to tell me before that moment that you and Devi were more than just friends, I do not know. Did you really think I would not approve that your partner was another woman? I

313

would hope you understood me better. If I'd known, I obviously wouldn't have been so thoughtless with my words. This is my apology to you, alas I realise twelve months late.'

'Thank you, Grandpa,' Rose whispered. Her eyes were shiny as she added to him and the rest of the room, 'We're having a baby.' She grinned. 'In April.' She put her hand to her flat stomach. 'Devi, not me. She's doing great, but I can't wait to see her again this evening. We know the sex and we've chosen a name: Eddie Luddenham. I knew really, Grandpa,' she added, turning back to the screen. 'I'm sorry I kicked off like that and didn't let you tell me to my face until now.'

'Ahem.' Edward cleared his throat. 'So let's get the whole inheritance thing out of the way shall we? My natural heirs, Helena and Rose, you will of course receive what I hope is a helpful sum each, including to Rose an additional legacy for any child that results from your current or future relationships. The full details are all in my will in the safe possession of my solicitor. The will also, duly witnessed and signed, states that I, Edward Luddenham, being of sound mind, do bequeath the majority of my estate including Bracestone House, its surrounding acres and a proportion of my business interests and financial investments to my beloved Mrs L.'

There was silence in the room, broken only by a babbling outburst from Mrs Linden. 'I couldn't possibly! No, no, I don't want it. Whatever would people think? No, I insist ...'

'Shh,' said Sara, pointing to the screen, 'he hasn't finished.'

There was a mischievous smile on Edward's lips. 'By which I mean of course my dear companion, lover and, for the last six months, my darling wife, Mrs Dinah Luddenham.'

This time the silence was so profound that it seemed it might never be broken. On the video screen, Edward raised a glass of port and said, 'I'll give you all a few moments.'

Helena was already on her feet, glaring at the older woman,

314

wrapped in her shawl, lap covered with yarn animals, who asked placidly, 'Is there a problem?'

'I knew it,' said Helena. 'He was acting very oddly that last summer when we came to visit. He was so dismissive of our plans and my suggestion that he might invest. He talked about other "considerations", other "interests" that he had to take into account. He meant you, didn't he? Tell me,' she almost spat, 'when did you, Dinah, owner of a third-rate craft shop in a middle-of-nowhere market town, realise that you were irresistibly attracted to my incredibly wealthy father?'

'I think it was when he came over to me at the Saltbay Folk Festival ceilidh and said that he had to find out how a woman with eyes as blue as the northern sky and a smile like an ocean breeze didn't have a partner for Strip the Willow,' said Sara, who hadn't moved from her position by the fireplace.

Helena whirled round.

'Sara?' she asked in confusion.

'Dinah actually,' the woman with grey-blue eyes replied. 'Dinah Luddenham née Garnett, technically your stepmother but don't feel you have to call me Mum. And my "third-rate craft shop" is a thriving local business with a strong online presence. It won Best Overall in the small shops category at this year's National Handicrafts Show.'

'If you're Dinah,' said James. He turned to the woman in the armchair, who had gathered up the woolly bundles in her lap and placed them on the floor.

'Sara Slade,' she said. 'Proprietor and chief investigator of Slade's Private Detective Agency, former Detective Inspector with the Northumbria Police.' She stood up and brushed strands of yarn from her skirt. 'Can I just say what an utter relief it is not to have to carry on pretending I can crochet?' She smiled at Dinah. 'You did your best, hun, but I was never going to get the hang of it.'

'*You* were giving *her* lessons?' said Rose, looking from Dinah to Sara. 'Not the other way round!'

Dinah nodded. 'I always swore anyone could learn but you are a hopeless case, Sara.'

She crouched down. 'Give me back my babies. I'll see if there's anything salvageable. Hmm.' She held up a thick pink tube. 'I promised my three-year-old niece a "cool flamingo" for Christmas. Do you think I can persuade her that worms are cool too?'

The rest of the guests watched on in silence, jaws gaping.

'You'll manage,' said Sara, who had settled back in the armchair and was very much enjoying the reactions to the news. 'And well done you for remembering all the details of my Snow Goose case. And for adlibbing the bits you forgot. It was very convincing.'

'Why the great switcheroo?' asked Stuart angrily. 'Why the deception? Bad enough having a private dick openly in our midst without you sitting there in disguise.'

'I'm hardly in disguise,' said Sara, 'this is what I always wear, unless I genuinely am under cover.' She tugged at her hair, the heavy locks coming away in her hands to reveal a neat but mousey bob. 'Though granted, the wig was a theatrical touch. You knew there was an investigator here. Did it matter which one of us it was?'

'Yes,' said Jon. 'I believe it does. One of us might have said something to you that was not intended for the ear of a professional detective.' He turned to Dinah who had her arms wrapped protectively round her slim body. 'So you're the person who had most to gain from Edward's death?'

'That's right,' chimed in Helena. 'It's not looking good for you, Dinah, is it?'

'The innocent have nothing to fear,' said Edward from the momentarily forgotten video screen. 'The majority of you do, I believe, belong to that category, in relation to my death at least. I hope you are all fully up-to-date with my marital situation and if not happy, at least resigned to it. I hope, as well, that you have given due condolences to my beautiful widow. Sorry, my darling, it is because of you that I have tried my hardest to stave off my doom.'

Dinah blew a kiss at the screen.

'Now,' continued Edward. 'I still have a few more suspects to tick off my list. With any luck before today, by which I mean my Christmas Eve here and now, is over, one of them will be apprehended, before they end my life. And this video will never have to see the light of day. Meanwhile I apologise in advance for revelations that will be uncomfortable for some. But needs must when the devil drives, to paraphrase Shakespeare.'

'Wait a minute,' said Judy. 'Could someone please press pause?' Barney obligingly jumped up. 'Didn't you investigate the snow globe thing, Sara?'

'I did,' she said. 'I even saw it for myself. There were no manufacturer's details on it, but Edward gave me the phone number he'd got from the packaging. After he was killed I told the police it might be significant. However, as the globe and the packaging it had been sent in were nowhere to be found, I wasn't convinced that they followed it up. I had rung the phone number. The call rang out and further enquiries drew a blank. It appeared that the company did not exist.'

'But Edward said he spoke to someone there,' said Judy.

'To "someone", yes,' said Sara, 'but we don't the person's name or even their sex.'

As if the word was somehow a cue, Mrs Linden re-entered the room. She must have been down to the kitchen because she was carrying a tray laden with champagne glasses and two bottles of prosecco. In her wake followed Linden, stately as

317

ever, bearing a Christmas cake decorated with miniature fir trees in one hand and a plate of Wensleydale cheese in the other.

'Thought we could do with some half-time refreshments,' said Mrs Linden, 'after all that excitement. And as a belated celebration of your nuptials, Mrs Luddenham,' she said, smiling at Dinah. 'To think he even kept the news from myself and Linden.' She shook her head. 'Never bringing you to the house. He was a man of many depths.'

Dash, apparently fully understanding the word 'refreshments', had jumped to his feet and was weaving steadily around the room as if it was a slalom course. Stuart rewarded him with a bone-shaped biscuit at the end.

After everyone had been provided with a filled glass and a slice of cake, with or without cheese, Barney restarted the video.

'I'd like to begin with a thank you,' said Edward. 'To Judy for her many years of help with my local history projects, which after my semi-retirement became almost an obsession. You seemed to enjoy the process as much as I did. I should have given you more credit and when *Notorious Northerners* comes out next year, God willing I'm granted the time to get that final chapter finished, you will be named as its co-author. It's the least I can do. I like to hope that my hitherto neglect would not alone be enough to make you want to kill me.'

Judy smiled and raised her glass to the screen, 'Thank you, Edward. It would have been an honour to have completed the book with you.'

'However,' Edward continued, 'your lack of credit wasn't your only concern, was it?'

Judy's smile wavered.

'You knew that I'd spotted you, didn't you?' Edward continued. 'That Saturday on the station platform at Middlesbrough. I thought perhaps the young man was your son. The one in the army that you always spoke of so proudly. Then you kissed and I realised, though half your age, he was your lover.

'That was the same day you introduced me to your husband. A jolly boozy lunch at the Yorkshire Rose tearooms. Strained though after I mentioned that I'd come in on the eleven o'clock train, earlier than expected, and asked if I'd been mistaken in seeing you when I'd changed trains at Middlesbrough. "Not me." You laughed. "I've been at work all morning. Must have been some other beautiful Black woman in a floral-print dress." We all laughed, Michael embracing you and saying that unless I'd seen the most beautiful black woman in the world in a flowery dress, I'd not got the right girl. Things were never quite the same between us after that and I cursed myself for having spoken up. I blame the wine, my shock at my discovery, after all your talk of family loyalty. But none of us really know, do we, what lies behind our friends' apparent contentment. The unexpected choices that people make. Are you waiting outside this bedroom right now, about to make another such choice, Judy? Are you afraid I won't keep my silence? I hope we know each other better than that.'

'It's over,' Judy protested to the room full of people she barely knew. 'I couldn't deal with the subterfuge. The guilt.'

'Still, would be awkward,' said Helena, 'if your husband found out.'

Judy raised one finely arched eyebrow.

Helena put up her hands. 'Your secret's safe with me.' She looked around the room. 'By the end of this I have a feeling we are all going to have things we want to stay in this room.'

'James,' said Edward. 'How's your book going, old chum? Hit the bestsellers chart yet? Quite a scoop for an old hack, no? A scandalous exposé of a much-loved man. We had some good times, didn't we, rootling around our respective sections of the archives? Each following our own trails, me hot on the heels of northern folk turned bad and you …?' He leaned in towards the camera. 'What exactly were you looking for, James? Your focus seemed to switch from week to week until of course your big discovery, nestled in the record vaults in Scarborough. A lost diary. Written in code, which is why nobody else had spotted its value. But once you got your mitts in it, well it will have changed quite a few perspectives on post-war British politics. "Explosive", "Revolutionary". Are those the words your publisher has put on the cover?'

Barney held up a copy of *Private Life of a Public Man* that James had artfully displayed on a bookshelf. It did indeed say 'Explosive' on the cover, as well as 'Iconoclastic' and 'Cataclysmic'.

'It was a fake though, wasn't it, James? Or at least mostly. What was the code again? Mirror writing? Done with his left-hand I think you said. I was there – do you remember? – when you found it. I only had a quick glimpse, but the entries were sparse, not chockful as in the version you made public.' Edward held up a rumpled square of yellow paper to the camera. The letters of the alphabet were printed on it in block capitals and then in lower case. 'I met you for a drink a few weeks later. You got there early and were writing on a napkin when I arrived. You squirrelled it away, said it was notes for an article. This fell out of your pocket as we were leaving. It probably looks just like ordinary writing on the screen if I'm right about how these things work, but looking at it here,' he smoothed out the napkin, 'it's obviously an exercise in mirror-writing. I imagine you kidded yourself you were just filling in the gaps. Shame those "gaps" were where all the juicy stuff was. When you got home and realised you'd lost the napkin, was that when you decided to kill me? The fear of lawsuits, libel charges, a long stretch in prison, a chapter even in *Notorious Northerners 2*?'

'James!' said Judy. 'Really? That's what you were looking for in Edward's bedroom? We've bought copies of your book for all our libraries; the reserves are off the scale. The large print edition is proving particularly popular. Is Edward right? Did you make most of it up?'

James's face was stony. 'There's no proof. It's a dead man's word against mine.'

'Rather convenient,' said Sara, 'the only witness to your fraud being dead.'

'It's a bestseller,' he said, pathetically. 'You can't take that away from me. Whatever happens.'

'I've bought you a copy for Christmas darling,' said Jon, patting Helena's knee. 'Maybe James could sign it. In mirror script of course.'

Before James or Helena could respond, Edward had begun talking again.

'Barney Yorke,' he said. 'Whatever your father might think I know that you are a very talented and resourceful young man.'

Barney looked nervous. Dash whimpered at his feet. The boy gestured for him to jump up and began to run his fingers through the dog's bristly fur.

'Film-making is a competitive field, Barney. Who knows if you have what it takes. You certainly know your way round the technology. My ideas for a series of documentary shorts, or even a full-length feature, based on my *Notorious Northerners* project have seemed more feasible since I chatted with you in the summer and we mocked-up some scenarios together. I think we share a similar aesthetic. You also showed me enough of the basics to give me the confidence to film this all by myself and to trust that when I save it as you showed me how to, I will be able to email it to my solicitor.

'You aren't relying on films about spooky trees and northern criminals to make your fortune, though, are you? Did you realise I had seen what else you've got on your laptop, Barney?'

There was a gasp from Helena.

'We'd been trying out some shots of me reading at my desk.' said Edward. 'You said it was too dark and popped out of the room to get another lamp. I was checking through the edits of what we'd recorded previously on your laptop. I must have pressed the wrong button, because what came up on the screen certainly wasn't footage of me striding across the moors in my wellingtons talking about highwaymen.'

'Oh dear lord,' said Stuart. 'Please, no, Barney. You haven't?'

Rose shifted away from the young man, who was fidgeting nervously with Dash's ears.

'Is it very bad?' Stuart asked his son gently. 'Or just a bit …'

'Just a bit what!' Helena almost screeched. 'If your boy has been making porn or, good grief, anything …' her voice dropped, 'illegal … I can't believe we've been sharing our family's house with him.'

Rose got up and went to sit next to her aunt, who put an arm round her waist.

'Itsntpn,' said Barney, his voice muffled in Dash's fur.

'Speak up,' snapped Stuart.

Barney lifted his head. His eyes hard, his teeth gritted. 'It's not porn, Dad. Jeez, what do you think I am?'

'Names,' said Edward, from the video screen, 'long lists of names with bank details, national insurance numbers, links to what looked like medical records.'

'You're a hacker?' said Rose, eyes wide. 'Oh my god! Have you been like blackmailing global organisations and threatening to bring down the internet?'

'No,' said Barney. 'It was just a bit of messing about.'

'The kind of messing about where people send you money in return for you not making their personal information public?' questioned James. 'I covered a story like this for the *Argus*. Couple of teenagers went down for ten years each.'

'Nobody died,' muttered Barney.

'I deleted the files,' said Edward. 'It was all I could think to do. I'm no tech wizard, so I didn't know if they were gone for ever. You might have made back-ups. I wanted to talk to you about it but when you came back in your laptop screen was frozen. You must have suspected that I'd tampered with it. You said it did that sometimes and you'd have to take it to a tech guy you knew to sort it. As you were packing everything away, avoiding my eyes, your father came through dangling his car keys and saying it was time you were both off. I didn't see you again until this morning and haven't had chance to speak to you today. Did you do the right thing Barney? Did you wipe your hard drive? Or have you decided to wipe me out instead?'

Sara watched the faces around her. What had begun as unease among the occupants of the room was now widening through a whole range of emotions. She saw disgust, confusion, fear and, her detection nerves quivering, among all that an unmistakeable anxiety that hinted at guilt.

Edward had continued. 'I realised reading through my list of people who might fancy taking a pop at me, that while you all might hold grievances or fears or expectations, not all of you would necessarily be willing to kill to get what you wanted. Not this type of cold, calculated, premediated kill anyway. Of course, the gift of the snow globe might just be a warning, a threat rather than a promise. I was perhaps clutching at straws.

'In addition to motivation I also examined my list for opportunity and predilection. The former I dispensed with by giving you all equal opportunity, inviting you to share Christmas with me as the clock ticked down to the second full moon. Safety in numbers? I thought witnesses too might be helpful in the aftermath, but I suspect you, whoever you are, may be too clever for that. I've even invited Dinah, who will be arriving here tomorrow in time for Christmas lunch, her first visit to Bracestone. All being well, we will be breaking the news of our marriage over the cheese and biscuits. In the less happy scenario, my solicitor will ask her to continue to keep our union a secret until it is revealed through the power of modern technology, by me. But back to the matter in hand.

'One of you, I knew, had killed before and had so far got away with it. Is there movement out there among you? Is anyone making a bolt for the door? Stuart,' he said, 'do you find yourself in urgent need of a visit to the little boys' room?'

Stuart, who had indeed partially risen from his chair, sat back down again.

'I understand, old friend, if you are feeling particularly miffed at being so late to find out about my wedding. You might have had expectations of being my best man again. A repeat performance of your hilarious speech back when we were both fresh-faced youths and I married my lovely Isobel. You'd have even more insights to give, wouldn't you, as so much has happened in the almost fifty years in between.

'You didn't ask me to be your best man when you got married the following year. A bit odd, I thought at the time, although after hearing the banal speech from one of your work colleagues who seemed to hardly know you, I got an inkling of why you hadn't asked me to step up to the role. And as your second wedding was on a Barbadian beach, I suppose a best man was the least of your worries.

'Stuart Yorke, always rising to the top of his game, but never staying there for long. Fingers in pies, without fully knowing their ingredients. Never able to be tied down about what he does for a living. You rode high on it at times, those knife-edge deals working out for you more often than not. But at what price? Did you tell our esteemed company about our trip to Andermatt? When Ben Gipal joined us? A colleague of mine, worked for me for a few years until I caught him selling copies of our R&D to a competitor. I had to let him go. Thought I'd heard the last of him. Not so, Stuart. You kept in touch, didn't you? Dropping out of your nascent law career, you found in Ben a common interest in shady deals and quick-buck schemes. Sorry, Barney, this is probably news to you. I imagine it would be news to your mother too. I wouldn't be talking about it now if it wasn't for that devil holding the reins. You see, Stuart, of all my friends and relations, you are the only one who I know for certain has killed before.'

Stuart clutched the arms of the chair. His face rigid.

'He looks like he's having a stroke,' said Mrs Linden, wafting her hand in front of his face. 'I'll fetch him a glass of water.'

'I don't know the details,' said Edward. 'When you came to me with your dilemma in June, bringing an oblivious Barney along for the ride, you said I didn't need to know the whos and whys. Only that the bad people who were inextricably bound up in your latest scheme had taken things up a notch. The long and the short of it was that you had been "forced" to take someone out. The result of which was that the bad people were demanding half a million pounds for their silence or they would send you floating down the same sewer in which you had deposited their associate. Half a million pounds, Stuart. You said it as if you expected me to have that as small change in my pocket. I observed that, while I had given you money in the past when you were desperate, this was a different order of magnitude. What did you say in reply, Stuart? Do you remember?'

'It's all sorted,' said Stuart his usually commanding voice a mere squeak. 'I got rid of them. By which I don't mean got *rid* of. I arranged a loan from elsewhere to cover it. I'm working with some other people now, not necessarily good people, but not as bad.' He looked beseechingly at Barney. 'Please don't tell your mother. I'm almost through the woods, just a couple more months and I can leave it all behind, start afresh.' He laughed nervously. 'We could maybe set up our own little film company, Barney. A couple of documentaries, some true crime ...'

'What you said,' continued Edward, 'was that if I couldn't help, you or one of your "friends" might have to take extreme action? What would you call that, Stuart, if not a direct threat? Was the snow globe just a gentle reminder?'

Stuart licked at his dried lips. 'Did someone mention a glass of water?' he asked.

'Here, have this,' said Rose, passing him her wine glass. 'This is all so horrible; I can't drink anything.'

Stuart took a long gulp. 'I was desperate,' he said. 'But I didn't kill Edward. It was an empty threat. Last Christmas, while the rest of you were singing and he was making that video, I was already in the car. We'd got a phone call from Louise, Barney's mum. There'd been an incident at our former family home, where she still lived. A brick through the window. She was beside herself. Barney, Dash and I jumped in the car and left immediately. We only found out Edward had died when we heard it on the news the next day. I was fifty miles away when he was killed.'

'It's true,' said Barney, but he was staring at his father in horror. 'You killed someone, Dad? Who? What happened?'

'Just a minute,' said Sara stepping into the centre of the room. She tapped the keyboard of the laptop; behind her, on the screen, Edward Luddenham's face froze.

'Before we discuss your father's past crimes, Barney, could we please wrap up the murder in hand? I've messaged the local constabulary and the detective who has been handling this case. If I'm not much mistaken,' she tilted her head, 'they are pulling up in the driveway as I speak. I've drawn my conclusions based on everything I've observed and heard over the last few days, adding to them my notes from my earlier investigations and the revelations brought to us from beyond the grave. Before I go on, however, let's just hear if Edward has anything else to add.' She tapped the keyboard again.

On screen, Edward Luddenham carefully wrapped and adjusted the knot of his tie. 'I will in a few moments email this video to my solicitor and join your past selves around the tree. Hopefully I'll be in time for "Silent Night". More fervently, of course, I hope that I am a foolish man speaking into a void. My words become destined never to reach your ears. This video deleted as unnecessary at the dawn of a new year. I hope that I am, in fact, celebrating a second Christmas with you all. Possibly singing carols, pulling crackers or simply hugging you each in turn. Glad to be alive. Glad to have been wrong.' His voice caught and he paused to rub a finger against his forehead. 'Only time will tell,' he continued. 'For now, over to you, Ms Slade.' The video came to a sudden stop.

'Thank you, Mr Luddenham,' said Sara in reply. She turned to the pool of expectant faces. 'In the course of my investigation I began to understand that it was not a question of who had the most to gain from Edward's death, but who had the most to lose if he continued to live.'

There was a noise from the hallway, a shout and the scuffle of feet. Unperturbed, Sara continued. 'Edward was correct in deducing that his killer would be among those assembled here at Bracestone House last Christmas Eve, although he did not want to believe that any of you would be capable of such a betrayal, or such violence. His "list of suspects" was based on the potential motives that he could clearly see, and yet by focusing on the obvious, the secrets and resentments that many of you sadly hold and of which he was fully aware, he was blinded to what should have been staring him right in the face. A deadly threat much closer to home.'

An unfamiliar voice called out, 'Through here I think.' The study door opened and in stepped a man in a suit.

There were puzzled looks and mutterings all around the room. Sensing excitement, Dash began to bark.

'Aha,' said Sara, addressing the newcomer. 'DCI Jones, welcome. You've arrived in the nick of time. If you'll pardon the pun.'

Rose got to her feet. 'You mean the person who killed Grandpa has been here all along? But who?'

She looked around at the gathering. Two people were missing.

'For that we must turn to Edward's book,' said Sara. 'His *Notorious Northerners*. He'd done some deep delving into a murky world and was getting close to uncovering a well-hidden secret. The clues were there in the work he left behind. I saw it for myself in one of the old photographs Helena found in his desk. He put himself in danger the minute he began to peel back the layers of deception. His book would have revealed a cleverly constructed lie. You can hide in plain sight, if the motivation is strong enough. And they hid behind the façade of respectability for years. But disguises can so easily slip – an unguarded look, a telling accent can be all it takes. Edward was all set to expose them. He said he just needed to put the final pieces in place. And I believe he had. With a fatal result. Am I right, DCI Jones?'

The man in the suit nodded. 'They were trying to escape when we arrived. They've got a bunch of dead bodies to their name. One more would have made little difference. Bring them in,' he called.

The door opened once more, revealing two officers, each struggling with their captive.

'Nice of you to join us,' said Sara, giving them an ironic smile. 'I think we can drop the whole charade now. Ladies and gentlemen, I present the final piece in the puzzle.'

THE FINAL PUZZLE

If you have completed all of the puzzles correctly so far you should have a list of eleven words and names. They are the key to deciphering the coded message below. In order to activate the key you will need to draw a grid like the one below, but with all the squares in the bottom row left blank.

Starting in the cell beneath 'A', fill in the letters of the words from your clues in the order that they appeared in the book. (So your first word is the answer to the main puzzle at the end of the first story.)

As you fill in the squares, do not repeat any letters that have already been used. Keep going until you have used all of the clues.

For example, if your first two clues were banana and peaches, the start of your key would look like this:

A	B	C	D	E	F	G	H	I	J	K	L	M
b	a	n	p	e	c	h	s					

N	O	P	Q	R	S	T	U	V	W	X	Y	Z

To decode the final puzzle, substitute each letter in the coded message with the letter that appears below it in your key. (In the above example key, the code word AEBFG would be deciphered as 'beach'.)

Fill in your grid with your gathered clues to decode this message and reveal who killed Edward Luddenham:

FCXINC XID ROQQFC ZH YFNNH IEC PQINI QOUF KLF LMUZFNDOCF ZBEEOF IEC PQHCF XLB LIJF ZFFE QOJOEA IK ZNIPFDKBEF LBMDF ID UND QOECFE IEC LFN PINFVMQQH DOQFEK LMDZIEC

PUZZLE ANSWERS

GOOSE EGGS AND MINI-PUZZLES

BRACESTONE HOUSE

On the card that welcomed the guests to Bracestone House, each of the letters in the coded house rule had been substituted with the letter three places further down from it in the alphabet (thus D, E and F, as indicated by the Wi-Fi code DEF123, would represent the first three letters and A, B, C would be at the end, as in the key below:

D	E	F	G	H	I	J	K	L	M	N	O	P
a	b	c	d	e	f	g	h	i	j	k	l	m

Q	R	S	T	U	V	W	X	Y	Z	A	B	C
n	o	p	q	r	s	t	u	v	w	x	y	z

So, Edward's final rule:

QR PXUGHUV WKLV BHDU SOHDVH

translates as:

'No murders this year please'

A SLIPPERY SLOPE

Goose Egg

The names you were looking for are all anagrams of traditional Christmas food items:

STUART YORKE – Roast Turkey

BEN 'STINKS' GIPAL – Pigs in Blankets

PIP SARNS – Parsnips

BEAU DASCER – Bread Sauce

HERR FLISTERY – Sherry Trifle

BENEATH THE STREETS

Goose Egg

The major tunnels to be found in the story are:

The Channel Tunnel, the Marmaray Tunnel (Turkey), Eisenhower Tunnel (Colorado, USA) and SMART tunnel (Kuala Lumpur, Malaysia)

THE MASKED CAROL SINGER

Goose Egg

The sisters share their first names with four of the Mitford sisters – Pamela, Diana, Jessica and Deborah. The name of their street is also that of a fifth Mitford sister, Unity and the novel that Pam was reading, *The Pursuit of Love* was written by the sixth Mitford sister, Nancy.

THE MAN WHO MADE LISTS

Mini Puzzle

The hidden message reads:

'Ted scares me'

THE BIG CHIP

Goose Egg

Those fictional cats hiding in Dash's story were:

Mog	– Judith Kerr's creation is name-checked repeatedly as Dash talks about the 'mogs'.
Snowball	– the Simpsons' cat(s) 'as much chance as a snowball on a barbecue' (ouch!).
Macavity	– the Mystery Cat from T. S. Eliot's *Old Possum's Book of Practical Cats*, the proud owner, perhaps, of Macavity's Grill.
Mr Bigglesworth	– from Austin Powers, the name of Lance's owner.
Felix	– the cartoon cat remembered in the name of Stuart's father, 'Grandpa Felix'.

DEATH ON THE BIGBUS EXPRESS

Goose Egg

The answers to the crossword clues are all poisons or contain toxins:
1. Belladonna
2. Cyanide
3. Foxgloves
4. Destroying Angel
5. Hemlock

IT'S ELEMENTAL

Goose Egg

The initial letters of the words in the message spell out NOTHING FOR NOTHING - a hint from Uncle Monty that his nephew would need to put some work in to earn his inheritance.

MAIN PUZZLE ANSWERS

A SLIPPERY SLOPE

A Cook's Conundrum

These are the ingredients in Hedy's biscuit recipe.

150 g	sieved plain flour
125 g	grated parmesan cheese
125 g	fridge cold butter
1 tbsp	Dijon mustard
1 tbsp	sweet paprika
½ tsp	sea salt flakes
1 tsp	ground black pepper
1 tbsp	sesame seeds

If you fancy making the biscuits yourself, mix together all the ingredients except for the seeds to form a firm ball. Roll this into a 'sausage' approx. 25 cm long and 15 cm in diameter. Cover in cling film and chill in the fridge for at least an hour.

Remove cling film and slice the dough into about 25 'rounds'. Place these on greaseproof paper on a baking tray (they will spread out slightly in the oven so leave some spaces between). Sprinkle sesame seeds on top of each one and press lightly into the dough.

Bake at 190°C for 10 minutes.

Remove and leave to cool on a cooling rack. Enjoy with a glass of Christmas fizz, or, although Charlie Sarns wouldn't approve, a nice German Riesling.

The name of the French town in Hedy's recipe is Dijon, which was the birthplace of Philip the Good.

The first word that will be needed to solve the Final Puzzle is: GOOD

BENEATH THE STREETS

Janey's Adventure Underground
the code for the keypad at the bottom of the steps is
$$5 \times 6 \times 144 = \mathbf{4320}$$
multiplied by
her successful three dart score
$$40 + 51 + 50 = \mathbf{141}$$
$$141 \times 4320 = \mathbf{609120}$$
then minus
the number of strokes it took her to cross the lake
24 strokes per minute, so 1128 strokes in total
$$609120 - 1128 = \mathbf{607992}$$
and add
the number of letters in the dwarf's name on the correct door.
Answer: **Sneezy 607998**

The result of the sum before adding the letters in the dwarf's name is 607992, which makes Sneezy 607998 (with six letters in the dwarf's name) correct and Doc 607990 (with three letters) close, but wrong)

Clue to take forward to the Final Puzzle is: SNEEZY

THE MASKED CAROL SINGER

Muddled Carols
1. God Rest Ye Merry, Gentlemen + A
2. Good King Wenceslas + V + T

3. Silent Night + E
4. Once in Royal David's City + D
5. We Three Kings + N

And the extra word that is your third clue for the Final Puzzle is:
ADVENT

THE TELL STONE

The New Year's Eve Dash
Colin the Clipper finished in forty minutes in his green vest.

Bella was a Flier in green and blue stripes and finished in fifty-one minutes.

Davina, a Hurrier, finished in fifty-eight minutes, in a red and white vest.

Abel the Strider finished at one hour two minutes, in his blue and white checked vest.

Clue to take forward to the Final Puzzle is: HURRIERS

THE MAN WHO MADE LISTS

A Question of Connection
The five groups are:

2D Shapes: Circle, Square, Octagon, Rhombus

British Birds: Hobby, Crane, Jay, Wren

Crustaceans: Crab, Krill, Barnacle, Lobster

Stages at Glastonbury: Pyramid, Acoustic, Marquee, Other

Constellations: Hercules, Scorpion, Triangle, Phoenix

Clue to take forward to the Final Puzzle is: CONSTELLATIONS

SOME LIKE IT HOT

Goldilocks and the Four Bears

Daddy Bear likes his porridge at 15°C in a glass bowl with sugar.
Mummy Bear likes her porridge at 28°C in a wood bowl with fresh berries.
Zak Bear likes his porridge at 20°C in a metal bowl with cream.
Mia Bear likes her porridge at 35°C in a ceramic bowl with raisins.
Goldilocks likes her porridge at 68°F, which is equivalent to 20°C.

The word you need for the Final Puzzle is: ZAK

SNOW GOOSE

Missing Birds

Christopher	ROBIN	Hood
Stool	PIGEON	Toes
Hand	RAIL	Way
Spruce	GOOSE	Bumps
Bombay	DUCK	Tape

The word you need for the Final Puzzle is: PIGEON
The band Lieutenant Pigeon was number one in the UK Singles Chart for 4 weeks in 1972 with 'Mouldy Old Dough'.

THE BIG CHIP

Lost in Translation

All the vowels have been changed to the consonant that follows them in the alphabet, e.g. a has been changed to b, e has been changed to f and so on. Then the final letter of each word has been moved to the front of that word. So the conversation reads:

'Nice weather for ducks,' said Sally.

'The sun shines on the righteous,' Alan replied.

Satisfied that he is not an imposter, Sally continued. 'Have you brought the key'?

'No,' he replied. 'But it is safe with the fishes.'

Susie looked out at the pond. 'Which fishes?' she asked.

'I fed it to a giant dogfish at the aquarium.'

'How am I supposed to get it back?' she asked.

'Just ask him for it nicely,' said Alan, who was actually working for the other side.

The word you need for the Final Puzzle is: AQUARIUM

THE LADS OF CHRISTMAS

Christmas Chaos

Hamza wanted A STUFFED PINK EMU,

which was mistakenly given to Roxy (as an anagram).

Luka wanted a TROMBONE (the French word for a paperclip), which was mistakenly given to Hamza (a T-bone, containing ROM).

Roxy wanted a WIND UP TRICERATOPS (literally 'three-horned lizard),

which was mistakenly given to Jenny (with the vowels missing).

Felix wanted the board game CLUEDO, which is exactly what he got.

Jenny wished for A CHEMISTRY SET (as an anagram),

which was mistakenly given to Luka (cryptically Pasteur = 'A Chemist' – preceding '-ry set', which sounds like 'reset' (an adjustment).

338

The name you need for the Final Puzzle is: FELIX

DEATH ON THE BIGBUS EXPRESS

A Puzzle of Two Cities

1. Aberdeen and Leicester
2. Liverpool and Belfast
3. Newport and Milton Keynes
4. Glasgow and Winchester
5. Norwich and (Port) Stanley

The name you need for the Final Puzzle is: WINCHESTER

IT'S ELEMENTAL

An Elementary Message

The numbers in the message were the atomic weights of chemical elements, and the letters they represented were the chemical symbols of those elements. The message read:

WELCOME, MY FAMILY AND FRIENDS.
I WILL BE BRIEF, BUT WHEN YOUR OWN TIME COMES WE MAY TALK AGAIN. A SURPRISE TO ME, A MAN OF SCIENCE.
BUT, AS THE AXOLOTL AND THE JERBOA NEVER MEET OUTSIDE OF A ZOO, SO MAY YOU BE ON THE PATH TO A DIFFERENT PLACE.
IT IS NOT TOO LATE TO CHANGE THAT PATH.
I HOPE WE MEET AGAIN.

The last clue needed for the Final Puzzle is: JERBOA

THE FINAL PUZZLE

The final message read:

EDWARD WAS KILLED BY JERRY AND CLARA LIME, THE
HUMBERSIDE BONNIE AND CLYDE, WHO HAVE BEEN
LIVING AT BRACESTONE HOUSE AS MRS LINDEN AND
HER CAREFULLY SILENT HUSBAND

ACKNOWLEDGEMENTS

This book could not have happened without my brilliant editor Sarah Bauer whose faith in me and the whole concept kept me going through long days of plotting and scribbling. *The Twelve Murders of Christmas* wouldn't be in such great shape without her editorial genius and that of Avon's editorial director Emma Grundy Haigh. I felt I was in safe and incredibly talented hands from the very start to the very end. I'm also grateful for the ingenuity and hard work of the excellent marketing and publicity teams. A special thank you to my amazing publicist Laura Sherlock.

I have felt so welcomed by the whole the Avon team, particularly publishing director Helen Huthwaite – who as well as being a superb publisher is also lovely and generous company. I will always be grateful for her making sure I got back to my campervan okay, accompanying me through the dark streets of Harrogate, during my first Theakston's Crime Writing Festival.

The combination of stories of murder and other crimes with puzzles has a long history, which isn't too surprising as a puzzle lies at the heart of every mystery. In Greek myth Oedipus sets out to solve the whodunnit of the murder of King Laius, only to discover in a tragic twist that he himself was the killer. And part of his story involves him solving the riddle of the Sphinx. The tradition has continued to the present day, including along the way, the cryptic clues of Agatha Christie, the ciphers of Arthur Conan Doyle and M. R. James, the symbology of Dan Brown and the riddles employed by Vaseem Khan. All of which have fed my love for ingenious conundrums set within brilliant storytelling. Not forgetting of course Nancy Drew and the Famous Five – whose mystery and puzzle solving adventures were among my earliest influences.

I have dedicated this book to my Dad, a stalwart champion of my writing, who always seems to have a puzzle to hand and helped stoke my love for brain-teasers in all their forms.

As a professional verifier I know the importance of having every detail of a question or puzzle checked. When playing with words, numbers, ciphers and logic a single letter or digit in the wrong place can collapse a whole carefully constructed house of cards. I am therefore massively thankful for my merry band of puzzle checkers, Jim and Tamsin Cooke, Tim and Eliza Brooks and Geoff Sweaney who between them not only weeded out any errors but also gave feedback on whether or not each of the puzzles 'worked'.

I feel very fortunate to be surrounded by great friends who have supported me at all points along the way, sometimes shaking their heads at the hours I have put in but also recognising the joy I have felt in writing this book. So a big thank you to the Discerning Lobsters, the Boozehounds, Saturday Chum runners, Toddies packrunners, the Unravelled knitters, my Sisters in Literature and the Monday morning coffee gang. Thank you for putting up with me both wittering on about my book and being prone to staring into space with a wicked gleam as I plot another murder.

For most of my life, if asked, I would have said I was a cat person. But since Digger the cockerpoo joined our family I have jumped ship to the canine crew. Dash's story, 'The Big Chip', although primarily a huge nod to my love of Chandler and Hammett, was inspired by Digger and his pals, particularly Ozzy, Fred, Ernie and of course Betsy who in characteristic fashion appears as her own brazen self in the tale.

And of course, although they have already had a mention above, a very special thank you to my husband Tim and daughter Eliza who throughout this fabulous journey have between them kept me fed, watered, loved and sane.